The Last Map Is The Heart

an anthology

WESTERN CANADIAN FICTION

DATE DUE

The Last Map Is The Heart

an anthology

WESTERN CANADIAN FICTION

Forrie, O'Rourke, Sorestad, Editors

Thistledown Press

Canadian Cataloguing in Publication Data

Main entry under title:

The Last map is the heart

  ISBN: 0-920633-64-1

1. Short stories, Canadian (English) - Canada, Western*. I. O'Rourke, Patrick,
1943-. II. Sorestad, Glen A., 1937-. III. Forrie, Allan, 1948-.

PS8329.5.W4L388 1989 C813/.01/089712 C89-098128-0
PR9198.2.W42L388 1989

Book design by A.M. Forrie
Cover by Ann Newdigate: *Followed by a projective taste/You see what you are*
(from the *Look At It This Way* series), Tapestry (Gobelin style), 1988,
180.0 x 90.3 cm. Courtesy of the Susan Whitney Gallery, Regina, Saskatchewan.
Transparency by A.K. Photos, Saskatoon, obtained with the assistance of the
Mendel Art Gallery, Saskatoon.
Typeset by Thistledown Press Ltd.

Printed and bound in Canada by
Hignell Printing Ltd., Winnipeg

Thistledown Press Ltd.
668 East Place
Saskatoon, Saskatchewan
S7J 2Z5

Acknowledgements

Special thanks to David Arnason and David Carpenter for their valuable sugges-
tions, to John Lent for suggesting the title of this anthology, to Donna Bergren
for reading the proofs, and a particular thanks to Sue Stewart for her invaluable
editorial assistance.

This book has been published with the assistance of The Canada Council and
the Saskatchewan Arts Board.

CONTENTS

Introduction

Writers from Western Canada have over the years made a considerable mark on the development of short fiction in this country. From the traditional realistic short story that presented a "slice of life," a dramatic encounter or sequence of events, short fiction has evolved in various directions—into the surreal, the bizarre and the fantastic, into magical realism, into mini-fictions and prose poems, into the various forms or metafictions that we find being published at present. The traditional short story, as so skillfully crafted by writers like Sinclair Ross and Ethel Wilson, is still very much with us, as will be seen in many of the contemporary stories of this anthology, such as those by Bonnie Burnard or Mel Dagg; but also included are fictions that extend the boundaries of what we have come to regard as short fiction. *The Last Map Is the Heart* brings together a diverse sampling of short fiction from writers from the four Western provinces into an anthology that, while neither comprehensive nor definitive, represents something of where Western short fiction has come from and perhaps might even signal where it is going. As much as any limited selection of writers and stories can, this anthology tries to map the geography of short fiction over the past fifty years in Western Canada with representative writing that articulates those ageless conflicts involving the human heart.

The landscape of Western Canada, in its incredible diversity and its often awesome presence, has been a powerful and dominant feature of fiction from this part of the country. Whether it is an obvious physical presence, such as the prairie landscape is in traditional stories like Ross's "The Painted Door" or Kreisel's "The Broken Globe", or as the coastal fog becomes in Wilson's story, it seems that the landscape, and particularly the rural landscape, still does much to shape the interior motivations of characters in the fiction of the West. Landscape in contemporary Western fiction is more often internalized and much less obtrusive, as in Rosta's "Hunting Season" or Arnason's "The Event"; but the presence of the landscape is still felt. Edna Alford's "Head" becomes a definitive example of this internalizing of landscape.

Though the population of Western Canada grows increasingly urban and the majority of writers tend to live in urban centres, the shorter fiction, especially from the prairies, has been slow to reflect this population shift. It would seem that even in the growing urban centers of the prairies the urban geography has not been able to supplant the overwhelming presence of the landscape. Just as the fictional Manawaka was for Margaret Laurence a spiritual and emotional geography for her work, so it appears the rural presence still is a powerful motivating presence and source for many of today's prairie fiction writers.

Writers from British Columbia have, on the other hand, apparently been less influenced by the physical geography of mountains and sea than prairie writers have by their landscape, though certainly landscape is a presence in the fiction of many West Coast writers. Historically, fiction from the West Coast has differed from the fiction of the rest of Western Canada to such an extent that Edward McCourt chose to exclude British Columbia fiction from consideration altogether in his 1949 work, *The Canadian West in Fiction*. Short fiction from here has been and remains far more diverse in its influences, more experimental, perhaps more reflective of a landscape that is fantastic in its diverseness. In the fiction of Andreas Schroeder, Sandy Frances Duncan, or Ernest Hekkanen we see writing that draws its influences from other sources; and in Lionel Kearns's "Blue Moon", especially, we see an example of what Geoff Hancock describes as a post-modern fiction, a form that "calls attention to the artifice of stories." As a favoured location for the influx of newcomers from within Canada and without, British Columbia, and its short fiction, is marked by the diversity that comes from the influence of writing and writers from all over the world, perhaps to a greater extent than has been generally so in the rest of Western Canada.

The writers included in *The Last Map Is the Heart* are themselves indicative or representative of the people who make up Western Canada. We have all come from somewhere. The writers may be descendants of the First People, who were themselves immigrants, exciting new Native writers like Thomas King and Shirley Bruised Head; they may be native

Western Canadians, the offspring of immigrant stock several generations into this country; they may be more recent immigrants to this country from the United States, as are Dave Margoshes or Leon Rooke, or from other countries, as is Brenda Riches, writers born elsewhere, but who have lived most of their lives in Western Canada. Wherever they or their ancestors have originally come from they have usually brought with them their cultural sensibilities and sensitivities that help to create the wonderfully different voices, styles and approaches that make the short fiction of Western Canada so interesting and unique. The stories included by Ken Mitchell, Gertrude Story and Guy Vanderhaeghe provide us with evocative insights into the historical and human mapmaking of the West by the immigrants and their children, insights that help us to see ourselves clearly as important parts of that human geography of the heart. In fact, the very act of becoming a citizen in this country is the focus of attention in Lesley Lum's story, "Old Age Gold". Immigrants bring with them their myth and lore and weave them into the fabric of the new land, something that we can see in several stories in this anthology—David Arnason's "The Event", Kristjana Gunnars's "Ticks" and Henry Kreisel's "The Broken Globe", to cite a few. It might be suggested that the forging of new myths is a necessary part of writing a new country into existence and that this is something our writers like Sandra Birdsell and Jack Hodgins are doing now. The physical geography of Western Canada may be the same, but the mapmaking goes on and our writers are forging their own trails into new territory, bringing with them the directions and signals of their own personal backgrounds to help them blaze their way into ever newer terrains of the heart.

Any anthology can only hope to provide a very basic map of a fictional terrain and *The Last Map Is the Heart* is no exception. As Geoff Hancock suggested, ". . . though maps fix a place, they recognize no limits where a traveller can wander." What we have tried to do is to offer the reader a means of beginning to explore the richness and originality of Western short fiction. We have gathered this selection of stories with a view to offering entertaining and provocative fictions by some of our best writers from the past and from the present. The stories we have chosen are not necessarily the "best" stories written by these writers, although some of them might be argued to be so. We offer a few stories that might be argued to be "classics" or "chestnuts" in Canadian literature. We have looked for variety and originality in style and treatment, from the serious to the ironic and light-hearted. We have tried to keep the reader in mind in selecting and arranging the stories that comprise this fictional map; the alphabetical arrangement of stories by author is admittedly arbitrary, but convenient. We have tried to include as many writers and stories as we could within the limitations of anthology size. Of course, there are other stories that we would like to have included, but the forty-two stories that comprise *The Last Map Is the Heart* are a testimony to the rich and diverse literary inheritance of writing in Western Canada.

Allan Forrie
Patrick O'Rourke
Glen Sorestad
Saskatoon, August 1989

Head

Edna Alford

Coming home I discovered there was no home left nor would there ever be again. Spruce and poplar and scrub were all in place along the way exactly as I had left them but my head was not where I had left it. I left it on a rock in the sun at the corner of the home quarter, the part not yet broke although I see there's been some breaking done on the next quarter to it. I left it on the big rock because I had never in all the years of my growing up seen the snow cover that rock. I don't know why. Maybe it had something to do with the wind.

At first I thought I might nestle it between some of the smaller rocks in the stone pile but then I remembered the snow even though it was very hot that day I left the head out in the field. And the head could smell the buffalo beans and the mustard and the stubby growth of wolf willow barely poking up out of the tall slough grass.

I wouldn't be so upset if I had thought about it before, about the chance the head might not be there when I got back. But I always kind of banked on its being there all that time looking out over the fields toward the sky, clear and cold most of the time. The clarity is what I mostly thought about. That there still was a place somewhere in the world where I could see things clear and from a long way off, like stars, I guess, or trees along the coulee hill, things like that and maybe more.

For it always seemed to me that if you could see one kind of thing clear and from far off—real things, natural things, trees and stars and such— then you could probably see the other kinds of things too, things you couldn't touch, ideas and feelings and who knows what, clear and from a long way off. I thought about that for years after I left the prairie, right up to now in fact. And I wasn't the only one who had that notion. Most of us did.

I met a fellow once in a Vancouver bar and he was reading a paper and he read me a story about city dwellers, how after a long time living in the city, they lose what they call their long-distance vision. These experts had figured it out. It's apparently because city people don't have to look so far, because they've always got something in the way of their looking, like brick buildings or glass skyscrapers or things like that. They get used to looking close; some of them, it seemed to me when I was there, got so bad they pretty well looked at their shoes most of the time or maybe it was the cracks in the sidewalk they were looking at and some of them in fact didn't seem to be looking out at anything at all. They seemed to be looking at themselves, as if their eyes had kind of revolved inside their heads and faced the wrong way altogether—toward their own insides—which is about as far away from long-distance vision as a person can get.

I was pretty smug in those days, knowing all the time I had my head back there on the bald-headed prairie—looking out at the sky and the fields any time I felt like it. Never anything to get in its way, maybe a storm some days, snow or rain or something, but always afterward the sun came back and all the clear clear sky lit up fine and green or even better, white and clean and fiercely clear. And all the time in the city when I'd see folks on their way to work looking at the grey pavement or the cracks in the concrete sidewalks or the buildings made of marble or cement like headstones, or maybe even at windows that gave them back a likeness of themselves, flat, without flesh, and sometimes wavy like the mermaids in the sea might look to a drowning man, I'd think to myself: *Now if only you could see the world the way I see it.*

I even told the guy in the bar in Vancouver about it. About the prairie and the way a man could see better there than anywhere and he laughed and picked up his glass and made a toast to the province of Saskatchewan and then he laughed again and emptied his glass, said the whole coast was nothing but a haven for prairie dogs like me and he said if things were so much better back there, how come the coast's full of all you stubble-jumpers. Half the province of British Columbia is from the province of Saskatchewan. Which is why he was toasting it in the first place he says. And he says he doesn't mind having to look at the buildings or the roads, which he hears still aren't so hot back there, much less cedars and mountains and such—anything, he says, has got to beat nothing six different ways. And he says he's from around Swift Current himself and why don't I tell him another one.

I never gave a second thought to him or what he said till now. When the mill shut down this fall, I finally come back to the prairie, to see the folks mostly. Then too, I guess I had it in the back of my mind I'd take a drive out to the home place and poke around some. And also I guess I had it in my mind to just take a quick check on the head while I was out there.

Which was how I come to see they'd burned the home place down and planted rape. And when I come to the stone pile down by the slough, I see the birds have picked my whole head clean as a whistle, like one of those buffalo skulls you see in the museums. And in the holes that used to be the eyes, I see somebody took a couple of little stones from the pile and stuck them in. They'd hung a pair of spectacles with wire frames on it. Only there was no glass in them, no glass at all. Nothing a fellow could see through even if he did have eyes.

The Event
David Arnason

The sun had just climbed out of the lake so that its rays poured horizontally through the kitchen window on a morning in early August. The orange that Paul had cut into segments lay on the table, and the rays of the sun saturated each section, making it more brilliant than the sun itself. The coffee, strong, as Paul liked it, and made the Icelandic style, weighted the air of the room with its aroma. He ran his hands over the smooth polished back of a wooden chair. It was his birthday. Seventy-eight, he reflected, and felt grateful that his senses could still react to the world with such intensity.

He was thinking of Helgi, his youngest son, who had drowned in a storm forty years ago. He had been thinking a lot about Helgi in the past few days, and he wondered why. His memory, for which he had feared, and whose loss he had sensed as a progressive and inevitable thing, had come back to him over these past days with an intensity and accuracy that amazed him. Helgi's face was as sharp in memory as if he were sitting in this very room, or had just left it a moment ago intending to return. Paul remembered the very words he himself had spoken to Helgi when he was teaching him how to set a gill net, how to keep your eye always on the sky whatever you were doing, so that you would never be caught by a storm. That was a lesson Helgi had not learned well enough.

Paul remembered the urgent sense that there was something he had forgotten when they had come to tell him of Helgi's death. He had remembered then that Helgi had come to him in a dream the night of his death and told him not to worry. He had believed that fiercely for forty years, but now he wondered. Had that dream ever happened? Was the thing he had to remember something else? The news of his dream had spread through Gimli, and people had been in awe of him because of his power, because he had dreamed the dream. Now, he wasn't sure that the dream had ever happened, or if it happened, when.

Paul decided that this morning he would walk to the edge of the lake before breakfast. He opened the door and sunshine poured in, a palpable presence that seemed to have its own density, quite separate from the darker air inside the room. The dark blue of the lake, when he stepped out the door, met with a sharp line the deeper blue of the sky. Usually, Lake Winnipeg was an ambiguity. The greyness of the lake met the greyness of the sky so that there was no horizon. Today was different. Today every tree stood out, every blade of grass was individual, recognizable. The tern that drifted in the sky was sharply defined and separated from everything else.

Paul walked across the narrow green stretch of lawn to the broad ochre beach that separated land from lake. Birds of all kinds chirped and whistled and fluted, yet each note was separate and identifiable. The sweep of beach along the bay was completely empty from the north point to the south point, except that halfway down the slope to the lake, directly in front of him, was a naked girl. She was sitting on the sand, her arms curled around her knees, staring out over the water. In spite of all the sunshine, there was a small breeze, and Paul thought that she must be chilly. Her long black hair reached nearly to her waist. He moved past her, circling, uncertain what he should do. Her skin was the purest white he had ever seen. She paid no attention to him, but continued to look out over the lake. He could see now that she was crying. Bright tears flowed from under her dark lashes and down her cheeks.

"What's the matter?" he asked, as gently as he could. She glanced up at him and he was certain she was the most beautiful girl he had ever seen.

"I don't know," she said. "I'm waiting."

"Who are you waiting for?"

"I don't know."

"What is your name?" Paul asked her. "Who are your people?"

She looked at him, her eyes as blue as the lake, as blue as the sky. "I don't know," she said. "I don't remember my name. I don't remember how I came here. I am waiting, but I don't know why. Perhaps I was waiting for you."

"Come," Paul said, and he reached out his hand to her. She stood, and he saw that she was nearly as tall as he was. He took her hand and marvelled at its whiteness and the gnarled brownness of his own. He led her up the beach to the house and into the kitchen, leaving her standing there for a moment while he went to get her a blanket. The marvellous sun through the window made her body golden. In the bedroom that he had shared with Martha, he looked for a blanket that would be right to wrap her in. He remembered that in the closet was the white blanket that they had been given as a wedding present, but which in the fifty years of their marriage they had never used because Martha had always said that it was too good. Now, he took it down from the shelf and carried it into the kitchen. The girl wrapped it around herself, carefully tucking it in to conceal her breasts, as if she had just discovered her nakedness. Paul took two mugs down from the cupboard and poured them each a cup of coffee. The steam from the coffee hung like smoke in the sunlight. The girl tasted her coffee and said, "It is very bitter."

"Perhaps you would like cream and sugar," Paul said.

"Yes," she replied, "perhaps."

He went to the fridge, took out a carton of cream and poured some into her coffee. He stirred in a large teaspoonful of sugar, then, remembering his own children, stirred in another spoonful.

"Yes," she said, "that's much better."

They sipped their coffee in silence, and Paul thought about Helgi and the dream. That day when they told him that Helgi had fallen from the boat and had not been found, he had remembered something. He told them it was the dream, but now it seemed that he had been wrong. It wasn't the dream after all. He had remembered something else, and he had told them about the dream because they would not have understood. What was it he had remembered?

"Today is my birthday," he told the girl.

"It is my birthday, too," she answered. Paul thought, "It is my birthday, and it is forty years since my son drowned. It was my birthday when they brought me the news," and he wondered if that was correct, if it had been his birthday. Martha would have remembered. She always remembered birthdays. He thought of Martha in the kitchen, singing. She hadn't sung more than other people, but when he remembered her, he always remembered her singing.

"I'll have to call the police," he told the girl. "They will be able to find out who you are and return you to your people."

"Yes," she answered, "the police will know."

"Or," he continued, "I could take you to the hospital. The doctors could find out, could help you remember."

"Yes," she said, "or we could stay here and drink coffee."

"Yes, we could do that." But Paul knew that they couldn't do that. The girl on the beach was like a fantasy, but she was undeniably real. In the sunlight, the tiny hairs on her upper lip were golden, and her straight nose made a triangular shadow on her cheek. Stray hair drifted across her eyes. Paul stared out the window. He could see the government pier stretching out into the lake, its high concrete wall preventing him from seeing the boats on the other side that were moored to it. To the left and down the beach a small way was the lifeguard stand that had been installed for the tourists. Soon, the first few swimmers and sunbathers would begin to gather with their blankets. By afternoon, the beach would be crowded, and instead of the sound of birds, he would listen to the sound of mothers scolding children, the shouts of young people dunking each other, and the roar of outboard motors pulling water skiers. The beach had once been his, a place where he launched his boats and spread out his nets to dry. Now, he owned it only in the early morning, and sometimes all day long in the early spring and late fall.

When Helgi had been young, he had loved the beach and played in the water all day, but had never learned to swim. Paul could not swim himself. All the young people who came to the beach now could swim, and Paul wondered how they had learned the secret. Swimming was a mysterious thing. Though you sank in the water, you could will yourself to stay at the top, to move across the surface. None of the other fishermen he had worked with could swim either. What they did with the lake had nothing to do with swimming, nothing to do with the casual joy of water on naked skin.

If Helgi had known how to swim, maybe he would not have drowned. But Helgi had drowned at night, in the worst norwester of the season, five miles from any shore. He would have had nowhere to swim to. And if he could swim, would he have come to Paul in the dream?

If there had been a dream. If Paul hadn't made up the dream so that he could say I have not forsaken my son. In his hour of peril he reached out to me across the water and I understood. But what had he understood? Only that his son was dead and all his possibilities were over, that the lake had claimed him as a sacrifice without any meaning. Paul moved suddenly in his chair, changing his shape so that the girl was frightened and asked, "What's the matter?"

"Nothing," he answered. Then, knowing that the police would come and take the girl and return her to her people, he added, "I have been thinking about my son. It is forty years since he drowned, and I have forgotten something important about his death. After forty years it is hard for an old man to remember what he should have remembered when he was young." Outside, the sun hung in the sky just above the lake. It didn't seem to have moved. The tern was etched white against blue exactly where it had been before. The trees were still as sharply distinct as if they had been made by fine craftsmen.

The girl said, "Sometimes it's better not to remember."

"No," Paul answered, "you always have to remember. It is all you have. They can take everything else away from you, but they can't take that."

Paul went to the stove to get them more coffee. His shadow against the wall was as alive as he was, shortening and lengthening as he moved. Helgi had imagined things when he was young. Once he had told Paul that he had seen a mermaid sitting on a rock at the north point, combing her long black hair. Martha had tried to explain that there were no such things as mermaids, but Paul had stopped her. He'd told Helgi that you could believe anything you wanted to, and he'd told Martha that children needed dreams. Now Martha was dead and Helgi was dead, and even the dream was dead. Paul sipped at his coffee.

"You'd better hurry," the girl told him. "Soon there will be people and it will be too late."

Then, quite suddenly, and as if he had known it all along, he remembered.

"Come, quickly," he told the girl, and took her by the hand, led her out the door and across the individual blades of grass of the lawn, past the secular trees, down to the beach.

"Hurry," he told her, and pulled her across the millions of grains of sand to where the water lapped on perfect white stones. The lake was a smooth mirror with nothing but sky in it. Then, the surface of the water broke and Helgi stood up straight and tall, moving toward the shore where they stood. Thousands of sparkling drops of water streamed from his blue jacket. The tern wheeled in the sky above his head, flashing white against the rising sun. The breeze tousled Paul's hair, and whipped the girl's long hair across her face like a veil. Helgi surged through the water to the shore, the dripping water singing in the brilliant light, making him silver. Paul felt his chest expanding with the memory that was beneath the dream, till he felt that he would be unable to contain it, that his heart would explode with the knowledge that was in it. Helgi strode on to the shore and put his arm around the girl, claiming her.

"Father," he said, "this is my bride." The blanket slipped from the girl and she looked up into Helgi's face. Then, Helgi put his arm around Paul's shoulders and said, "I'm home."

Paul looked down at his hands. The blue veins had disappeared, his knotted knuckles were smooth and strong, the shrunken skin was ruddy with health. He could feel the renewed power in his legs, the force in his back, his shoulders. They started up the beach to the green blur of the trees. Before them, the nets glistened on the reels still wet from that morning's fishing. The corks were brilliant orange and blue and red. As they crossed the soft carpet of lawn, they could hear Martha singing in the kitchen. The world filled with birdsong as it took on the shape of Paul's heart.

Flowers for Weddings and Funerals
Sandra Birdsell

My Omah supplies flowers for weddings and funerals. In winter, the flowers come from the greenhouse she keeps warm with a woodstove as long as she can; and then the potted begonias and asters are moved to the house and line the shelves in front of the large triple-pane window she had installed when Opah died so that she could carry on the traditions of flowers for weddings and for funerals. She has no telephone. Telephones are the devil's temptation to gossip and her God admonishes widows to beware of that exact thing.

And so I am the messenger. I bring requests to her, riding my bicycle along the dirt road to her cottage that stands water-marked beneath its whitewash because it so foolishly nestles too close to the Red River.

A dozen or two glads please, the note says. The bride has chosen coral for the colour of her wedding and Omah adds a few white ones because she says that white is important at a wedding. She does not charge for this service. It is unthinkable to her to ask for money to do this thing which she loves.

She has studied carefully the long rows of blossoms to find perfect ones with just the correct number of buds near the top, and laid them gently on newspaper. She straightens and absently brushes perspiration from her brow. She frowns at the plum tree in the corner of the garden where the flies hover in the heat waves. Their buzzing sounds and the thick humid air makes me feel lazy. But she never seems to notice the heat, and works tirelessly.

"In Russia," she says as she once more bends to her task, "we made jam. Wild plum jam to put into fruit pockets and platz." Her hands, brown and earth-stained, feel for the proper place to cut into the last gladiolus stalk.

She gathers the stalks into the crook of her arm, coral and white gladioli, large icy-looking petals that are beaded with tears. Babies' tears, she told me long ago. Each convex drop holds a perfectly shaped baby. The children of the world who cry out to be born are the dew of the earth.

For a long time afterward, I imagined I could hear the garden crying and when I told her this, she said it was true. All of creation cries and groans, you just cannot hear it. But God does.

Poor God. I squint at the sun because she has also said He is Light and I have grown accustomed to the thought that the sun is His eye. To have to face that every day. To have to look down and see a perpetually twisting, writhing, crying creation. The trees have arms uplifted, beseeching. Today I am not sure I can believe it, the way everything hangs limp and silent in the heat.

I follow her back to the house, thinking that perhaps tonight, after the wedding, there will be one less dewdrop in the morning.

"What now is a plum tree but a blessing to the red ants and flies only?" She mutters to herself and shakes dust from her feet before she enters the house. When she speaks her own language, her voice rises and falls like a butterfly on the wind as she smooths over the guttural sounds. Unlike my mother, who does not grow gladioli or speak the language of her youth freely, but with square, harsh sounds, Omah makes a sonatina.

While I wait for her to come from the house, I search the ground beneath the tree to try to find out what offends her so greatly. I can see red ants crawling over sticky, pink pulp, studying the dynamics of moving one rotting plum.

"In Russia, we ate gophers and some people ate babies." I recall her words as I pedal back towards the town. The glads are in a pail of water inside my wire basket. Cool spikelets of flowers seemingly spread across my chest. Here I come. Here comes the bride, big, fat and wide. Where is the groom? Home washing diapers because the baby came too soon.

Laurence's version of that song reminds me that he is waiting for me at the river.

"Jesus Christ, wild plums, that's just what I need," Laurence says and begins pacing up and down across the baked river bank. His feet lift clay tiles as he paces and I squat waiting, feeling the nylon filament between my fingers, waiting for something other than the river's current to tug there at the end of it.

I am intrigued by the patterns the sun has baked into the river bank. Octagonal shapes spread down to the willows. How this happens, I don't know. But it reminds me of a picture I have seen in Omah's Bible or geography book, something old and ancient like the tile floor in a pharaoh's garden. It is recreated here by the sun on the banks of the Red River.

"What do you need plums for?"

"Can't you see," he says. "Wild plums are perfect to make wine."

I wonder at the tone of his voice when it is just the two of us fishing. He has told me two bobbers today instead of one and the depth of the stick must be screwed down into the muck just so. Only he can do it. And I never question as I would want to because I am grateful to him for the world he has opened up to me. If anyone should come and join us here, Laurence would silently gather his line in, wind it around the stick with precise movements that are meant to show his annoyance, but really are a cover for his sense of not belonging. He would move further down the bank or walk up the hill to the road and his bike. He would turn his back on me, the only friend he has.

I have loved you since grade three, my eyes keep telling him. You, with your lice crawling about your thickly matted hair. My father, being the town's barber, would know. Laurence. But I defied him and played with you anyway.

It is of no consequence to Laurence that daily our friendship drives wedges into my life. He stops pacing and stands in front of me, hands raised up like a preacher's hands.

"Wild plums make damned good wine. My old man has a recipe."

I turn over a clay tile and watch an earthworm scramble to bury itself, so that my smile will not show and twist down inside him.

Laurence's father works up north cutting timber. He would know about wild plum wine. Laurence's mother cooks at the hotel because his father seldom sends money home. Laurence's brother is in the navy and has a tattoo on his arm. I envy Laurence for the way he can take his time rolling cigarettes, never having to worry about someone who might sneak up and look over his shoulder. I find it hard to understand his kind of freedom. He will have the space and time to make his wine at leisure.

"Come with me." I give him my hand.

Omah bends over in the garden. Her only concession to the summer's heat has been to roll her nylon stockings to her ankles. They circle her legs in neat coils. Her instep is swollen, mottled blue with broken blood vessels. She gathers tomatoes in her apron.

Laurence hesitates. He stands away from us with his arms folded across his chest as though he were bracing himself against extreme cold.

"His mother could use the plums," I tell Omah. Her eyes brighten and her tanned wrinkles spread outwards from her smile. She half-runs like a goose to her house with her apron bulging red fruit.

"See," I say to Laurence, "I told you she wouldn't mind."

When Omah returns with pails for picking, Laurence's arms hang down by his sides.

"You tell your Mama," she says to Laurence, "that it takes one cup of sugar to one cup of juice for the jelly." Her English is broken and she looks like any peasant standing in her bedroom slippers. She has hidden her beautiful white hair beneath a kerchief.

She's not what you think, I want to tell Laurence and erase that slight bit of derision from his mouth. Did you know that in their village they were once very wealthy? My grandfather was a teacher. Not just a teacher, but he could have been a professor here at a university.

But our heads are different. Laurence would not be impressed. He has never asked me about myself. We are friends on his territory only.

I beg Laurence silently not to swear in front of her. Her freckled hands pluck fruit joyfully.

"In the old country, we didn't waste fruit. Not like here where people let it fall to the ground and then go to the store and buy what they could have made for themselves. And much better too."

Laurence has sniffed out my uneasiness. "I like homemade jelly," he says. "My mother makes good crabapple jelly."

She studies him with renewed interest. When we each have a pail full of the dust-covered fruit, she tops it with a cabbage and several of the largest unblemished tomatoes I have ever seen.

"Give my regards to your Mama," she says, as though some bond has been established because this woman makes her own jelly.

We leave her standing at the edge of the road shielding her eyes against the setting sun. She waves and I am so proud that I want to tell Laurence about the apple that is named for her. She had experimented with crabapple trees for years and in recognition of her work, the experimental farm has given a new apple tree her name.

"What does she mean, give her regards?" Laurence asks and my intentions are lost in the explanation.

When we are well down the road and the pails begin to get heavy, we stop to rest. I sit beside the road and chew the tender end of a foxtail.

Laurence chooses the largest of the tomatoes carefully, and then, his arm a wide arc, he smashes it against a telephone pole.

I watch red juice dripping against the splintered grey wood. The sun is dying. It paints the water tower shades of gold. The killdeers call to each other as they pass as silhouettes above the road. The crickets in the ditch speak to me of Omah's greenhouse where they hide behind earthenware pots.

What does Laurence know of hauling pails of water from the river, bending and trailing moisture, row upon row? What does he know of coaxing seedlings to grow or babies crying from dewdrops beneath the eye of God?

I turn from him and walk with my face reflecting the fired sky and my dust-coated bare feet raising puffs of anger in the fine warm silt.

"Hey, where are you going?" Laurence calls to my retreating back. "Wait a minute. What did I do?"

The fleeing birds fill the silence with their cries and the night breezes begin to swoop down onto our heads.

She sits across from me, Bible opened on the grey arborite, cleaning her wire-framed glasses with a tiny linen handkerchief that she has prettied with blue cross-stitch flowers. She places them back on her nose and continues to read while I dunk pastry in tea and suck noisily to keep from concentrating.

"And so," she concludes, "God called His people to be separated from the heathen."

I can see children from the window, three of them, scooting down the hill to the river and I try not to think of Laurence. I haven't been with him since the day on the road, but I've seen him. He is not alone anymore. He has friends now, kids who are strange to me. They are the same ones who make me feel stupid about the way I run at recess so that I can be pitcher when we play scrub. I envy the easy way they can laugh at everything.

"Well, if it isn't Sparky," he said, giving me a new name and I liked it. Then he also gave me a showy kiss for them to see and laugh. I pushed against his chest and smelled something sticky like jam, but faintly sour at the same time. He was wearing a new jacket and had hammered silver studs into the back of it that spelled his name out across his shoulders. Gone is the mousy step of my Laurence.

Omah closes the book. The sun reflects off her glasses into my eyes. "And so," she says, "it is very clear. When God calls us to be separate, we must respond. With adulthood comes a responsibility."

There is so much blood and death in what she says that I feel as though I am choking. I can smell sulphur from smoking mountains and dust rising from feet that circle a golden calf. With the teaching of these stories, changing from pleasant fairy tales of far-away lands to this joyless search for meaning, her house has become a snare.

She pushes sugar cubes into my pocket. "You are a fine child," she says, "to visit your Omah. God will reward you in heaven."

The following Saturday, I walk a different way to her house, the way that brings me past the hotel, and I can see them as I pass by the window, pressed together all in one booth. They greet me as though they knew I would come. I squeeze in beside Laurence and listen with amazement to their fast-moving conversation. The jukebox swells with forbidden music. I can feel its beat in Laurence's thigh.

I laugh at things I don't understand and try not to think of my Omah who will have weak tea and sugar cookies set out on her white cloth. Her stained fingers will turn pages, contemplating what lesson to point out.

"I'm glad you're here," Laurence says, his lips speaking the old way to me. When he joins the conversation that leaps and jumps without direction from one person to another, his voice is changed. But he has taken my hand in his and covered it beneath the table. He laughs and spreads his plum breath across my face.

I can see Omah bending in the garden cutting flowers for weddings and funerals. I can see her rising to search the way I take and she will not find me there.

Golden Eggs
Lois Braun

A bump and giggle meant the girls were up. Two for sure, probably
Moses and Violet, who slept side by side in a single cot at the head of the
stairs. Every morning they awoke with the first rasp of the pump beside
the kitchen sink and then quarrelled in whispers under the comforter.

Sarah let her hand rest on top of the woodstove for a moment, feeling
it heat up as the oak kindling started to crackle and hiss. Summer was over
now. In one night, the weather had turned almost winter-cold. Her girls
would need their coats and stockings this morning. She was lucky, they'd
needed only sweaters all September, though she had seen them squatting
in their skirts on the street, after the sun had gone down, to keep their
bare legs warm.

Bare feet padded on the cold upstairs floor. A balled-up pair of brown
wool stockings bounced down the steep staircase, and after it, Violet,
wearing a man's suit-jacket over her nightgown. She fished the stockings
from under the chair with no back and rolled them up to her ankles. "Can
I cut the bread?"

Sarah threw the knife down beside the bread on the wooden table and
turned her back on it, but then regretted her surliness. Violet always came
down the earliest and cut the bread the straightest. Sometimes she peeled
the potatoes or helped Betty-Ann get dressed. But mostly she liked to tell
stories, stories from thick books she read at school, about hags and genies
with hair as long as ladders. She painted the stories in thrilling colours
and textures for her cloistered listeners. Violet's teacher was a girl from
across the river where they had no religion. At first Sarah worried that the
stories might be heathen. And then, her worry became guilt when she

realized she enjoyed the flow of glass coffins and castle towers and magic kisses and dogs with eyes like saucers. Not that lions' dens and fiery furnaces weren't picturesque enough. It was just that her father had imparted all Bible stories with solemn reproach, with the burden of Old Testament sin heavy in his voice. Every villain was the Devil.

Sarah popped a slice of raw potato into Violet's mouth and said, "Have they started fighting yet?" Over the stockings. There were never enough whole stockings on any chilly morning. Knitting as fast as she could, Sarah could not keep up with the girls' toes and heels bursting through the brown wool. And they were often one pair short. She wished for the magic spinning wheel from Violet's story.

"Not yet. They don't know how cold it is." Violet measured the slices with her eye before cutting into the new loaf. "Except Bowlie. She slept with hers on. Scratch came to the yard yesterday and told her secretly that it was going to get terrible cold overnight. Don't ask me how he knew." Bowlie wore her stockings night and day all winter long. When they got holes, she'd get up after her sisters had fallen asleep at night and ransack the bottom bureau drawer for the newest pair, replacing them with her holey ones. So the sisters made fun of her bowed legs, and told their friends at school that she was "bowl-egged". Bowlie didn't care. She was an odd, self-contained child who had formed a curious bond with the skinny, ragged boy they called Scratch. Most of the townspeople thought Scratch was a demon, but both Sarah and Bowlie respected his omniscience.

"Anybody sick today?"

"No. Lulu's crying as usual."

More bumps from above. This time with whimpering and sniffling. Lulu always cried in the morning because her bed-partners pinched her to get her awake.

Sarah pumped water into a basin and carried it to the tiny bathroom at the back of the house where the older girls washed and put on their lipstick. A calendar with a kitten on it hung on the bathroom wall. September had been torn off. Ben's letter said he'd be coming home on the train around the fifteenth. It had been over nine months since her husband had been home. He'd arrived a few days after Christmas, complaining that his work had kept him back. Sarah didn't believe that the Alberta oil company he worked for had its men working on Christmas Day. His delay had only inflated the girls' excitement, and when he'd shown up with silk stockings for Alma and Esther and Katherine, and fur muffs for the young ones, they'd taken turns sitting on his lap for the rest of the evening. Except for little Betty-Ann, who didn't recognize her father. He would bring gifts now, too, but would leave again before Christmas. This year the girls would have to be satisfied with nuts and candy and home-made mittens and tams.

When Sarah came back into the kitchen, Violet was trimming the crusts from one of the bread slices. She had carved them into neat squares and triangles and circles and arranged them in a pattern on the table. All was play to her. Why couldn't she, Sarah, have learned such play as a child? Her father had enslaved her as soon as she could pump well-water and learn Bible verses, and now Ben, who soldiered in foreign lands, could not endure the confines of her small life.

Sarah's anger rose again like boiling milk. "Violet, I told you not to cut the crusts off the bread!"

"Just one, Mama! Lisa always leaves hers over anyhow. Might as well cut them off ahead of time."

"I always eat Lisa's crusts!"

"Well, here then." Violet jumbled the little collage in her hands and held them out to her mother.

Sarah wanted to grab Violet's fists and squeeze until her fingers opened and the crusts fell to the floor. But instead, she gestured to the shelf beside the sink and said, "Put them in my cup. I'll soak them in my coffee. And bring me the plates."

They heard the train whistle just as the sun made a starburst on the gilded rim of the teacup Ben had given Sarah for Christmas. It sat unused on the sill of the window above the sink. Sarah was at the stove, stirring a mixture of potatoes and lard and water in two big black skillets. When she heard the whistle, she stopped and looked at the window. Violet was there, washing herself. The child bent her dripping face towards the gold star at the teacup's edge, then held a wet hand in the sunbeam to see if the light would make stars on the droplets suspended from her fingertips.

Sarah went back to her stirring. Violet dried her face. "When's Daddy coming?"

Sarah hadn't told anyone about the letter, but they always started asking about their father just before he came home. "Soon." She went to the foot of the stairs and called, "Girls!"

The last time Ben was home, Sarah had tried to get him to sleep on the decrepit sofa in an alcove just off the kitchen. Betty-Ann was used to sleeping with her in the double bed in the back room of the tiny house, she said, and the little girl couldn't be expected to sleep alone in a space she wasn't used to. But Ben had given Betty-Ann a bright new nickel and she became an easy traitor to her mother. By pure luck, Sarah had not become pregnant last time Ben had been home, nor the two times before that. She didn't plan to, ever again.

For twenty-six years he'd been leaving her in this shack while he spent long months on jobs in far-away places, coming back on the train only long enough to make her pregnant and put stars in his daughters' eyes. They'd had two sons as well as the twelve girls: the first- and second-born had been boys. As soon as they were old enough, their father had found them work with the oil company, and now Sarah saw them less often than she saw Ben. The boys didn't like coming home to a crowded house filled with girls.

Take me, Ben. Take me this time. Sarah put her hand to the tight knot of hair at the back of her neck, a smooth, petrified knot that was out of her sight during the long days, but became in the mirror at night a girlish auburn spill of light on her breast. When he was home, she turned out the lamp before he could see it.

Looking at the sofa now, Sarah wondered how she might engineer her husband to sleep on it this time. Perhaps now that the lumps and sags were out of it . . . In May she had gone to see Kaminsky, the storekeeper, who also sold and repaired furniture. Kaminsky was bald and had tufts for eyebrows. He reminded Sarah of the genie in Violet's book.

"How much to have that old red sofa of mine restuffed?"

"Five dollars, if you want new springs."

Five! That took a big chunk out of grocery money. Violet kept pennies in a cigar box . . .

"Two for stuffing and my time."

"Forget the springs. Who needs springs?"

A few days later, he was at her door with an enormous sack on his shoulder. While she ironed little cotton dresses, he pulled old clothes, perfectly wearable old clothes, and straw out of the sack, and crammed them into the seat and back of the couch.

Unlike the other merchants in town, who were too friendly and traded their gossip for your business, Kaminsky was a haughty, cold man. His eyes narrowed when she gave him the two dollars, but he'd hardly said a word all afternoon. When he left, after sewing up the seams with a huge needle, Sarah felt as though she'd had a divine visitation.

There was a large thump and a wail from the upstairs room, and an impatient banging of drawers. "Girls!" Sarah called again. She could hear another muffled thumping somewhere, at first she thought in the cellar. "The devil's at the door," she muttered to herself. But then she realized it was coming from the closet under the stairs. Violet was in there looking for the coats, probably intending to get the best one before her sisters came down. She emerged wearing a pretty one that was much too big for her. "There are only eight," she announced, with two or three draped over her arm.

"There are some in my bedroom closet."

"Teacher told us a story yesterday," said Violet as she and Sarah sorted through the eight coats in the narrow passageway between the kitchen and the back rooms. "It was about a fish that could talk. It was quite—" she paused, her hand in one of the coat pockets, "—smashing," she said, as though she'd found the word in the pocket. "It was about this fisherman and his wife who were very, very poor and lived in a horrible old shack.

"One day the man meets a fish in the ocean who—well, he doesn't meet the fish, he catches it, and then the fish says—I think the fish was beautiful with gold scales—the fish says, 'If you let me go, I'll grant you a wish.'" Violet crossed her eyes and changed her voice so that it sounded bubbly. Sarah scratched at a spot on one of the coats and tried not to laugh. "So the man did it. Moses says it was stupid for the man to believe that a fish could grant wishes, but I said that if a fish could talk—I mean, talk English—then it was ob'iously magic." Moses was a pious, practical, old-womanish child and therefore Violet's opposite. Moses never went anywhere without her tree-branch walking staff, and on Sundays, a Bible under her arm. Her real name was Rose.

"So the man asks his wife what to wish for and she tells him to wish for a new cottage. The man goes back to the ocean and asks for a new cottage. Well, first he has to say this little poem. And when he gets home, there it is, a new cottage with his wife in it. But she keeps sending him back to ask for more and more, and finally they live in a huge castle. Pretty soon the wife says she wants to be the lord of the sun and the moon, and when the man tells the fish, the fish says, 'Go home', like always, and when the man goes home, it's a shack again."

"You'll have to let Anna have that coat, Violet. It doesn't fit you."

"But you know what, Mama? The man goes back to the beach one day and he finds the fish dead on the shore and he cuts it open with his knife and you know what he sees?"

"Guts."

"No. A golden egg!"

"Violet, you made that up. Last week you told me about cutting a goose open to look for golden eggs."

"Well—I felt sorry for him." The train whistle blew again, on the track at the other end of town.

One by one the girls came into the kitchen to wash at the sink and eat their mushy, salty potatoes and bread smeared with lard. Once they were all down, Violet, who never ate breakfast, went upstairs to dress, so she could have the dresser mirror to herself. She took a coat with her. Betty-Ann, cheeks shiny with warm lard, followed her up to explore the many perfume- and urine-scented beds.

"When's Daddy coming?"

"Soon." THWACK! The wooden spoon hit the bottom of each plate as Sarah measured out the potatoes. She had never gone anywhere with Ben on the train. He'd whisked Joseph and young Ben away on the train, and the older girls had all, at some time or other, stolen a trip to Winnipeg in a boxcar. Last spring, a rumour had trickled down the street that Anna had given her favours to the brakeman in return for a ride up front in the engine. Sarah hadn't been on the train since the time she was thirteen when her own mother had taken her to the city to escape from a smallpox epidemic. How many trains would it take to get to the ocean? These days, Sarah got only as far as Emerson and St. Joe, when the neighbours took her visiting in their Packard. She never went away for very long. It seemed dangerous to leave the house bristling with twelve females.

One by one, the children finished their breakfasts, and after Sarah had inspected their clothing for stains and torn seams, the younger ones scampered to the bathroom to have their hair braided by Katherine and Esther. Sarah herself brushed Lulu's curls. When she was about two, Lulu had smashed her head against a red-hot stove-pipe one bitter evening when her sisters had taken turns tossing her around the kitchen. Her hair had never grown back there. Sarah made sure every morning that the scar was well covered. "What about the stockings?" she whispered in Lulu's ear so as not to open that can of worms.

"One is missing," Lulu whispered back. "Alma only had enough for one leg."

"Did she cut it in half?"

"No. She's wearing her Daddy-stockings." Usually, only Katherine and Esther wore their silk stockings because they had jobs and were both engaged to be married.

"I'll knit like the devil tonight."

A kind of frenzy built up in the kitchen now, with everyone fed and dressed and invigorated by the prospect of the splash of cold air, everyone ready to fly from the house like so many jaunty balloons. But Sarah, who was at the counter beside the sink sliding puffy bits of leftover potatoes into another plate, her plate, had floated out into an ocean brimming with magic fish. She was the fisherman, not the old wife in the horrible shack, and there was a promise of golden eggs in the ocean's bright surface. At her elbow, the cool, scummy water in the sink rippled with the thumps and footsteps of the children behind her. Ripples in her ocean.

"Mama, there aren't enough coats." Violet stood just at the entrance to the passageway across the room. Her words rose above the other voices.

Who . . . ? There was Bowlie, sitting on the old sofa, looking as though she would gladly walk across town to school with no coat on, if that's how things would end up. She wore her favourite short-sleeved floral-print dress and neat brown stockings. The other girls were dressed in wool coats of navy, dark green, black, chocolate, maroon. Katherine had bought her own coat last winter. She tied a yellow scarf around her neck and left the house.

Sarah's bedroom was dark and cold and peaceful. The privacy of the closet was seductive. Several times over the years she'd been startled when, after the chaos of getting everyone to bed, she'd opened the door to hang up her dress and found a daughter huddled inside, clutching a doll or sucking on a chicken bone.

Three coats hung in the closet, hers, and two very small coats that were big enough only for Molly and Betty-Ann, who didn't go to school yet.

Sarah went back to the kitchen. When she arrived empty-handed, the children fell silent. Then the younger ones began to hurry, in case they should somehow lose the coats they were already wearing. Violet said, "Mama, if you would let Alma or Esther wear your coat just for today, we would have enough."

Sarah stared at Bowlie on the sofa. *Give up her own coat?* "What about tomorrow. So what good would it do? Besides, my coat is a big, black, fat coat. People would think the devil had come to town."

"We can borrow one tonight. Just give us yours for today."

"We will not borrow clothes from our neighbours! I need my coat! I—have to go to buy wool for stockings. And I have to go to the post office. There might be—there might be a letter from your father."

"You could go to the post office after we get home from school."

"I will not be stuck here without my coat!" Sarah was answering Violet, but she was talking to Bowlie, who still sat on the sofa. Lulu and Molly began to cry.

"Well, what can we do then?"

Bowlie did not cry. She was a peaceful flower patch against a nubby red background.

Sarah picked up the breadknife still lying in a bedlam of crumbs on the breakfast table. "There will be enough coats."

With her left hand, Sarah pushed Bowlie off the sofa, and with her right, she plunged the knife into the seam in the middle of the back-rest. She hacked away at the red cloth until straw and stuffing bulged through the gash. No golden eggs, no emeralds or crowns, not even a piece of silk. What riches would she receive for rescuing Bowlie from the simple cold of an autumn morning? Sarah reached in and pulled out musty-smelling pieces of cotton and chintz and felt, frayed shirts, half-skirts, dress-sleeves, patched trousers. The large eyes of her children glowed at their mother's sudden wizardry. Closer they came and closer as the treasure chest spilled remnants of strangers' lives.

At last Sarah pulled out a green wool bundle that, when shaken out, looked like a coat.

"It's all wrinkled," said Moses in her low, old-woman voice.

Sarah held it up to Bowlie's shoulders. "Maybe a little small, but it will do until your father comes home with the money."

While the girls draped themselves in patchworks of cloth remnants, a paisley dress-sleeve here, a tweed pant-leg there, Sarah pulled the ironing board out of a cupboard and lifted one of the sad-irons from the stove. Violet picked straw off the new old coat.

"It just came to me that it was there," Sarah said to herself as she ran the iron along the green fabric. "It's funny how a person remembers things she thought she didn't ever know."

In twos and threes, the girls left the house and shouted down the street and to the new cold air. At the front of the yard, Scratch leaned against a maple tree, smoking a cigarette butt he'd found on the street. Soon only Violet and Bowlie remained in the kitchen.

"He brings us fancy teacups as though we were princesses living in a castle." Sarah's iron thumped on the board and she plucked at wisps of straw caught in the weave. Bowlie and Violet day-dreamed at the table with their chins on their hands.

At last Bowlie put the coat on. A button was missing and the sleeves did not quite touch the bones of her thin wrists. She opened the kitchen door and stood in the cold air for a moment, and watched Scratch puff on the stubby cigarette.

"What's for supper?" asked Violet.

"Fish."

"If they talk, listen."

Sarah went to the window to see the girls leave the yard. The glass was steamed up now and she had to wipe the moisture away with her hand. In a month or so, a layer of ice would coat the window, and she would have to press a hot iron to it to melt it away so she could look out while washing the plates.

The sun was higher and brighter now, and Sarah could see a piece of straw shining in Bowlie's dark hair. The other daughters were strung along the road like coloured wooden beads. All wore their brown woollen stockings. Violet walked by herself at the end, her head tilted up to catch the sunlight on her face. Her coat, a little too long, flapped at her knees. The whistle blew one last time as the train took on water before floating back into the clouds.

The Thing That Grows in the Gasoline Tank
Brian Brett

The series of tacked-together buildings were made of old, dirty pine, and he doubted if any man had the stamina to live in such remarkable decay. Three crows walked the roof of the first. It was a grocery store: closed, deserted. His heart sank into his stomach as he peered through the dirt-caked windows at a home for spiders, its walls cobwebbed into an enormous nest.

A man ambled from behind the structure, an Indian—old and wrinkled like last year's apples. His filthy, long white hair covered his shoulders. "Fine day for a stroll," the Indian said.

Levy was taken aback. "My car broke down." He pointed to the dead vehicle on the crest of the hill.

"It sure picked a good place. This is the only garage for thirty miles in either direction."

"Garage?" Levy examined the ancient buildings cobbled together with dust and Drink 7-Up signs. Around the corner he noticed a rusted gas pump. "So this is a garage." He scratched his head, and managed to resemble what he was—a puzzled bureaucrat. The Indian smiled.

"What's the problem?"

"It just died."

"Let's check it out then."

They climbed the hill. The unbearable heat sapped the salt from their skin, or at least Levy's. The old man didn't perspire at all, and once again Levy thought of apples—dried, wizened, forgotten, yet lurking in the basement. A pathetic cloud scurried for the horizon while the hellish sun sat like a big, red egg in the middle of the sky. "You're not from these parts," the old man said, halfway up the hill.

"No, I came here to negotiate with the tribe in Windridge, about forty miles down the road—settle the complaints over that new housing project outside of town."

"How'd it go?"

"Awful."

"The houses were no good?"

Levy stopped climbing, and caught his breath. He thought about it for a minute. "No, the houses weren't any good."

"Then those people back there, they should get their homes fixed."

Levy hurried to catch up. "Sometimes, unfortunately, it's not as simple as that. The contractor knows how to use the law."

When they reached the car the old man pushed and pulled a few wires and tried the ignition. It wouldn't come alive. "We'll roll it to the garage. I got tools there."

At the garage, that ramshackle monstrosity of a building, the man leaned into the machinery again. Levy rested his back against the building, supervising. If the old man got it fixed, he might yet make it to Vancouver tonight.

Levy watched the Indian take the carburetor off and set it on the fender. "No, it's not the carb," he said, diving under the hood again. Then he removed the battery after carefully inspecting the terminals. "It might be the battery, but if it's the battery, it's caused by something else." Soon the condensor, the voltage regulator, and the distributor were lying in the dust at the side of the car.

"Are you sure you know what you're doing?" Levy asked as the alarming pile of parts grew beside the car.

"If you don't like my work, go to another garage," the man replied, yarding out the starter. "It ain't the starter." The starter was joined by the fuel pump and the alternator. "It's not the alternator either. I think this is serious."

"Serious?" Levy smiled, contemplating the machinery spread around the man's feet. "I did nothing to you."

"I never said you did."

"Then why take my car apart?"

"Broken things, they must be fixed. That's my job."

"What's wrong with my car?"

"It's serious."

"What's wrong with my car?" Levy repeated calmly, "Besides all the parts taken out?" Years of government experience had taught him how to appear placid, no matter what the crisis.

"It's the thing that grows in the gasoline tank."

Levy felt helpless. The sun beat at his eyes, and he leaned against the building again, knowing the dirt coated the shoulders of his shirt, a new kind of jacket. "The thing that grows in the gasoline tank?" He wanted to laugh. He'd been taken apart by a crazy man. How long would it be before he greeted the welcome lights of Vancouver now? It was a long walk out.

The Indian disappeared around the side of the building, and Levy thought he wouldn't see him any more. He was wrong. In a few minutes the man returned with a fishing rod and a disgusting, sour piece of meat. He stuck the meat on a large hook. "You're not going to fish in my gas tank?" The Indian did. He popped the cap off and stuck the meat in. Then he stared at Levy. He fed out some line. After a few seconds he sat in the dust, legs crossed, rod straddling his knees.

Levy could have hit him, could have done many things, but they would do little good at this point. Besides, there might be others around. Unmoving, he attempted to appear as contemptuous as possible. There was no sense giving the old goat satisfaction. If there was a phone . . .

While he was wondering what to do, a cloud of dust puffed into sight on the horizon. It grew. It was a car—a ride? They were driving towards Bella Coola. At least there he could catch a plane and send the police after this crazy. The car roared ahead of its funnel of dust, gradually assuming noise and size. He was about to step onto the road when he noticed it slowing down. They were going to stop anyways. He didn't move. It was full of Indians.

A big, heavy-faced man leaned out the window. "How's the fishing, chief?"

"Slow."

Everyone in the car laughed, their toothless mouths open and facing Levy. One of the women pointed at the pile of parts. They laughed again until the car shook.

The nearest woman stuck her head out the rear window. "What are you fishing for, chief?"

"This government man, he's got the thing that grows in the gasoline tank."

Silence. Levy felt nauseous. "That's bad," a voice said inside the car.

"Very bad," nodded the old man.

"Well, good fishing." Everybody waved. The driver threw the car into gear, and they sped down the road, enveloping the old man and Levy in their dust cloud. Levy remained leaning against the ramshackle building with his arms folded as the dust settled like dry snow. The Indian also remained motionless. "I'll wait him out," Levy thought, "maybe he'll give me a break and put it back together once the joke's finished."

They didn't move for half an hour under the blistering sun. The Indian took out his makings and rolled himself a cigarette. He was licking the paper when he got a strike. Tobacco, paper, and arms went flying into the air. The thing inside jerked at the rod, reminding Levy of a big ling cod fighting to return to the deep. The old man reeled in line. Levy didn't move. He watched, fascinated, as the old man fought the bending rod. Suddenly, the line snapped, and the fisherman flipped backwards, landing on his shoulders. With his arms still crossed, Levy walked to the side of the car while the Indian rolled to his feet—looking even older now.

"He got away," the Indian said.

Levy gawked at the strand of line hanging from the gas tank. Everything was placid. Then something splashed inside, and the line disappeared like a snake being sucked into a hole.

"It's a big one, all right." The Indian brushed himself off, walking around the side of the building. Levy was afraid the man would leave him alone. It was true; there was something in his gas tank. The old man returned with a narrow gaff hook and a second piece of meat. He pulled another fishing hook out of his vest pocket, tied it to the line, jabbed the meat onto the steel barb, and dumped it in.

"This time when he bites, you take the rod and I'll gaff him," he said to Levy who nodded mindlessly in agreement.

Time passed. They waited almost an hour until the rod curved again, and the old man fought the thing, not quite reeling in hard enough to break the line. The fight lulled for a second, and he adroitly handed the rod to Levy, then grabbed the gaff. Levy pulled as hard as he could, his head back, the sun gouging his eyes. He felt the line separate, and he collapsed into the dust. Jumping up, he saw the man had the gaff in the tank, was heaving, trying to jerk something out. There was a loud pop, and the gaff leaped towards them, seemed to stand on end in front of the sun. Levy gaped at the shadow as the sunspots seared his eyes.

It was a dismembered hand, slowly opening and closing, two hooks and the gaff embedded in the flesh; a piece of meat dangled between the gesturing fingers.

Levy sat down in the dust and began to vomit. Everything went grey . . . black . . . grey again . . . and he was conscious once more. There was wet stuff on his shirt front. The Indian stood beside him, holding the gaff with the constantly moving hand.

"It's a man's hand!"

"That's what grows in the gasoline tank."

Levy splashed dust onto his soggy shirt, drying it. "Do you get much of this sort of thing around here?" This was a dream. He knew it was a dream. Besides, nothing as big as that hand could get through the narrow neck of the tank, unless it were elastic. He was going to play along with it. He'd wake up soon.

"Once in a while," the old man said. "On your feet, and I'll show you something. This business can add up."

"How does it eat meat if there's no mouth?"

The Indian shrugged. "Maybe the way a plant eats sunlight."

They walked around to the back of the dusty, worn-down building. The old man asked with an air of concern, "How's your stomach now?"

"Better."

"Good. I want you to have a look at this."

They entered the building. It was dark, windowless and smelled of oil and gas. The old man set the gaff on the cement floor, and the hand slithered away, dragging the wooden handle across the floor with a slow, frightening scrape. There was a flashlight on the table near the door, and the man turned it on. The weak batteries fed a faint light that settled on the hand which seemed to take forever crawling across the dark, dirty floor. At last, the thing came to the edge of a tank and went over the side, landing with a splash.

Levy and the old man approached the edge, and peered down. Within the dim light of the gasoline liquid Levy saw hands scuttling around the bottom, swimming and crawling in every direction. He stepped back, raising his chin towards the dark rafters of the building, attempting to hold onto whatever dignity he had left. "What kind of dream is this? How come it doesn't stop?"

The Indian smiled. "Look closer," he said, "these are the hands of my dead people." Then he gave a soft, sad laugh. "Yet you can never cling to what is already lost."

Levy peeked over the edge at the hideous hands in the gasoline almost ten feet below the cement rim. The old man pushed hard, and he fell. He came to the surface, gasping, choking on the gas, above him the faint silhouette of the Indian's head.

The batteries were growing weaker in the flashlight. Something touched Levy's side, and he brushed it off. He saw them bouncing from the walls, speeding through the gasoline towards him. Five thick fingers tightened around his throat. They were trying to pull him down.

The head of the old man disappeared from the edge.

As if from a great distance, he heard the Indian walk away. And distantly, he heard him say: "Goodbye, government man."

An Afternoon in Bright Sunlight

Shirley Bruised Head

Ayissomaawa . . .

The Porcupine Hills look soft and brown as we stand gazing out over sunburnt prairie grass.

"Come on, guys. Let's go for a ride," says Hank.

Hank is boss. At least he thinks he is. He is a year older than Anne and me and is the only boy in the family. We let him get away with it, sometimes.

Anne agrees with him. She always agrees with him, especially when we have nothing to do. "We'll ask Mom to make some sandwiches."

"Good idea. Tell her we're going to hunt arrowheads."

Hank decides Anne will ride Brownie, a twelve-year-old bay gelding, same age as Hank. He chooses Hoss for me. Hank says, "Hoss needs some kinks worked out, and this is as good a day as any." He chooses Buck, because Buck is his horse and Buck understands him.

Mom packs enough food to last a week, and, as we make our way back to the corral, she comes to the door and yells, "Don't go too far into the coulee, and watch out for rattlesnakes." She mangles a dish towel. "Keep an eye open for that bear Jerry saw last week. He says he spotted it down by the old school and later saw it moving toward the hills." She shakes out the towel and waves it. "Get home before dark." She smiles. "Have a good time."

"Alright," I yell. "We'll be careful."

"Don't let her worry you." Anne picks up the sack. "There are no rattlesnakes in the coulee, and you know Jerry lies a lot."

"I know Jerry lies. I'm not worried."

Hank has the horses saddled and ready to go. He takes the sack and ties it to the back of his saddle.

A wide streak of dust rises, billows out, and kind of hangs in the air. "There's Dad," says Hank. He pats Buck's neck.

Mom doesn't look too pleased. The dust mushrooms. We hear Dad's loud laughing voice, "Hello Dawlink!" Mom takes a swipe at him with her dish towel. "I brought company," he says.

"Isn't that old Sam?" says Hank.

Mom shakes hands with Sam. Her voice carries on the breeze. "Come in. I'll make you something to eat."

Everybody treats Sam with respect. I remember walking in front of him one time, and, boy, did I ever get it from Dad. I stay out of his way, now.

Hank is all excited. "There's Les!"

Les comes running. We all think Les is the greatest. Dad picks him up whenever he needs help. He trains horses for Dad. He trained Hoss, and helps out during calving season. He travels with Dad, and, sometimes, he even drives. He seems older than fourteen.

"Hey, Les," says Hank. "You can ride Hoss."

"Where you going?" Les lengthens the stirrups.

"Hunting arrowheads."

Anne and I stand there listening. They ignore us. They always ignore us.

"Hey! You kids!" shouts Dad from the house. Hank shoves me and Anne up on Brownie, and we take off. We can hear Dad shouting. We reach the coulee, and Hank reins in. Les looks at him.

"Your Dad was calling."

"I know."

"You guys are in trouble."

"He wants us to stay home."

"Well," says Les. "We might as well keep going now. We'll catch heck for one thing or another."

"I know, but maybe if we stay out late, he'll cool off."

"Yeah, he'll get worried," says Anne.

"Yeah, he'll just have more to get mad about," I say.

They just look at me.

We wander into the coulees, stopping every now and then to pick cactus berries. They are green and plump, the size of grapes. Their juice is sweet and sticky. They are easy to find in the short grass, and we go from patch to patch.

As we near an outcropping of rock, Anne says, "Mom said to watch out for rattlesnakes."

"Don't be silly. Everybody knows there are no rattlesnakes in these coulees. Right, Hank?"

Hank and I agree.

"Well, how about that bear Jerry saw?" says Anne.

"Jerry didn't see no bear," laughs Les.

"Are you sure?" Hank licks his lips whenever he's worried. He does it now.

"Sure I'm sure. There hasn't been a bear in these coulees for years."

"Well, a bear could have come down from the hills."

"Look," says Les, "there are no bears in this coulee."

That settles the bear question. We stay away from the rocks. Everybody knows that snakes sun themselves on rocks. None of us likes snakes, especially Hank and Anne.

Hank licks his lips. "Jerry lies a lot."

"You still worried?" says Les.

"I just remembered Dad said he saw something out here."

"I remember, too," says Anne eagerly. "It was the day before Jerry came to visit."

"It was after," I say.

"It was before," says Hank.

Anne smiles at me. "I told you," she says.

"Come to think of it," says Les, "just before we came out, we were at the pool hall in town. Your dad, Sam, and some other men were talking about seeing something out here."

"What did they see?"

"Do you know anything about Sam?"

"Yeah. He's old, and he lives by the school," says Hank.

"You're not supposed to walk in front of him," I say. "Did you know that?"

Anne wants to know more. "What about him?"

Les looks at Hank. "Do you know why he lives there?"

"No."

"He guards the coulees."

We look at Les. He looks back. He isn't smiling. His eyes sweep over us. Then he turns and carefully guides Hoss around a clump of brittle reeds down onto a dry creek bed.

"What do you mean, he guards the coulees?"

"Just that."

"Why should he guard the coulees?" Les has me curious, too.

"Oh," says Les. "There's things out here."

"What kind of things?"

"Animals . . . other things that live in the coulee."

"You've got to be kidding. Only animals live in the coulee." Hank shakes his head and laughs.

"What kind of things?" I insist.

"You don't have to know," Hank cuts in. "What did old Sam have to say?"

In a matter-of-fact tone, Les says, "He thinks a wolverine may have moved in."

"A wolverine? No kidding!" Hank's eyes light up. He moves closer to Les. "Maybe we should forget about arrowheads and go hunting."

"I don't think so."

"But, I've never seen a wolverine. It would be fun."

"We better wait until Sam figures out what to do."

"What does Sam have to do with anything?"

"Sam knows a lot. He says they're dangerous."

I break in. "That's what Emma said."

"Yeah? What did Emma have to say?"

"You're not supposed to listen to Emma," says Anne.

"Well, she says they're dangerous and evil, too."

"Forget about Emma," Hank says, licking his lips. "She's a crazy old lady. Just how dangerous are wolverines?"

"Well, you know that bear?" says Les.

"Yeah?"

"Well, wolverines hunt the hunter."

Hank looks over his shoulder. Anne and I smile.

It is hot. Horse tails switch lazily at slow-moving flies. Saddle leather squeaks. Hooves thud dully on dry grass. An occasional sharp crack echoes down the coulee.

She stands listening to the children's voices. An outcropping of rock hides her den. Inside, it is cool and dry.

Ayissomaawaawa . . . I must be careful, I waited long. Need to grow. Strong. Strong. Strong as when I was young. It was good. Our power was strong. Must be careful. Haste betrays. I must wait. Come, boy. Come alone. Do not fear. There is nothing to fear.

"Hank!" Anne yells. "Look at the chokecherries!"
Low chokecherry bushes grow halfway up the side of the coulee. Their branches hang with thick clusters of black cherries.
"Let's pick some for mom," I say.
Hank dismounts. "Good idea, Girlie. Here, you hold the horses."
"Why do I always have to hold the horses?"
"Because I tell you to."
I look down at him. "We can't pick berries, anyway."
"Why not?"
"We have nothing to put them in."
"We can put them in the lunch sack," says Anne.
"Good idea," says Hank. "We can tie the horses up down by those bushes."

I must wait. Cannot hurry. Wait. Not strong. Stronger must I get. Soon. Soon. So close.

The bushes are low and evenly spaced. They look as if they were planted by someone. Anne and I fill our hats and empty the berries into the sack. We begin filling our hats again, when Anne spots some raspberries growing near the outcropping of rock.
"Come on, Hank. Let's get some of them, too."
"I'm not going over there."
Anne looks at me. I shake my head.
"Just look at them!"
"Go and get them, then," says Les.
"Yeah." Hank and I agree.
"I don't know." Anne looks at the rocks.
"Nobody's stopping you," says Les.
"There might be snakes."
"Snakes won't kill you. These snakes are just ordinary snakes," says Les.
"Then you go and get them."
"I don't like raspberries."

Ayissomaawa . . . Patience. Must have patience. Soon I will have them. I must have them. Must be careful. Not move. Too soon. Wait. Time. Old woman. Now old woman. Do not frighten.

"Let's go, then. You girls wait for us here. Okay?"

"Why do we have to wait?"

Hank is real nasty. "Alright. If you want to walk down, I'm not stopping you."

"I'm not going anyplace." Anne drops to the ground. "You guys can get the horses."

Hank and Les run down the coulee.

"Do you smell something funny?" says Anne.

"Yeah, it smells like sage."

"No. Sage doesn't smell like that."

"Maybe it's dry mint."

"No. Mint doesn't smell like that, either."

"Maybe its a snake den. Snakes like rocks, you know."

"No. It isn't snakes."

"How do you know?"

"I know," says Anne. "Now quit. You're giving me a headache."

We sit there. The sun is beating down. It is quiet. Flies drone. I feel sleepy. The sun is warm on my back.

Ayissomaawa . . .

"Anne! Girlie! Get over here."

Les and Hank have the horses. They wait while we bring the sack of berries.

"Come on. Hurry up!"

"I don't feel so good, Hank," says Anne. "I have a headache."

"Me too."

Hank and Les look at each other. "So do we."

"Maybe we should just go home."

"We can't let a stupid headache stop us from hunting for arrowheads."

Anne and me stand there, looking at Hank. Nobody says anything. Hank looks at us. "Just around the bend is where we found them last time."

"I wonder if there are any left," says Les.

"There should be plenty."

"What happened to the other ones we found?"

"Mom still has them. She takes them out every once in a while."

Ayissomaawa . . . Horses. Horses know us. Must be careful.

"Are we going to hunt arrowheads or stand around here all day?" I say.

"We're going. Now get on that horse."

Hank lifts Anne and me up on Brownie and ties the sack to his saddle. "Ready to go?"

"Yeah."

The horses walk sideways. Their ears flick back and forth. Their eyes roll, and they jerk their heads up and down. We don't go very far.

"What's that smell?"

"Smells like sage to me."

"No, it doesn't." Anne is emphatic. I agree with her.

"Well, it doesn't smell half-bad. It sure is strange, though. Wonder what's causing it." Les looks around.

"What's that?" Anne points to the rocks. I try to see over her shoulder.

"Where?"

"Over there. See?"

"It's just a shadow."

"There's something there," says Anne.

The horses balk. Hoss backs into Brownie.

"Let's go see. Let's find out what it is. Come on, Hank."

Hank licks his lips. "Do you think we should?"

We look at him.

"Well, the horses don't want to go."

Les stands up in his stirrups to get a better view. A surprised look crosses his face.

"It's an old woman."

Brownie whirls. Takes off down the side of the coulee. Anne and I hold on tight. I didn't know Brownie had that much speed. As we hit the bottom of the coulee, I see two riders loom up in front of us. Brownie stumbles, and both of us fall.

"Are you hurt?" Dad sounds worried.

"No," I say, and he pulls me off Anne.

"Anne, Anne, you alright?"

"Yeah, Dad. I'm okay." Anne lies back and starts to cry.

Before Hank and Les can slide to a stop, Dad is already yelling. "How many times have I told you not to run the horses like that?"

"We didn't do nothing." Hank points back to the rocks. "The horses . . . they just took off when they saw that old lady in the coulee."

"What are you talking about?"

"An old woman . . . in the coulee." Hank looks at Les.

"She spooked the horses," says Les.

Dad looks back and forth, eyeing each of us. He knows we wouldn't dare lie to him.

"Did you see her?"

"We didn't get a good look," says Les.

Dad looks at us and then at Sam.

"It was near those rocks," says Hank.

"Yeah, and it smelled kinda like sage," says Les.

"You kids get home right now," says Dad. He shoves me and Anne back up on Brownie. "Get going! Stay there till I get back."

We know an order when we hear one.

Too late. Must move. Always moving. He'll come. Tired. Tired. He has power. He will come. No more.

Dad stands at the mouth of the coulee holding the two horses.

Sam walks into the coulee.

The Knife Sharpener
Bonnie Burnard

"Now tell me again," Janet said, wrapping the yellow scarf around her daughter's neck. Erin was dark, like her mother, with unruly curly hair framing an open face. She began her singsong.

"Don't dawdle, don't play with the dogs, don't talk to anyone I don't know. Go right to Kathleen's house." Kathleen was the twelve-year-old daughter of a friend and she had agreed to walk Erin to school the first year.

"Right," Janet opened the back door. "Off you go. See you at lunch." Mitsy ran up with Daniel in tow.

"Kiss and hug," she demanded. "Kiss and hug for me."

Daniel threw himself into the huddle, his arms raised and eager. After a minute Janet broke them up. "Okay, okay, enough." She herded the little ones back into the den. "Play," she said.

Erin stood hanging on the doorknob, waiting for her mother's hug. She accepted it like a talisman, safer after. "Love you Mom. Bye." She hurried down the steps.

Janet closed the door. She walked back up through the kitchen, grabbed her cigarettes and went to the living room window. From there she could watch Erin march down the driveway and across the street, making her way to the corner, where she turned out of sight. The neighbour, the older woman whose children were grown, sometimes watched Erin too. She'd told Janet that the child walked just like her mother. It was a kind of hurried saunter, a shuffle, anything but graceful. Janet lit her cigarette. Here and there, patches of the road had been worn by traffic to blue-black ice. The smaller kids on the street ran to those patches, sliding as fast and as far as they could, but always later in the morning, when the neighbourhood traffic had ceased and the street was quiet. For the past few years Janet and the other mothers had taken informal turns supervising the play and even when she was not on patrol, pacing and jumping in her parka and mukluks, she watched from the living room window. This year Erin would not be involved in the games. She was off, on her own.

Mitsy and Daniel stood with Janet now, their hands pressed against the cold window. Mitsy wrapped her arms around her mother's leg. "Time for toast," she said.

Daniel joined in, happy to hear a word he could echo. "Toast," he said. "Toast, toast, toast and jam."

"Okay." Janet took a hand in each of her own. "Let's do it."

The kids hauled themselves up to their places at the table while Janet dropped some bread into the toaster and eased the handle down to catch. She got the peanut butter and jam out and cleared Erin's cereal and juice away. The kids sat quietly, eyeing each other. Any minute some squabble would break out and then in another minute they would be best friends again. It would go on like that all day. She wondered when real long-lasting malice would begin. She'd seen hints of it in Erin, big hints.

The toast popped up.

"There it is," Daniel yelled.

She made herself a cup of coffee and sat down with them. Erin will be in school by now, she thought, will be taking off her coat and scarf and boots and sitting down at her desk, ready.

When the kids had finished eating she took them to the TV in the den. They settled down in front of "Romper Room", waiting for their instructions from the young woman who would lead them through their romps. Janet looked at the woman's perfect face. "You do a fine job," she said. "You're a good broad."

She spoke to the backs on the floor. "I'm going up to shower now. I'll leave the bathroom door open." They ignored her.

She hurried upstairs and made the beds. One of her husband's jackets hung on the bedroom door. That meant it needed a button; the button would be in the pocket. She stripped in the hall, tossing her nightie down the chute before going to the bathroom to turn on the water. Then back to the top of the stairs to listen for any noise other than the voice of Miss whatever-her-name-was on TV. Then into the shower. She sudsed her hair and groaned into the steamy water. Someday she would stand there for an hour, just stand, steaming, wasting water.

Afterwards, downstairs to check the kids and downstairs again to the wash in the basement. Left, right, white, coloured; left, right, white, coloured. She threw the white into the washer. Then upstairs to the bananas. They were past eating raw, ready to be made into muffins. She'd do this, check the mail, have another coffee. Then the kids. Hold them. Tell them there would be muffins.

She was mashing the bananas when the back doorbell rang. Oh go away, she thought, leave me be. But she went to the door and opened it. It was an old man.

"Yes?" she said.

"Morning." He tipped an imaginary hat to her. "I was wondering if you'd have any knives that could use sharpening?"

He was tall but his shoulders were stooped under the sloppy sleeves of a heavy grey curling sweater. It was not zippered and she could see suspenders. They held up dingy brown draped pants, the kind the young guys were wearing again now, but these were from some former life in the world of fashion. A satchel hung over his shoulder, bulky with something heavy. His face, fleshier than the rest of him, was a sickly, ashen colour. Her eyes finally settled on his. They were clear and alert, under bushy grey eyebrows. Well, he's not a drunk, she thought.

"Knives?" she asked.

"Maybe you've heard from your neighbours. I come round every March. Do mowers as well." He bundled his sweater around his chest, moving his weight from one foot to the other.

"Come in," Janet said. "You're cold." She closed the door behind him. "I guess I likely have some that aren't as sharp as they might be. How much do you charge?"

"That's up to you, Mrs.," he said.

Janet started toward the kitchen. "Come this way. I'll give you the knives. The mower's in the basement."

Mitsy and Daniel erupted from their play trance. "Hi," Mitsy said. "Who are you?"

Janet shooed them away from the knife sharpener. She led him to the kitchen drawer and handed him the knives, one after another. "These, I guess."

Downstairs in the basement, she pointed to her husband's workshop. "The mower's in there. I'll leave you to it."

She watched him look around. He dragged a lawn chair over to the workbench, opened his satchel and took out his whetstone.

Janet went to the washer, emptied the white load into the dryer, threw in the coloured and left him to go upstairs. The kids were busy with Lego. She finished the muffins.

Then Mitsy was at her knees.

"Hi, sweetheart," she said. "I'm coming to sit with you." She led her by the hand down into the den. They sat on the floor with Daniel and he pointed to the abstraction he'd built. "Tree," he said.

She played with them, letting them roll over and around her like bear cubs. Between squeals, she could hear from the basement the rhythmic scrape of steel against whetstone. She wondered if he could hear the squeals. The timer buzzed.

"Muffins!" she said.

The kids ran ahead of her, stopping just short of the stove. She pushed them back so she could open the oven door. "They have to cool a bit." She dumped the pans upside-down on the counter. Steam rushed up to her face and a sweet banana smell filled the kitchen. The kids danced around her. "In a minute," she said.

She put the kettle on for tea. He can likely smell the muffins, she thought. She reached for the cups and got the tray out from behind the spices. Two hands reached up over the counter and she put a steaming muffin in each. "Blow on them," she warned. "I'm going downstairs. You eat your muffins with Big Bird." They wandered off, watching their muffins as they carried them.

When the tea was ready, she arranged the pot and cups on the tray with a plate of muffins and carried it down to him. He was bent over his work, his knees braced under his thickly muscled arms. He didn't see her until she was right in front of him. He jumped a little.

"Thought you might like some tea and muffins." She put the tray on the workbench.

"Don't mind if I do," he said. He set the knife he was working on down beside him on the floor, the whetstone on his lap. "This is one fine old house," he said. "Tell by the shape of the basement." He waited for her to pour his tea.

"Yes," she said. "It's got some creaks and cracks but we like it." She leaned against the wall.

He took a muffin. "What line of work's your husband in?" he asked.

"He's an architect," she answered.

"That'd be interesting," he nodded.

"Are you retired from something?" Janet asked. "I'm guessing this is sort of a hobby?"

He leaned back to give her room as she poured his tea. "Retired from a lot of things," he chuckled. "Never been very lucky with a career." He took a sip of tea and added some milk. "Had jobs, though. Some good, some not so good."

Janet thought about her father. He'd been lucky; he'd made it. All the men in her life had made it, one way or another.

"I quit regular work when my wife died," he said. "She needed money more than I ever did."

"I'm sorry," Janet offered.

"Oh, that's all right," he said. "We didn't get along anyway. She spent most of her time hanging over a bingo card, anxious for the big win. Did make a good pot of tea, though. Like you. I miss a woman pouring my tea."

"You have children?" Janet asked.

"Two," he said. "The young lady took off with the scum of the earth when she was sixteen and my boy's over in the North Sea, drilling for oil. He don't write much but I follow the papers to see what's going on over there. His mother used to worry over him but I don't. He's a hell of a swimmer. If the thing threatened to blow, he'd be the first one off, guaranteed." He broke a muffin open and wiped his mouth with the sleeve of his sweater.

Janet saw that the cuff was unravelling, eating away at itself. "That would be a good high-paying job for a young man," she said.

"He's not so young," he said. "He came home two years ago to bury his mother and he was thirty-five then."

Janet was sorry she'd poured a cup for herself and she finished it quickly.

He put his teacup on the tray. "Thanks a million," he said. He picked up his whetstone. "I better get to work here."

"And I better get back upstairs," Janet said. "My oldest will be home soon. I'll leave the muffins for you."

"How old's she?" the knife sharpener asked.

"Six," Janet answered.

"That's a nice age," he said.

She left him to finish, got the clothes out of the dryer and put the coloured load in. Upstairs, she dumped the clothes on the floor with the kids and began to fold. The back door flew open.

Erin ran across the rug and threw herself into the mess of clothes and arms on the floor. "I'm home," she said.

"Boots off," Janet said. "How was school this morning?"

Erin trudged back to the door, kicking off her boots. "We did art," she said. "Real art."

The kids looked at something behind Janet. It was the knife sharpener.

"Finished," he said.

"Oh, good," Janet got up from the floor. "I'll get my purse."

Erin came back into the room. "You're not the plumber," she said.

"No," he answered. "I just had tea with your mommy and sharpened some things for her."

Janet stood beside him, offering a ten dollar bill. "Is this all right?"

"That's good, Mrs. Thank you."

Erin had come to stand in front of her mother, wrapping Janet's arms around her chest.

"I was wondering if you'd like to stay and have lunch with us?" Janet asked. "Just soup."

"No, " he said. "I'll be off, thank you." He walked over to the door, turning to wave at the kids as he let himself out.

They all admired Erin's school work, her bold triangles and shaky circles, then Janet went up to put the soup on to heat. She saw the knives on the counter. She was glad she'd had them sharpened. They were overdue. She gathered them up in a bunch and put them into an upper cupboard. They'd have to stay there for a while; the kids wouldn't know how sharp they were until one of them was cut and bleeding.

After lunch, Janet stood at the living room window again, watching Erin, admiring the way she swung her book bag. As the child crossed the street, she took a good run at a sheet of ice, skidding across it and tripping up onto the sidewalk. Erin, the name book said: a fair jewel set in a tranquil sea. Janet wondered if hard work and luck would bring her a good old age with her children. She wondered about the places downtown that offered some warmth, some company. Old hotels, there were six or seven of them, close to the Bay.

She saw him clearly, standing at the corner, his hand outstretched to Erin. Erin gave a little skip then took his hand; Janet had seen her take her grandfather's hand just that way. They walked together around the corner.

She ran back to Mitsy and Daniel in the den. They were watching "Mister Rogers". "Don't move," she said. "I just have to go out for a minute."

She grabbed her coat from the closet and was out the door and half-way down the driveway before she had it on. She ran as hard as she could, down to the corner and around it. Nothing. They were gone. There were two lanes mid-way down the block, one going south, one north, back toward the house. Don't call her name, she told herself. Don't call her name. There are garages, empty yards, shrubs to hide in. She decided on the lane going south. That's where he'd take her. She ran across the street. Her slippers were slapping hard on the icy pavement, loud. She kicked them off and started down the lane in her stockinged feet. She looked in the yards on each side as she ran, looked in every filthy garage window, in every overgrown space between house and fence.

She saw Erin's scarf snagged around the stuccoed corner of a garage twenty yards ahead. She let loose, let everything she had go to her legs.

She found Erin tucked into an evergreen hedge. The knife sharpener was crouched down talking to her in a gentle old man's voice. Janet pulled her away from him, turning the small face into the front of her coat.

The knife sharpener stood up and started to back away from them. "I wouldn't have hurt her, Mrs."

"Just what the hell would you have done with her then? Just what the hell do you think . . ." Janet heard the ugly edge to her voice and she knew she'd have to stop. Erin had taken her hand.

The knife sharpener was edging back, along the wall of the garage. "Please don't call the police," he said.

"What choice do I have?" Janet asked. She saw Erin watching, listening.

They turned their backs on him, walking down the lane and out into the street. She found her slippers there, overturned in the snow and she put them on. Erin hadn't said anything. Just keep quiet, Janet told herself, let her questions sort themselves out. She'll ask the right one. They were nearly at Kathleen's house.

"I shouldn't have gone with him, should I?" Erin looked down at her boots. "He was a stranger."

"No," Janet said. "You shouldn't have. You can know strangers a little bit but they're still strangers."

Erin kicked at the snow. "I thought he was a friend of yours."

Kathleen ran noisily toward them. "Where've you been?" she asked. "My mom's been phoning. We're late. C'mon."

"Hi," Erin said calmly, as though nothing had happened to her. She took her friend's hand. "See you later, Mom."

"Wait, Kathleen," Janet put her hand on the girl's book bag. "You be sure you don't talk to anyone you don't know. All right?"

"I never do. What's wrong?" she asked.

"Just make sure, that's all. I'll talk to your mom this afternoon." Janet watched the two of them go off down the street. Erin was leaning, just slightly, into Kathleen's shoulder. She turned back toward the house and, remembering Mitsy and Daniel, began to run again.

They were fine. They had all the muffins, some half eaten, spread out around them on the floor. "Mister Rogers" was still on. Janet looked at the screen, at his kind face, at his kind cardigan sweater. She felt her feet stinging from the cold.

She went to the living room window with her cigarettes. The snow on the lawns was blue-white in the sun and the black ice on the street had been covered with a light dusting of snow she hadn't seen fall.

She had choices. She could call her husband, who would likely call the police. She could describe the knife sharpener. She could make it so bad for him that he'd never show his face in their world again. Or she could say absolutely nothing, to anyone, ever.

She could take a calm liberal stance. She could get in the Toyota and find him, talk to him, listen to him. She could remind him of his own daughter, when she was small and trusting on his knee. Before she took off with the scum of the earth.

Or she could take the grey ceramic ashtray from the coffee table and hurl it across the room at the fireplace where it would shatter and come to rest in pieces among the ashes.

The Museum of Man
Mel Dagg

Smitty is crazy. Quite mad. I see that now. It has taken four and a half days locked in the cab of this van with him, listening to his constant ravings as we speed across Canada, to come to this conclusion—definitely crazy.

I'm his assistant. I take photographs, handle equipment, attend to details, arrangements, and like all assistants, feed his craziness. That's my job. That's what I get paid for. Still, it beats working on newspapers. Better to feed the refined craziness of an anthropologist, than the daily hunger of thousands of newspaper readers.

Smitty's craziness is more civilized, more intricate, more complex. It centres around what has become the consuming passion of his life, his mission, his personal fantasy. And the government has granted him unlimited funds to realize that fantasy—The Museum of Man. Five concentrated years of collecting. Totem poles cut down in the Queen Charlottes and shipped to Ottawa, medicine bundles from the prairies. Eskimo carvings, relics, beadwork, and now, his crowning achievement, his, as the Indians would say, *coup*, Victoria Red Plume. He has heard she is dying, this old woman, the last of the quillworkers, and we have travelled day and night to reach her.

"Preserve, Danny, don't you see? It all has to be preserved, before it's too late, before," his eyes now completely off the road as he turns to me, his voice rising, "before the culture is dead."

"For Christ's sake," I scream, "*we'll* be dead if you don't watch your driving."

He swerves back into our lane just as the transport truck bearing down on us hits the gravel shoulder. Smitty isn't concerned about details. He has his own private vision, his Museum of Man. I close my eyes, trying to catch some sleep as he drones on, reassured by the fact that we're almost there.

Funny though, now that he mentions it, I haven't seen any dying culture, or dead Indians, for that matter. In Kenora, much to the discomfort of the rest of the town, they seemed unavoidably alive. In fact, one of them nearly knocked me over as I walked through the bar door trying to get a little relief from Smitty. Later, on the highway, I tried counting trees, but they began to shrink, smaller and smaller, until there weren't any at all, just Manitoba scrub. Then it was gone and there was nothing, nothing but the inescapable prairie sky. Suddenly I felt small, vulnerable, threatened, dwarfed by a barren nudity that stretched forever, drowning under the immensity of a clear blue flooding sky. It reached down to touch the tips of fence posts, and it reached down to touch me. I shifted uncomfortably in my seat, feeling its presence.

"It all has to be preserved," he said, still overcome by seeing his first live Indians in Kenora. He hadn't noticed the sky. In the evening I pointed the van toward the gigantic orange globe flaring against the western rim of the earth.

He would have shipped them all back to Ottawa, alive, enclosed in his goddam glass museum cases, if he had had the chance. I jammed the accelerator to the floor and hurtled into the consuming flames of the setting sun, me thinking maybe seeing the old woman will change him.

The van shakes me awake and I hear Smitty say "we're almost there" as we bump up over the railway tracks and enter the reserve. An old man weaves drunkenly ahead of the children straggling along the roadside. He is waving stupidly at us and I can feel eyes staring out of windows as we rattle down the dusty pothole-pitted road. Finally Smitty swerves in at a house set apart from the others by a row of poplars and we lurch to a halt in the yard.

We sit staring out through our insect-smattered windshield at the collection of farm machinery, rusted out shells of cars, gas and diesel barrels, tractors, and rolls of barbed wire surrounding us. A wisp of smoke rises from a barrel of smouldering garbage. Three thin half-wild dogs sniff at the base of the barrel, eyeing us nervously. A green plastic garden hose snakes out past the smoking barrel and disappears into an old bath-tub overflowing with water. Staring at us dumbly through the distance, a small herd of cattle shiver in the heat as they shake the cloud of mosquitoes clinging to them.

"Well, what are we waiting for?" I ask Smitty. "Let's go," I repeat, grabbing my equipment, opening the door of the van.

"Grannie, there's some men here to see you," calls a small girl, running ahead of us as we pick our way through the yard.

"Yes, I know, child. Now run along and play," a voice answers from the other side of a hedge.

Then, inside the hedge, suddenly we see her. She is sitting on a faded red blanket, her quills neatly arranged before her in rowns, and as we move toward her it seems she has always been here under this tree, working with her quills, waiting for us. Or maybe she's just squatting on the ground out here because she doesn't want us in her house. And me, I'm starting to wonder what right we have to be here anyhow.

Watching her long white braids trail down her arched back, her whole body bent in concentration upon the brightly coloured beads, quills, and scraps of leather spread before her, I see that she is much older than I expected. Her brown hands are wrinkled, yet they don't shake. Her fingers move steadily, surely, as she handles her materials. She has passed beyond age. We do not exist. She is oblivious to our presence here, involved in the detail, the creation of a pattern of which we form no part.

"Mrs. Red Plume?" asks Smitty.

"Yes," she answers, not looking up at us.

"We've come from Ottawa," announces Smitty, fiddling with his pen and note-pad, "to make a permanent record of you doing your quillwork. My name is Edwin Schmidt, Doctor Edwin Schmidt, and this is my assistant, Danny Stone," he adds, waving at me.

I'm kneeling in front of her, trying to get a reading on her face, watching the dial of the light meter wave back and forth between the dark brown of her skin and the shining creases catching the sunlight. It's impossible, I'll just have to guess.

"Now, Mrs. Red Plume," continues Smitty, speaking slowly, deliberately, "our research shows that you are one of the last living quillworkers in Canada. It is very important that we record and gather a specimen of your work, before it is too late, before . . ." searching for the words he speaks so easily to me, "before it becomes a lost art. Do you understand?"

"Gathering specimens? No. I don't understand. Every summer men like you come to our reserve with cameras, tape-recorders, typewriters. Why? Everything has been taken from us except this land we are enclosed on. There is nothing left here now. What do you want? For years we were told it was wrong to live as Indians, to forget the old ways, the hunt, the Sun-dance, our religion, to farm as whites. But now you come caring only about this single thing, the few sacred remains that remind us of the time when we moved with freedom upon the land. You don't care about us, how we live now."

"But of course we care, Mrs. Red Plume," soothes Smitty, carefully pronouncing her name correctly. "That's why we're here."

"No, you're here because you want this single thing. You do not care whether we are able to put up the thousands of bales of wild reserve grass needed to feed our cattle through the winter. You do not know we can't borrow money on reserve land, like white farmers, to increase our herd or buy better equipment. You do not live on bannock and sell prime beef in Calgary to pay off debts on farm machinery that is already old. You do not live from day to day. You do not know. You only care about this single thing. You have taken everything else, and now you want this too. You have no right to ask for this small thing, this little that remains. I do not think you understand that when the legends and myths we speak, telling them through the night, through the years, telling them differently each time, are printed in your children's books, they change, they die. Oh, you will give me a ten dollar bill, or send me copies, but my name is never on the book. And my name is nothing. You are nothing."

"But the civilized world, Ottawa waits . . ." Smitty splutters into silence as the old woman continues talking right through him.

"My skill at working with quills is a gift, a sacred right given to a chosen few, passed down to only one daughter in each generation. The dyes, the designs, the symbols, none of these are mine. They were given to my grandmother just as she gave them to me. I know which pattern was taken in a *coup* against the Sioux, which was stolen in a raid on the Crees. I am only the receiver, the last small bead sliding down a waxed thread, fixed forever in a design that reaches back to a time when my people moved freely, shifting across the prairie, following the buffalo. When I hold this small medallion the beads move to tell me their story."

The bright coloured beads flash in the palm of her brown hand, swirling in their spiralled, contained design. She is connected to something outside us, outside herself.

I try to think what that might be, on this reserve, a woman of prestige, an elder, a member of the *Moto-kiks* society, a Holy Woman. As sure as Smitty and I have without ceremony sacreligiously opened, ransacked, photographed and framed in glass dozens of them, there's a medicine bundle in that house she will not have us enter, and into which, even as she sits before us, she's already entered, connected to it. My god, while Smitty mumbles officiously and I fumble with my camera, she's rummaging around inside her medicine bundle.

"Do you understand?" repeats Smitty, not understanding, unable to reach her.

A young girl is dancing with the women, weaving a circle, a human mandala of loping, fringed, beaded buckskin, her arched moccasined feet gently touching the prairie with each rhythmic beat of the drum. The smell of fresh smoking meat drips over the fires, drifting through the camp, mingling with the chant of the drummers.

"Yes," she replies finally in a quiet monotone, "I understand," looking up for the first time, right at Smitty, her brown, wizened face expressionless, as if she is looking through him, as if he isn't there. Then slowly, bending in concentration, she begins working with the quills.

She picks up the first red hollow quill, places it in her mouth, draws it through her teeth, then the next, flattening them one by one, drawing them through, placing them over the two strips of sinew, carefully overlapping the quills so they seem one, a continuous band of red, growing slowly at first, now more quickly.

Smitty nudges me, wanting photographs, but I can't get the f-stop right, feeling that medicine bundle pulling, tugging at her back, drawing her out until she is lost in something that has never stopped. Someone else, another woman, directs her hands, draws the quills through her teeth, links them together. And as the strip of red grows, the bond grows, strengthens until they are one, bound together as each of the quills are bound.

The orange embers of the fire flicker across the dark swaying faces of the elders, blending with the humped figures of buffalo painted on the inside of the lodge-skins.

The girl watches as the moving shadows of the old people weave among the painted figures of the animals, becoming a single movement. Suddenly the grey long hair of an old woman shines in the firelight as she leans out of the semi-darkness, into the flames, plunges a willow fork into the fire, and removes on the end of her tongs a bright coal that in the darkness becomes a thin orange line as the old woman traces out her pattern, waving the ember through the lodge, holding it aloft on the end of her willow fork. Four times the bright orange line moves upward to the sky, four times it arcs out of the darkness toward the girl, and four times it moves downward, to the earth. Finally it is stilled, becomes again a stationary spark on the end of a willow stick. The cord of a leather bag is undone and the dry sweet-grass, twisted into a golden braid, is handed to the old woman. Again the spark at the end of her willow tong moves, touching the braided sweet-grass until a thin sweet-smelling column of smoke begins to rise from the grass. In the silence the girl closes her eyes, breathing in the sweet heavy incense that hangs hovering within the closed cone of the teepee. A hand touches her forehead in the darkness. Quietly the whisper of many voices rises gradually to a soft chant, filling the wind-hushed stillness of the prairie night with prayers.

The pages of Smitty's note-book flap in the hot summer wind as the old woman works on, oblivious to the constant flick of my shutter as I try to freeze each rapid movement, the blur of her brown wrinkled hands lost in repeated, familiar ritual.

Through air heavy with heat, the buzz of flies, water overflowing from a bath-tub, the faint distant drone of a tractor, the low guttural murmur of her voice speaks not to us, but beyond, to her connection.

"Each time I work a quill into place I lengthen the band begun by my grandmother. I hold a quill in my hand and I am with her. We are the two strips of sinew running parallel to each other, joined by the quills that cross over them, joined through time. Now there is only one quill remaining to fit into place, to complete the pattern."

A hot gust of wind lifts the poplar leaves, brushes the grass, bends the dry brown blades almost to the ground. The light keeps changing.

"That's lovely, really lovely, Mrs. Red Plume," says Smitty. "We're just in time."

She is holding the quill, turning it between her fingers against the setting sun. She stares at the quill, turning it slowly, as if she doesn't hear him. The thin shaft's sharp tip catches the sun, flaring into the lens of my

camera, blinding, bright as the electric white arc at the end of a welder's
rod, still it turns.

*Tinder-dry late September grass crackles under the soft soles of the old woman's
moccasins. Beside her the girl walks lightly. These are her favourite days, spent
alone with the old woman, apart from the crowded constantly moving life of the
camp. For a moment they stand together at the top of the ridge, looking down into
the gently sloping small valley. In its lower-most dip, the brown grass is broken by
a fringe of green bushes bordering the small creek that slowly trickles, snaking
through the centre of the valley. They have waited for this, the day after the first
evening of fall frost to lightly brush against the bushes. She cannot contain herself.
She begins to run, feeling the seeds of the tall grass flick against her bare legs, the
slope of the hill pulling her forward, carrying her faster and faster. At the bottom,
breathless, she lies waiting by the creek bed, hearing the faint laughter of the old
woman slowly move down the hillside.*

*The thin supple branches swoop downward, heavy with the weight of the ripe
berries hanging in clusters at their tips. The girl reaches up, her hand closing
around the smooth branch. Like blood the berries fall from the shaking leaves, slowly
covering the grandmother's blanket.*

*The old woman kneels down, scooping a handful of berries into a small
buckskin bag, setting them aside for dye. Then the four corners of the laden blanket
are tied together and they begin their journey back to the camp. As they slowly climb
the hill, both carrying the heavy knapsack of ripe fruit, the girl listens as for the
first time she is told of the quillwork; how it is a sacred gift given only to those
chosen by the old people; how the fingers of women who work the quills without their
blessing become swollen and ugly, so that they are known to everyone, how
Lightning in anger once blinded a woman who had not been chosen, who attempted
to work the quills without permission.*

*At the edge of the camp the old woman and the girl stop for a moment, resting
near the horses. From within the folds of her large dress the grandmother removes
the small leather bag. Placing some quills in with the berries, she pulls the draw-cord
tight and hands the bag to the girl, telling her to sleep with it.*

*For two nights the girl tosses in her sleep, shifting uncomfortably, feeling the
small lump beneath her body. Then on the third night, startled, she awakes, not
feeling the leather bag under her. At her feet sits the old woman. One by one she
removes the quills from the bag, rubbing them in bear fat until they shine, scarlet
against the coals of the fire.*

She is still holding the quills to the sun, staring at the pin-point, the small concentrated nimbus flaring at its tip. I close the lens opening to cut the glare, taking advantage of her pause to get a portrait.

"What an exhibit this will make for the museum!" says Smitty, looking down at the quillwork resting in the folds of her faded cotton print dress.

"I went to a museum once, many years ago in Calgary, with my husband. It was called a foundation, designed to preserve the history of the West. Crowfoot, the chief who surrendered our land to the C.P.R., was called a 'wise statesman.' The R.C.M.P., they said, arrived just in time to save us from ourselves. I have never forgotten the feeling as we stood looking in at objects of our own culture exhibited in glass display cases for whites. Many of them were sacred to our religion. Medicine bundles that could never be recreated, except in a vision, and were only to be opened by their owner, lay undone. I read the neatly lettered card inside the glass case telling of the contents spilling out of the opened medicine bundle. To us, the patterns on the beadwork only lived, moved, if they were worn, the bundles only held meaning for their owners. My husband cursed in our language. A choking dust was settling on everything. We felt death all around us as we left.

"Now I sit here staring west, this almost completed quillwork in my lap, and your museum returns to me. I am beginning to see." She squints into the horizon, pointing two miles away at a yellow school bus.

The highest thing on the horizon, I watch the bus hump across the edge of the earth and disappear, a burnt dot devoured by the blazing globe setting behind it.

"That is the bus returning children for the weekend from the white schools in the city," she says. "Rachel, my granddaughter, will be on that bus. I know that this last quill I hold in my hand must be given to her, as my grandmother gave it to me, not stifled in your glass cases. There is so much to do, so little time. The hide I left soaking in the old bath-tub is not yet ready for tanning and in the morning she will come. How the child loves the smell of the soft, smoke-tanned leather as I guide the needle in her hands."

Ignoring her, Smitty licks the flap of a long envelope. He bends forward and picks up the quillwork resting in the folds of her dress.

"But it isn't finished," she says. "Without the last quill in place, the two sinews joined together so the red band narrows to a fine point, it holds no meaning."

"It's perfect, Mrs. Red Plume, just what we want," Smitty says, slides the quillwork into the envelope, seals it.

It is as the old woman leans forward slightly, the lines in her face suddenly sharpening in the camera's frame, that I see for the first time what I should have known all along. That the rapid sequence of film, the record of each movement and detail of her work, shot on the automatic setting, was never quite in focus.

"We've got it Danny. We've done it!" Smitty beams, ecstatic in the cab of the truck, holding the precious envelope, his career, in his hands.

"We don't have anything," I say, for once unable to humour him. "Not even a photograph."

A Plague of Armadillos

James Michael Dance

Armadillos. Everywhere. There was just no getting around it. They were everywhere.

It hadn't been so bad at first; one here, one there, one in the corner or the one on the sofa, the one in the garden as regular as morning coffee—then it wasn't so bad. Now they were everywhere. Armadillos. Everywhere.

Joe Burns was a businessman. He did not have much use for armadillos, yet he tolerated them and did not even mind them very much at first. But that was before.

Joe Burns drank. A lot. He liked to drink, it got him through his days and nights, early mornings and late evenings. He also had a wife and a home and, although he did not know them very well, he did appreciate them. That was why he resented this invasion of his privacy, these armadillos, that is; they were everywhere.

Joe first caught sight of one early one morning just as he was leaving for work. There it was in the garden, an armadillo watching him. There was no expression on its face, no wrinkling of its nose or curl of the mouth, no sign of fear and no emotion in its beady eyes. It merely stared balefully at him just as he stared back at it. Deciding on a stand-off, Joe muttered, "Ridiculous looking thing," under his breath, turned away from it and got into his car, whereupon he promptly opened the glove compartment and took a deep swig of a bottle of whiskey he kept there, as a sort of pacifier of his nerves. That made things all right again.

"Getting low," he thought and, with a glance at the armadillo that still looked back at him just as silently and as solemnly as ever, he drove off to work, stopping only to pick up a bottle and some gum for the office.

Joe chewed a lot of gum. He found that people often averted their faces with surprising alacrity when he spoke to them, and, assuming them to be abstainers but having to deal with them anyway, he chewed gum. A glorious compromise, he thought.

It was not so easy with the armadillos, however. He saw no more that day but when he returned home, tripping as lightly as ever, there was that same armadillo in the same spot, the same expressionless gaze, just sitting there.

As usual Joe ate little and turned in early. It was a habit with him; too much food tended to upset his stomach, while too little sleep made it difficult to get up. Joe looked forward to waking up in the morning, to his early drop or three of spirits, to fresh packages of gum, and even the possibility (always exciting) of cracking a new bottle. He had never reckoned with armadillos, though.

When he first opened his bleary, dream-clouded eyes next morning, he thought he saw an armadillo looking him straight in the face. The apparition vanished with wakefulness, but the impression did not.

Leaving the house brought more surprises. In the garden where before there had been only one armadillo, there were now two. They both stood silent, motionless, and ever watchful, as if frozen into a position of eternal immobility, as if waiting for something. The morning paper perhaps? Joe shook his foggy head. That was ridiculous.

"Scoundrels," he thought and glared at them for a moment before going to work.

As he drove Joe sipped happily on his bottle, capped it, and suddenly swerved to avoid hitting a ratlike creature with a shell (an armadillo) that ran out in front of his car.

"Stupid thing. I might have spilled something," was his immediate reaction. He drove the rest of the way without incident but at the office they began to show themselves more and more. After that there was simply no getting away from them. They were in the hall, on his desk, waiting for him in his car. There were three in the garden when he got home and even one at the dinner table, but that he could brook. Food was not of primary importance anyhow. But in his bedroom. It was beginning to go too far. Why soon the darn things would be sleeping with him and his wife. Joe could not accept that; he liked to sleep with his wife, or beside her anyway.

The next day at work he kicked one of them that got underfoot (they always got underfoot, blast them), but the thing just leered back at him.

In his office they sat and gazed at him, pitilessly, like buzzards, but as slow and steady as a lot of silent turtles, and they multiplied. He even imagined that they talked among themselves in low tones, but about what he could not even guess.

Joe was glad to leave the office but outside things were not better. They were in his car, on his car, all around his car, they were everywhere. Armadillos. Everywhere.

There were more in the garden and in his home, and there was even one perched on his wife's shoulder at dinnertime, which he stared at unhappily for some time, much to his wife's discomfort.

The more of the things he saw, the more he drank and the more unhappy he became. Not even the strongest whiskey could give him solace. He ferried dozens of armadillos to the office very day, and there seemed to be hundreds of them in the streets. He worked and drank all day long under their penetrating gaze and spent most of his nights in a bar, as he was often accustomed to do, still surrounded by the awful things. They slept with him and they woke up with him, they went to work with him and gave him no peace, not for a moment. Joe dreamed of armadillos, Joe saw armadillos, everywhere. In short they made his life miserable.

"It's all so unfair," he thought, blubbering into a bottle. "It's not even fair. There's just no way out of it, no solution to be found." And with that he tossed off a large portion of the bottle, even large for Joe, and contemplated the inanity of it all, of his whole ugly situation.

Things were fast coming to a head.

The climax came when Joe was seated in his office, in front of the desk, drinking and working. His office seemed much smaller now, having become quite crowded with armadillos. The supreme moment of despair and frustration came when one of them (fancy, just fancy the gall) actually tried to jump on his shoulder. This sudden action took Joe so completely by surprise and so horrified him that he nearly choked on a mouthful of good liquor, and even spilled a quantity of it on his tie and clean shirt, leaving him speechless with rage, such was the shock. Was it not enough that they constantly surrounded him, haunted him, had invaded his home, his garden, his office, and even his bed? Was there no end to it? And now in their boldness they even dared to sneer at him, even touch him and rest on his shoulder? Making him spill good liquor was the final straw, so to speak, a tragedy that he could not let go by.

"Oh, those damned armadillos," he gasped, still stunned by their audacity and even their rudeness.

But Joe Burns was no fool. He immediately got hold of himself, took a drink and decided on action. Joe was a man of strong will, of quick judgement, able to make decisions; no armadillo was going to get the best of Joe. The situation had become unbearable, and something had to be done.

Well, that was it then. No more armadillos, none, no more. He simply would not accept them, would not even recognize their existence. And sure enough they went away and bothered Joe Burns no more.

Joe drank, ate, slept and drank happily for the next few days. He forgot all about armadillos, and it seemed as though the sun was shining on his world once again. All was fine.

Except for one thing. Badgers. One day there was a badger in Joe's garden, the next day there was one in his office. Badgers were all right, though. Anything but armadillos. They were in fact (the badgers, that is) quite agreeable creatures—quiet, solemn, and never in his way, never any sudden movements, always calm and collected, considering all the possibilities.

They looked almost friendly in a way, and Joe even offered them drinks from time to time, but they were sober sorts. "Just as well," Joe thought. "Enough drinkers in the world, heh heh." They even reminded him a bit of his father, but no, wait a minute, that was ridiculous. "Why they're not at all like my father, not a bit," and that was that.

But they multiplied, it seemed, though not quickly, they didn't do anything quickly, yet they grew in number, but that was all right, badgers were all right, and they weren't armadillos.

✳   ✳   ✳

Badgers. Everywhere. There was just no getting around it, they were all right, but they were everywhere, everywhere. Badgers. Everywhere.

Flowers for the Dead

Sandy Frances Duncan

They planted Amanda with the usual pomp and ceremony. They washed and dressed her in her best green dress, put her in the satin-lined casket, said ashes to ashes, etc., and lowered her into the ground.

The box was very soft and smooth. Amanda spent the first little while waiting for God to fly her up to Heaven. She'd always thought He (or an angel) came before the box was closed. That's what she'd told the children. But she was willing to wait if He'd been delayed. The thought that maybe it was the Devil who had been delayed made her shiver. Then, being of a pragmatic nature, she decided to stick around and see.

She started to get uncomfortable and twitchy. It was boring lying in a box in the ground and no matter how elegant the blue satin was, it didn't allow her much room to wriggle. Her buttocks were numb and she shifted regularly from one side to the other. For lack of anything else to do she practised sighing, and eventually decided God (or the Devil) and His emissaries had forgotten about her.

The day (or night) she resigned herself to being forgotten she felt damp. When she inhaled for a sigh, at which she was becoming marvellously adept, she smelled earth: deep and acrid and clinging. Too clinging. She couldn't move her feet. But her dress was warm and such an expensive casket should be well insulated. Sighing, she went to sleep.

When she awoke she realized rather groggily that her toes had grown through the end of the box. She thought God had finally come and she was going to Heaven feet first—or more likely Hell, since it was feet first, but then she felt that her toes had branched out in different directions. She wiggled them and they grew farther. It was fun. She did it again. A pleasant sensation crept up her legs, tickling and vibrating. It made her think of her husband and she laughed.

Gradually Amanda noticed that the pressure had shifted from her buttocks to the soles of her feet, or rather, to the tips of her toes, with which she was quickly losing touch. It seemed she was inclined on a sharp angle. She laughingly dismissed this as fancy produced by the darkness of the box, but of course, couldn't be sure since there was no light with which to get her bearings. But when her forehead, some time later, butted against the top of the casket, she was relieved she had not been hallucinating.

She sensed rather than heard a noise—a series of constant little belches. Suddenly the horrible pressure on her forehead stopped and the top of the box fell away. The dribbles of earth being shifted around her tickled. "Worms," she sighed, trying to get comfortable in her new position. One worm crawled across her face and nibbled her eyelash. She told him angrily where he could go and he went. She was very relieved, having always thought that if one didn't go to Heaven (or Hell) one was eaten by worms.

Now her arms didn't want to stay across her chest where they'd been placed. They wanted to be over her head. With resignation, she let them go. One finger felt warm. She tried to pull it back, but it wouldn't come. Up went a finger, then another, then the hand, then the other hand. It was too warm. She wiggled her fingers and, like her toes, they grew.

For the first time in her life, Amanda felt thin. The rolls around her middle had been stretched. She thought it a great technique and relatively painless. She even thought when she got out she'd start a reducing salon. But her dress was very tight and she wondered if she just felt thin and was really fatter. How could that be lying in a box in the ground—and dead, to boot. It was all so confusing.

Her hands eventually got used to the warmth which sent shivers down her arms. Again, her head started pushing on something which kept bulging and bulging and she got a headache. Just when she thought it was turning into a migraine, the top of her head broke through and the pressure stopped. Now all her arms to below the elbows and the top two inches of her head extruded. She thought she'd die of suspense, not knowing into what they extruded. She'd always been the sort who read the last chapter of a mystery first.

It took a while for her head to work through some more and then she couldn't see anyway because of the dirt in her eyes. She drew down slightly and tried to jump, pushing with the ends of her toes. She grew a little more. By this method Amanda managed to work her way nine inches out of the ground. But it was exhausting and she drooped her arms and head for a rest. Something red was hanging over her left ear. She felt with her left leaf—hand, she corrected. Petals covered her head.

Amanda straightened up and looked around. She was in the middle of a wreath of withered carnations and chrysanthemums which rested against a grey headstone. New grass grew in front of her and the lime-green of the well-tended cemetery plots stretched away like fallen soldiers with stone heads. A sudden noise made her swivel. Two men with shovels approached. One kicked at the wreath, catching Amanda in the armpit.

"Lookit that tulip, will ya? These perpetual graves're a pain in the ass. Folks're always bringin' new flowers, but they never think t'take the dead ones away. They'd be here forever if it wasn't f'r us." He bent down. "It's stuck. There." Amanda shrieked as her top half came off in his hand. "Wind comin' up? Thought I heard somethin'."

"Hearing ghosts, George. Only ghosts."

They were still chuckling when they tossed the flowers in the garbage.

How I Spent My Summer Holidays

Cecelia Frey

The Home squats obscenely in the middle of a field. Around us houses form a distant circle. This is after catastrophe and construction is beginning again. Still, no one dares this strip we walk on or the thing that sits like a raised boil at its centre.

In my mind now, as I sit amongst my bottles of blood, we cross and recross that no man's land of thistle and quackgrass. It must have been green sometimes, if only for a short while in the spring, but I always see it as brown and feel it as prickly. Endlessly, we trudge to and from school, eyes bent to the ground. We do not remember why we are here; our brains are seared bare as the landscape we move across.

Marlene speaks in her high whine. "What's wrong with you? What's wrong with a person like you anyways? Are you crazy or something?"

My response is silence.

"Why did you shout, 'I can't see, I can't see?'" Marlene shrills on. Then, disgusted, "You were weird."

"That's what happens when you faint." My foot deftly avoids a pile of dog shit which steers me toward a broken beer bottle. I swerve again.

Even though I have these explanations and the distinction of being the only kid in the Home with the experience of fainting, I feel inadequate, especially with Marlene. Marlene is the Wonder Woman of the Home. She has the biggest mouth and can hold water in it the longest, all the way from the toilet sink to where we crouch in the dirt by the playhouse. We need this water for our brick dust pies. We are not allowed to take containers such as cups outside. Sometimes, someone finds a tin can. Then that person has something to bargain with and the rest of us watch with envy. We constantly sift through garbage for such treasures, but this is during rationing and short supply. To scrape the bricks, which we dig from the playhouse foundation, we use nails or shards of glass gleaned from rubble. After use, these are placed carefully on a special ledge. In spite of such restrictions, we construct our pies as best we can, and take pride in them, too, not having experienced how grand they might be with more sophisticated tools.

So we walk always watching the ground for broken or torn bits of string or metal. We walk together, seven or eight of us, the big kids. They do not tell us our ages but we do have grades at school. I am in grade five; Eddie is in grade six. If we raise our heads, we can see another group, the little kids, their dark outlines merging into one shape.

Eddie speaks. He is the one who always comes to my rescue. "What *you* should be saying," he says to Marlene, "is 'I can't find my brain.'"

We walk slowly. We do not want to arrive. Constantly, we are aware of the thing in front of us, three stories, red brick, wooden verandah. Inner boundaries are only half-heartedly established, a caragana hedge at the front, a wire fence along the playground side, three strands of barbed wire along the garden side. These aren't necessary, because no one ever wants to get in, and the difficulties of getting out have nothing to do with wire fences. We are told that no one has escaped. What they mean is escapees are always found, sleeping in the bus depot or lifting something from Woolworth's.

Eddie and Ray often go out at night, just to be free, they say. They take in a movie or watch the drunks on 97th Street. They always have money. Possibly they roll those bodies that lie limp in alleys and doorways. They always return because where else is there to go? They speak of adventure, but then everybody here tells lies, especially when faced with authority. We'll say anything to save ourselves. But when they get caught escaping, there is nothing they can say. Then, it's the strap for sure. Mr. Epsom does the boys. But that isn't why Eddie hates him.

Mr. Epsom is supposed to be the gardener, but he only got the job because of Mrs. Epsom who is the cook and saves the Board piles of money with hot water she calls soup and cold water with bits of floating bread she calls pudding. As to the gardening, the kids do most of it, while Mr. Epsom shuffles around with his evil eye. The kids, naturally, don't do any more than they have to, which is why the marigolds are always rusty and the grass splotchy, worn to the dirt in some places, overgrown in others.

In looks the Epsoms are the tall and short, the lean and fat. She is bustly and minds her own business, especially where the Board and the Head are concerned. Her biggest job is keeping Mr. Epsom on the straight, scrubbed and pruned. But sometimes he gets away from her. Once a week he has his Legion night, and then if you stay awake long enough you can spot him from the dorm window, weaving his way across the field. You can hear him fumbling for the gate latch and swearing to himself.

Everyone at the Home knows certain facts of survival. No one speaks of these things. They are transferred amongst us by a process something like osmosis. We know how to sneak down the fire escape; we know to try and get a kitchen job because then you can give yourself the biggest helpings of what you like and the smallest of what you don't; we know to watch out for Mr. Epsom. We know to stay away from the garden shed because that is where he keeps his dirty pictures and sits playing with himself.

All this isn't why Eddie hates Mr. Epsom, though. The reason Eddie hates him is because Mr. Epsom is the one who hacked Mr. McGregor to bits.

The voices come again. As I push yet another needle into a vein raised blue and irresistible beneath the skin, I hear Eddie's long drawn-out 'hey' full of admiration and wonder. I see Mr. McGregor coiled and sunning himself in the field, except at first I do not see him. What I see is his movement near my foot as he whips open in a shimmer of light. I have no picture of my reaction. As my psychologist friend would say, I've probably repressed it.

Right away, Eddie picks him up.

"What if he's poison," says Marlene.

Eddie doesn't care. He would rather die than not touch him.

"Garter," says someone.

"Rattler," says another.

"None of those," says Ray, who's an Indian and knows.

"What then?"

"I dunno," says Ray. "I never saw one of them before."

All the rest of the way that snake curls up and down Eddie's arms. He's about four feet long, greyish beige with patches of rust. He holds onto Eddie's arm so tightly we can't get our fingers in beneath the two skins. We take turns trying. At first I won't do it. I don't want to touch anything cold and slimy. But I can feel Marlene's appraising eyes, her eagerness to tell the world about my cowardice. As it turns out, Mr. McGregor is smooth and soft and warm from the sun. He is incredibly strong, his body a thick, hard muscle, frightening because of the way it has its own life and can turn so quickly. Eddie calls him "he" but Mr. McGregor's delicate face and black tongue furling out so gracefully make me think of Lily.

Lily of the almond eyes and toffee skin. Lily with holes in her ears threaded with finely spun gold. One recess she tells me she is twelve, her birthday is February nineteenth. She tells me she is Hungarian. I detect a slight accent.

I go home with her once, even though it is against the rules. It means starvation and solitary but it is worth it, if only for the smells, cinnamon, other spices I do not recognize. In the kitchen a grandmother with jiggly arms rolls dough. Milk, icy and creamy, foams up out of tall glasses. Cookies, row upon row, cool on wire racks. A strange language, quick, fierce, loving, is spoken without effort. On the wall a clock ticks. I thought school was the only place with clocks.

In the living room it doesn't seem to matter if Lily touches things or sits in the chairs. She shows me glass figurines like jewels and painted wooden dolls, each fitting perfectly inside the others, each with a mouth in the shape of a heart. Upstairs, in her bedroom Lily sleeps alone in a bed that has four pillars and an umbrella. A closet is full of dresses, any colour you can think of. I touch everything, the pebbly bedspread, the wiry doll's hair. A white rug lies on the floor beside the bed. I take off one shoe and sock and put my foot into its soft thickness. On the bedside table there is another clock, this one made of pink shells.

At the Home we know time through Roxy. She is the one who calls us to stand in lines, for wash-up, for meals. She tells us when to leave for school and when to go to bed. Roxy is scrawny as a mauled cow. She struts around on turned-out ankles and worn down heels, waving a long stick and shouting. "Okay, everybody to their lockers!"

These doorless lockers line the playroom. In the past we must have each been assigned one. Sometimes, I think I spend my whole childhood sitting in mine, staring at nothing, memorizing the details of my teeth.

I *have* to start at the top left molars, inside. I work my way across the smooth surface to the extreme right edge, then return to the bottom inside left. Then I do the same with the outside, first top, then bottom. I work my tongue slowly; time is no object. There is something about their slipperiness, their solid feel, that I like. Outside in the playground, I often perform the same sort of ceremony with stones. I pop one into my mouth and roll it around and around with my tongue. My psychologist friend calls this repetition compulsion.

Returning, too, she says, to a place you once knew.

And I do wonder why I do this, return to this void where I feel such discomfort. In my more penetrating moments, I know I go back to try and change things, but I also know nothing can be changed. Why repeat? The terrible need to have things come out right.

And so again during the endless heat of that summer, Eddie scrounges alleys for chicken wire and builds a pen for Mr. McGregor down beyond the garden. A line of scraggly trees and overgrown shrubs make this the only place on the compound where you can not be seen, even from third floor windows. There's a shallow ditch where we sit and smoke and read comics. It must be nearly summer holidays when we find Mr. McGregor, because I spend long days down there watching Eddie clean the pen, watching Mr. McGregor curl himself like bracelets around Eddie's arms. I can never bring myself to let him do that to me, although part of me wants to.

Mr. McGregor is both beautiful and horrible. I mean in the way he takes his food. Eddie catches mice and gophers in the field. He lets them go into the pen, and Mr. McGregor squeezes them and swallows them whole, then goes off into a corner for three days to sleep it off. At first a big lump rounds out his stomach. You can see this get smaller and smaller. Then you know he needs to eat again.

I cannot stand watching. One quick squeeze would not be so bad. But it takes a few. At each squeeze, the victim lets out air until finally there is no space left for air to go in. As I sit in the playroom or spoon tapioca into twenty-seven sherbets lined up on the kitchen counter, I do not think about what is happening down in the garden. I do not think of the way the mouse scurries and the final frozen look on its face.

Otherwise, I'm with Eddie every chance I get. When I finish in the kitchen, I slip away and cross the short space of grass. I can feel eyes watching me from behind, Mrs. Epsom maybe, or maybe the Head in his office. I try to become invisible.

As I go along the path, I meet Mr. Epsom. I shrivel myself and move around him. I keep my head down and try not to let anything bounce. Even if I don't actually meet him on this journey, I'm aware of him, his shadow in the yard or garden, or waiting in his shed. I think of him looking at his pictures. I turn sharply and walk quickly. I control my legs so they will not run.

"What's wrong with you?" Eddie asks when I arrive. "You're not going to faint are you?"

When Mr. Epsom catches me, though, it is in the kitchen, where I do not expect it. For one thing, Mrs. Epsom is usually there. But also, the kitchen is large and airy and white. Windows on two sides let in lots of light. There isn't a speck of dirt or a drip of food anywhere, not if Mrs. Epsom can help it. When I hear the screen door close and look up to see Mr. Epsom, my mind instinctively reaches for Mrs. Epsom, but she has gone to consult with the Head. My chest tightens. I keep my eyes on the eternal tapioca, glassy fish eggs in grey blue.

Mr. Epsom sits down on the bench near where I'm standing. I am wearing shorts Roxy gave me from the communal clothes cupboard and about two sizes too small. On my bare leg, I feel something wet, something being moved up and down, being stroked along skin, leaving a trail of wetness. This is a situation I cannot think about. Although the room is starting to turn about me, I keep spooning out tapioca.

Mrs. Epsom is the one who saves me. The instant she barges in through the swinging door from the dining room, the thing on my leg disappears. In a matter of seconds, Mr. Epsom is gone. Mrs. Epsom looks at me, at my legs, and says something about young girls who run around half-naked. I feel queasy and unclean. Why did I not move to the other side of the table? Why did I not escape through the door? There is something wrong with me, something that forces me to submit, something that will not let me defend myself. And Mr. Epsom knows. After that, I live in terror. As long as Mr. Epsom is around, I am in danger, so when Eddie suggests getting rid of him, I'm all for it.

We are kneeling in the grass staring down at the bloody remains of Mr. McGregor. Mr. Epsom, shovel in hand, is heading back towards his shed mumbling something like, "Don't want no goddamn giant worm. Get ridda that chicken wire, too," he growls across his shoulder. "Too much goddamn junk around this place."

I can see the tears just back of Eddie's eyes. "What I'm gonna do," he says through clenched teeth, "I'm gonna get ridda him."

"How?" I ask. "How?"

At first Eddie talks of hacking up Mr. Epsom so he can see what it's like. Next day, he decides it will be more subtle, not so much chance of getting caught, to simply give him a push at the top of the stairs. The trouble with this is Eddie lacks occasion. He never comes upon Mr. Epsom at the top of a suitably long flight of stairs. Finally, he settles upon scaring him to death.

We paint ourselves all over, faces, legs, arms, with this special paint that glows in the dark. We smear it on some clothes we got from the rag cupboard. We glue our hair so it sticks straight up. We paint gashes and holes with blood dripping out of them all over our faces. We stick feathers and fur on our bodies. One thing about Eddie, he can get anything, just don't ask any questions.

We hide in the caragana hedge on Legion night and wait for Mr. Epsom to come home drunker than a hoot owl. "He'll think we're his DT's, larger than life," says Eddie with satisfaction.

The night is dark. Skinny fingers of clouds cover most of the moon. We wait, crouched, not daring to look at each other, scarcely daring to breathe. We hear something at the gate and Mr. Epsom going through his list of curse words. We hear his footsteps coming closer. Then, it cannot be more perfect. Just as we leap into his path, arms raised, mouths wide in silent screams, tongues stretched to our chins, the clouds blow across the moon.

There we are in all our glory, in the spotlight. Mr. Epsom stops. His eyes bug out. He does a little dance, first one way then the other. He catches himself, balances on one foot, lurches toward us with his arms outstretched. His hands go for our throats. We step aside. His face twists. It is a strange colour. He staggers past us, then backward again, then forward, then sideways.

We watch until the final pitch into his own bed of drooping petunias. Then, we move fast. We do not look back. Next morning at breakfast comes the solemn announcement. Mr. Epsom has passed away in the night. The gossip is poison. Where he got it is a mystery. Someone says moonshine, someone says chicken, someone says Mrs. Epsom's cooking.

When I hear the word poison, I can only repeat to myself thank you, thank you, thank you, to some invisible decision-maker who lifted the whole thing out of my irresponsible hands. Eddie, however, is disappointed. We are in the smoking ditch, hiding from the sun. "We didn't do nothing," he says. "It wasn't us at all. We thought we looked shit hot.

Some great Hollywood production, when all the time we were just a couple of kids with a feather or two and some paint. Pitiful." His voice is angry. At first I think he is angry with me, or Mr. Epsom. Then I realize he is angry with himself.

Patsy Arnold gave me the farm idea. She sat directly in front of me. Already, she was busy writing. I stared at the back of her head. Then it happened, the miracle. The flecks of white scalp showing between those tight French braids transported me. There was something, too, about the braids themselves, the perfection of the way they were woven, the taut hairs held in marvellous tension. Probably, it also had something to do with Patsy's stories before morning bell.

Patsy had a million relatives, all on farms. She had uncles and aunts, grandmothers and grandfathers, first cousins, second cousins, third cousins. She had relatives I had never even heard of. "Second cousin once removed," she recited in a high piping voice. Her mother came from a family of thirteen, her father from a family of eleven. My mind boggled. She related family picnics, weddings, family ball games. I was left gasping. She spoke of driving tractors, running with dogs, riding horses. She may as well have been talking about riding balloons beyond the clouds.

The problem was I could not tell the truth. The truth was I had done nothing during the summer. How could I talk about dishing out tapioca, picking raspberries, sitting in my locker, making brick dust pies? It was too shameful.

The teacher told us to take our stories home for homework and bring them back the next morning. All that evening I sat in the toilet writing. It was quieter than the playroom. Once I got started I couldn't stop. It was crazy. The lies compounded so easily. I told things I didn't even know I knew. I told about my non-existent grandmother who kept forgetting things like where she was and where she had left her teeth. I revealed my imagined aunt's moustache—fine dark hairs springing out of pulsating pores just above moist lips, drooping down to faint fleshy jowls, soft and alive.

Where my words came from is a mystery. Perhaps they were of another life that I could not remember. Perhaps they were inside me, lying waiting. All I know is, as I scribbled furiously on, they possessed me. They told a story of sounds and smells and visions, bells echoing, hay freshly cut. Horses in impossible green pastures suddenly become possible. Dogs barked in air so pure it shone as with a white light. They ran, they jumped, they twisted bodies so sleek that the words *copper* and *satin* took on new meanings.

But I have to admit my forte was people. I assumed so easily the story of my fabricated uncle's toenails: he always cut his toenails in the living room, which my aunt said was uncouth. One day, my little boy cousin crawling around on the floor was seen to be chewing something which turned out to be my uncle's toenail, and my aunt really screamed at my uncle, but he hollered back that toenails would make a man of him. "If it's toenails you want, kid," he said, "there's lots more where them came from. I'll start saving 'em up for you!"

When I was finished, I read it over. There was something wrong. It lacked romance. That was where Clarabelle came in. She was my cousin who was tragically in love with this guy my uncle couldn't stand who worked on the oil rigs and walked around town with his boots and his leather jacket open. On Saturday night coming home from the dance their car went off the road, which was like grease because of the rain, and they didn't get home until morning and there was a terrible row with my uncle shouting and waving his fists and my cousin wringing her hands and crying and saying what had she done so wrong anyway, all they did was sleep in the ditch.

Somewhere in the distance Roxy was shouting. I had forgotten about Roxy and the cubicle in which I sat, its cement floor, its leaky pipes, its damp odours. The call was for bed and lights out. I had to stop writing, but my fingers refused to stop twitching. For hours I kept leaping up in the darkness to find my scribbler, to kneel in the moonlight at the foot of my bed, to add, to correct, to delete.

The next day I did not want to abandon my composition to the immaculate hands of Adelaide. Adelaide was the person for whom I reserved a special contempt. She dotted all her i's and crossed all her t's. She always collected papers and handed out pencils and got out early on days we reviewed test papers. When that perfect hand was stuck in front of my face, a hand so clean you could see into every white pore, I suddenly knew that my story was not acceptable. It contained the sweaty imprints of my hand, the wrinkles of that impossible position perched on the toilet edge having to make hurried exits when someone knocked on the door calling was I going to be in there all night and maybe a dose of castor oil would fix me up.

There was something else too, something about betraying my relatives to people like Adelaide, people who would not understand them. But I had no choice. I gave them over. A couple of days later when the papers were returned, mine wasn't among them. Disaster hung heavy over my head. Had I been lost? Or simply forgotten? Or perhaps mine had been so bad the teacher had thrown it, in disgust, into the waste paper basket. Then I heard my name and could I stay at recess. This was having the accusatory finger pointed. My lies must have been discovered. This was calamity.

At recess, as I approached the teacher's desk, I saw my story in all its defects, lying exposed on top of a pile of other papers. It looked even grubbier than I remembered. Red pencil marks were all over it, like my face with measles. Angry scratches crossed out whole paragraphs. I'll never forget the teacher's fingernails, so squarely pruned, so highly buffed, the cuticles so precise. By the end of that session, I had memorized them. I was right about the lies. How could I have been so dumb? Of course, all the teachers knew the Home kids. It was down in their registers. And even if it wasn't, all you had to do was look at us. We all had the same haircut, straight bangs, straight around the bottom edge. You could tell by our clothes, every year the same ones, only on different bodies. You could tell by the impetigo scabs and the ever-present smell of seven-year itch powder.

"There's nothing wrong with writing a story," the teacher's voice said, "as long as we don't pretend it's the truth." Then she couldn't resist the question. "You do know, don't you, that this isn't real? It's important to keep things separate, in our own minds, that is."

I said nothing. After a moment, her voice changed gear. She started talking about my story being well done, in a way. She talked about some sort of writing competition for young Canadians. She said how my story was too long and how it needed some style and some smoothing over. She said she would show me how to do this. She gave me a note so I could stay after school the next day. I can see now that what we did to that story was tone it down a couple of notches. We didn't exactly remove my uncle's temper and Clarabelle's ditch romance but we subdued them. And what we did to the spelling and grammar was out of this world. By the time we were finished, I scarcely recognized myself at all.

I didn't win a prize, but I got honourable mention. All the winners plus the honourable mentions got put into the newspaper, one every week, on the Saturday Children's page. Mine didn't come up for several weeks, and I never saw it anyway because we never got to look at a paper. I know it appeared, though, because the Monday morning after, the teacher said did I like seeing it and my name in print and I said yes.

I thought that was the end of it, but I was doomed to be haunted by that story. A few months later, it was winter because I remember the caragana hedge as bare twisted branches growing out of the Head sitting in front of the window, Roxy told me I was wanted upstairs. Upstairs did not mean the kitchen, the dining room, or the dormitories, which were all, also, upstairs. It meant the *Office* with everything contained in that word. Sometimes, kids returned from the office looking like torture victims, their faces numb, their bodies moving like sleepwalkers. Sometimes, kids would disappear into the office never to be seen or heard of again. Occasionally it was good news, a visitor, especially good if the visitor brought candy. But sometimes the call came because a kid had done something so bad it was beyond Roxy's stick. So it was with mixed looks of envy and relief that the other kids watched me walk past them and start up the steps. It was more terrible than I could have imagined. I was faced with my lies. My characters had come to life. There was an aunt with a moustache, there was a blustery uncle, I could only assume he had toenails, there was even a cousin called Clarabelle. They were all there, in pulsating flesh. Even before anyone spoke, I was struck by dismay at what I had done. These were my people. I had created them. Yet they were unfamiliar and definitely unfriendly.

Now, as I watch another vein collapse and another vial fill with purplish blood, I hear their voices, full of accusation and denial, come at me again in a clamouring rush.

My uncle: "How could you do this to us, smear us all over the paper like that?"

My cousin: "Making us sound like hicks."

My aunt: "My house never looked like that. I keep my house clean as anybody."

My cousin advances, head high, pointing at her chin. "You call that a double chin? Ah!" She turns away in disgust. "You don't even know what a double chin is!" This is in regard to a slight descriptive reference in which I was only trying to give her a unique appearance.

My aunt speaks of spite and my uncle of suing if I weren't a child.

After a long and stunning trial came the sentence delivered by the Head, a blank skull shape against a square of light. The voice was detached. It seemed to descend from the ceiling. "What's done is done. The best we can do now is an apology and a promise that this will never happen again." So I apologized and promised, my words echoing those of the Head. Then I slunk away, back downstairs, and went and sat in my locker. I thought about things. How could I have done that? How could I have told the truth when I didn't know what it was? Maybe I had some special power. I thought of Mr. Epsom. Maybe it had not been poison. Maybe if I could make people live, I could also make them die. This was too horrible to think about for long. I made a solemn vow to myself to stop sticking pins in dolls. Never, never again would I chant magic formulas of either life or death. Such acts, even such thought of such acts, are too dangerous.

Eddie builds a snow cave in the ditch. A tarp covers the floor where we sit. It is warm and cozy and peaceful in that hollow white space alone with Eddie. We are half-way through a bottle of scotch, another one of Eddie's finds. Now the taste of scotch rises up in me and threatens my system. But then I am where I want to be, with Eddie. He takes a long pull on his cigarette and draws the smoke deep into his lungs. I watch in admiration. I never inhale; I would pass out. Eddie speaks, "That's what you gotta learn, that's what you gotta remember. There's no relief, no miracles." His voice is already dead.

Would it have made a difference if I had been able to tell him about magic? But then how could I? I had already turned away from belief. Once, from some vague source, I heard how Eddie made out later, on the outside. He did a lot of breaking and entering, aggravated assault, drug selling. I heard he died of an overdose, methadone, which he gave to himself, but I can't remember where I heard it.

None of this is true. Or some of it may be true. But I never brought people to life. I never killed people. I'm not that powerful or dangerous. Sometimes, I think I make up everything. Years ago, I began to suspect myself. I began to wonder about hearing that gate latch, about waiting, shivering in the hedge, about the sound and feel of those footsteps coming closer. I began to suspect I was dreaming, that the picture I have in my mind of Mr. Epsom falling is from something else, something I have read, maybe. I began to wonder if Eddie and I dressed up and hid in the hedge at all. It seems to me now that I dreamed up this story after the announcement of Mr. Epsom's death. But did Mr. Epsom ever live?

Why then do these voices haunt me? These people cannot come to life and accuse me, Marlene of her big mouth, Mr. Epsom of his evil ways. And Eddie. How can he accuse me of not giving him what he needed? And how can I get caught up in my own fictions, to think it matters?

I find the safest thing to do is simply go on with my blood-letting. This I can be sure is real—my white uniform, my sterile instruments, the spotless counters, the glistening vinyl. And at the end of a good day's work, as I close the door on the small room they allow me in this place, I feel a satisfied glow seeing my vials of blood, all sitting neatly in racks along the wall, all tagged and labelled with black ink.

Ticks

Kristjana Gunnars

July twenty-first.

The ticks must be gone now. In the Wasagaming Museum they say the active time for ticks is between the middle of June and the middle of July. They had a bloated one in a plastic box. It was bigger than a lima bean. They said it came from a dog and was finished sucking up the lymph and blood. It must be the stupidest insect. It's got no head at all, just a large bloated torso. The disgusting thing about ticks is that they're parasites. Some insects spin webs or dig burrows or build honeycombs. But this one can't do anything except latch onto an animal and suck the life out of it.

June seventeenth must be just the time for ticks. We never think of that. We always have to celebrate June seventeenth in the country by Pense. There have to be open fires in the dusk and races in burlap sacks in the afternoon and walks down a country road. It's dusty and crickets croak in the tall grass by the wayside. Far away a tractor pokes into a field in a dust cloud. Behind you someone laughs loudly. A joke about Gudbrandur Erlendsson whose cow sank into a quagmire in 1880. The air is dry. Straws crack, blackbirds fidget. Grasshoppers pounce across the road. For once the *huldu*-people are visible. People you've heard about and never seen. That day you see them. Next day they're gone. It's like that every year. They say things don't last in Canada. They're wrong.

Stories get told on June seventeenth. Stories that never made it into English or into print. I know why. It's the odd people they show. You think your great-grandparents must have been superstitious. I guess they were. That Jóhannes Bjarnason from Stykkishólmur, say. He stayed with Jónas Schaldemoes in a cabin by Lake Winnipegosis in 1916. I heard that story five weeks ago in Pense when we got together for our yearly fest. They say Canada's too new for folktales and legends. They're wrong.

I'm sitting on the bank of the Lake Waskesiu panhandle in north Saskatchewan. I'm here alone. I brought no provisions except for a tent and a sleeping bag. There are patches of wild strawberry just below my tent site and saskatoons closer to the lake. My plan was to pick those and fish for the rest of my needs. I've got a license and it's a good fishing lake. I just haven't made the gear yet. I've picked the branches and root fibres, but it's still raw in the camp. This morning I put a sheet of birch bark into the lake to soften it up. I'm going to make a spoon and a bowl with it when it's smooth enough. I'm back to feel it, but it's not ready. I planned this trip a month ago. Now that I'm here I'm angry. Maybe I didn't sleep well enough. It was the first night. You have to expect to be nervous on the first night, but it's made me bad. I feel bad.

Maybe it's the ugly ticks. You come up here to think about beauty. To hear warblers in the morning and wind in the birch leaves overhead. But then you end up thinking about mites and ticks with lymph-sucking pipes that cut open your skin and dig inside. There they hang, getting big on your own blood. You don't think of purple hyssops or scarlet shootingstars or swallows swooping by. You think of white and yellow or brown ticks that don't have any shape or colour or character. It's mean. The whole thing is mean. Those pests don't have a right to lay eight thousand eggs all over the grass with nothing to do but climb onto a straw and wait for you to walk by.

Maybe you get that way when you're by yourself and everything is raw. That Jóhannes Bjarnason up in Lake Winnipegosis was like that. He got strange. Maybe it's in the family. He's supposed to be related on my mother's side. He stayed in this cabin with Schaldemoes's family, a wife and daughter, on a promontory into a lake. He was new in Manitoba, fresh from Iceland. The idea was that he'd help Jónas put the nets into the lake in the fall and gather firewood for winter. They were going to fish the nets out when the lake froze over. To do that, they hacked out holes in the ice and threaded a string underneath. Later they pulled the nets out of the holes, took the fish out, and put them back in. They had almost seventy nets and they lifted twenty of them every day.

If my folks knew about this they'd have a search party out for me. Maybe they've got one out anyway. It's a big argument with them, that I don't know enough to do something like this. It's dangerous for a girl

who's only seventeen. But what about the first pioneers? What did they
know about fishing in prairie lakes or camping in poplar stands? There
isn't anything remotely like this in Iceland. You've got to be brave about
life. You can't test yourself unless you step outside. So, I don't know what
I'm doing, but I'll learn. I figure I'll be able to catch northern pike or
yellow perch here. Pike are supposed to get so big that one catch might
do me for a couple of days. They come where the water is shallow in the
morning. You can probably just pick them up from the waterweeds.
Otherwise, you can put a worm on your hook and use a button for a lure.
A shiny one, anyway. And perch is supposed to be around all the time.
You can catch it from the banks, especially at noon or in the evening. It
shouldn't be hard.

This Jóhannes, my great-uncle. In November, the Schaldemoes family
went to Winnipegosis town and he stayed in the cabin alone while they
were gone. It was on Hunter's Island, twenty miles away and three miles
from the nearest neighbour. Jónas Schaldemoes kept asking him if he felt
all right about being alone, and told him not to work after dark and to
stay overnight in the neighbour's cabin instead of sleeping alone. Friday
morning the family left and Jóhannes went to work on the lake. It was
slow work, lifting nets alone, but he didn't want to quit until he'd done
enough to call it a day's work. So he didn't get back to the cabin till after
dark. He was uncomfortable when he got there, but the discomfort
vanished as soon as he started preparing supper for himself. He made the
lunch-pack for the following day and went to sleep.

Next morning he went to work early and stayed on the lake till it was
dark again. The hoar-frost was thick in the air and there was a dark heavy
fog when he got back. He tried to open the door to the cabin, but it was
as if someone pushed it against him from inside. He tried to get in twice,
but both times the door slammed shut in his face. He thought about
following Jónas's advice and going to the neighbour's cabin, but then he
decided that would be cowardly. He'd slept all right in this one the night
before. So he collected his energy, opened the door and walked in. As
soon as he'd lit the lamp, he stood for a while and looked around. It
occurred to him that he wasn't alone in the cabin. He couldn't see
anybody else, but he felt sure he wasn't alone.

They say a tick goes through three stages. It's as if it's got three lives
and in each one it has to latch onto an animal and gorge itself with blood.
First it's the larva, then it's the nymph, then it's the adult. Each time it's

bigger and takes more blood than before, and in the end it's so big that the shield on the outside of the body just about cracks. That's when it drops to the grass again. Then it's had enough. The lousy parasite. It isn't enough to have thousands of eggs from each one, but every one of those eggs gets you three times before it's dead. They're all over. There's no such thing as being alone in the wilds, is there. There's lots of company.

Jóhannes pulled himself out of his cowardice and started preparing supper. Stewing catfish, maybe. He knew he wouldn't get any sleep so he sat down to write a letter home. He didn't finish the letter till after midnight, but by that time he felt calm and tired. So he went to bed. There was a window over his bed and the stove stood on the other side of the room, a few feet away. He turned his face to the wall and lay still for a while. Then he looked over his shoulder onto the floor. There stood a man, half-way between the bed and the stove. Half a man, because the top half was missing. The legs, feet, and hips were there, but the rest was gone. He sat up in bed and stared at the apparition, but then it vanished.

You'd think he was getting bush fever already on his second night. Maybe it doesn't take longer than that. The trick is to stay organized and keep your mind on something specific. Like the birch bark. Even if a tree is dead, you can use the bark. The bark stays alive in a way. You just have to soak it in water and it'll work. Anything can be made with it: cups and bowls and plates. Pots too, with the dark side out so it won't catch fire. I'm going to fold this piece up into a rectangle and glue the ends with sap. Then I'll roll up a small wad for a spoon and slide it into the slit of a twig. I'll tie it with roots. It's easy.

That man. He should have thought of something else when he lay down again after the figure was gone. Keeping your mind on something like that makes it come again. Sure enough, a little later he saw the same half-man on the floor. When he stood up, the vision was gone. He lay down for the third time, and soon he saw it again. Three times it came to him during the night. After that he couldn't stay in bed. He got up and paced the floor for the rest of the night. By six in the morning he was so tired that he lay down. Just as he was about to fall asleep, he heard a man call outside his window: "Ho, ho, ho." He thought it was Hjálmar, Jónas's cousin from the next cabin. Hjálmar used to visit on Sunday mornings. But then he realized it was too early for a visitor. Jóhannes went outside and walked around the cabin, but he didn't see anyone. The strange voice had sounded most like an Indian's call.

By noon the family was back home at the cabin. They asked Jóhannes how he'd been and he said nothing about what he'd seen. Some days later, when they were at work on the lake, Jónas asked again if he hadn't seen anything while they were gone. Then Jóhannes told him everything. After all, they said he'd acted strange when they got back. Jónas got more thoughtful after hearing the story of the split man in the cabin. Then he told his guest what it was he'd seen.

That's the way ticks are. You don't see them on the grass. You walk into them and they jump on you. You don't see them until they're burrowing into your skin and you have to get them out. The only way to do it is to stick a burning twig at the insect. That'll make it curl up and drop off. If you force it out or pull it, the mouthparts stay in your skin. But the whole thing doesn't sound as dangerous as they make it out to be. A few bloodsuckers can't do anything when they're that small. I guess they can give you diseases or sores or ulcers. That's what happens to cows and sheep. In the Rockies, the chipmunks and rabbits have spotted fever from ticks. People can get that too. But it sounds worse than it is. Just put some oil on the pest and it'll let go.

That birch bark still isn't ready. I didn't realize there were so many layers to a piece of bark when I cut it off the tree. Where do you stop with all those layers? They keep going. You don't know where the bark ends and the meat of the trunk begins. Maybe I didn't peel off enough layers. You peel one sheet, then another, some darker, some lighter. They alternate, but they always come back. Maybe I took too many and that's why it's so stiff. Maybe it's never ready.

Like that Indian on Lake Winnipegosis. He may never stop calling. Jónas said that a few years earlier, an Indian had been working on the lake during the winter. He moved fish bundles across the lake on a sled pulled by two horses. It was early in the winter and the ice was rotten. He disappeared on that trip and people said he'd fallen through. But no one knew what really happened. Next spring, when the ice loosened up, a man's corpse washed up just below Jónas's cabin. They decided it must have been the Indian who had vanished, but they couldn't be sure. The body wasn't recognizable any more. It was cut in half. All they found was the bottom half.

You'd think it was the top half calling for the bottom half. Looking for itself forever. But what harm can half a ghost do anybody? Without a head, without arms, it has to be harmless. There's no real body there. Even if it were a whole ghost, it's be easy to shrug off. Just light a fire in the hearth and you won't see it any more. But what if it keeps coming back? Every spring it's there and you have to listen to the calls and the knocks clattering on your floor. By winter it's under the ice again. It only comes around when somebody's alone in a cabin and it wants to talk.

Maybe I've got my information wrong. Maybe you don't soak the bark in water at all. I guess I'll try a young tree next time, one with soft moist bark you can just rip off. Maybe I'm too mad to do anything right. It's only the second day. I'll come around. I didn't sleep after all. This sort of thing takes time. You have to move one step at a time. First you set up a tent, then you make a fire. Then you make the implements, one at a time. Soon you'll have them all. Bowls and spoons and plates and knives'll be dangling on the branches all around your tent. Like the sheep ticks. You don't see them, don't hear them, hardly feel them. But suddenly they're there. Right on you. They say in Europe the cows can have so many ticks hanging on them that they clatter and rattle when they walk. What a load. Think of having to take them off, one at a time. Burning them off with brands.

The whole thing is mean, like the name they gave me. Kolla. That's short for Kolbrún. I got it because I'm darker than the rest of them, as if I were the black sheep or something. Maybe they got the idea I'd be moody already when they had me in the crib. Kolbrún, which means brown as coal. Coal. That's a burnt forest, isn't it?

The Fatal Error

Ernest Hekkanen

A man leans closer to examine an engraving by Dürer, for at first glance he thinks he sees a screwdriver implanted in the forehead of the diminutive skull at the horses' forehooves; however, on second glance he believes himself to be mistaken. The skull does not seem to be a skull at all, but rather a lump of wood or the figure of a small animal. He shrugs off his first impression and turns to go to the next engraving, but as he turns he notices the skull and screwdriver again, in the periphery of his vision, and he turns abruptly back to examine the engraving again. This time the impression of the skull with the screwdriver implanted in the forehead remains somewhat longer, and then it fades as before, the same way the impression on a television screen will fade once the set has been switched off. Has Dürer managed to leave this impression or has the viewer superimposed it? The viewer cannot determine which; however, now he perceives that he is feeling rather guilty at having taken so much time away from the office in order to indulge his passion for art, and he proceeds to leave the museum.

The city coughs up numerous sounds and smells; he walks along the sidewalk in an absent-minded manner, a condition he understands as having been induced by the impression of the screwdriver driven through the forehead of a skull that might very well have been a lump of wood or the figure of a small animal. He waits in an eddy of pedestrians for a signal light to change, and realizes if he continues along his present route he must pass an enormous pit being dug in the centre of the downtown area and that his senses will be assailed by a myriad of abrasive noises. For a moment he ponders whether to conduct a detour, which will mean a walk of several blocks, but suddenly the light changes, the crowd pushes forward and the matter is decided for him.

✻ ✻ ✻

In another part of the city a man sits behind a steering wheel, watching a car in front of him conduct an illegal left-hand turn. He tries to decide whether to pursue the driver. While he is trying to make up his mind, he receives a call on his radio informing him of a mishap some dozen blocks away. He secures the beacon on the car's dash, traverses several lanes of traffic and proceeds to the area of the accident. When he gets there he finds a large crowd milling around, hoping to get a glimpse of the body. Flashing his credentials, he pushes through the crowd to where the victim is stretched out on the sidewalk next to a barrier erected to keep pedestrians from falling into the enormous pit out of which the rusty skeleton of a future office building towers toward the sky. A screwdriver is implanted up to the yellow plastic handle in the man's forehead, somewhat up from the nose; and two tiny rivulets of blood are running down into the eye sockets.

Only two junior officers are on the scene and they are valiantly trying to hold back spectators who surge forward in successive waves in order to see the mess the victim has made on the sidewalk. Certain members of the crowd are engaged in exchanging loud invectives, as well as fists, in their eagerness to see the gore.

✻ ✻ ✻

When I got there only two officers were on the scene, trying to hold back spectators who kept pushing forward to get a glimpse of the victim. I asked the nearest one to give me a description of what had happened and he told me that a screwdriver had fallen from a beam that the crane was swinging into position on the building. Indeed, when I looked up there was a beam swaying back and forth some thirty storeys above me. On seeing it I felt a chill scurry down my spine.

Meanwhile, two paddy wagons had arrived; officers from each of the vehicles began to disperse the spectators, and those who would not leave voluntarily were dragged bodily away, often flailing and screaming, and were disposed of in the paddy wagons. Even then many of them exhibited extraordinary feats of contortion, casting forth arms and legs in final last-ditch attempts to link themselves with the gore on the sidewalk.

Half an hour later the scene was finally cleared of onlookers and we were able to examine the victim in relative quiet. I say relative quiet because in this part of the city the traffic never ceases, even for death; and, of course, work continued unabated in the enormous pit beyond the barrier. Indeed, since my arrival, the building had grown by what seemed at least another storey. The growth was independent of the workmen who scaled the numerous beams and girders and was occurring at such an accelerated pace that it left me a little bewildered. But such is the state of modern technology: it overwhelms the senses to such an extent that it leaves one in a dazed, thoughtless state.

✻   ✻   ✻

After several seconds spent contemplating the construction, the Inspector turns his attention back to the victim lying at his feet. It is the look of horror that impresses him: features that would otherwise be quite ordinary have been contorted in such a way as to seem inhuman, an effect that is more than a little enhanced by the screwdriver implanted in the forehead and the two rivulets of blood that flow down into seemingly fathomless eye sockets.

✻   ✻   ✻

I was ready to conclude that the death was accidental. However, when I examined the victim's personal identification I found it to be that of one Geoffrey Milds. That in itself was unimpressive; but when coupled with the fact that the initials G.M. appeared in the butt of the screwdriver, I was given cause to wonder.

I told one of the junior officers to get on the radio to headquarters. "I want a squad from the forensic lab down here on the double. Then I want the owner of that screwdriver found. Meanwhile, make sure no one leaves the construction site."

The questioning lasted all day; and because work on the building could not stop, even for death, we had to scale the girders in order to approach witnesses to the accident. It seems many had seen the screwdriver fall; several, in fact, had tried to net it as it was descending. Those who had tried to net it had gotten relatively close glimpses, so close they could identify the initials in the plastic butt. On each floor there was at least one witness to the descent of the screwdriver so that we were able to establish an uninterrupted path from the thirtieth floor to the first floor and then to ground level where a passerby, approaching the victim from the opposite direction along the sidewalk, had seen the screwdriver about to strike the victim.

"That was the odd thing," said the witness, "for while I saw the screwdriver about to strike him, I did not actually see it penetrate; because at that moment he jerked up his head—perhaps having heard a shout—and his face changed so horribly I was distracted. The next thing I knew he was lying on the sidewalk at my feet."

"You say his face changed. How?"

"That I can't tell you, Inspector. Not with any accuracy. All I know is it went through these changes, each one a little more horrible than the last, then his eyes rolled back and they seemed to sink out of sight."

✻ ✻ ✻

Although the questioning resulted in many witnesses to the accident, it did not produce the owner of the screwdriver. Several men remembered seeing it on the site. One in particular remembered using it for some purpose he could not recall the exact nature of, but no one remembered leaving it on the beam; in fact, several had distinct impressions of somebody removing it, although they could not remember the face of the person.

"We're always careful not to leave on the beams anything that might fall or hurt anybody," said the superintendent of the site; but nonetheless, the screwdriver had found its way onto the beam; it had been hoisted nearly thirty-one floors and had fallen with pinpoint accuracy on the victim.

When it began to look as if our questions were not going to meet with any success, we suddenly found a man who admitted to having brought the screwdriver onto the site. Although this man admitted to having brought it with him to work, he maintained quite stubbornly that the screwdriver was not his.

"You mean you stole it?"

"No. I picked it up on my way to work. You see, I saw it lying on the ground. I thought someone had lost it."

"Did you lend it to anybody while on the site?"

"Yes, several people. In fact, I remember lending it to the driver of the truck, the one who brought the beams onto the site. But after that I don't know what became of it. I was too busy, and besides I didn't place that much value on it."

Questioning in this manner seemed fruitless, so we asked him to take us to the place where he had found the screwdriver. He took us to an intersection in the east end of the city, only a few blocks from his home.

"You see, I catch a ride with another fellow, and we come to work together. I saw this screwdriver lying in the grass of the boulevard and I simply put it in my pocket."

* * *

Inspectors, by nature, are thorough, meticulous men, and in this respect I am no different. A man taught to distrust coincidence must by necessity find causality when confronted by seemingly random facts or events. Simply because an event seems accidental is no reason not to suspect something more heinous. Cause and effect underpin all matters seemingly inconsequential and unrelated, and this I felt must be the case with Mr. Geoffrey Milds and the screwdriver.

Ultimately, after much time spent walking sidewalks and knocking on doors, we found that the screwdriver had been in the possession of a man who had used it to install a tail-light in his car the night previous to the accident. He had placed the screwdriver on the fender, had forgotten about it after being distracted by a neighbour and had, the next morning, driven off with it lying there, whereupon he had heard a clatter and had glanced in the rear-view mirror just in time to see it fly off, and that had been about six blocks from his house. He had not sought to retrieve the screwdriver as he was in a hurry, and anyway he had come by it by accident. Apparently he had found it on his patio where his son and another boy had left it after making repairs to their bicycles. The son, in turn, told us that the screwdriver had belonged to his friend and that his friend had had it in a tool kit he always carried on his bike. On asking the son's friend where he had come by it, we found it had been left at his house by a furnace repairman and that the boy had claimed it for his own. The furnace repairman worked for an outfit downtown and he had accidentally included the screwdriver among his tools while rebuilding a furnace a year or two before. For some reason the furnace repairman had found himself to be without a screwdriver, possibly having left his own somewhere else, and seeing it in the basement of the house where he was rebuilding the furnace he had simply picked it up and started using it and had forgotten to replace it. Each person up to this point had had the screwdriver in his possession several weeks or months, and recalled it instantly on seeing the initials emblazoned in the butt of the plastic handle.

The man who had the furnace rebuilt lived next door to the victim. He told us that one afternoon several years before he had found the screwdriver lying on the lawn between the adjacent properties. He remembered seeing Milds tinkering with the carburetor of his lawn mower earlier in the day and decided to pick up the screwdriver and return it the next time he saw his neighbour.

"I remember putting it on the hall table, and after that I don't know what became of it. One day I noticed it wasn't there and I assumed my wife had given it back to him."

On questioning his wife, we learned that she had grown tired of seeing the screwdriver on the hall table, which was a rather ornamental piece and considered by her to be a show-piece, and had taken the screwdriver downstairs and had put it on her husband's workbench where such items belonged.

At this point we went next door to the victim's house. We found in the basement an array of tools that had been initialled in the same manner, apparently with the red-hot tip of a soldering iron.

"My husband was always very careful with his tools, Inspector. He felt by initialling them they would stand a better chance of getting back to him if ever they were lost."

In the basement, we also discovered a wooden model of Dürer's *Demonstration of Perspective*, a device the victim's wife could not adequately account for, other than he was always tinkering with one project or another.

✽   ✽   ✽

A man sits in an office he suddenly finds uncomfortable and contemplates the enormity of events. He feels perhaps because of some law of causality not yet fully understood that certain things are bound to occur; he ponders the identity of a man found with a screwdriver implanted in his forehead and considers the fact that his initials were found in the plastic butt of the screwdriver's handle, and he feels underlying this is a relationship that is too vast, too ambiguous and too imponderable for his mind to fully grasp and appreciate. He remembers the look of horror on the man's face, for it was not ordinary horror; no, it was the sort of horror that allows one to think a vision has been glimpsed, a vision too frightening to be fully communicated. In looking up and seeing the screwdriver about to impale him, the victim must have glimpsed the horrendous nature of his act when, quite by accident, several years before, he had misplaced this same screwdriver after making repairs to his lawn mower. A man who had desired things to come back to him, he had, by the small exertion of will it took to emblazon his initials on the plastic handle, shaped his own end. No wonder the horror on his face! No wonder his eyes had rolled back into the sockets! For on glimpsing the screwdriver he must have also felt impelled to look inside himself, over the vague terrain of his own interior; and he must have realized the fatal error he had commited: that of exceeding a hitherto unknown law of causality. In recognizing this he had made himself vulnerable, he had allowed a small fissure to develop in his skull, whereupon the screwdriver, finding its way prepared, had slotted itself conveniently into the hole, the tip lodging deep within the manifold tissue of the brain.

✿   ✿   ✿

It is the closing night of the Dürer Exhibition when the crime is detected; apparently a vandal, one exhibiting a great deal of stealth, for there is a guard on duty twenty-four hours a day, has unhung the engraving of *Knight, Death and Devil* and has driven a screwdriver through the lower left-hand corner and has added certain artistic embellishments of his own: namely a dash of blood and two eye sockets. The police are called in and the Inspector who arrives to assess the crime immediately gives way to laughter. This laughter strikes the curator as rather coarse, for the engraving by Dürer is priceless and this crime has occurred in a museum under his management. He admonishes the Inspector, who in turn tells the curator that he knows who the culprit is, a surrealist living in the neighbourhood. That surrealist is then hauled kicking and screaming from bed and is charged with gross mischief, destruction of property and corruption of the public's sensibilities. At the same time that this occurs, a man half-way around the world finds he has suddenly lost his faith without knowing why, except that he has seen in a dream a man with a screwdriver implanted in his forehead and since then he has found it impossible to believe.

Rumours of Foot

Rick Hillis

Twenty years without direct word, and then out of the blue, a phone call.

"I need you," his voice said.

I rested the receiver against my chest. What do you tell a man whose dreams you betrayed in the bursting seconds of youth? How do you answer for something like that?

"Tell me where," I said, "and when."

Hours later I am flying. My wife, alone in the terminal waving, is a confused citizen of my life. I am up in the air, returning to regain something.

Memory

serves like a tennis pro acing a teacup. You won't be able to make a clean return, and if you try to reach back you may be struck by shards of the past, and it will hurt. Still, there are times when the world feels like a baseball in your palm. You can do anything. That's how I felt: there was a feeling inside that had been gone a long time.

Foot and Buddy, Buddy and Foot. Left wing and centre, forward and guard. God, we were good. Baseball, whacking homeruns into backyards. Hockey, slap-shots ringing off goalposts, snicking through the net. Basketball, dominating the boards over the tall thin boys with change-purse collar-bones and futures in the college ranks. Football . . .

But let me tell you about Foot Rose. He was the dreamer and the dream, the champion of desire, the harbinger of youth. Truly a beautiful man. He paid a price along the way—he lost some things. But he didn't lose me, not in spirit he didn't. I don't care what the rumours say because I loved the Foot. I always will.

Rumours

Nobody knows where they come from. Origin unknown. But they descend on us and we gather, pass them around like photographs.

"Did you hear the latest on wonderboy? . . . Well," tucking a loop of fat under the belt, "apparently he's jogging the Great Chinese Wall."

"The Wall of China? No."

"This is what I understand. On top of it yet. Not getting paid a red penny, either."

"Sounds like Rose to me."

"Vintage Foot all right."

"Foot Rose is Foot Rose etc., and so on."

"Always was, always will be. Won't never grow up."

I admit it, we in his hometown mocked him. But you see when all you have left are the diminished dreams of middling health, early retirement and peaceful far-away death, you hold on to these hard. Foot was something gone in us now, and I guess we were jealous, but I know we waited for those rumours like the rest of a song heard passing under a bridge.

Foot Rose skiing the spine of the Alps
Playing semi-pro soccer in Brazil, drinking with Pele
Pacing Sherpas up K2's stone-studded slopes

The plane set down in a city in the south where drooping cedars leaned across streets, touching leaves like old friends shaking hands. It was a place of ancient frame houses, snapping flags, humidity. I taxied to Foot's address and stood on the street in front of a motorhome raised up on blocks.

As the taxi pulled away I bent for my bags, and a scab-coloured station-wagon with half moons of rust above the wheels swerved around the corner and nearly hit me. It could have killed me, but it didn't stop. Several gap-toothed youngsters laughed at me through the smudged rear window as the car roared away.

Memory (of the game)

Last day of the season, last year of high school. Late October, late afternoon. Field blue and hard as a sheet of steel, snow smoking across it. My feet are hammerheads welded to my ankles and I hobble when I run.

Hard to believe, but we are losing. Down by two. Third and ten from our own 40. Barring penalty, the last play of the game. I search the sidelines for a call and see the coach fling his clipboard in the air. We huddle, helmets clicking together. Some of us are crying, eyes blue chips of ice. I can't throw into this wind, and my eyes implore my men for forgiveness for what I'm about to do: sink to a knee behind a horseshoe of linemen, wait for the gun. Slump off the field, back to school, in a few months, into adulthood.

"Don't quit on me," Foot whispers in my earhole. "Let me try a fieldgoal."

On the sidelines, Coach was exploding his arms. We had never re-sorted to a fieldgoal before, but Foot was our kickoff man. I made a split-second decision, the correct one. Punt formation. I knelt on the snow, *saw the referee's eyes on the watch on his blue wrist, barked out the cadence, ball wobbling from between the centre's legs, hard as a frozen Javex bottle in my hands* . . .

The motorhome was locked, but from behind it I heard a strange rhythmical noise that can only be described as what it was. I rounded the rear bumper and saw an old woman prone on a padded bench, straining beneath a barbell. She looked like a child wearing a soiled body-stocking and a fright mask. Her neck tendons bulged like worms moving brain-ward, breath shattering from her false teeth. She had on nylon running shorts, Nike shoes, a mesh tank top that flapped on her bones like a flag. She placed the barbell in the bench's metal palms and sat up.

"You must be Buddy," she said. "From what I heard about you, I'm surprised you kept your word."

Memories (of the kick)
The sound of a single piston sparking life in a machine that would never stop
of a missle bursting the skin of the sea, losing itself in space
of my head exploding

Where was the ball? We gawked at the sky. Then there—a flake of ash hanging in the wind over the hashmarks, arcing between the uprights, burying itself in an endzone snowdrift. *Eighty yards*, I remember thinking, *not even George Blanda . . .*

The old woman's name was Ma Bird. She told me Foot was at the stadium and jabbed the barbell in its direction.

When had I begun to grow old? Not long after that football game, I guess. A cheerleader placed a hammerlock on my heart, and there was a weird security in losing some freedom. Her name was Maureen and she made me quit hockey for my teeth. I took to sitting around with her. Got a part-time job, put my money into a car. Maureen made me give up basketball because she said my knees looked like a chicken's. Badminton, she told me, was lame. So I threw everything away and more or less started to become what I thought was a man.

Meanwhile, Foot was becoming famous. *Sports Illustrated* got wind of the eighty-yarder and published his photo in their "Look Out" section beside a five-year-old pool shark who shot a perfect game of snooker, wheeling himself around the table on a castered office chair. Scholarship offers poured in.

The stadium lifted out of the trees and homes like a volcanic cone. Inside was emptiness, but I heard a ticking sound and followed it around until I spotted the distant back of a runner pounding up the endzone steps. When I got close, I could see the hamstrings bulge, arms shoot forward and back, muscles rippling like heavy ropes making shapes under the tight skin like wishbones. At the crest, Foot turned, and time flaked away like cells of dead skin. He hadn't changed at all. We raced toward each other and embraced like guys.

In June, Foot took me into the locker-room and said he was getting a lot of good scholarship offers. I told him I suspected as much and that he deserved them.

"What I'm saying is, we're a team. If anybody gets me, you get a free ride too."

"Me?" I said. "Why?"

"Foot and Buddy, Buddy and Foot," Foot said. "Because you were there—"

I knew what he meant, that I'd been there all along, but things were different now. I made a face and waved my hand as if to frighten something off. "So were a lot of other people there," I said.

"You pinned the ball, though."

I shook my head. "I have my own life," I said. "Let me live it."

A few days later Foot hauled me away from a crowd of smokers in front of the school and asked me to jog a few laps with him. We were side by side for a few moments, then my lungs started scratching, my feet clumping. Pretty soon Foot's back was disappearing. I hobbled to the showers.

I was towelling off when Foot clacked in in his cleats.

"Pin some for me?" he asked.

Water dripped from the sag of my belly. "I'm getting married," I said, "Maureen and me."

"You and Sub*marine*?"

"I'd be proud if you'd be my best man."

"What about football, though?"

"What about it? Football's over."

"When?"

"Now! *Forever!*"

Foot swung open his locker and held a sheaf of papers. "Washington State," he said dully. "The Crimson Tide—" He was licking his thumb and flinging the papers one by one into the water at my feet, his scholarship offers becoming diaphanous on the floor. We stood ankle-deep in a stack of dream places. "—Clemson, Boston College, Miami of Florida, the Cornhuskers, Oklahoma Sooners . . ." He could have gone on and on, but he just pitched the remaining pages down and clacked out of the locker-room and out of my life. He didn't write his final exams, so he blew his chances for college. The rumours have him burning his cleats in a trash barrel outside the bus depot and leaving town.

But you can't trust rumours.

The motorhome was a mausoleum for old athletes. Photos of Gordie Howe, Muhammad Ali, Tony Esposito, Wilt Chamberlain, Phil Niekro. Above the sit-up ramp, a blow-up of George Blanda, his boot cleat lifting a small clump of lawn, hands thrown up as if describing the size of a fish. Somewhere off-camera, the ball splitting the uprights.

Foot revved his blender, began ramming fruit in. He measured out a portion of odious powder and poured everything into an empty peanut-butter jar.

"So what's Submarine say about you coming?" He was sipping from the jar.

"She wasn't too happy."

Foot looked pleased. "You did the honourable thing," he said. "This time."

I followed Foot to the window and we looked outside. The old weight-lifter from that afternoon was twisting, coiling herself into painful-looking yoga-like positions.

"Sixty-eight years old. Can you believe it?" Foot said in a tone that indicated he was amazed.

Her moans were audible through the glass. She looked every second of 68 to me, but I couldn't say that to Foot.

"We met on a jogging trail," Foot told me. "She's my old lady."

I pictured Foot and the old woman together. Then I tried not to, but I couldn't.

"She moved in right away and we decided we'd band together and push for my dream. Now or never was the way we saw it."

"Your dream?" I said.

Ma Bird

Foot told me her story. This is it: a few years before she and her husband retired and headed south. Before they made a hundred miles, a tire on the motorhome blew. Ma's husband pranced out, jacked up the vehicle, cranked on the spare and had a heart attack. He passed away right there on the shoulder of the road. Ma must have been a naïve old woman because when she saw him lying there like a stick, her eyes opened on death for the first time. She was furious. You trust your dreams with a guy and he dies on you. Since there was no one else, she fed him into the local incinerator and pointed the motorhome down the road.

Foot's Dream
was to play football.

"No team would look at a guy your age," I said.

"Just tell me if you're standing by me or not."

"*Come on, Foot!* You might be in good shape, but you're still how old you are. Those college kids would shatter your bones!"

"Not college," said Foot. "Pro."

"*PRO!*"

"Just give me tomorrow, Buddy. Give me a chance is all I ask. And if I don't measure up after that, you can walk away guilt-free."

What could I say? We watched Ma Bird's luminous running-shoes wobble into the night, moving down the street where traffic loomed and tires screamed.

I didn't sleep until dawn. All night I lay cramped on the couch listening to Foot and Ma sleep like an audience of clapping hands. It was a weird picture, believe me. Finally I drifted into a dream of myself and Maureen.

"Pin it."

I am on the fifteen-yard line. This is pathetic, a lineman could kick a fieldgoal from here. Solemnly, Foot strides toward the uprights, swiping bits of paper out of his path with the toe of his cleat. When he turns to look at me, I can't meet his eyes. It's that embarrassing.

"You're on the wrong side," Foot says to me.

I look up. Foot is pointing at the *other* uprights. From where I'm kneeling they look like a tuning-fork. Gulls whirling over the endzone are only specks on my glasses. Foot moving towards me, a blur.

Diary (of the next several weeks)

Arise at dawn. Foot climbs five miles of stadium steps.

Noon: Kicks 1000 fieldgoals (I learned to handle the balls like cobs of corn, setting them down with factory exactness). Ma Bird, in the endzone, shags balls, sprints them back. Longest stretch without a miss: three weeks.

Evenings: Pasta, vitamins, protein drink, cool down with a street game of aerial football, crowd noise simulated by traffic hums. (Twice a week phone Maureen—don't let Foot know about this.)

In early May we are ready. Take the motorhome down off the blocks, hit the road.

Recounting the rest is like explaining dream logic. It doesn't make sense. Suffice it to say nobody wanted an aging free-agent with no college experience in their training camp.

Team after team, city after city, the same. Ma rubs Foot down with Antiphlogistine, sends him out with the other boys fighting for the kicking job.

"Who's that geezer?" one of them would say.

"Kind of looks like Tab Hunter."

"Yeah? Who's Tab Hunter?"

A team lackey would putt out in a golf cart.

"I'm Foot Rose. I'm a free-agent," Foot would say.

"You'll have to leave, sir."

"Why?"

"Medical reasons."

"I'm fit as a fiddle, though."

"It's out of my hands. We're not covered."

At first we chuckled it off and got psyched for the next camp, but time made Foot angry. In Cincinnati, he had to be forcibly removed from the playing surface by security officers, two linemen, Ma Bird and myself. He didn't even get a chance to warm up.

It wasn't fair. Here was possibly the greatest leg of all time, a man with reckless ability and the heart of a child. But the world wouldn't let him play. There wasn't fairness.

Depression banked up. Twenty towns, twenty rejections.

One night, feeling snarly, we unwound with a game of street football. It was dark, there was too much traffic, we shouldn't have played. I have nothing more to say about it.

The next day things changed. When Foot was asked to leave the field, he saw a football cupped in a plastic tee in front of the warm-up net that looks a bit like a wall of nylon mesh. Foot took a step toward it and blasted through an oblong hole.

I watched the peak of the head coach's cap flip up as the aluminum frame of the warm-up net folded in a kind of curtsy to the ground. The lackey who had sent Foot away U-turned his golf cart mid-field, but the reporters were already there with their microphones.

Foot kicked ten fieldgoals in three pre-season games. After he single-handedly defeated Chicago, Jim McMahon joked on "Letterman" that oldsters shouldn't be allowed to play in the NFL.

There is a "60 Minutes" piece that ends with two child actors, one pinning a football, the other kicking in a cinder schoolyard. This is superimposed by myself pinning for Foot on the practice field, once again being superimposed by actual game footage of Foot's five fieldgoals against the Bears.

As Foot is being slow-motion swarmed by his teammates, Dianne Sawyer recites.

and dreaming just comes natural
like the first breath from a baby
like sunshine feeding daisies
like the love hidden deep in your heart

and my face superimposes the everyman in the crowd.

The dream
died somewhere along the way. Foot suggested a game of street football. We were wired, tense. It seemed like a good idea. Foot defended Ma. I was quarterback. The ball went deep on a post pattern at the same instant backup lights flicked on in a driveway. Ma went up for the ball, out of reach. Foot, leaping, twisting in mid-air (he must have heard me scream), knocked Ma to the pavement. He let the ball go, which was not instinctive. Maybe that's as good as we got maybe.

The Sunday after the "60 Minutes" clip, during the last pre-season game, the unexpected reared. Or perhaps the inevitable. In Foot's case, maybe the desired. I didn't say that.

After a completed fieldgoal, Foot, bouncing, bouncing, watching the ball sail over the catch net, announcers going:

—Rose did not play college football, but back in high school, which judging by the hair under that helmet must have been a fair distance ago ... Foot bouncing, bouncing, it almost seemed *waiting* for some name-hungry defensive back built low and heavy like a hog to come in and blind side him like a pin setter.

And he came. *A dark streak, low from the left, Foot's cleats gripping the artificial turf. Knee an explosion. The gun.*

Foot Rose would never play football again. That's what the doctors told the press. But on the basis of his knowledge of kicking technique and his short burst of media attention (so short you might have missed it), he was offered a position in China teaching soccer players how to meet the ball. Later he became the first non-Russian football coach in the Soviet Union.

At least, these are the rumours.

As a sign of bereavement, which I now consider bizarre, I bought a cage full of pigeons from a kid and set them free in a kind of Olympic salute.

"Dreaming just comes natural," I said as I slid back the slat roof of the cage. Pigeons rushed past me in an explosion of white and grey, whirled once over top of me and returned to their box. Not even one tried to escape.

"What did they have her in?" Foot asked me on the day I left. We were in a seedy bar. He was wearing a stained brown trenchcoat, leaning on an umbrella for a cane, looking very much the wino.

"Running togs," I said.

"I thought so." Foot tipped his head and emptied his glass. He wiped his mouth with a sleeve, fixed his liquid eyes on me. "I figured you'd lie to save me."

Rumours

We need them like the young need sleep and we pass them around like drinks. We mow our busy lawns, watch sports on the satellite, wait for it to happen. We deaden ourselves.

Once in a while a friend will ask for the story I am telling, and I'll do my best, though to be honest—it's hard. Sometimes Foot is toiling in an industrial semi-pro league in the Northeast, sometimes we nearly make it on "Donahue." One time three adults scrimmaged in the street after dark. Usually I falter before the end because I don't know how to finish this story.

How do you explain youth slipping by?

By the River
Jack Hodgins

But listen, she thinks, it's nearly time.

And flutters, leaf-like, at the thought. The train will rumble down the valley, stop at the little shack to discharge Styan, and move on. This will happen in half an hour and she has a mile still to walk.

Crystal Styan walking through the woods, through bush, is not pretty. She knows that she is not even a little pretty, though her face is small enough, and pale, and her eyes are not too narrow. She wears a yellow wool sweater and a long cotton skirt and boots. Her hair, tied back so the branches will not catch in it, hangs straight and almost colourless down her back. Some day, she expects, there will be a baby to play with her hair and hide in it like someone behind a waterfall.

She has left the log cabin, which sits on the edge of the river in a stand of birch, and now she follows the river bank upstream. A mile ahead, far around the bend out of sight, the railroad tracks pass along the rim of their land and a small station is built there just for them, for her and Jim Styan. It is their only way in to town, which is ten miles away and not much of a town anyway when you get there. A few stores, a tilted old hotel, a movie theatre.

Likely, Styan would have been to a movie last night. He would have stayed the night in the hotel, but first (after he had seen the lawyer and bought the few things she'd asked him for) he would pay his money and sit in the back row of the theatre and laugh loudly all the way through the movie. He always laughs at everything, even if it isn't funny, because those figures on the screen make him think of people he has known; and the thought of them exposed like this for just anyone to see embarrasses him a little and makes him want to create a lot of noise so people will know he isn't a bit like that himself.

She smiles. The first time they went to a movie together she slouched as far down in the seat as she could so no one could see she was there or had anything to do with Jim Styan.

The river flows past her almost silently. It has moved only a hundred miles from its source and has another thousand miles to go before it reaches the ocean, but already it is wide enough and fast. Right here she has more than once seen a moose wade out and then swim across to the other side and disappear into the cedar swamps. She knows something, has heard somewhere that farther downstream, miles and miles behind her, an Indian band once thought this river a hungry monster that liked to gobble up their people. They say that Coyote their god-hero dived in and subdued the monster and made it promise never to swallow people again. She once thought she'd like to study that kind of thing at a university or somewhere, if Jim Styan hadn't told her grade ten was good enough for anyone and a life on the road was more exciting.

What road? she wonders. There isn't a road within ten miles. They sold the rickety old blue pickup the same day they moved onto this place. The railroad was going to be all they'd need. There wasn't any place they cared to go that the train, even this old-fashioned milk-run outfit, couldn't take them easily and cheaply enough.

But listen, she thinks, it's nearly time.

The trail she is following swings inland to climb a small bluff and for a while she is engulfed by trees. Cedar and fir are dark and thick and damp. The green new growth on the scrub bushes has nearly filled in the narrow trail. She holds her skirt up a little so it won't be caught or ripped, then runs and nearly slides down the hill again to the river's bank. She can see in every direction for miles and there isn't a thing in sight which has anything to do with man.

"Who needs them?" Styan said, long ago.

It was with that kind of question—questions that implied an answer so obvious only a fool would think to doubt—that he talked her first out of the classroom and then right off the island of her birth and finally up here into the mountains with the river and the moose and the railroad. It was as if he had transported her in his falling-apart pickup not only across the province about as far as it was possible to go, but also backwards in time, perhaps as far as her grandmother's youth or even farther. She washes their coarse clothing in the river and depends on the whims of the seasons for her food.

"Look!" he shouted when they stood first in the clearing above the cabin. "It's as if we're the very first ones. You and me."

They swam in the cold river that day and even then she thought of Coyote and the monster, but he took her inside the cabin and they made love on the fir-bough bed that was to be theirs for the next five years. "We don't need any of them," he sang. He flopped over on his back and shouted up into the rafters. "We'll farm it! We'll make it go. We'll make our own world!" Naked, he was as thin and pale as a celery stalk.

When they moved in he let his moustache grow long and droopy like someone in an old, brown photograph. He wore overalls which were far too big for him and started walking around as if there were a movie camera somewhere in the trees and he was being paid to act like a hillbilly instead of the city-bred boy he really was. He stuck a limp felt hat on the top of his head like someone's uncle Hiram and bought chickens.

"It's a start," he said.

"Six chickens?" She counted again to be sure. "We don't even have a shed for them."

He stood with his feet wide apart and looked at her as if she were stupid. "They'll lay their eggs in the grass."

"That should be fun," she said. "A hundred and sixty acres is a good-size pen."

"It's a start. Next spring we'll buy a cow. Who needs more?"

Yes who? They survived their first winter here, though the chickens weren't so lucky. The hens got lice and started pecking at each other. By the time Styan got around to riding in to town for something to kill the lice a few had pecked right through the skin and exposed the innards. When he came back from town they had all frozen to death in the yard.

At home, back on her father's farm in the blue mountains of the island, nothing had ever frozen to death. Her father had cared for things. She had never seen anything go so wrong there, or anyone have to suffer.

She walks carefully now, for the trail is on the very edge of the river bank and is spongy and broken away in places. The water, clear and shallow here, back-eddies into little bays where cattail and bracken grow and where water-skeeters walk on their own reflection. A beer bottle glitters where someone, perhaps a guide on the river, has thrown it— wedged between stones as if it has been there as long as they have. She keeps her face turned to the river, away from the acres and acres of forest which are theirs.

Listen, it's nearly time, she thinks. And knows that soon, from far up the river valley, she will be able to hear the throbbing of the train, coming near.

She imagines his face at the window. He is the only passenger in the coach and sits backwards, watching the land slip by, grinning in expectation or memory or both. He tells a joke to old Bill Cobb the conductor but even in his laughter does not turn his eyes from outside the train. One spot on his forehead is white where it presses against the glass. His fingers run over and over the long drooping ends of his moustache. He is wearing his hat.

Hurry, hurry, she thinks. To the train, to her feet, to him.

She wants to tell him about the skunk she spotted yesterday. She wants to tell him about the stove, which smokes too much and needs some kind of clean-out. She wants to tell him about her dream; how she dreamed he was trying to go into the river and how she pulled and hauled on his feet but he wouldn't come out. He will laugh and laugh at her when she tells him, and his laughter will make it all right and not so frightening, so that maybe she will be able to laugh at it too.

She has rounded the curve in the river and glances back, way back, at the cabin. It is dark and solid, not far from the bank. Behind the poplars the cleared fields are yellowing with the coming of fall but now in all that place there isn't a thing alive, unless she wants to count trees and insects. No people. No animals. It is scarcely different from her very first look at it. In five years their dream of livestock has been shelved again and again.

Once there was a cow. A sway-backed old Jersey.

"This time I've done it right," he said. "Just look at this prize."

And stepped down off the train to show off his cow, a wide-eyed beauty that looked at her through a window of the passenger coach.

"Maybe so, but you'll need a miracle, too, to get that thing down out of there."

A minor detail to him, who scooped her up and swung her around and kissed her hard, all in front of the old conductor and the engineer who didn't even bother to turn away. "Farmers at last!" he shouted. "You can't have a farm without a cow. You can't have a baby without a cow."

She put her head inside the coach, looked square into the big brown eyes, glanced at the sawed-off horns. "Found you somewhere, I guess," she said to the cow. "Turned out of someone's herd for being too old or senile or dried up."

"An auction sale," he said, and slapped one hand on the window glass. "I was the only one there who was desperate. But I punched her bag and pulled her tits; she'll do. There may even be a calf or two left in her sway-backed old soul."

"Come on, bossy," she said. "This is no place for you."

But the cow had other ideas. It backed into a corner of the coach and shook its lowered head. Its eyes, steady and dull, never left Crystal Styan.

"You're home," Styan said. "Sorry there's no crowd here or a band playing music, but step down anyway and let's get started."

"She's not impressed," she said. "She don't see any barn waiting out there either, not to mention hay or feed of any kind. She's smart enough to know a train coach is at least a roof over her head."

The four of them climbed over the seats to get behind her and pushed her all the way down the aisle. Then, when they had shoved her down the steps, she fell on her knees on the gravel and let out a long unhappy bellow. She looked around, bellowed again, then stood up and high-tailed it down the tracks. Before Styan even thought to go after her she swung right and headed into bush.

Styan disappeared into the bush, too, hollering, and after a while the train moved on to keep its schedule. She went back down the trail and waited in the cabin until nearly dark. When she went outside again she found him on the river bank, his feet in the water, his head resting against a birch trunk.

"What the hell," he said, and shook and didn't look at her.

"Maybe she'll come back," she said.

"A bear'll get her before then, or a cougar. There's no hope of that."

She put a hand on his shoulder but he shook it off. He'd dragged her from place to place right up this river from its mouth, looking and looking for his dream, never satisfied until he saw this piece of land. For that dream and for him she had suffered.

She smiles, though, at the memory. Because even then he was able to bounce back, to resume the dream, start building new plans. She smiles, too, because she knows there will be a surprise today; there has always been a surprise. When it wasn't a cow it was a bouquet of flowers or something else. She goes through a long list in her mind of what it may be, but knows it will be none of them. Not once in her life has anything been exactly the way she imagined it. Just so much as foreseeing something was a guarantee it wouldn't happen, at least not in the exact same way.

"Hey you, Styan!" she suddenly calls out. "Hey you, Jim Styan. Where are you?" And laughs, because the noise she makes can't possibly make any difference to the world, except for a few wild animals that might be alarmed.

She laughs again, and slaps one hand against her thigh, and shakes her head. Just give her—how many minutes now?—and she won't be alone. These woods will shudder with his laughter, his shouting, his joy. That train, that kinky little train will drop her husband off and then pass on like a stay-stitch thread pulled from a seam.

"Hey you, Styan! What you brought this time? A gold brooch? An old nanny goat?"

The river runs past silently and she imagines that it is only shoulders she is seeing, that monster heads have ducked down to glide by but are watching her from eyes grey as stone. She wants to scream out, "Hide, you crummy cheat, my Coyote's coming home!" but is afraid to tempt even something that she does not believe in. And anyway she senses—far off—the beat of the little train coming down the valley from the town.

And when it comes into sight she is there, on the platform in front of the little sagging shed, watching. She stands tilted far out over the tracks to see, but never dares—even when it is so far away—to step down onto the ties for a better look.

The boards beneath her feet are rotting and broken. Long stems of grass have grown up through the cracks and brush against her legs. A squirrel runs down the slope of the shed's roof and yatters at her until she turns and lifts her hand to frighten it into silence.

She talks to herself, sings almost to the engine's beat—"Here he comes, here he comes"—and has her smile already as wide as it can be. She smiles into the side of the locomotive sliding past and the freight car sliding past and keeps on smiling even after the coach has stopped in front of her and it is obvious that Jim Styan is not on board.

Unless of course he is hiding under one of the seats, ready to leap up, one more surprise.

But old Bill Cobb the conductor backs down the steps, dragging a gunny sack out after him. "H'lo there, Crystal," he says. "He ain't aboard today either, I'm afraid." He works the gunny sack out onto the middle of the platform. "Herbie Stark sent this, it's potatoes mostly, and cabbages he was going to throw out of his store."

She takes the tiniest peek inside the sack and yes, there are potatoes there and some cabbages with soft brown leaves.

The engineer steps down out of his locomotive and comes along the side of the train rolling a cigarette. "Nice day again," he says with barely a glance at the sky. "You makin' out all right?"

"Hold it," the conductor says, as if he expects the train to move off by itself. "There's more." He climbs back into the passenger car and drags out a cardboard box heaped with groceries. "The church ladies said to drop this off," he says. "They told me make sure you get every piece of it, but I don't know how you'll ever get it down to the house through all that bush."

"She'll manage," the engineer says. He holds a lighted match under the ragged end of his cigarette until the loose tobacco blazes up. "She's been doing it—how long now?—must be six months."

The conductor pushes the cardboard box over against the sack of potatoes and stands back to wipe the sweat off his face. He glances at the engineer and they both smile a little and turn away. "Well," the engineer says, and heads back down the tracks and up into his locomotive.

The conductor tips his hat, says "Sorry," and climbs back into the empty passenger car. The train releases a long hiss and then moves slowly past her and down the tracks into the deep bush. She stands on the platform and looks after it a long while, as if a giant hand is pulling, slowly, a stay-stitching thread out of a fuzzy green cloth.

Blue Moon

Lionel Kearns

Whenever Harvey hears the song he thinks of Sybil Chalmers, who in 1949 came into the grade seven class, and sang it, astonishing them all.

"We have a new face with us this morning," the teacher had said. "This is Sybil." She was a middle-sized girl with her red hair in a kind of page-boy perm, a common style in those days. "Sybil wants to sing us a song," added the teacher.

This was something out of the ordinary. No one sang songs to the class. It was unheard of. It was unthinkable. Even so, it might be better than getting into the morning's Social Studies lesson. So the boys did not jeer at this point, as they might have done, had they had more time to consider what was happening.

"What are you going to sing, Sybil?" asked the teacher.

"Blue Moon," said Sybil, and after a little pause, she began to sing: "*Blue Moon/ You saw me standing alone/ Without a dream in my heart/ Without a love of my own/*" and so on, right through the whole song, including the choruses.

Sybil belted it out in a deep, rich, sexy, crooning voice that should have been coming over the radio or out of the mouth of a movie star, but should definitely not be occurring here in this time and place. The class was stunned. What was happening? One of themselves, even though she was a newcomer, was standing there revealing herself to be something very strange and threatening—a non-child, a young woman, a sexual being, or was it a kind of parody? No one knew how to respond, so they stared at her, noticing her small breasts pushing out her sweater front as

she sang with all that husky-throated self-assurance and conviction about
the unmentionable, about romantic love.

When she finished there was silence. The class was in a state of shock.
Even the teacher was upset. She had agreed to Sybil's suggestion, thinking
that it would be a children's song, executed in the customary thin high
pitch of a schoolgirl. But Sybil's rendition of "Blue Moon" seemed almost
obscene. After a long pause someone began to clap, and then there was
general applause. But that grade seven class was never the same again.

Three years later Harvey is on a train with the other members of his
Midget B hockey team. They are headed for Regina, the site of a minor
hockey tournament. Walking through the train with some of his team-
mates on the way to the diner, Harvey sees Sybil Chalmers. Wham! He
passes her without speaking, pretending he does not recognize her. She
is sitting with her mother. *"Blue-moon-blue-moon-blue-moon,"* the words race
through his mind's ear as he moves quickly on through the door at the
end of the train car. His friends behind him have also noticed her, and
one of them gives a whistle before Harvey can close the door and move
quickly on through the next one into the diner.

"Did you see that cutie?" someone says, as they are shown to their seats
by the dining car steward.

"Hey, stupid, that's her mother she's with," says one of the others.

"Let Harvey have her mother," says someone.

Harvey, of course, does not let on that he knows her, though he can
feel his cheeks turning hot. He has a sudden moment of terror, thinking
the others will notice his blush, but this passes. While he eats his lunch
he tries to convince himself that he has been mistaken. The girl in the
next coach is much too beautiful to be Sybil Chalmers. But the song is
going through his head. *"Blue moon/ You saw me standing alone . . ."*

"You watch me," says Ed. "I'm going to make a date with her when we
go back through her coach. I'll bet she's getting off at Regina too."

"Bet she ain't," says someone.

"Five bucks says you don't even speak to her," says somebody else.

"Ten bucks she doesn't speak to him!" says one of the others.

Harvey is feeling a bit sick. What should he do? He is not participating
in the merriment of his team-mates. "The stupid bunch of jerks," he
thinks to himself. "If I was alone I'd speak to her for sure."

When they finish their lunch Harvey is the first one up and through the door at the end of the diner. He knows that Sybil and her mother are facing the other way, so if he walks through fast enough she won't have a chance to recognize him. He can hear the laughter and loud remarks of the others behind him.

"Excuse me, do you know the time?" Ed is saying, trying to sound serious.

"What's the matter with your watch, Ed?" someone shouts.

"Hey lady, you have to watch this guy. He's got lover's nuts," someone is hooting amongst the uproar.

Harvey is at the end of the train car and shutting the door on their noise and laughter. Sweating and cringing, he is relieved to be out of that space and finally into the safety of his own seat. He sits there alone, asking himself why he is such a chicken. If he played hockey like that he certainly would not be on this team or this trip. By now the others are coming through the door and down the aisle in quick succession.

"Boy, did she ever tell Ed," says one of them, a little subdued.

"That's five bucks you owe me anyway," says Ed.

"Bullshit! You didn't talk to her. You talked to her mother! Ha ha ha, and did her mother ever put you down," says one of the others.

"You're a bunch of jerks!" says Harvey.

For the next two hours Harvey sits looking out the window at the monotonous prairie landscape. The train comes to several stops, once at a siding, twice at small prairie towns that seem to have no more than a few empty box cars waiting on sidings, one or two grain elevators, and a cluster of houses.

"Can you imagine living in a dump like that?"

"They don't even have a rink."

"Prairie kids skate on ponds, stupid. They use magazines stuffed in their pants for shin pads. Wait till you see them on the ice in Regina."

"But they sure have classy women."

"She ain't from the prairies, stupid."

All afternoon Harvey looks out the train window and thinks about Sybil Chalmers, and the words of the song keep going through his head " . . . *without a dream in my heart/ Without a love of my own . . .*" in time to the rhythm of the wheels of the train on the track. He wonders whether she recognized him. Of course she did. Then why didn't she say something? Because he didn't give her a chance. Was that all? No. Maybe she was embarrassed too? Not if she was the Sybil Chalmers from grade seven. Nothing seemed to embarrass her. Was that true? He remembers how he avoided her at school. Everyone avoided her. Did she have any friends? Harvey remembers seeing her once or twice on the street with her mother. He too referred to her as "Blue Moon", as everyone did, even when she could overhear it. Sometimes they called her "Blue Moon" to her face. That must have hurt. What finally happened to her? Harvey remembers that she did not return to school in grade eight. She and her mother must have left town.

These are the thoughts that are going through Harvey's mind as he sits quietly looking out the train window. When he thinks of grade seven he feels sad and ashamed, but when he thinks of Sybil Chalmers sitting one train car away from him he feels excited. Perhaps he will be able to somehow wipe away all that teasing and ridicule she had to endure. And Harvey begins to think that he should walk back there and apologize to her. Wouldn't his team-mates be amazed if they saw him sitting there chatting to her and her mother like old friends? But Harvey decides that it would be safer to do it when they are not around. He begins to rehearse the scene in his imagination.

"Excuse me, but didn't you go to Kootenay Junior Secondary one time?"

"Why yes, how did you know?"

"Well, I'm Harvey Santini, and I used to be in your class."

"Why you're not the Harvey Santini I used to know. I mean he was just a little fellow."

"Yes I am, and I want to apologize."

"Oh don't be silly, Harvey."

"We treated you very badly . . ." Harvey spends the rest of the day trying to get the dialogue to go right, and to generate enough courage to put his plan into effect. By late afternoon he has made up his mind. His plan is to stay behind when the rest of the team goes down to the diner for dinner.

"Not hungry right now," he says. "Maybe I'll go later."

So Harvey sits alone for twenty minutes, and then gets up and moves towards the door at the end of the train car. He is frightened. His heart beats fast and loud. He pushes open the first door and stands waiting in the noisy platform area between the cars. Then he draws in his breath and pulls open the second door. He begins to walk casually down the aisle, keeping his eyes unfocussed until he is close to them, to where he thinks they are sitting. But when he looks at the seat where Sybil and her mother were sitting, they are not there. The seat is now occupied by an old couple. Harvey is relieved, and begins to breathe easier. Then he wonders if perhaps Sybil and her mother are in the diner. This thought troubles him. The diner, full of his own team-mates, is not the place to carry out this plan.

"Leave it till later," he says to himself, turning around and going back through the train to his own seat, where he waits for his friends to return.

"Ed must have driven that chick and her mother off the train," someone remarks after they get back.

"What, you mean she's gone?" asks Harvey. It is the first time he has mentioned her.

"Sure has, Harvey, and her mother too."

Some years later Harvey is blowing trombone in a local dance band. It's not a very good band, but it is the best one in the district, and so they play regularly every weekend. They play mostly tunes and arrangements out of the swing era; you know the kind of thing: "Tuxedo Junction," "Pennies from Heaven," . . . "Blue Moon".

Of course that tune always makes Harvey think of Sybil Chalmers. He remembers how beautiful she looked on the train, and he regrets his cowardice in not speaking to her the first time he saw her. He wonders if he will ever see her again.

The band needs a female vocalist, and Harvey thinks of her singing "Blue Moon" whenever they play it, which is at least once a week. He has been thinking of her now for years. She grows more and more voluptuous and desirable in his imagination. And she is always connected with that song: *"Blue Moon/ You saw me standing alone/ Without a dream in my heart/ Without a love of my own/ Blue Moon . . ."* Sometimes he dreams of her spontaneously, without the aid of the musical cue.

Harvey wonders how he can track her down. He worries that if he does not find her soon they will both be so old that they will be repulsive to each other when they finally meet. Already he is approaching middle age. What should he do? He has tried to forget her, but whenever he thinks he has rid himself of that troublesome memory, he hears the tune, "Blue Moon", and there she is, back in his head again.

Somehow he expects her to turn up as a famous singer in a big name band in the States, or maybe to surface suddenly as a star in a Hollywood musical. But he never hears of her. Perhaps she is dead. This thought makes him very depressed. It is as though part of his own life has been suspended. The idea of tracing her becomes more and more obsessive.

In a final effort to locate Sybil Chalmers, Harvey Santini writes a story and sends it to Thistledown Press. That story is what you are reading at this moment. The third person hero is only a literary device. I am Harvey Santini. That is why I know so much about this situation. My goal is to reach Sybil Chalmers, wherever she may be. Surely she will notice the title of this story and be intrigued enough to read it and find out that I am writing about her. Or, even if she does not see it immediately, someone else will read it and tell her about it, and she will eventually contact me. Surely she will. That is why I have gone to the effort of writing this story.

But Reader, I beg your indulgence to let me return again to the ease of third person narration, so that I may tell you in a more detached manner what happens next. Shortly after the story is published, Sybil Chalmers discovers it. However, instead of making contact with Harvey directly, she chooses to send her lawyer, who lays libel charges against Harvey and the editors of *The Last Map is the Heart.*

Why has Sybil responded in this way? Harvey has written this story as a tribute to her magnificent voice and her beauty. He has written it as an apology for the way he treated her in grade seven. He has written it to confess his cowardice on the train. He wants to tell her that her song has touched him more deeply than any other song has touched him. Yet she is bringing libel charges against him. She does not deny that the first part of the story is essentially correct. She is the same Sybil Chalmers who sang "Blue Moon" in the grade seven class of the Kootenay Junior Secondary School. She is the Sybil Chalmers who travelled with her mother on the train through the prairies three years later. However, the second part of the story is completely false. It seems that it has somehow looped ahead of itself, for she has not yet brought charges against the writer of this story or the editors of this anthology. It is this strangeness in the story that constitutes the grounds for her libel action.

Harvey has a number of possible responses open to him. He can claim that all names in the story bear no relation to anyone living or dead. He can change the names of the principal characters and the name of the song. He can even change the offending ending of the story. He considers

would render the whole work meaningless. Falsification would commit
these words and images back to the flux and swirl of unorganized and
unintegrated experience. It would push the song and the girl and part of
Harvey Santini himself into the oblivion of never having actually occurred, where no one stands alone among strangers without a dream,
without a love of his or her own, where this feeling, where feeling itself,
is unconnected and so unbearable.

There is also the other problem. If Harvey changes the name of the
song, or the name of the girl, or the school, or even his own name, Sybil
will not read the story and recognize herself and him and their situation.
The pattern will remain incomplete and so the story will not make sense.

In the end he cannot change the story or retract the truth. Sybil sues
Harvey and the publisher, winning a devastating court settlement.
Neither he nor the company can find the money to pay. Thistledown Press
folds and Harvey changes his name and goes underground. What else can
he do? Years later he starts a small literary press devoted to enigmatic
reminiscence. The name of the press is *Blue Moon.*

Magpies

Thomas King

for Chrisula

This one is about Granny. Reserve story. Everyone knows this story.
Wilma knows it. Ambrose knows it. My friend, Napioa. Lionel James. Billy
Frank knows it, too. Billy Frank hears this story in Calgary. He hears it
three times. Maybe six. Boy, he tells me, here comes that story again.

Sometimes this story is about Wilma. Some people tell it so Ambrose
is all over the place. The way I tell it is this way and I tell it this way all the
time.

Sometimes I tell you about those Magpies first. With those noses. Good
noses, those ones. Magpies talk all the time, you know. Good gossips,
those. Hahahahaha. Good jokes, too. Sometimes I start that way.

Okay. Here comes that story again.

Granny falls and hurts her leg. So, that leg is pink. Then it looks blue.
Another time it is black. Yellow for a long time. That leg. Granny's leg.

Granny looks at that leg and thinks about dying. So she talks about
falling over dead. When that Granny starts talking about being dead,
Wilma says no, no, no. That is just a bruise. Yellow bruise. Those ones are
okay.

Granny talks to everyone she see about dying. I'm going to die, she
says to me and I say yes, that's right. Old people know these things. It
happens. Maybe that blood thing. Maybe cigarettes. Maybe a truck. Maybe
that bottle. Granny likes to talk of dying. I'm going to be dead real soon,
she says. Going to rot and nobody comes by but those birds tell all those
stories and laugh.

Watch those Magpies, that old woman tells Ambrose. You see them?

Sure, says Ambrose.

They smell death, she says. Isn't that right?

Yes, I says, that's true.

Those ones take the eyes first, she says, soft parts. Nice round parts they like first. Ripe. That's why you got to wrap them tight.

That's right, I says.

You listening Ambrose? That old Granny shake Ambrose so he is awake. They smell death, those birds, like you smell chokecherries on the boil. When I die, they'll come to me like that.

You can count on me, says Ambrose.

I'm going to die, then, Granny tells me, and I says okay.

Wilma takes that old woman to the hospital to see two, maybe five white doctors. They look at the leg. They look at that leg again. They do it some more times, too. Ummmm, ummmm, ummmm. That way. In the mouth. They don't dance. They don't sing. They think they talking to Granny. Ummmm, ummmm, ummmm.

Granny says to me there are good places to die. River is a good one. Coulees is okay, too. Maybe a mountain. Bad places, too, she says. Grocery store. Shopping mall. Movie show. Hospital.

That hospital is one bad place to die. See-po-aah-loo. See-po-aah-loo is like a hole. In the ground. See-po-aah-loo is one old word. Where you put stew bones. Where you put old things that are broke. Where you put old things that smell bad. Where you put beer cans. Coffee grounds. Fish guts. Milk cartons. Newspapers. Tractor oil. That black dog Walter Turnbull hit with his truck. Everything you don't want people to see. You put them there. See-po-aah-loo.

Then you cover it up. Go someplace else.

Hospital.

Those doctors tell Granny, ummmm, ummmm, ummmm. Maybe you better stay here. One day. Four days. Maybe we see something. Ummmm, ummmm, ummmm. Ambrose says Whites go to that hospital to get a new nose. Get good breasts. Fix up that old butt. Haul out things you don't need no more. Ambrose tells me that. Fix you up. Like a car. Run better. Ummmm, ummmm, ummmm.

Those ones don't fool Granny. I can tell you that.

That Granny nod her head. Look at that floor. Look at that door. Shuffle her feet. Like a Round dance. Ho-ho-ho-ho, that one dances out of See-po-aah-loo. Don't want to be in no hole, she says.

God loves you, Granny, Wilma says. Good woman, that Wilma. Loves Granny. Fixes her food. Washes her clothes. Wilma is mostly Catholic in the middle. Knows about dying. Reads those papers you get from church. In that wood pocket. Near that water.

When God takes you, Momma, you'll be real happy. This is how Wilma talks. Dead is okay, Wilma says. That God fellow just waiting for you. Good to see you. Howdy-do.

Don't put me in that grave, See-po-aah-loo, Granny tell Wilma.

Garbage hole.

Hospital.

One word. You see?

Yes, says Wilma, that's the modern way. You need a priest. He can make it clean.

Holes are cold, Granny says.

God will keep you warm, Wilma says.

So, Granny finds Ambrose.

Ambrose is a big man. Big chest. Big legs. Big head. Friendly man that Ambrose. Have a joke. Have a story. Always thinking about things to do. Going to fix this thing. Going to fix that thing. Granny finds Ambrose. You fix this thing for me, she says. Yes, that one says, I will do it. You can count on me.

Granny brings that boy to my house. Ho, I says, you got your big boy with you. Yes, she says, we come to see you, talk with you. Sit down, I says. Coffee is here. Tea, too. Sit down and eat some food.

You must talk to my big boy, Granny says. Tell him the way. Show him how to do this thing. You listen to this old one, Granny says. You can count on me, Ambrose says.

Granny squeeze her eyes. You be here when I die. You tell Wilma how to do this thing. You look out for me, take care of me, my big boy.

You can count on me.

I'm counting on you, says Granny. In that cottonwood at Heavyshield's cabin. Aoo-lee-sth. That's the one. Other ways that hole will get me and I'll come back.

You can count on me.

That leg get better. Granny's leg. But Granny dies anyway. Later. Not right now. Two, maybe four years. Maybe more. She falls over dead then. Like that. It is finished.

Ambrose is not there when Granny dies. Someone says he is in Edmonton at those meetings. Someone says, no, he is in Toronto. Someone says he is across the line. Wilma sniff her nose this way and that one sniff her nose that way. We can't wait for that Ambrose maybe come along. We going to do this thing right, Wilma says. We going to do this thing now.

So they get a priest.

So they put Granny in a box.

So they stick Granny in the church.

So they throw her in a hole.

Just like that. Pretty quick. They put her in that hole before Ambrose comes home. Everyone stands there. Ho ho ho ho. All of them feel bad, Granny in that hole. Wilma cries, too. Smack her hands and says, that's okay now. Everything is done now. It is finished.

Aoh-quwee.

That's the end of the story.

No, I was just fooling.

There's more.

Stick around.

Okay. Ambrose comes home. Everyone figures out this part, Ambrose comes home. No smile. No happy joke. Momma is with God, Wilma says. She's happy. Nothing for you to do.

I gave her this promise, Ambrose says, and I says, yes, that's right.

Keep your promise in your pocket, Wilma says. Momma don't need that promise. Everything is pretty good. God's got her.

God don't live in a hole, says Ambrose.

God is everywhere, says Wilma.

Those two talk like that. One day, maybe two, three weeks. Talk about God. Talk about that promise. You make lots of promises, Wilma says. Those things are easy for you to make. They fall out of your mouth like spit. Everybody got three or four of them.

That part is true. I can tell you that. Ambrose is generous with those things. Those promises. I help you chop wood for winter, Ambrose tells my friend Napioa. Fix that truck for you, he says to Billy Frank. Going to dig that ditch tomorrow, he tells his uncle.

You can count on me.

Keep that promise in your pocket, Wilma tells that one.

Ambrose comes to my house. Ho, he says, we got to fix that window. Yes, I says, it is broke alright. Maybe I'll bring some tools out next week, he says. Yes, I says, that would be good.

That Ambrose sits down and starts to cry. Hoo hoo hoo hoo. Like that. That big boy cries like that. Sit down, I says. Have some tea.

You got to help me, he says. Sure, I says. I can do that.

Granny's in that hole, he says. She's going to come back. You got to help me do this thing. We got to get her out and do it right. Put her in that tree. Heavyshield's tree. In the mountains. Like she said.

Boy, I says, lots of work that. They put her in pretty deep. Way down there. With that God fellow.

I can dig her up, Ambrose says. You don't have to do anything. I'll dig her up and get you and you can tell me how to do this thing. Got to keep that promise.

Okay, I says.

So.

That Ambrose gets everything we need. Wilma watches him and sniffs with her nose. Tonight I'm going to do it, Ambrose says. But he doesn't. Flat tire, he says.

Tonight I'm going to do it, that one tells me. But he doesn't. No moon.

Tonight I'm going to do it. That big boy has one good memory. But he doesn't do it then either. Got the flu.

Ambrose gets a skin and he keeps that skin in the back of his truck. Green. Getting to smell, I think. Maybe not. Those Magpies hang around that truck. What you got in that truck, Wilma says. Nothing, says Ambrose. Just some stuff.

But you know, he does it. That big boy comes to my house early in the morning. With his truck. With that skin. With Granny sewed up in that skin. Just like I said. Ho, I says, you got that Granny. Yes, says Ambrose, I dig her up last night. Now we can do it right.

So we do. Ambrose drives that truck with Granny sewed up in the skin to Heavyshield's cabin and that good boy climbs that tree and that one drags Granny up that tree with a rope. High. On those skinny branches. Near the sun. He puts that old woman. Then he climbs down. There, he says, and smacks his hands together. That does it.

I make some tea. Ambrose sits on the ground, watches Granny in the tree. Pretty soon he is asleep.

Let's see what happens.

Well, pretty quick those Magpies come along and look in that tree. And they fly in that tree. And they sit in that tree. Talking. They sit on that hide has Granny hid inside and talk to her. Hello. Nice day.

Then that sun comes down. Into the tree. With those birds. With Granny. Ho, that sun says, what we got here? Granny and a bunch of Magpies. That's right, I says.

Then that big dust ball comes along, right up to the house. Heavy-shield's place. Rolls into the yard.

Then Wilma gets out.

Then the RCMP gets out.

Then Benny Goodrunner, tribal policeman, gets out.

Out of that dust ball.

Boy, those birds are some fast talkers.

Where's Granny, Wilma says. Where's Ambrose? She says that, too. Where's Ambrose Standing Bull, RCMP says. Benny don't say nothing. He just stand there. Look embarrassed.

Ambrose wakes up. Wilma sees him wake up. There he is, she says. There is that criminal. There is that thief. Then she uses words I don't understand.

Ambrose stands right up. I'm just doing what Granny asked. Nothing wrong with that.

That RCMP got his bright uniform on. Body-stealing is against the law, he says.

This is reserve land, Ambrose says.

Benny's going to arrest you, Ambrose, says Wilma. Going to put you in jail for digging up Granny.

Lots of Magpies in the tree now. They just listening. All ears.

Wilma looks in that tree. She sees those birds. She sees that sun. She sees that hide. He's already stuck her in that tree. We got to bring her down.

RCMP man looks at Wilma and looks at Benny. Wilma looks at Benny. Ambrose looks at Benny. Maybe you boys want some tea, I says. Nice evening. Maybe you want to sit and have some tea.

No time for tea, old one, Wilma says in our language. My mother's in that tree. We got to get her down.

So. Benny is the one. Have to climb that tree. All the way. So, he starts up. Those birds stop walking on Granny and watch Benny. Ambrose watches Benny. Wilma watches Benny. RCMP man watches Benny. That

Benny is a rodeo man, rides those bulls. Strong legs, that one. He climbs
all the way to Granny. Then he sits down. On a limb. Like those birds.
Hey, he says, I can see the river. Real good view.

Look for Granny, says that Wilma.

Leave her alone, says Ambrose.

Boy, those Magpies are jumping around in that tree. Dancing. Choosing sides. Singing songs. Telling jokes.

Milk carton comes out of that tree.

Peach can comes out of that tree.

Bottle of Wesson cooking oil comes down. Empty.

Carburetor.

Magazine.

Hey, says Benny. Granny's not here. She's not in this skin. She's gone.
Nothing here but garbage. Benny comes down that tree.

Everybody looks at Ambrose.

Must be magic, says Ambrose and he walks into that cabin and closes
the door.

Wilma stands up straight and she looks at that RCMP man. Benny has
his clothes all dirty. That RCMP is mostly clean. Nothing but garbage in
that tree, Benny says. Alright, says Wilma. She gets back in the truck, that
one. Benny gets in that truck. RCMP gets in that truck.

Boy, pretty exciting.

That sun gets down behind the mountain. Ambrose comes out of that
house, says, everybody gone? Yes, I says. Good trick, that one, he says. Yes,
I says, that one had me fooled. My shovel broke, says Ambrose. I'm going
to get her tonight. Nobody will see me this time. I would have got her that
other time but my shovel broke. You got a shovel I can borrow? Sure, I
say, you can use my good shovel.

You watch, says Ambrose. This is my plan. Benny saw that bag of
garbage. So now I get Granny and put her up there. Take that garbage
down and put Granny in that tree like I promise. No one will look there
again. That's my plan.

That's a good plan, I says. That should fool them. Good thing you got
some of that garbage out of the ground.

You got to promise me you won't tell anyone about my plan, Ambrose
says. Watch out for those birds, I says. They told Wilma about your bag of
garbage, I bet. They got good ears, those ones. You got to sing that song
so they can't hear. So they won't remember. You know that song?

No, say Ambrose. You better listen then, I says. Otherwise those birds will tell everyone what your plan is. So I show Ambrose the song and he sings it pretty good, that boy. And he borrows my shovel. My good shovel. And I don't see him for a long time. And I don't see Wilma either. And I don't tell Ambrose's plan.

But I know what happened.

But I can't tell.

I promised.

You can count on me.

The Thrill of the Grass

W.P. Kinsella

1981: the summer the baseball players went on strike. The dull weeks drag by, the summer deepens, the strike is nearly a month old. Outside the city the corn rustles and ripens in the sun. Summer without baseball: a disruption to the psyche. An unexplainable aimlessness engulfs me. I stay later and later each evening in the small office at the rear of my shop. Now, driving home after work, the worst of the rush hour traffic over, it is the time of evening I would normally be heading for the stadium.

I enjoy arriving an hour early, parking in a far corner of the lot, walking slowly toward the stadium, rays of sun dropping softly over my shoulders like tangerine ropes, my shadow gliding with me, black as an umbrella. I like to watch young families beside their campers, the mothers in shorts, grilling hamburgers, their men drinking beer. I enjoy seeing little boys dressed in the home team uniform, barely toddling, clutching hotdogs in upraised hands.

I am a failed shortstop. As a young man, I saw myself diving to my left, graceful as a toppling tree, fielding high grounders like a cat leaping for butterflies, bracing my right foot and tossing to first, the throw true as if a steel ribbon connected my hand and the first baseman's glove. I dreamed of leading the American League in hitting—being inducted into the Hall of Fame. I batted .217 in my senior year of high school and averaged 1.3 errors per nine innings.

I know the stadium will be deserted; nevertheless I wheel my car down off the freeway, park, and walk across the silent lot, my footsteps rasping and mournful. Strangle-grass and creeping charlie are already inching up through the gravel, surreptitious, surprised at their own ease. Faded bottle caps, rusted bits of chrome, an occasional paper clip, recede into the earth. I circle a ticket booth, sun-faded, empty, the door closed by an oversized padlock. I walk beside the tall, machinery-green, board fence.

A half-mile away a few cars hiss along the freeway; overhead a single–
engine plane fizzes lazily. The whole place is silent as an empty classroom,
like a house suddenly without children.

It is then that I spot the door-shape. I have to check twice to be sure
it is there: a door cut in the deep-green boards of the fence, more the
promise of a door than the real thing, the kind of door, as children, we
cut in the sides of cardboard boxes with our mother's paring knives. As I
move closer, a golden circle of lock, like an acrimonious eye, establishes
its certainty.

I stand, my nose so close to the door I can smell the faint odour of
paint, the golden eye of a lock inches from my own eyes. My desire to be
inside the ballpark is so great that for the first time in my life I commit a
criminal act. I have been a locksmith for over forty years. I take the small
tools from the pocket of my jacket, and in less time than it would take a
speedy runner to circle the bases I am inside the stadium. Though the
ballpark is open-air, it smells of abandonment; the walkways and seating
areas are cold as basements. I breathe the odours of rancid popcorn and
wilted cardboard.

The maintenance staff were laid off when the strike began. Synthetic
grass does not need to be cut or watered. I stare down at the ball diamond,
where just to the right of the pitcher's mound, a single weed, perhaps two
inches high, stands defiant in the rain-pocked dirt.

The field sits breathless in the orangy glow of the evening sun. I stare
at the potato-coloured earth of the infield, that wide, dun arc, surrounded
by plastic grass. As I contemplate the prickly turf, which scorches the
thighs and buttocks of a sliding player as if he were being seared by hot
steel, it stares back in its uniform ugliness. The seams that send routinely
hit ground balls veering at tortuous angles, are vivid, grey as scars.

I remember the ballfields of my chilhood, the outfields full of soft
hummocks and brown-eyed gopher holes.

I stride down from the stands and walk out to the middle of the field.
I touch the stubble that is called grass, take off my shoes, but find it is like
walking on a row of toothbrushes. It was an evil day when they stripped
the sod from this ballpark, cut it into yard-wide swathes, rolled it,
memories and all, into great green-and-black cinnamonroll shapes,
trucked it away. Nature temporarily defeated. But Nature is patient.

Over the next few days an idea forms within me, ripening, swelling,
pushing everything else into a corner. It is like knowing a new, wonderful

joke and not being able to share. I need an accomplice.

I go to see a man I don't know personally, though I have seen his face peering at me from the financial pages of the local newspaper, and the *Wall Street Journal,* and I have been watching his profile at the baseball stadium, two boxes to the right of me, for several years. He is a fan. Really a fan. When the weather is intemperate, or the game not close, the people around us disappear like flowers closing at sunset, but we are always there until the last pitch. I know he is a man who attends because of the beauty and mystery of the game, a man who can sit during the last of the ninth with the game decided innings ago, and draw joy from watching the first baseman adjust the angle of his glove as the pitcher goes into his windup.

He, like me, is a first-base-side fan. I've always watched baseball from behind first base. The positions fans choose at sporting events are like politics, religion, or philosophy: a view of the world, a way of seeing the universe. They make no sense to anyone, have no basis in anything but stubbornness.

I brought up my daughters to watch baseball from the first-base side. One lives in Japan and sends me box scores from Japanese newspapers, and Japanese baseball magazines with pictures of superstars politely bowing to one another. She has a season ticket in Yokohama; on the first-base side.

"Tell him a baseball fan is here to see him," is all I will say to his secretary. His office is in a skyscraper, from which he can look out over the city to where the prairie rolls green as mountain water to the limits of the eye. I wait all afternoon in the artificially cool, glassy reception area with its yellow and mauve chairs, chrome and glass coffee tables. Finally, in the late afternoon, my message is passed along.

"I've seen you at the basball stadium," I say, not introducing myself.

"Yes," he says. "I recognize you. Three rows back, about eight seats to my left. You have a red scorebook and you often bring your daughter . . ."

"Granddaughter. Yes, she goes to sleep in my lap in the late innings, but she knows how to calculate an ERA and she's only in Grade 2."

"One of my greatest regrets," says this tall man, whose moustache and carefully styled hair are polar-bear white, "is that my grandchildren all live over a thousand miles away. You're very lucky. Now, what can I do for you?"

"I have an idea," I say. "One that's been creeping toward me like a first baseman when the bunt sign is on. What do you think about artificial turf?"

"Hmmmf," he snorts, "that's what the strike should be about. Baseball is meant to be played on summer evenings and Sunday afternoons, on grass just cut by a horse-drawn mower," and we smile as our eyes meet.

"I've discovered the ballpark is open, to me anyway," I go on. "There's no one there while the strike is on. The wind blows through the high top of the grandstand, whining until the pigeons in the rafters flutter. It's lonely as a ghost town."

"And what is it you do there, alone with the pigeons?"

"I dream."

"And where do I come in?"

"You've always struck me as a man who dreams. I think we have things in common. I think you might like to come with me. I could show you what I dream, paint you pictures, suggest what might happen . . ."

He studies me carefully for a moment, like a pitcher trying to decide if he can trust the sign his catcher has just given him.

"Tonight?" he says. "Would tonight be too soon?"

"Park in the northwest corner of the lot about 1:00 A.M.. There is a door about fifty yards to the right of the main gate. I'll open it when I hear you."

He nods.

I turn and leave.

The night is clear and cotton warm when he arrives. "Oh, my," he says, staring at the stadium turned chrome-blue by a full moon. "Oh, my," he says again, breathing in the faint odours of baseball, the reminder of fans and players not long gone.

"Let's go down to the field," I say. I am carrying a cardboard pizza box, holding it on the upturned palms of my hands, like an offering.

When we reach the field, he first stands up on the mound, makes an awkward attempt at a windup, then does a little sprint from first to about half-way to second. "I think I know what you've brought," he says, gesturing toward the box, "but let me see anyway."

I open the box in which rests a square foot of sod, the grass smooth and pure, cool as a swatch of satin, fragile as baby's hair.

"Ohhh," the man says, reaching out a finger to test the moistness of it. "Oh, I see."

We walk across the field, the harsh, prickly turf making the bottoms of my feet tingle, to the left-field corner where, in the angle formed by the foul line and the warning track, I lay down the square foot of sod. "That's beautiful," my friend says, kneeling beside me, placing his hand, fingers spread wide, on the verdant square, leaving a print faint as a veronica.

I take from my belt a sickle-shaped blade, the kind used for cutting carpet. I measure along the edge of the sod, dig the point in and pull carefully toward me. There is a ripping sound, like tearing an old bed sheet. I hold up the square of artificial turf like something freshly killed, while all the time digging the sharp point into the packed earth I have exposed. I replace the sod lovingly, covering the newly bared surface.

"A protest," I say.

"But it could be more," the man replies.

"I hoped you'd say that. It could be. If you'd like to come back . . ."

"Tomorrow night?"

"Tomorrow night would be fine. But there will be an admission charge . . ."

"A square of sod?"

"A square of sod two inches thick . . ."

"Of the same grass?"

"Of the same grass. But there's more."

"I suspected as much."

"You must have a friend . . ."

"Who would join us?"

"Yes."

"I have two. Would that be all right?"

"I trust your judgement."

"My father. He's over eighty," my friend says. "You might have seen him with me once or twice. He lives over fifty miles from here, but if I call him he'll come. And my friend . . ."

"If they pay their admission they'll be welcome . . ."

"And *they* may have friends . . ."

"Indeed they may. But what will we do with this?" I say, holding up the sticky-backed square of turf, which smells of glue and fabric.

"We could mail them anonymously to baseball executives, politicians, clergymen."

"Gentle reminders not to tamper with Nature."

We dance toward the exit, rampant with excitement.

"You will come back? You'll bring others?"

"Count on it," says my friend.

They do come, those trusted friends, and friends of friends, each making a live, green deposit. At first, a tiny row of sod squares begins to inch along toward left-centre field. The next night even more people arrive, the following night more again, and the night after there is positively a crowd. Those who come once seem always to return accompanied by friends, occasionally a son or young brother, but mostly men my age or older, for we are the ones who remember the grass.

Night after night the pilgrimage continues. The first night I stand inside the deep green door, listening. I hear a vehicle stop; hear a car door close with a snug thud. I open the door when the sound of soft-soled shoes on gravel tell me it is time. The door swings silent as a snake. We nod curt greetings to each other. Two men pass me, each carrying a grasshopper-legged sprinkler. Later, each sprinkler will sizzle like frying onions as it wheels, a silver sparkler in the moonlight.

During the nights that follow, I stand sentinel-like at the top of the grandstand, watching as my cohorts arrive. Old men walking across a parking lot in a row, in the dark, carrying men who have slipped away from their homes, skulked down their sturdy sidewalks, breathing the cool, grassy, after-midnight air. They have left behind their sleeping, grey-haired women, their immaculate bungalows, their manicured lawns. They continue to walk across the parking lot, while occasionally a soft wheeze, a nibbling, breathy sound like an old horse might make, divulges their humanity. They move methodically toward the baseball stadium which hulks against the moon-blue sky like a small mountain. Beneath the tint of starlight, the tall light standards which rise above the fences and grandstand glow purple, necks bent forward, like sunflowers heavy with seed.

My other daughter lives in this city, is married to a fan, but one who watches baseball from behind third base. And like marrying outside the faith, she has been converted to the third-base side. They have their own season tickets, twelve rows up just to the outfield side of third base. I love her, but I don't trust her enough to let her in on my secret.

I could trust my granddaughter, but she is too young. At her age she shouldn't have to face such responsibility. I remember my own daughter, the one who lives in Japan, remember her at nine, all knees, elbows and missing teeth—remember peering in her room, seeing her asleep, a shower of well-thumbed baseball cards scattered over her chest and pillow.

I haven't been able to tell my wife—it is like my compatriots and I are involved in a ritual for true believers only. Maggie, who knew me when I still dreamed of playing professionally myself—Maggie, after over half a lifetime together, comes and sits in my lap in the comfortable easy chair which has adjusted through the years to my thickening shape, just as she has. I love to hold the lightness of her, her tongue exploring my mouth, gently as a baby's finger.

"Where do you go?" she asks sleepily when I crawl into bed at dawn.

I mumble a reply. I know she doesn't sleep well when I'm gone. I can feel her body rhythms change as I slip out of bed after midnight.

"Aren't you too old to be having a change of life," she says, placing her toast-warm hand on my cold thigh.

I am not the only one with this problem.

"I'm developing a reputation," whispers an affable man at the ballpark. "I imagine any number of private investigators following any number of cars across the city. I imagine them creeping about the parking lot, shining pen-lights on licence plates, trying to guess what we're up to. Think of the reports they must prepare. I wonder if our wives are disappointed that we're not out discoing with frizzy-haired teenagers."

Night after night, virtually no words are spoken. Each man seems to know his assignment. Not all bring sod. Some carry rakes, some hoes, some hoses, which, when joined together, snake across the infield and outfield, dispensing the blessing of water. Others cradle in their arms bags of earth for building up the infield to meet the thick, living sod.

I often remain high in the stadium, looking down on the men moving over the earth, dark as ants, each sodding, cutting, watering, shaping. Occasionally the moon finds a knife blade as it trims the sod or slices away a chunk of artificial turf, and tosses the reflection skyward like a bright ball. My body tingles. There should be symphony music playing. Everyone should be humming "America the Beautiful."

Toward dawn, I watch the men walking away in groups, like small patrols of soldiers, carrying instead of arms, the tools and utensils which breathe life back into the arid ballfield.

Row by row, night by night, we lay the little squares of sod, moist as chocolate cake with green icing. Where did all the sod come from? I picture many men, in many parts of the city, surreptitiously cutting chunks out of their own lawns in the leafy midnight darkness, listening to the uncomprehending protests of their wives the next day—pretending to know nothing of it—pretending to have called the police to investigate.

When the strike is over I know we will all be here to watch the workouts, to hear the recalcitrant joints crackling like twigs after the forced inactivity. We will sit in our regular seats, scattered like popcorn throughout the stadium, and we'll nod as we pass on the way to the exits, exchange secret smiles, proud as new fathers.

For me, the best part of all will be the surprise. I feel like a magician who has gestured hypnotically and produced an elephant from thin air. I know I am not alone in my wonder. I know that rockets shoot off in half-a-hundred chests, the excitement of birthday mornings, Christmas Eves, and home-town doubleheaders boils within each of my conspirators. Our secret rites have been performed with love, like delivering a valentine to a sweetheart's door in that blue-steel span of morning just before dawn.

Players and management are meeting round the clock. A settlement is imminent. I have watched the stadium covered square foot by square foot until it looks like green graph paper. I have stood and felt the cool odours of the grass rise up and touch my face. I have studied the lines between each small square, watched those lines fade until they were visible to my eyes alone, then not even to them.

What will the players think, as they straggle into the stadium and find the miracle we have created? The old-timers will raise their heads like ponies, as far away as the parking lot, when the thrill of the grass reaches their nostrils. And, as they dress, they'll recall sprawling in the lush fields of childhood, the grass as cool as a mother's hand on a forehead.

"Goodbye, goodbye," we say at the gate, the smell of water, of sod, of sweat, small perfumes in the air. Our secrets are safe with each other. We go our separate ways.

Alone in the stadium in the last chill darkness before dawn, I drop to my hands and knees in the centre of the outfield. My palms are sodden. Water touches the skin between my spread fingers. I lower my face to the silvered grass, which, wonder of wonders, already has the ephemeral odours of baseball about it.

The Broken Globe
Henry Kreisel

Since it was Nick Solchuk who first told me about the opening in my field at the University of Alberta, I went up to see him as soon as I received word that I had been appointed. He lived in one of those old mansions in Pimlico that had once served as town houses for wealthy merchants and aristocrats, but now housed a less moneyed group of people—stenographers, students, and intellectuals of various kinds. He had studied at Cambridge and got his doctorate there and was now doing research at the Imperial College and rapidly establishing a reputation among the younger men for his work on problems which had to do with the curvature of the earth.

His room was on the third floor, and it was very cramped, but he refused to move because he could look out from his window and see the Thames and the steady flow of boats, and that gave him a sense of distance and of space also. Space, he said, was what he missed most in the crowded city. He referred to himself, nostalgically, as a prairie boy, and when he wanted to demonstrate what he meant by space he used to say that when a man stood and looked out across the open prairie, it was possible for him to believe that the earth was flat.

"So," he said, after I had told him my news, "you are going to teach French to prairie boys and girls. I congratulate you." Then he cocked his head to one side, and looked me over and said: "How are your ears?"

"My ears?" I said. "They're all right. Why?"

"Prepare yourself," he said. "Prairie voices trying to speak French— that will be a great experience for you. I speak from experience. I learned my French pronunciation in a little one-room school in a prairie village. From an extraordinary girl, mind you, but her mind ran to science. Joan

McKenzie—that was her name. A wiry little thing, sharp-nosed, and she always wore brown desses. She was particularly fascinated by earthquakes. 'In 1755 the city of Lisbon, Portugal, was devastated. Sixty thousand persons died; the shock was felt in Southern France and North Africa; and inland waters of Great Britain and Scandinavia were agitated.' You see, I still remember that, and I can hear her voice too. Listen: 'In common with the entire solar system, the earth is moving through space at the rate of approximately 45,000 miles per hour, toward the constellation of Hercules. Think of that, boys and girls.' Well, I thought about it. It was a lot to think about. Maybe that's why I became a geophysicist. Her enthusiasm was infectious. I knew her at her peak. After a while she got tired and married a solid farmer and had eight children."

"But her French, I take it, was not so good," I said.

"No," he said. "Language gave no scope to her imagination. Mind you, I took French seriously enough. I was a very serious student. For a while I even practised my French pronunciation at home. But I stopped it because it bothered my father. My mother begged me to stop. For the sake of peace."

"Your father's ears were offended," I said.

"Oh, no," Nick said, "not his ears. His soul. He was sure that I was learning French so I could run off and marry a French girl ... Don't laugh. It's true. When once my father believed something, it was very hard to shake him."

"But why should he have objected to your marrying a French girl anyway?"

"Because," said Nick, and pointed a stern finger at me, "because when he came to Canada he sailed from some French port, and he was robbed of all his money while he slept. He held all Frenchmen responsible. He never forgot and he never forgave. And, by God, he wasn't going to have that cursed language spoken in his house. He wasn't going to have any nonsense about science talked in his house either." Nick was silent for a moment, and then he said, speaking very quietly, "Curious man, my father. He had strange ideas, but a strange kind of imagination, too. I couldn't understand him when I was going to school or to the university. But then a year or two ago, I suddenly realized that the shape of the world he lived in had been forever fixed for him by some medieval priest in the small Ukrainian village where he was born and where he received an education of sorts when he was a boy. And I suddenly realized that he wasn't mad, but that he lived in the universe of the medieval church. The earth for him was the centre of the universe, and the centre was still. It didn't move. The sun rose in the East and it set in the West, and it moved perpetually around a still earth. God had made this earth especially for man, and man's function was to perpetuate himself and to worship God. My father never said all that in so many words, mind you, but that is what he believed. Everything else was heresy."

He fell silent.

"How extraordinary," I said.

He did not answer at once, and after a while he said, in a tone of voice which seemed to indicate that he did not want to pursue the matter further, "Well, when you are in the middle of the Canadian West, I'll be in Rome. I've been asked to give a paper to the International Congress of Geophysicists which meets there in October."

"So I heard," I said. "Wilcocks told me the other day. He said it was going to be a paper of some importance. In fact, he said it would create a stir."

"Did Wilcocks really say that?" he asked eagerly, his face reddening, and he seemed very pleased. We talked for a while longer, and then I rose to go.

He saw me to the door and was about to open it for me, but stopped suddenly, as if he were turning something over in his mind, and then said quickly, "Tell me—would you do something for me?"

"Of course," I said. "If I can."

He motioned me back to my chair and I sat down again. "When you are in Alberta," he said, "and if it is convenient for you, would—would you go to see my father?"

"Why, yes," I stammered, "why, of course. I—I didn't realize he was still . . ."

"Oh, yes," he said, "he's still alive, still working. He lives on his farm, in a place called Three Bear Hills, about sixty or seventy miles out of Edmonton. He lives alone. My mother is dead. I have a sister who is married and lives in Calgary. There were only the two of us. My mother could have no more children. It was a source of great agony for them. My sister goes to see him sometimes, and then she sometimes writes to me. He never writes to me. We—we had—what shall I call it—differences. If you went to see him and told him that I had not gone to the devil, perhaps . . ." He broke off abruptly, clearly agitated, and walked over to his window and stood staring out, then said, "Perhaps you'd better not. I—I don't want to impose on you."

I protested that he was not imposing at all, and promised that I would write to him as soon as I had paid my visit.

I met him several times after that, but he never mentioned the matter again.

I sailed from England about the middle of August and arrived in Montreal a week later. The long journey West was one of the most memorable experiences I have ever had. There were moments of weariness and dullness. But the very monotony was impressive. There was a grandeur about it. It was a monotony of a really monumental kind. There were moments when, exhausted by the sheer impact of the landscape, I thought back with longing to the tidy, highly cultivated countryside of England and of France, to the sight of men and women working in the fields, to the steady succession of villages and towns, and everywhere the consciousness of nature humanized. But I also began to understand why Nick Solchuk was always longing for more space and more air, especially when we moved into the prairies, and the land became flatter until there seemed nothing, neither hill nor tree nor bush, to disturb the vast unbroken flow of land until in the far distance a thin, blue line marked the point where the prairie merged into the sky. Yet over all there was a strange tranquillity, all motion seemed suspended, and only the sun moved steadily, imperturbably West, dropping finally over the rim of the horizon, a blazing red ball, but leaving a superb evening light lying over the land still.

I was reminded of the promise I had made, but when I arrived in Edmonton, the task of settling down absorbed my time and energy so completely that I did nothing about it. Then, about the middle of October, I saw a brief report in the newspaper about the geophysical congress which had opened in Rome on the previous day, and I was mindful of my promise again. Before I could safely bury it in the back of my mind again, I sat down and wrote a brief letter to Nick's father, asking him when I could come out to visit him. Two weeks passed without an answer, and I decided to go and see him on the next Saturday without further formalities.

The day broke clear and fine. A few white clouds were in the metallic autumn sky and the sun shone coldly down upon the earth, as if from a great distance. I drove south as far as Wetaskiwin and then turned east.

The paved highway gave way to gravel and got steadily worse. I was beginning to wonder whether I was going right, when I rounded a bend and a grain elevator hove like a signpost into view. It was now about three o'clock and I had arrived in Three Bear Hills, but, as Nick had told me, there were neither bears nor hills here, but only prairie, and suddenly the beginning of an embryonic street with a few buildings on either side like a small island in a vast sea, and then all was prairie again.

I stopped in front of the small general store and went in to ask for directions. Three farmers were talking to the storekeeper, a bald, bespectacled little man who wore a long, dirty apron, and stood leaning against his counter. They stopped talking and turned to look at me. I asked where the Solchuk farm was.

Slowly scrutinizing me, the storekeeper asked, "You just new here?"

"Yes," I said.

"From the old country, eh?"

"Yes."

"You selling something?"

"No, no," I said. "I—I teach at the University."

"That so?" He turned to the other men and said, "Only boy ever went to University from around here was Solchuk's boy, Nick. Real brainy young kid, Nick. Two of 'em never got on together. Too different. You know."

They nodded slowly.

"But that boy of his—he's a real big-shot scientist now. You know them addem bombs and them hydrergen bombs. He helps make 'em."

"No, no," I broke in quickly. "That's not what he does. He's a geophysicist."

"What's that?" asked one of the men.

But before I could answer, the little storekeeper asked excitedly, "You know Nick?"

"Yes," I said, "we're friends. I've come to see his father."

"And where's he right now? Nick, I mean."

"Right now he is in Rome," I said. "But he lives in London, and does research there."

"Big-shot, eh," said one of the men laconically, but with a trace of admiration in his voice, too.

"He's a big scientist, though, like I said. Isn't that so?" the storekeeper broke in.

"He's going to be a very important scientist indeed," I said, a trifle solemnly.

"Like I said," he called out triumphantly. "That's showing 'em. A kid from Three Bear Hills, Alberta. More power to him!" His pride was unmistakable. "Tell me, mister," he went on, his voice dropping, "does he remember this place sometimes? Or don't he want to know us no more?"

"Oh, no," I said quickly. "He often talks of this place, and of Alberta, and of Canada. Some day he plans to return."

"That's right," he said with satisfaction. He drew himself up to full height, banged his fist on the table and said, "I'm proud of that boy. Maybe old Solchuk don't think so much of him, but you tell him old Mister Marshall is proud of him." He came from behind the counter and almost ceremoniously escorted me out to my car and showed me the way to Solchuk's farm.

I had about another five miles to drive, and the road, hardly more now than two black furrows cut into the prairie, was uneven and bumpy. The land was fenced on both sides of the road, and at last I came to a rough wooden gate hanging loosely on one hinge, and beyond it there was a cluster of small wooden buildings. The largest of these, the house itself, seemed at one time to have been ochre-coloured, but the paint had worn off and it now looked curiously mottled. A few chickens were wandering about, pecking at the ground, and from the back I could hear the grunting and squealing of pigs.

I walked up to the house and, just as I was about to knock, the door was suddenly opened, and a tall, massively built old man stood before me.

"My name is . . ." I began.

But he interrupted me. "You the man wrote to me?" His voice, though unpolished, had the same deep timbre as Nick's.

"That's right," I said.

"You a friend of Nick?"

"Yes."

He beckoned me in with a nod of his head. The door was low and I had to stoop a bit to get into the room. It was a large, low-ceilinged room. A smallish window let in a patch of light which lit up the middle of the room but did not spread into the corners, so that it seemed as if it were perpetually dusk. A table occupied the centre, and on the far side there was a large wood stove on which stood a softly hissing black kettle. In the corner facing the entrance there was an iron bedstead, and the bed was roughly made, with a patchwork quilt thrown carelessly on top.

The old man gestured me to one of the chairs which stood around the table.

"Sit."

I did as he told me, and he sat down opposite me and placed his large calloused hands before him on the table. He seemed to study me intently for a while, and I scrutinized him. His face was covered by a three-day's stubble, but in spite of that, and in spite of the fact that it was a face beaten by sun and wind, it was clear that he was Nick's father. For Nick had the same determined mouth, and the same high cheekbones and the same dark, penetrating eyes.

At last he spoke. "You friend of Nick."

I nodded my head.

"What he do now?" he asked sharply. "He still tampering with the earth?"

His voice rose as if he were delivering a challenge, and I drew back involuntarily. "Why—he's doing scientific research, yes," I told him. "He's . . ."

"What God has made," he said sternly, "no man should touch."

Before I could regain my composure, he went on, "He sent you. What for? What he want?"

"Nothing," I said, "nothing at all. He sent me to bring you greetings and to tell you he is well."

"And you come all the way from Edmonton to tell me?"

"Yes, of course."

A faint smile played about his mouth, and the features of his face softened. Then suddenly he rose from his chair and stood towering over me. "You are welcome in this house," he said.

The formality with which he spoke was quite extraordinary and seemed to call for an appropriate reply, but I could do little more than stammer a thank you, and he, assuming again a normal tone of voice, asked me if I cared to have coffee. When I assented he walked to the far end of the room and busied himself about the stove.

It was then that I noticed, just under the window, a rough little wooden table and on top of it a faded old globe made of cardboard, such as little children use in school. I was intrigued to see it there and went over to look at it more closely. The cheap metal mount was brown with rust, and when I lifted it and tried to turn the globe on its axis, I found that it would not rotate because part of it had been squashed and broken. I ran my hand over the deep dent, and suddenly the old man startled me.

"What are you doing there?" Curiosity seemed mingled with suspicion in his voice and made me feel like a small child surprised by its mother in an unauthorized raid on the pantry. I set down the globe and turned. He was standing by the table with two big mugs of coffee in his hands.

"Coffee is hot," he said.

I went back to my chair and sat down, slightly embarrassed.

"Drink," he said, pushing one of the mugs over to me.

We both began to sip the coffee, and for some time neither of us said anything.

"That thing over there," he said at last, putting down his mug, "that thing you was looking at—he brought it home one day—he was a boy then—maybe thirteen-year-old—Nick. The other day I found it up in the attic. I was going to throw it in the garbage. But I forgot. There it belongs. In the garbage. It is a false thing." His voice had now become venomous.

"False?" I said. "How is it false?"

He disregarded my question. "I remember," he went on, "he came home from school one day and we was all here in this room—all sitting around this table eating supper, his mother, his sister and me and Alex, too—the hired man like. And then sudden-like Nick pipes up, and he says, we learned in school today, he says, how the earth is round like a ball, he says, and how it moves around and around the sun and never stops, he says. They learning you rubbish in school, I say. But he says no, Miss McKenzie never told him no lies. Then I say she does, I say, and a son of mine shouldn't believe it. Stop your ears! Let not Satan come in!" He raised an outspread hand and his voice thundered as if he were a prophet armed. "But he was always a stubborn boy—Nick. Like a mule. He never listened to reason. I believe it, he says. To me he says that—his father, just like that. I believe it, he says, because science has proved it and it is the truth. It is false, I cry, and you will not believe it. I believe it, he says. So then I hit him because he will not listen and will not obey. But he keeps shouting and shouting and shouting. She moves, he shouts, she moves, she moves!"

He stopped. His hands had balled themselves into fists, and the remembered fury sent the blood streaming into his face. He seemed now to have forgotten my presence and he went on speaking in a low murmuring voice, almost as if he were telling the story to himself.

"So the next day, or the day after, I go down to that school, and there is this little Miss McKenzie, so small and so thin that I could have crush her with my bare hands. What you teaching my boy Nick? I ask her. What false lies you stuffing in his head? What you telling him that the earth is round and that she moves for? Did Joshua tell the earth to stand still, or did he command the sun? So she says to me, I don't care what Joshua done, she says, I will tell him what science has discovered. With that woman I could get nowhere. So then I try to keep him away from school, and I lock him up in the house, but it was not good. He got out, and he run to the school like, and Miss McKenzie she sends me a letter to say she will send up the inspectors if I try to keep him away from the school. And I could do nothing."

His sense of impotence was palpable. He sat sunk into himself as if he were still contemplating ways of halting the scientific education of his son.

"Two, three weeks after," he went on, "he comes walking in this door with a large paper parcel in his hand. Now, he calls out to me, now I will prove it to you, I will prove that she moves. And he tears off the paper from the box and takes out this—this thing, and he puts it on the table here. Here, he cries, here is the earth, and look, she moves. And he gives that thing a little push and it twirls around like. I have to laugh. A toy, I say to him, you bring me a toy here, not bigger than my hand, and it is supposed to be the world, this little toy here, with the printed words on coloured paper, this little cardboard ball. This Miss McKenzie, I say to him, she's turning you crazy in that school. But look, he says, she moves. Now I have to stop my laughing. I'll soon show you she moves, I say, for he is beginning to get me mad again. And I go up to the table and I take the toy thing in my hands and I smash it down like this."

He raised his fists and let them crash down on the table as if he meant to splinter it.

"That'll learn you, I cry. I don't think he could believe I had done it, because he picks up the thing and he tries to turn it, but it don't turn no more. He stand there and the tears roll down his cheeks, and then, sudden-like, he takes the thing in both his hands and he throws it at me. And it would have hit me right in the face, for sure, if I did not put up my hand. Against your father, I cry, you will raise up your hand against your father. Asmodeus! I grab him by the arm, and I shake him and I beat him like he was the devil. And he makes me madder and madder because he don't cry or shout or anything. And I would have kill him there, for sure, if his mother didn't come in then and pull me away. His nose was bleeding, but he didn't notice. Only he looks at me and says, you can beat me and break my globe, but you can't stop her moving. That night my wife she make me swear by all that's holy that I wouldn't touch him no more. And from then on I never hit him again nor talk to him about this thing. He goes his way and I go mine."

He fell silent. Then after a moment he snapped suddenly, "You hold with that?"

"Hold with what?" I asked, taken aback.

"With that thing?" He pointed behind him at the little table and at the broken globe. His gnarled hands now tightly interlocked, he leaned forward in his chair and his dark, brooding eyes sought an answer from mine in the twilight of the room.

Alone with him there, I was almost afraid to answer firmly. Was it because I feared that I would hurt him too deeply if I did, or was I perhaps afraid that he would use violence on me as he had on Nick?

I cleared my throat. "Yes," I said then. "Yes, I believe the earth is round and that she moves. That fact has been accepted now for a long time."

I expected him to round on me but he seemed suddenly to have grown very tired, and in a low resigned voice he said, "Satan has taken over all the world." Then suddenly he roused himself and hit the table hard with his fist, and cried passionately, "But not me! Not me!"

It was unbearable. I felt that I must break the tension, and I said the first thing that came into my mind. "You can be proud of your son in spite of all that happened between you. He is a fine man, and the world honours him for his work."

He gave me a long look. "He should have stayed here," he said quietly. "When I die, there will be nobody to look after the land. Instead he has gone off to tamper with God's earth."

His fury was now all spent. We sat for a while in silence, and then I rose. Together we walked out of the house. When I was about to get into my car, he touched me lightly on the arm. I turned. His eyes surveyed the vast expanse of sky and land, stretching far into the distance, reddish clouds in the sky and blue shadows on the land. With a gesture of great dignity and power he lifted his arm and stood pointing into the distance, at the flat land and the low-hanging sky. "Look," he said, very slowly and very quietly, "she is flat, and she stand still."

It was impossible not to feel a kind of admiration for the old man. There was something heroic about him. I held out my hand and he took it. He looked at me steadily, then averted his eyes and said, "Send greetings to my son."

I drove off quickly, but had to stop again in order to open the wooden gate. I looked back at the house, and saw him still standing there, still looking at his beloved land, a lonely, towering figure framed against the darkening evening sky.

The Loons

Margaret Laurence

Just below Manawaka, where the Wachakwa River ran brown and noisy over the pebbles, the scrub oak and grey-green willow and chokecherry bushes grew in a dense thicket. In a clearing at the centre of the thicket stood the Tonnerre family's shack. The basis of this dwelling was a small square cabin made of poplar poles and chinked with mud, which had been built by Jules Tonnerre some fifty years before, when he came back from Batoche with a bullet in his thigh, the year that Riel was hung and the voices of the Métis entered their long silence. Jules had only intended to stay the winter in the Wachakwa Valley, but the family was still there in the thirties, when I was a child. As the Tonnerres had increased, their settlement had been added to, until the clearing at the foot of the town hill was a chaos of lean-tos, wooden packing cases, warped lumber, discarded car tires, ramshackle chicken coops, tangled strands of barbed wire and rusty tin cans.

The Tonnerres were French half-breeds, and among themselves they spoke a *patois* that was neither Cree nor French. Their English was broken and full of obscenities. They did not belong among the Cree of the Galloping Mountain reservation, further north, and they did not belong among the Scots-Irish and Ukrainians of Manawaka, either. They were, as my Grandmother MacLeod would have put it, neither flesh, fowl, nor good salt herring. When their men were not working at odd jobs or as section hands on the CPR, they lived on relief. In the summers, one of the Tonnerre youngsters, with a face that seemed totally unfamiliar with laughter, would knock at the doors of the town's brick houses and offer for sale a lard-pail full of bruised wild strawberries, and if he got as much as a quarter he would grab the coin and run before the customer had time to change her mind. Sometimes old Jules, or his son Lazarus, would get mixed up in a Saturday-night brawl, and would hit out at whoever was nearest, or howl drunkenly among the offended shoppers on Main Street, and then the Mountie would put them for the night in the barred cell underneath the Court House, and the next morning they would be quiet again.

Piquette Tonnerre, the daughter of Lazarus, was in my class at school. She was older than I, but she had failed several grades, perhaps because her attendance had always been sporadic and her interest in school-work negligible. Part of the reason she had missed a lot of school was that she had had tuberculosis of the bone, and had once spent many months in hospital. I knew this because my father was the doctor who had looked after her. Her sickness was almost the only thing I knew about her, however. Otherwise, she existed for me only as a vaguely embarrassing presence, with her hoarse voice and her clumsy limping walk and her grimy cotton dresses that were always miles too long. I was neither friendly nor unfriendly towards her. She dwelt and moved somewhere within my scope of vision, but I did not actually notice her very much until that peculiar summer when I was eleven.

"I don't know what to do about that kid," my father said at dinner one evening. "Piquette Tonnerre, I mean. The damn bone's flared up again. I've had her in hospital for quite a while now, and it's under control all right, but I hate like the dickens to send her home again."

"Couldn't you explain to her mother that she has to rest a lot?" my mother said.

"The mother's not there," my father replied. "She took off a few years back. Can't say I blame her. Piquette cooks for them, and she says Lazarus would never do anything for himself as long as she's there. Anyway, I don't think she'd take much care of herself, once she got back. She's only thirteen, after all. Beth, I was thinking—what about taking her up to Diamond Lake with us this summer? A couple of months' rest would give that bone a much better chance."

My mother looked stunned.

"But Ewen—what about Roddie and Vanessa?"

"She's not contagious," my father said. "And it would be company for Vanessa."

"Oh dear," my mother said in distress, "I'll bet anything she has nits in her hair."

"For Pete's sake," my father said crossly, "do you think Matron would let her stay in the hospital for all this time like that? Don't be silly, Beth."

Grandmother MacLeod, her delicately featured face as rigid as a cameo, now brought her mauve-veined hands together as though she were about to begin a prayer.

"Ewen, if that half-breed youngster comes along to Diamond Lake, I'm not going," she announced. "I'll go to Morag's for the summer."

I had trouble in stifling my urge to laugh, for my mother brightened visibly and quickly tried to hide it. If it came to a choice between Grandmother MacLeod and Piquette, Piquette would win hands down, nits or not.

"It might be quite nice for you, at that," she mused. "You haven't seen Morag for over a year, and you might enjoy being in the city for a while. Well, Ewen dear, you do what you think best. If you think it would do Piquette some good, then we'll be glad to have her, as long as she behaves herself."

So it happened that several weeks later, when we all piled into my father's old Nash, surrounded by suitcases and boxes of provisions and toys for my ten-month-old brother, Piquette was with us and Grandmother MacLeod, miraculously, was not. My father would only be staying at the cottage for a couple of weeks, for he had to get back to his practice, but the rest of us would stay at Diamond Lake until the end of August.

Our cottage was not named, as many were, "Dew Drop Inn", or "Bide-a-Wee", or "Bonnie Doon." The sign on the roadway bore in austere letters only our name, MacLeod. It was not a large cottage, but it was on the lakefront. You could look out the windows and see, through the filigree of the spruce trees, the water glistening greenly as the sun caught it. All around the cottage were ferns, and sharp-branched raspberry bushes, and moss that had grown over fallen tree trunks. If you looked carefully among the weeds and grass, you could find wild strawberry plants which were in white flower now and in another month would bear fruit, the fragrant globes hanging like miniature scarlet lanterns on the thin hairy stems. The two grey squirrels were still there, gossiping at us from the tall spruce beside the cottage, and by the end of the summer they would again be tame enough to take pieces of crust from my hands. The broad moose antlers that hung above the back door were a little more bleached and fissured after the winter, but otherwise everything was the same. I raced joyfully around my kingdom, greeting all the places I had not seen for a year. My brother, Roderick, who had not been born when we were here last summer, sat on the car rug in the sunshine and examined a brown spruce cone, meticulously turning it round and round in his small and curious hands. My mother and father toted the luggage from car to cottage, exclaiming over how well the place had wintered, no broken windows, thank goodness, no apparent damage from storm-felled branches or snow.

Only after I had finished looking around did I notice Piquette. She was sitting on the swing, her lame leg held stiffly out, and her other foot scuffing the ground as she swung slowly back and forth. Her long hair hung black and straight around her shoulders, and her broad coarse-featured face bore no expression—it was blank, as though she no longer dwelt within her own skull, as though she had gone elsewhere. I approached her very hesitantly.

"Want to come and play?"

Piquette looked at me with a sudden flash of scorn.

"I ain't a kid," she said.

Wounded, I stamped angrily away, swearing I would not speak to her for the rest of the summer. In the days that followed, however, Piquette began to interest me, and I began to want to interest her. My reasons did not appear bizarre to me. Unlikely as it may seem, I had only just realized that the Tonnerre family, whom I had always heard called half-breeds, were actually Indians, or as near as made no difference. My acquaintance with Indians was not extensive. I did not remember ever having seen a real Indian, and my new awareness that Piquette sprang from the people of Big Bear and Poundmaker, of Tecumseh, of the Iroquois who had eaten Father Brébeuf's heart—all this gave her an instant attraction in my eyes. I was a devoted reader of Pauline Johnson at this age, and sometimes would orate aloud and in an exalted voice, "*West Wind, blow from your prairie nest; Blow from the mountains, blow from the west*"—and so on. It seemed to me that Piquette must be in some way a daughter of the forest, a kind of junior prophetess of the wilds, who might impart to me, if I took the right approach, some of the secrets which she undoubtedly knew—where the whippoorwill made her nest, how the coyote reared her young, or whatever it was that it said in *Hiawatha*.

I set about gaining Piquette's trust. She was not allowed to go swimming, with her bad leg, but I managed to lure her down to the beach—or rather, she came because there was nothing else to do. The water was always icy, for the lake was fed by springs, but I swam like a dog, thrashing my arms and legs around at such speed and with such an output of energy that I never grew cold. Finally, when I had had enough, I came out and sat beside Piquette on the sand. When she saw me approaching, her hand squashed flat the sand castle she had been building, and she looked at me sullenly, without speaking.

"Do you like this place?" I asked, after a while, intending to lead on from there into the question of forest lore.

Piquette shrugged. "It's okay. Good as anywhere."

"I love it," I said. "We come here every summer."

"So what?" Her voice was distant, and I glanced at her uncertainly, wondering what I could have said wrong.

"Do you want to come for a walk?" I asked her. "We wouldn't need to go far. If you walk just around the point there, you come to a bay where great big reeds grow in the water, and all kinds of fish hang around there. Want to? Come on."

She shook her head.

"Your dad said I ain't supposed to do no more walking than I got to."

I tried another line.

"I bet you know a lot about the woods and all that, eh?" I began respectfully.

Piquette looked at me from her large, dark, unsmiling eyes.

"I don't know what in hell you're talking' about," she replied. "You nuts or somethin'? If you mean where my old man, and me, and all them live, you better shut up, by Jesus, you hear?"

I was startled and my feelings were hurt, but I had a kind of dogged perseverance. I ignored her rebuff.

"You know something, Piquette? There's loons here, on this lake. You can see their nests just up the shore there, behind those logs. At night, you can hear them even from the cottage, but it's better to listen from the beach. My dad says we should listen and try to remember how they sound, because in a few years when more cottages are built at Diamond Lake and more people come in, the loons will go away."

Piquette was picking up stones and snail shells and then dropping them again.

"Who gives a goddamn?" she said.

It became increasingly obvious that, as an Indian, Piquette was a dead loss. That evening I went out by myself, scrambling through the bushes

that overhung the steep path, my feet slipping on the fallen spruce
needles that covered the ground. When I reached the shore, I walked
along the firm, damp sand to the small pier that my father had built, and
sat down there. I heard someone else crashing through the undergrowth
and the bracken, and for a moment I thought Piquette had changed her
mind, but it turned out to be my father. He sat beside me on the pier and
we waited, without speaking.

At night the lake was like black glass with a streak of amber which was
the path of the moon. All around, the spruce trees grew tall and close-set,
branches blackly sharp against the sky, which was lightened by a cold
flickering of stars. Then the loons began their calling. They rose like
phantom birds from the nests on the shore, and flew out onto the dark,
still surface of the water.

No one can ever describe that ululating sound, the crying of the loons,
and no one who has heard it can ever forget it. Plaintive, and yet with a
quality of chilling mockery, those voices belonged to a world separated
by aeons from our neat world of summer cottages and the lighted lamps
of home.

"They must have sounded just like that," my father remarked, "before
any person set foot here."

Then he laughed. "You could say the same, of course, about sparrows,
or chipmunks, but somehow it only strikes you that way with the loons."

"I know," I said.

Neither of us suspected that this would be the last time we would ever
sit here together on the shore, listening. We stayed for perhaps half an
hour, and then we went back to the cottage. My mother was reading beside
the fireplace. Piquette was looking at the burning birch log, and not doing
anything.

"You should have come along," I said, although in fact I was glad she
had not.

"Not me," Piquette said. "You wouldn't catch me walkin' way down
there jus' for a bunch of squawkin' birds."

Piquette and I remained ill at ease with one another. I felt I had
somehow failed my father, but I did not know what was the matter, nor
why she would not or could not respond when I suggested exploring the
woods or playing house. I thought it was probably her slow and difficult
walking that held her back. She stayed most of the time in the cottage
with my mother, helping her with the dishes or with Roddie, but hardly

ever talking. Then the Duncans arrived at their cottage, and I spent my days with Mavis, who was my best friend. I could not reach Piquette at all, and I soon lost interest in trying. But all that summer she remained as both a reproach and a mystery to me.

That winter my father died of pneumonia, after less than a week's illness. For some time I saw nothing around me, being completely immersed in my own pain and my mother's. When I looked outward once more, I scarcely noticed that Piquette Tonnerre was no longer at school. I do not remember seeing her at all until four years later, one Saturday night when Mavis and I were having Cokes at the Regal Café. The jukebox was booming like tuneful thunder, and beside it, leaning lightly on its chrome and its rainbow glass, was a girl.

Piquette must have been seventeen then although she looked about twenty. I stared at her, astounded that anyone could have changed so much. Her face, so stolid and expressionless before, was animated now with a gaiety that was almost violent. She laughed and talked very loudly with the boys around her. Her lipstick was bright carmine, and her hair was cut short and frizzily permed. She had not been pretty as a child, and she was not pretty now, for her features were still heavy and blunt. But her dark and slightly slanted eyes were beautiful, and her skin-tight skirt and orange sweater displayed to enviable advantage a soft and slender body.

She saw me, and walked over. She teetered a little, but it was not due to her once-tubercular leg, for her limp was almost gone.

"Hi, Vanessa." Her voice still had the same hoarseness. "Long time no see, eh?"

"Hi," I said. "Where've you been keeping yourself, Piquette?"

"Oh, I been around," she said. "I been away almost two years now. Been all over the place—Winnipeg, Regina, Saskatoon. Jesus, what I could tell you! I come back this summer, but I ain't stayin'. You kids goin' to the dance?"

"No," I said abruptly, for this was a sore point with me. I was fifteen, and thought I was old enough to go to the Saturday-night dances at the Flamingo. My mother, however, thought otherwise.

"Y'oughta come," Piquette said. "I never miss one. It's just about the on'y thing in this jerkwater town that's any fun. Boy, you couldn' catch me stayin' here. I don' give a shit about this place. It stinks."

She sat down beside me, and I caught the harsh over-sweetness of her perfume.

"Listen, you wanna know something, Vanessa?" she confided, her voice only slightly blurred. "Your dad was the only person in Manawaka that ever done anything good to me."

I nodded speechlessly. I was certain she was speaking the truth. I knew a little more than I had that summer at Diamond Lake, but I could not reach her now any more than I had then. I was ashamed, ashamed of my own timidity, the frightened tendency to look the other way. Yet I felt no real warmth towards her—I only felt that I ought to, because of that distant summer and because my father had hoped she would be company for me, or perhaps that I would be for her, but it had not happened that way. At this moment, meeting her again, I had to admit that she repelled and embarrassed me, and I could not help despising the self-pity in her voice. I wished she would go away. I did not want to see her. I did not know what to say to her. It seemed that we had nothing to say to one another.

"I'll tell you something else," Piquette went on. "All the old bitches an' biddies in this town will sure be surprised. I'm gettin' married this fall—my boyfriend, he's an English fella, works in the stockyards in the city there, a very tall guy, got blond wavy hair. Gee, is he ever handsome. Got this real classy name. Alvin Gerald Cummings—some handle, eh? They call him Al."

For the merest instant, then, I saw her. I really did see her, for the first and only time in all the years we had both lived in the same town. Her defiant face, momentarily, became unguarded and unmasked, and in her eyes there was a terrifying hope.

"Gee, Piquette—" I burst out awkwardly, "that's swell. That's really wonderful. Congratulations—good luck—I hope you'll be happy—"

As I mouthed the conventional phrases, I could only guess how great her need must have been, that she had been forced to seek the very things she so bitterly rejected.

When I was eighteen, I left Manawaka and went away to college. At the end of my first year, I came back home for the summer. I spent the first few days in talking non-stop with my mother, as we exchanged all the news that somehow had not found its way into letters—what had happened in my life and what had happened in Manawaka while I was away. My mother searched her memory for events that concerned people I knew.

"Did I ever write you about Piquette Tonnerre, Vanessa?" she asked one morning.

"No, I don't think so," I replied. "Last I heard of her, she was going to marry some guy in the city. Is she still there?"

My mother looked perturbed, and it was a moment before she spoke, as though she did not know how to express what she had to tell and wished she did not need to try.

"She's dead," she said at last. Then, as I stared at her, "Oh, Vanessa, when it happened, I couldn't help thinking of her as she was that summer—so sullen and gauche and badly dressed. I couldn't help wondering if we could have done something more at that time—but what could we do? She used to be around in the cottage there with me all day, and honestly, it was all I could do to get a word out of her. She didn't even talk to your father very much, although I think she liked him, in her way."

"What happened?" I asked.

"Either her husband left her, or she left him," my mother said. "I don't know which. Anyway, she came back here with two youngsters, both only babies—they must have been born very close together. She kept house, I guess, for Lazarus and her brothers, down in the valley there, in the old Tonnerre place. I used to see her on the street sometimes, but she never spoke to me. She'd put on an awful lot of weight, and she looked a mess, to tell you the truth, a real slattern, dressed any old how. She was up in court a couple of times—drunk and disorderly, of course. One Saturday night last winter, during the coldest weather, Piquette was alone in the shack with the children. The Tonnerres made home brew all the time, so I've heard, and Lazarus said later she'd been drinking most of the day when he and the boys went out that evening. They had an old woodstove there—you know the kind, with exposed pipes. The shack caught fire. Piquette didn't get out, and neither did the children."

I did not say anything. As so often with Piquette, there did not seem to be anything to say. There was a kind of silence around the image in my mind of the fire and the snow, and I wished I could put from my memory the look that I had seen once in Piquette's eyes.

I went up to Diamond Lake for a few days that summer, with Mavis and her family. The MacLeod cottage had been sold after my father's death, and I did not even go to look at it, not wanting to witness my long-ago kingdom possessed now by strangers. But one evening I went down to the shore by myself.

The small pier which my father had built was gone, and in its place there was a large and solid pier built by the government, for Galloping Mountain was now a national park, and Diamond Lake had been re-named Lake Wapakata, for it was felt that an Indian name would have a greater appeal to tourists. The one store had become several dozen, and the settlement had all the attributes of a flourishing resort—hotels, a dance-hall, cafés with neon signs, the penetrating odours of chips and hot dogs.

I sat on the government pier and looked out across the water. At night the lake at least was the same as it had always been, darkly shining and bearing within its black glass the streak of amber that was the path of the moon. There was no wind that evening, and everything was quiet all around me. It seemed too quiet, and then I realized that the loons were no longer there. I listened for some time, to make sure, but never once did I hear that long-drawn call, half mocking and half plaintive, spearing through the stillness across the lake.

I did not know what had happened to the birds. Perhaps they had gone away to some far place of belonging. Perhaps they had been unable to find such a place, and had simply died out, having ceased to care any longer whether they lived or not.

I remembered how Piquette had scorned to come along, when my father and I sat there and listened to the lake birds. It seemed to me now that in some unconscious and totally unrecognized way, Piquette might have been the only one, after all, who had heard the crying of the loons.

Old Age Gold

Leslie Lum

"What is your name?"

The first question is always the easiest. Mrs. Louie had told her about the Canadian citizenship hearing. In this fluorescent room with wood panel walls, Canadian wood, the first question was easy. There was a kind of order in the government pens and papers. The judge had her file in his hand. She recognized it, her name in print. Name. There was the sound of typewriters behind the wood walls, wood walls with swirls and curls, Canadian wood. Perhaps they were typing her name. The first question was always the easiest after the shock of arrival. They gave chances. They always gave chances, these Canadians. The judge would, this kind-looking man, only forty years or so with his brown glasses. So young a man to have glasses and government papers. He would understand her fright. She thought of the answer. Surname last, these funny westerners, surname last as it if did not matter at all, hidden behind the sound of given name. And surname must be given of husband, not father, another complication. How very contrived, a mystery, these westerners and their logic were. She rolled the syllables slowly over on her thin tongue before pronouncing. Everything seemed of the utmost importance as if even the breath must be checked before exhaling. The judge, he might notice some deviation, something that was not Canadian. Guy Mo Chiang. Slowly the words came out. It was easy. Merely reverse the name. Guy Mo Chiang.

"When did you come to Canada?"

It was difficult for Guy Mo Chiang to get over here from China. One had to attempt all means in those days, thirty years ago. Actually the fault fell completely on her husband. Completely. He arrived here first. It was he who bought the papers using the assumed name. Such a name too, so far from his own name, especially from hers. There was no other way. They had no relatives who had immigrated. It was necessary to leave China, then. It was necessary to make one's fortune and return. The return was beginning. Name was the first obstacle. Fortunately the government had allowed amnesty on names. For a period now, the procedure was quite simple. Merely go to the immigration office and report a change of name. They moved their hands about, these government people. They grunted angrily, demanded the final truth. Mrs. Chin, the Canadian-born translator, had asked her over and over again. Was this the truth? Did she have papers? Papers? No one in China had papers. When one was born, one was born. Mr. Woo down the hall had a friend vouch for him, had his friend say that he was born on such a date at such a place. Mr. Yee had to ask his older brother when he was born. Guy Mo Chiang was born. Her name reflected the occasion, the situation, the fortune of the family at the time. Papers were not necessary. Writing was not necessary. How could one possibly forget one's name? She gave her name. When it was given to her, she could not remember. Nobody was about who could testify to it. No elder brother, no friend. She was old now. She had out-lived many at sixty-nine. Sixty-nine. Was she sixty-nine? By Chinese calendar she was seventy, but nobody about could testify, put it down on paper, in print, in English print, using English calendars perhaps to make it even more official. Chinese documents were often made on the spur of the moment, even though the characters were carefully painted.

"Do you speak English?"

Of course she would answer yes. Yes, Mrs. Chin told her to say that she was taking night classes at the Catholic school. She wasn't, of course. What possible use could she find for English? Thirty years now, she had not needed it. And now when the return was beginning she finally needed it. The judge was looking at her from behind his huge wood desk filled with papers. He expected an answer. All the women who had passed their citizenship hearing had said yes. Yes, Guy Mo Chiang does speak English. Why was this room so bright? Perhaps the red rug and the red and white flag behind the judge. It had a golden brace on the bottom like dragon claws, something sacred no doubt. Red, the happy colour of the Chinese. Perhaps the westerners knew too. Happy, happy she could speak English. There was no need for it. Everybody in the neighbourhood spoke Chinese. That was why they had never moved out of there. There were many women in the neighbourhood who did not speak English and who had their citizenship papers. Say yes. Mrs. Chin was sitting there nodding at her. Say yes. She spoke enough English to get through this Canadian citizenship hearing. Yes. She did. English language of the barbarians, for Canadian-borns and westerners. English, not needed in her neighbourhood.

"Where do you live?"

In her neighbourhood the new immigrants always settled first. It was very nice before the government started putting in housing projects. There were only Chinese immigrants. Now there were westerners in the neighbourhood. Bad westerners. They stole and vandalized the neighbourhood. All the more well-to-do immigrants had moved out because of this. Only the poorer ones remained—as Guy Mo Chiang and her husband had, in their rooming house. The old rooming house in the middle of the block crowded by orange, green, yellow, and pink houses, the other houses painted bright phosphorescent colours by the Chinese. The government gave grants to improve the neighbourhood, to preserve the Chinese culture, probably an apology for having moved in the westerners. They lived in the green stucco rooming house across from a government housing project. At the project one could get a nice suite for very little. Three bedrooms, a refrigerator, stove. For very little, in the rooming house one got a room and use of the bathroom down the hall and the common kitchen with gas stove one lit by matches. Guy Mo Chiang had fixed her room up. There was the red sofa bought by her husband in one of his weak moments. She covered it with old rice sacks sewn together so as not to dirty it. There was the iron bed that came with the room and wooden chairs to put out in the hall when she wanted to speak with other women. Most visitors sat in the hall with her and spoke of everything. Perhaps a recent immigrant had married. That was success for them. Then there was the Canadian-born who had just bought a new car, a large car too. What extravagance. They talked in Chinese in this neighbourhood. This neighbourhood near Chinatown. Guy Mo Chiang could go and argue with the store clerks over which piece of meat they were giving her. She could choose her meat through the glass. They always gave too much fat. She could argue with them. This could change nothing but at least she could speak to them. She went to the supermarket sometimes. It bothered her, all the newness, the shiny freezers, the shelves with everything arranged just so, Western. Many of the stores in Chinatown were like that now but Guy Mo Chiang remained with the older ones, the ones run by the older immigrants and their sons. The supermarkets wrapped their meats already and she could not argue in Chinese.

"Do you work?"

She had worked all her life, all her life. When she first arrived here, there were many jobs, but money, money was scarce. She had worked in a restaurant cleaning dishes. Then like many of the other women she took to farm labour. It was difficult. Up at five o'clock in the morning and into the dark blue truck with Hon Wah Yeung written on the side in white letters. It was only as large as three cars and yet Hon Wah Yeung managed to fit as many as eighty people into the truck, on the hard wooden benches. In the summer, it was young children, teenagers not old enough to get a social insurance number, and the women. Hon Wah Yeung was paid for everybody that he brought onto the farm. He had a young Canadian-born girl punching cards for him during strawberry season. She was very pretty and spoke English. The owner of the farm bought her candy and pinched her cheek. Hon Wah Yeung said be nice to the boss man. He was fog-headed.

In the spring it was weeding, then strawberry picking, then beans, then potatoes every season for years and years. Although Guy Mo Chiang was once tall and straight, the years had bent her back. She walked around slightly stooped with her hands behind her back to keep her balance. Today Guy Mo Chiang wore a new black sweater from Hong Kong and a new pair of black pants. Luckily pants suits were in style. Before, Mrs. Chin insisted that all her female clients wear dresses to their hearings. Guy Mo Chiang wore black pants and, on fancy occasions, a flowered blouse, never dresses.

Guy Mo Chiang gave her occupation as babysitter. She did babysit for the two younger Chinese women in the rooming house. They worked in the sewing factory. She took their children during the day, five of them, all Canadian-born and not old enough to go to school. She wished they were her own grandchildren. That was success, to have grandchildren. She could have said strawberry picker. One summer she made five hundred dollars strawberry picking. She was very fast before her fingers became stiff. Guy Mo Chiang clutched her black purse and smiled at the judge with the mole on his cheek.

"What is your husband's name?"

Once a Canadian-born little girl had asked her why her husband's back was so bent. Guy Mo Chiang had explained that westerners stood straight because they never slept on boards, as in China. She forgot about the work he had done for the moment. He would have her forget, hoarding his money and letting it out only in little dribbles. Husband. Why bring him into this ordeal? The minutes. It was very cold in here. The judge did not seem to feel it. Mrs. Chin looked very hot and red. Mrs. Louie, her other sponsor, kept smiling and nodding after each question and answer. What a funny room this was with its brown wood walls and printing all over in picture frames. There were many pictures. The white woman in the gold frame on his desk. It was the judge's wife no doubt, so pretty. He was a good husband with his huge desk and papers. Ten minutes and it would be all over, perhaps six minutes now. She could claim Canadian citizenship. Something that weak man across the hall would never have the courage to do. He always made life difficult, leaving her in China for five years alone with his relatives while he came to make his fortune. And when she arrived, he brought her from the boat to the rooming house where they still lived. How disappointed she had been. Of course it was better than China; there was running water, food to eat, a room of her own and the rooming house was so close to others. Years ago. Guy Mo Chiang had lost count. It was of no significance, those years of disappointment. She had hoped; she had wished; the relatives had told her that there was nothing but good fortune to be found here. After the first week she had wanted to return. At least in Hong Kong she had worked for a rich family. She was that close to wealth. But then she had lived down those expectations through the years. She became accustomed to hard labour, as in China, as in Hong Kong. But this time there were westerners to tell how hard she was working, working for him. But it would all end now. He would no longer be an obstacle. He would no longer make her suffer.

Even in this final effort he could not help but thwart her attempts. If only he had applied for Canadian citizenship. It would all be so easy. She could then answer in Chinese, being married to a Canadian citizen. He knew English, the bent back, the old board. But no, he did not want to return. He would die here, away from China, not caring, hoarding all his money. At least he did not return to Hong Kong with his money and get another wife like Mr. Kwan did. How the whole neighbourhood had scorned his action. They talked about it in the hall. They laughed when Mr. Kwan returned penniless to his first wife. She did not take him back but stayed with her son and took care of her grandchildren. But no woman would have him with his bent back, the old board. He would rather leave all his money to their son, that stubborn bent man, than go back to China. She did not need him. She would have her Canadian citizenship and return to China with her fortune, her Canadian Old Age Gold. She would be able to live in luxury for the remainder of her life. Tomorrow she would get the young student down the hall to write another letter home, reporting final success. Guy Mo Chiang never learned to write in Chinese.

The judge was looking at her. He looked ferocious like the pictures of white bears he hung about his office. White bear carvings on the bookshelves above all the printed books. Strange for a man to have white bears in his office. Perhaps it was a western sign of good luck. White bears, strange. When she returned to China, nothing would be strange to her. She would be in place. In fact, she might be very special, having lived here in Canada, having felt western luxuries. She could display her papers. She could tell them of Canada, refrigerators, white bears, cars, every family had a car. She could flaunt her eighty dollars a month, live in leisure for the rest of her life and die peaceably among her relatives. This was success. After seventy years on this earth, life would be finally happy. She would finally have . . . place, a home. Ever since arriving here there had been nothing on her mind but returning to China with Canadian fortune. She, who could neither read nor write the language of China. She, who had spent her life envying her elder sisters who had learned to read a few characters. She would return. It was just a matter of ten minutes, perhaps five now. What would they say, to see her after receiving letters describing how she could not save, how that man had taken the money, drank some, gambled some and invested some in a grocery store which had burnt down a few years after. It was so difficult working in the store anyway, not speaking English. She could only smile and nod, smile and nod, knowing at night she would return to the rooming house and someone who would speak with her in Chinese. He remained at the store, so frightened his precious wares would disappear overnight, not even overnight. They closed the store at one o'clock in the morning and re-opened at seven the same morning. Perhaps thieves were faster here. She would not stay. She returned to the rooming house at nine, prepared her meal in the common kitchen and then she would sit in the hall and speak with other women about the downfall of the Canadian-born, their loss of heritage and their stupidity and rashness in spending. Sometimes there would be a wedding in the community. That was success, to get a good husband. But soon the couple would be buying cars and houses and television sets. How could they save enough to go back to China?

"How many children have you?"

Such nice pictures on his desk, this judge had. His children with golden hair and blue eyes. Two of them and so young. That was success, to have such lovely children. They had three children once. One son had died in China. It was too difficult. Their other son was making his fortune in San Francisco. His restaurant was doing much business. Often he wrote, often for such a busy man as he was. He sent money, sometimes. But that old board hoarded it like a cat with a captured feast. Their daughter remained trapped in China with her husband. Guy Mo Chiang would return there and her daughter would take care of her. They sent money to China often and wondered how much went to her and how much the Communists took. She would return with her Canadian Old Age Gold and they would live well. Grandchildren, she would see her grandchildren. Her son sent pictures up at Christmas. He had four children by a Christmas tree. She had wanted four children too, many children, but that old board said there was not enough money. And one had died. They should have had more. They would die. One died easily. More children, more would live. And her son did not have the time to bring her grandchildren up to see her. He had three sons and a daughter and the restaurant where he worked seven days a week. He was a very busy man, very successful.

Guy Mo Chiang had not see her daughter for years. They sent pictures out once every four years. They were not eating well, but they would not say so. If the Communists found out they had complained they would take their jobs away. They only had two children. Families were smaller in China, they wrote. What if they died? Who would carry the name? The Communists. They said China had changed now. They said it was different. It was not China like before. Perhaps that was just the north, near Peking. Guy Mo Chiang would return to Kwang Tung province with her daughter. There would be little change in the south.

The most difficult questions were coming now. How difficult they had been. Why was it necessary to learn the strange ways of this strange government? She remembered the exasperation of Mrs. Chin. Mrs. Chin's main occupation was helping people get citizenship. She charged seventy-five dollars but collected nothing if the attempt was unsuccessful.

Mrs. Chin must have been certain at the start that this attempt would be unsuccessful. Guy Mo Chiang did not speak English. It was never necessary to learn. It was so difficult to learn. She could not write nor understand the written characters so the phonetic equivalent of the answers could not be written down. At the beginning only private tutoring sessions were a means of grasping all these sounds which must come out in western logical order. But they took time and Mrs. Chin had many other clients. She wanted to charge extra money. Mrs. Chin was successful. She knew the meaning of money.

Guy Mo Chiang had never gone to school. She found it difficult to practise these sounds. She did not know how to. Mayors, premiers, prime ministers, senate and commons. All in Ottawa, another strange sound near Toronto where Mrs. Louie's son lived. Mrs. Louie was still nodding. It was a sign that Guy Mo Chiang was succeeding. Guy Mo Chiang continued to smile at the judge. She could not learn these sounds at first. Mrs. Chin never thought it possible, but that tape recorder had meant success. It had cost money, forty-nine dollars and ninety-five cents and the tax, part of the money she had saved for the trip across the Pacific, but she had learned by playing the sounds over and over again and repeating them over and over again until they corresponded. The judge spoke differently. He jumbled the sounds in different orders. Mrs. Chin was at the side repeating words silently, helping Guy Mo Chiang. It was seventy-five dollars if she succeeded. Mrs. Louie looked worried. She had stopped nodding. Guy Mo Chiang had forgotten nothing, perhaps a slight mistake here and there. The judge had looked up, puzzled a few times, but she was sure, quite sure that the sounds corresponded, but he spoke differently from Mrs. Chin on the tape recorder. The old board would laugh if he found out that she had failed after buying the tape recorder. He had scorned her then, saying it was a waste of money. He had laughed when she was learning to use it. So many squares to push. Red, black and white, for forward, backward, fast, and stop. The tape had been tangled a few times but the student down the hall had helped her fix it. Guy Mo Chiang gave him a box of ginger for his help. She would not fail. The questions were becoming difficult.

"Who represents the Queen in Canada?"

Guy Mo Chiang was silent for a long time. It was necessary to produce an answer so she could, six weeks from now, stand with fifty other new Canadians and mouth the Oath of Allegiance and take home the Bible and papers to China. The other women had told her about the ceremony. How one stood and repeated the sounds. There were speeches and tea after. It was necessary to find an answer. It was difficult. There were so many obstacles, lack of place, lack of time, lack of money, lack of success. But success was only a few minutes away. He looked like a kind man, the white bear. Perhaps he would overlook this one wrong answer, just one wrong answer. The sounds were becoming unfamiliar.

"Who represents the Queen?"

Queen. He emphasized the sound "queen". It was of some importance. The prime minister was an important sound. Was he not the centre of everything, like an emperor? They said China was different now. The new immigrants came back with stories of improvement of conditions, revolution. The prime minister was connected to it somehow.

Perhaps she could feign sickness. She had been sick just recently. The woman at the corner grocery store had to take her to the hospital. Guy Mo Chiang did not have to make signs to the doctors. The woman spoke for her. Guy Mo Chiang did not have to face the westerners. She could not understand their diagnosis, but it was not necessary. She had a Chinese body and a Chinese sickness. She must return home. That was all. The old board had worried that time. He had stood at the entrance of the rooming house when she came back. He had been too weak to bring her to the hospital but he waited there when she came back. He had even bought her a box of mandarin oranges, a whole box. But he was an old board. Her daughter would take better care of her in China. He did not think of returning but was content to spend his time in that dark brown room in Chinatown playing Mah Jong and cards. He would die there alone. He would never change.

There was an answer. It seemed right. The judge would excuse just one mistake. The ten minutes were over, just over. She was sure. She was counting with every breath since it began. He rustled the papers a little. The typewriters in the background had continued throughout the whole session. He had her papers in her file. She could read the print in large black letters. She could see her application for citizenship. Government papers giving. They gave housing projects, grants for homes, shiny books about Canada, Bibles and Old Age Gold cheques. They gave to Canadians, only to Canadians. Were they giving this time? The judge was speaking to her sponsors.

"Her English . . . her English . . ."

Mrs. Chin protested, "She had worked hard, very hard. It was very difficult for older people to learn it. She was taking classes at the Chinese Catholic School."

Mrs. Louie was nodding in agreement with what Mrs. Chin said. But the judge seemed uncertain. He looked at Guy Mo Chiang, the white bear.

"One more question . . . just one more question."

Mrs. Chin was looking at her. This was seventy-five dollars. Mrs. Louie was nodding. Guy Mo Chiang was expected to nod. She did. She did not understand.

The judge was shuffling the first paper on the top of the pile. She recognized it, having stared at it all through the hearing. Perhaps it might even be said that she had almost learned to read. All the facts about Canada ran through her mind and arranged themselves in logical western sequence. At the end of the path there was China. Population, Senate, House of Commons, the sounds were familiar because she was so near being a Canadian citizen. She could return home and pronounce the words for them. Perhaps she could even read about the Old Age Gold cheque. It was printed full with Canadian terms. It was all so close. The white bear was speaking.

"Where does the Queen live?"

Guy Mo Chiang stopped smiling. Mrs. Louie and Mrs. Chin sat upright in their chairs, silently mouthing words to her. The white bear was looking at her. There was silence and the only breathing was the white bear. He was looking at her in his brown suit and brown glasses. He was looking at Guy Mo Chiang as if she did not belong in Canada. He was stopping her from returning to where she did belong.

"Where does the Queen live?"

The white bear was speaking again. It was different in China, the Communists. Guy Mo Chiang was thinking of her daughter and her two grandchildren. She thought of her son who was too busy to visit her. It was too difficult to go down to visit him and her grandchildren. San Francisco was so far away and besides the old board would not come with her. She would have to travel alone. Back to China. Alone. The old board, he would be alone. Her daughter was not eating well. Perhaps the Communists would take away her Old Age Gold cheque. It was different now. The new immigrants laughed at the old ones. They said they had kept the customs of old China. There was no such China now.

The white bear was shuffling the papers again. He looked up at Guy

Mo Chiang. She looked as if she might cry. The poor old stooped lady.

"She's old. It is difficult for her to learn, but she has worked so hard."
Mrs. Chin was speaking loudly to him.

"I can see that. I can see that." The white bear was speaking.

"It is her greatest wish to become a Canadian, to belong to Canada."
Mrs. Chin folded her hands together and pleaded with the judge.

The judge looked at Guy Mo Chiang. Canada was a place for all. Equal
opportunity for all races, cultures and ages. It was in the glossy slick book
they handed out to all their applicants for citizenship. She was so old and
stooped. She looked as if she had no place in the world.

"I spoke English once like that." Mrs. Louie nodded at the judge. "I
learned better now. See. She was learning. She is very clever. She babysits.
She will pick it up from the children. When she stays a while longer in
Canada she will learn very well."

The white bear looked at them. He looked at Guy Mo Chiang. Guy Mo
Chiang watched China disappear. It was better this way. She could argue
with the store clerks. China, after thirty years, why had she ever thought
of it. She could never belong.

The white bear was speaking.

"Mrs. Chiang, I want you to come back in about a month for your
citizenship papers. We'll notify you when to come."

He looked at Mrs. Chin. Guy Mo Chiang looked at Mrs. Chin.

"Can you explain to her and tell her to bring pictures?"

Mrs. Chin nodded and smiled. She told Guy Mo Chiang that she must
bring pictures so that she could have a card made up showing her
Canadian citizenship. Canadian citizenship. Mrs. Louie was smiling at the
judge. Guy Mo Chiang looked at them all.

The white bear was speaking again.

"She has done very well . . . very well. We give the older ones more
chances. The names are hard to learn."

The white bear smiled. He pushed up his glasses. Such a nice man.

The red and white flag behind, the printing on the wall in black
frames, they all said something about Canada. They were all smiling.
Perhaps Guy Mo Chiang would go down to visit her son in San Francisco
now that she had her Canadian citizenship and Old Age Gold. China was
so far away.

The Caller

Dave Margoshes

Lewis was reading when the telephone rang and he hung on tenaciously to the sentence he was following, letting it pull him to the end of the paragraph before he grudgingly rose on the fourth ring. Judy was taking a shower and there was no one else but him to go. He spent a good part of his working day on the telephone and in the evening, at home, he hated to be drawn to the damn machine.

As he walked into the kitchen, and even as he was picking up the receiver, he was wondering who could be calling. They had only been in the house for two weeks, in the city one week more, and they had no friends yet, knew hardly anyone besides the people in his office. He couldn't remember a call yet on their slick yellow wall phone that hadn't been a wrong number. "Yes?" he said.

There was a silence for a moment on the other end of the line, a hesitation he knew the sound of his voice must have triggered, and he knew the call was a wrong number. Then a tiny, fuzzy voice whispered, "Is my mother there?"

It was a child's voice, whether boy or girl he couldn't tell. It sounded choked, distant, furtive, perhaps frightened. Lewis smiled warily. "No, honey, she isn't. I think you have the wrong number. Did you dial carefully?"

There was another hesitation, then the quavering voice again: "Is my mother there?"

Without meaning to, Lewis became impatient. "I'm sorry, honey, you have the wrong number. Dial again more carefully this time." He started to hang up but the voice pulled him back to the receiver, urgent this time, immediate. "Isn't this 624-1736?"

That *was* the number and Lewis was surprised to hear it, glanced at the phone just to make certain. "Yes," he started to say, but the voice cut him off: "Mrs. Andrews said my mother was there. Let me talk to her."

He was exasperated now; without reason, almost angry. "Listen, son," he said, sure now that his caller was a boy, "your mother isn't here . . ."

"You're a liar," the voice shouted and then the earpiece erupted into laughter. Then there was a click and the line went dead. Lewis hung up and stood for a moment staring at the phone before he shrugged and went back to the livingroom and his book. He found the paragraph he'd just finished and read it through again to get back into the action but found he couldn't get any farther. The call troubled him strangely, made him jittery and he got up from the couch to lock the front and rear doors.

The voice had sounded so much like that of a child, a little boy of perhaps five or six, frightened by something and wanting his mother, but he had acted so peculiarly. It was the accusation of lying, and that awful laugh, that had rattled him, Lewis knew. What a strange thing for a child to say, and what a strange laugh. And why the laugh at all, if the caller had indeed been a frightened child?

Perhaps it had been a child after all, he thought as he prowled around the house, listening to the fierce running of water in the bathroom, but not frightened, perhaps not as young as he had thought. A ten-year-old, calling numbers at random to amuse himself. Maybe even a teen-ager, killing time with a perverse joke. But the laugh, its memory still ringing in his ears, cold and unexpected, harsh and mirthless, nagged at him. A burglar, checking to see if anyone was home? An anonymous caller beginning a whole series of unsettling intrusions? Then again, he thought with some remorse, perhaps his caller had in fact been a child, a genuinely frightened child whose laugh and accusation was inspired by hysteria, and he chided himself guiltily for not having attempted to keep the boy talking, draw more out of him.

Lewis was not a timid man by nature, not a worrier especially, but he felt suddenly cold and vulnerable, as if someone were watching him from a dark corner of the house. He checked the doors again and made sure all the windows were locked and the curtains and drapes were drawn. He stood gazing through the kitchen window with comfort at the brightly shining porch light of a neighbor until he heard the shower turn off and he felt relieved a few minutes later when Judy came out of the bathroom, looking pink and fresh in her flowered bathrobe, a towel wrapped around her hair.

"Is that a great shower," she said, kissing him on the cheek. "It's such a luxury, I can't get enough of it. Never again will we live somewhere that doesn't have one."

She lit a cigarette and shook out her hair. "Who was on the phone?" she asked.

"Just a wrong number," Lewis shrugged. He went back to his book while she crawled into bed with a magazine. He felt better, as if having shrugged off the call to his wife he could now accept it that way himself. When he finished the chapter he was reading he took a shower and by the time he got into bed he'd forgotten the call.

Lewis was thirty-two, a native New Yorker and graduate of City College, a veteran of the pre-Vietnam Air Force. He worked as a public relations executive for a paper manufacturer and, after four years in the New York office, where he was one of many, had been transferred to San Francisco, where he was second man in the office, with a whole phalanx of "communications specialists" beneath him. The company he worked for, which grew thousands of acres of trees in the northwest, cut them down and ground them into pulp in order to make newsprint, napkins, writing paper and tissues, had become especially sensitive to the growing concern about the environment, and he had been put in charge of the counterattack against the critics. It was hard, stimulating work, involving the coming up with of ideas for campaigns and seeing to it that they were put into action. He had a good group of guys working with him and he was expecting a call from one of them three days after the night of his peculiar caller when the phone rang.

"I'll get it," he said, getting up from the table. They had just finished dinner and Judy was stacking the dishes in the washer while Lewis sipped at his second cup of coffee. "It's probably Stein."

He picked up the receiver and cradled it against his shoulder, reaching for a pad and pencil. "Hello? Stein?"

"Is my mother there?" a voice whispered and the memory of that laugh reverberated through Lewis's head. He snapped up straight, clenching the phone in his hand, his brow furrowing. Before he could say anything he realized how silly he was being and he relaxed, smiling, shaking his head at himself.

"Who is this?" Lewis asked gently.

"Bobby," the quavering little boy's voice said. "Can I speak to my mother?"

"Your mother isn't here, Bobby. You called here a few days ago, remember? You're dialing the wrong number. Now hang up and dial again, *carefully*."

There was a pause and Lewis smiled softly, picturing the puzzled frown on the boy's face. "Isn't this 624-1736?" the boy asked. He *did* sound puzzled, as if, somehow, he was being cheated by a force he couldn't understand, or a grown-up—just as bad. Lewis glanced at the number on the phone, as he'd done the first time, just to reassure himself, and nodded. "Yes, it is, Bobby, but your mother isn't here. Whoever wrote down the number for you got it wrong. Probably just one of the numbers is wrong." He was feeling proud of himself now, for being so calm when his first reaction had been irritation, and for being so reasonable and helpful to what was obviously just a little boy trying to call his mother. "Is there anybody there you can ask about the number?"

There was another confused pause, then the boy asked, demanded really: "Let me talk to my mother," and all of Lewis's calmness fled.

"Now listen, boy," he snapped into the receiver, "I told you your mother isn't here. Now I'm sorry but I have to hang up, I'm expecting . . ."

But he was cut off by the boy's high, piercing laugh, short and deadly sounding, before he could finish, and then a click and the inevitable buzz of the broken line. He slammed the receiver onto its cradle and shook his head violently.

"What was that all about?" Judy asked. She was standing behind him, beside the table, and when he turned he was startled by the expression on her face, realizing that he must have looked and sounded like a fool. His face flushed and he twisted his mouth into a crooked grin to hide his embarrassment. He and Judy had been married for only six months and they were still going through the sometimes wonderful, sometimes painful process of getting to know each other.

"Just a wrong number," he said.

"Some wrong number."

"Some silly kid, says he's trying to call his mother. He called a few days ago too. I think he's playing a game, dialing numbers at random, trying to shake people up."

"A little boy?" Judy said. She looked doubtful. "Trying to shake people up?" She smiled at him but there was something in her eyes that made his mouth pucker with annoyance. The phone rang before he could say anything. He hesitated, his hand just above the receiver, for a moment before picking it up. It was Stein, the man from his office. When he was finished with the conversation, Judy had forgotten about the boy's call, and they went out for a walk. But Lewis hadn't forgotten, and it preyed on his mind all that evening. He woke the next morning thinking of that terrible laugh.

They lived in a quiet, residential area at the base of Golden Gate Park, just a few blocks from the ocean, and they loved to walk along the beach in the evenings. It was springlike warm, unusually so for the city in April, the rains had all but gone and the days were getting longer. Lewis and Judy would usually go out for a walk after dinner and not be back until after dark, when the streets would become deserted of casual strollers. It was supposed to be unsafe to be on the streets after dark, but after New York, San Francisco seemed tame to them both and often Lewis wished they could walk all night, hating to go back to their house and the waiting for the phone to ring.

In the several weeks after the boy's first two calls he had become a persistent intruder in Lewis's evenings. His reaction to the individual calls oscillated between genuine concern, curiosity, annoyance and, occasionally, anger, but, in general, his uneasiness about the mysterious caller had deepened. Even Judy, who had been skeptical at first, then kidding, after answering the phone a few times before Lewis could get to it, became frightened. Concern for her prompted him to get in touch with the telephone company, but when the man he spoke to there heard that nothing obscene or threatening was being said by the caller he lost interest. Certain that he would be laughed at, Lewis dismissed the idea of talking to the police.

With the exception of the second time, when the boy had called just past dinner time, he invariably called sometime after dark, from as early as 7:30 to as late as midnight. Always, he began by asking to speak to his mother; always, he ended the conversation by laughing and cutting off the line. In between, what he actually said changed subtly from call to call, the message expanding, like a puzzle in which pieces are gradually, painfully filled in.

Lewis's feelings about the boy remained ambivalent even as he grew more apprehensive. Sometimes he would be convinced his caller really was no more than a small boy desperately trying to get through to his mother, thoroughly uncomprehending his difficulty; at other times, Lewis was sure he and Judy were being made the butt of some cruel, perverse prank, perhaps with danger lurking somewhere at the end, and he became frightened. It was an uncomfortable feeling for a grown man, a responsible man, a veteran, a man who had endured the bloodied noses and split lips of streetcorner brawls that seemed inevitably to accompany growing up in New York—to be frightened of a telephone call, of the voice of a small boy. But Lewis sensed poison in that feeble, fuzzy voice, tasted venom in his own mouth when he responded to it, and his heart skipped a beat and sweat stood out on his forehead when he heard the ringing each night.

The calls had become a nightly occurrence. Into them, fairly early, had slipped the character of the boy's father.

"Daddy's coming," the voice whispered. "I must tell my mother."

"Your mother isn't here, Bobby," Lewis said wearily, but he immediately became interested. "Your father is coming? Has he been away? Will he be home soon?"

But the boy would be drawn no further and the laugh came soon, that damned laugh, and the call was over.

"Daddy's coming, he'll be mad if my mother isn't here," the voice said a few calls later.

"Where does your daddy live?" Lewis asked. The boy wouldn't say.

Another time: "Call my mother to the phone, please, my daddy's coming home and I'm frightened."

Lewis, alarmed, spent a wearying five minutes trying to wheedle from the boy where he lived, only to evoke a sobbing, choking sound, screams that he was lying, that the boy's mother *must* be there, ending with the horrible laugh. Lewis, feeling drained and defeated, threw himself face down on the couch and had to struggle to keep sobs from breaking out from his own throat. Judy came and sat beside him, stroking his hair. She didn't ask him what had been said, she had heard half the conversation and she could see the conclusion.

"Let's get our number changed, get an unlisted number," she said. "I'm frightened."

"No," Lewis said. He had already thought about that. But along with the dread growing within him that was personal, directed toward himself and Judy, a fear focusing on the boy was developing. Although he hadn't

completely abandoned the idea that the caller was a grown-up or teen-
ager, a practical joker or a twisted tormenter, more and more he was
becoming convinced that the boy was real, that his calls were pleas for
help.

The final call came on a Sunday. It was late, past midnight when the
phone rang and Lewis was already in bed, having thought the boy would
perhaps spare him one night. He rose on the first ring, like a lifeguard
springing from his perch at the first sign of a floundering swimmer, and,
perhaps because the calls always made him feel so vulnerable, he took the
time to slip into his pants.

He got to the phone on the fifth ring. "Hello?"

He was greeted by a wailing he hadn't encountered before. It was the
boy's voice, Bobby's, he knew it well enough now to recognize it no matter
how distorted, but it was cracked with fear, swollen with bellowing.
"Mommy, Mommy," the voice cried, "save me, Daddy's coming, he's
coming up the stairs, he's at the door . . . ." The voice trailed off in a spasm
of sobs.

Lewis was alarmed but strangely calm. For once, despite the inco-
herence of the words which babbled on into his ear, the message of the
call was clear—it *was* a call for help, a frightened boy cringing from a
threat made of bone and flesh, falling back on the one place where he
knew there was a listener. It didn't matter whether his mother was there
or not, Lewis was there, and it suddenly dawned on him that, with the
possible exception of the first wrong number, the boy never had been
calling for his mother, he was calling for Lewis, the nice faceless man who
always answered when darkness had come and fear was around him.

"Bobby, Bobby, calm down," Lewis soothed. "It'll be all right, I'm here,
I'm listening. Stop crying and tell me what's the matter. What's happened, has your father come home? Is that it?"

But the boy would not be consoled. He kept on sobbing, hiccupping
out snatches of words: "Daddy's here . . . he's at the door . . . he's banging
. . . he's going to kill me . . . "

"No, no, Bobby," Lewis said softly, firmly, over and over again. Judy
had come up behind him, wrapping a robe around her and shivering in
the chilly kitchen. "What is it, Lew?" she asked but he didn't hear her, all
his attention, all his energy focussing on the telephone, the lifeless
receiver through which a life was reaching toward him.

Suddenly Lewis heard a banging, crashing sound in the background, and the boy's wail pitched higher. He froze, his lips quivering, and now, if he hadn't before, he believed the voice, shared the dread. "What's that noise, Bobby?" he shouted. "What is it? Is it your father?"

"Mommy, Mommy," the voice wailed, "he'll kill me, he'll kill me."

"Bobby, listen to me," Lewis commanded. "What's your name, where do you live? Tell me and I'll call help, I'll come and help you. Do you hear me? Do you understand? Where do you live, what's the address? Bobby, Bobby?"

His voice was drowned out by a heavy, crashing sound, like wood splintering, and the boy's scream. Then there was silence.

"Bobby!" Lewis shouted. "Are you there? Hello, hello, is anybody there? Do you hear me? Answer, for God's sake."

On the other end of the line, someone hung up the phone. The click rang in Lewis's ear like the shot of a pistol, like a hysterical laugh, like a cry of mortal dread. Then came the deadly, endless buzz.

"Oh, my God," Lewis said. He stood dazed, staring at the yellow receiver in his hand as if it were some strange, alien thing he had just discovered, or a powerful talisman which had finally failed him. Judy put her arms around him, draping herself around his bare back, but was silent, trembling. In a moment, he seemed to awaken, pulled himself up straight. Perhaps it wasn't too late, something could be done. If only he knew where the boy lived, knew his last name. Why hadn't he, in all these weeks, done more than just listen, why hadn't he pumped the information he needed so desperately now out of the boy? Why hadn't he cared enough to try to answer?

It didn't matter now, he knew; it was too late for bullying himself. He had to do something, *now*. What was that name? The boy, several times, had said he'd gotten the number from a woman. Mrs. Anderson? No, Andrews. That was it. Mrs. Andrews. He reached for the phone book, in a drawer beneath the phone but stopped before he had it out. There must be hundreds of Andrews. The number? Surely, the first time, the boy must have dialed the number wrong or, if he had it written down, it was written wrong. He looked at the number on the phone. Seven numerals, any one of them could be the key. Perhaps if he tried calling a few, changing a numeral each time? No, there were too many possibilities, thousands of alternatives.

He reached for the dial, meaning to call the operator and ask for the police, but shame stopped him. In the end, he went forlornly into the street, barefooted and shirtless, shivering in the cold, to stand in front of the house, staring up and down the dark, silent street as if there was something to see, as if something would be revealed in the light from the streetlamp, the neon at the gas station on the corner. He wanted to cry out but was silent. He wanted to walk barechested to the ocean and stare out across the dark water until dawn came up, but he was afraid. After a few minutes Judy came out, put her face against his chest and led him into the house.

Cranes Fly South
Edward McCourt

"They fly all night," the old man said. "First you hear a sound far off and you figger it's thunder—and it gits louder and nearer, and soon it's like a freight train passin' right over your head, and if there's a moon they fly across it and the night gits dark—"

"But I tell you I saw one!" Lee said. "Honest, Grandpa. Out at Becker's slough. I was looking for ducks—and all of a sudden—"

"Ain't no whoopin' cranes nowadays," the old man said disconsolately.

Lee spoke very slowly now, trying hard to be patient. "At Becker's slough. Honest. I saw the black tips of his wings just as clear!"

"And you feel like you want to go, too," Grandpa said. "Breaks your heart almost, you want to go that bad, when you hear the thunder right over your head—like a big, long freight train passin' in the nighttime."

His voice rose in an unexpected harsh croak. "At Becker's slough, you say? A whoopin' crane—a real, honest-to-gosh whooper? Boy, I ain't seen a whooper for forty years!"

"There's only twenty-eight whoopers left in the whole world," Lee said. "They fly south in the fall clear to Texas."

"Me, I'm going south, too," Grandpa said. "You can set in the sun all winter and see things besides flatness. Man gets mighty tired of flatness—after eighty years." HIs voice trailed off. He fell back in his chair and closed his eyes.

Lee remembered what his mother had said. "Grandpa is a very old man, Lee; he mustn't ever get excited." He knew a moment of paralysing fear. Maybe Grandpa was dying; maybe he was already dead! "Grandpa!" he shouted hoarsely. "Wake up, wake up!"

A convulsive shudder twisted the shrunken body in the chair. The old man stood up without laying a hand on the arm rest of the chair, and his voice was loud and strong. "Boy, I got to see it. I tell you I got to!"

Lee stared, fascinated and irresolute. "But Mum says—"

The old man's voice lost its tone of loud authority, dropped into feeble wheedling. "Aw, come on, boy. Ain't nobody goin' to see us. Your paw's workin' in the far quarter and Ellen she's off to a hen party somewheres. We can slip out and back just as easy."

"But it's three miles. And Mum's got the car."

Grandpa wrinkled up his face. "We got a horse and buggy, ain't we?"

"But the buggy hasn't been used for years and years," Lee protested. "And the harness—"

The old man caught up his stick from beside the chair. Fury chased the cunning from his puckered face. "You git along, boy," he screamed, "or I'll welt the hide off you!"

Lee retreated to the door. "All right, Grandpa," he said placatingly. "I'll hitch Bessie up right now."

Grandpa had a hard time getting into the buggy. But the moment he reached the seat he snatched the lines from Lee's hands and slapped the old mare's rump with the ends of the lines. Bessie broke into a startled trot and Lee held his breath. But Bessie slowed almost at once to a shambling, reluctant walk, and Lee felt a little easier. Maybe the buggy wouldn't fall to pieces after all.

They drove along the road a little way and turned off to a trail that wound across bleak open prairie. Grandpa stared straight ahead, and his eyes were bright. "Like I say, boy, they go south. Figger they see the Mississippi from a mile up. Sure like to see it myself. Will, too, some day."

The old man's chin dropped toward his chest. The lines fell from his fingers, and Lee caught them just before they slipped over the dashboard.

"Thanks, boy, for takin' me out. Maybe we'd better go home now. I'm tired—awful tired."

The boy's throat tightened. "We're near there, Grandpa," he said. "You can see the slough now."

"Ain't no whoopers any more," the old man mumbled peevishly. "Gone south."

Lee swung Bessie out of the rutted trail into the shelter of a poplar grove. He eased the old man down from the buggy and slipped a hand under his arm. "Come on, Grandpa," he urged. "We'll make it all right."

They advanced slowly from behind the sheltering bluff into the tall grass that rimmed the borders of the slough. The sun dazzled their eyes, but the wind blew strong and cold across the slough, carrying with it the rank smell of stagnant water and alkali-encrusted mud. Grandpa huddled under his greatcoat.

"What are you doin' to me, boy?" he complained almost tearfully. "You know what Ellen said. I ain't supposed to go out without she's along."

"Down, Grandpa—down!"

The old man crumpled to hands and knees. "Where is it, boy? Where is it?" His voice rose in a shrill, frenzied squeak.

"Come on—I can see his head!"

Something moved in the long grass. For a shuddering moment the boy lay helpless, beyond the power of speech or movement. Then his body jerked convulsively to life and he leaped to his feet and his voice rang wild and shrill.

"Grandpa—look—look!"

He wheeled to clutch at Grandpa, but the old man already stood upright, staring out of dim, fierce eyes at the great white body flung against the pale sky. "Great God in heaven!" The words were a strange, harsh cry of ecstasy and pain. "A whooper, boy—a whooper!"

They stood together, man and boy, held by an enchantment that was no part of the drab, flat world about them. The great bird rose steadily higher, the black tips of his wings a blurred streak against the whiteness of his body. He swung in a wide arc, flew high above the heads of the watchers by the slough, then climbed fast and far into the remote pale sky. For a minute or more he seemed to hang immobile, suspended in space beyond the limits of the world. Then the whiteness faded, blended with the pale of the sky, and was gone.

The old man's fingers were tight on the boy's arm. Again the harsh cry burst from his lips—"Great God in heaven!"—the cry that was at once a shout of exultation and a prayer. Then the light in his eyes faded and went out.

"He's gone south," Grandpa said. His shoulders sagged. He tried to pull the greatcoat close about his shrunken body. "They come in the night and you hear a sound like thunder and the sky gits dark—and there's the Mississippi below and the smell of the sea blown in from a hundred miles away . . . "

Lee's mother led the boy to the door, "He's raving," she said, and there were tears in her eyes and voice. "He's so sick. Oh, Lee, you should never—"

At once she checked herself. "The doctor should be here soon," she whispered. "Tell your father to send him up the minute he comes."

Lee fled downstairs, away from the dim-lit, shadow-flecked room where the only sounds to break the heavy silence were Grandpa's muttered words and his hard, unquiet breathing. Grandpa was sick—awful sick. He had no strength left to lift his head from the pillow, and his eyes didn't seem to see things any more. But he wasn't crazy; he knew all right what he was saying. Only no one except Lee understood what he meant. He did not regret what he had done. No matter what happened he was glad that Grandpa had seen the whooper.

"He just had to see it," he said stubbornly to his father. "He just had to."

His father nodded slowly from behind the paper he was pretending to read. "I know, son," he said. And he added, a queer, inexplicable note of pain in his voice, "Wish I'd been along."

Lee fell asleep on the couch after a while. When he awoke much later, he was alone in the living room and the oil lamp on the table was burning dimly. He sat up, instantly alert. The house seemed strange and lonely, and the noises which had troubled him even in sleep were still. Something had happened. You could tell.

His mother came downstairs, walking very quietly. Her face was set and calm. He knew at once what she had come to say. Her fingers touched his hair, to show that what he had done didn't matter any more.

"Grandpa is dead," she said.

Suddenly her voice choked and she turned away her head. A moment of anguish engulfed him. He couldn't bear to hear his mother cry. But when at last he spoke, the words sprang clear and triumphant from his throat.

"He's gone south," he said.

The Great Electrical Revolution

Ken Mitchell

I was only a little guy in 1937, but I can still remember Grandad being out of work. Nobody had any money to pay him and as he said, there wasn't much future in brick-laying as a charity. So mostly he just sat around in his suite above the hardware store, listening to his radio. We *all* listened to it when there was nothing else to do, which was most of the time unless you happened to be going to school like me. Grandad stuck right there through it all—soap operas, weather reports and quiz shows— unless he got a bit of cash from somewhere. Then he and Uncle Fred would go downtown to the beer parlour at the King William Hotel.

Grandad and Grandma came from the old country long before I was born. When they arrived in Moose Jaw, all they had was three children: Uncle Fred, Aunt Thecla, and my Dad; a trunk full of working clothes; and a 26-pound post mall for putting up fences to keep "rogues" off Grandad's land. Rogues meant Indians, Orangemen, cattle rustlers and capitalists. All the way out on the train from Montreal, he glared out the Pullman window at the endless flat, saying to his family:

"I came out here for land, b'Christ, and none of 'em's goin' to sly it on me."

He had sworn to carve a mighty estate from the raw Saskatchewan prairie, although he had never so much as picked up a garden hoe in his whole life before leaving Dublin.

So when he stepped off the train at the C.P.R. station in Moose Jaw, it looked like he was thinking of tearing it down and seeding the site to oats. It was two o'clock in the morning, but he kept striding up and down the lobby of the station, dressed in his good wool suit with the vest, as cocky as a bantam rooster in a chicken run. My Dad and Uncle Fred and Aunt

Thecla sat on the trunk, while Grandma nagged at him to go and find them a place to stay. (It was only later they realized he was afraid to step outside the station.) He finally quit strutting long enough to get a porter to carry their trunk to a hotel down the street.

The next morning they went to the government land office to secure their homestead. Then Grandad rented a democrat and took my Dad and Uncle Fred out to see the land they had come half-way around the world to find. Grandma and Aunt Thecla were told to stay in the hotel room and thank the Blessed Virgin for deliverance. They were still offering their prayers some three hours later, when Grandad burst into the room, his eyes wild and his face pale and quivering.

"Sweet Jesus Christ!" he shouted at them. "There's too much of it! There's just too damn much of it out there." He ran around the room several times in circles, knocking against the walls. "Miles and miles of nothing but miles and miles!" He collapsed onto one of the beds, and lay staring at the ceiling.

"It'ud drive us all witless in a week," he moaned.

The two boys came in and told the story of the expedition. Grandad had started out fine, perhaps just a little nervous. But the further they went from the town, the more agitated and wild-eyed he got. Soon he stopped urging the horse along and asked it to stop. They were barely ten miles from town when they turned around and came back, with Uncle Fred driving. Grandad could only crouch on the floor of the democrat, trying to hide from the enormous sky, and whispering hoarsely at Fred to go faster. He'd come four thousand miles to the wide open spaces—only to discover he suffered from agoraphobia.

That was his last real excursion onto the open prairie. He gave up forever the idea of a farm of his own. (He did make one special trip to Mortlach in 1928 to fix Aunt Thecla's chimney, but that was a family favour. Even then Uncle Fred had to drive him in an enclosed Ford sedan in the middle of the night, with newspapers taped to the windows so he couldn't see out.) There was nothing left for him to do but take up his old trade of brick-laying in the town of Moose Jaw, where there were trees and tall buildings to protect him from the vastness. Maybe it was a fortunate turn of fate; certainly he prospered from then until the Depression hit, about the time I was born.

Yet—Grandad always felt guilty about not settling on the land. Maybe it was his conscience that prompted him to send my Dad out to work for a cattle rancher in the hills, the day after he turned eighteen. Another point: he married Aunt Thecla off to a Lutheran wheat farmer at Mortlach who actually threshed about five hundred acres of wheat every fall. Uncle Fred was the eldest and closer to Grandad (he had worked with him as an apprentice brick-layer before they immigrated) so he stayed in town and lived in the suite above the hardware store.

I don't remember much about my father's cattle ranch, except whirls of dust and skinny animals dragging themselves from one side of the range to the other. Finally there were no more cattle, and no money to buy more, and nothing to feed them if we *did* buy them, except wild fox-tails and Russian thistles. So we moved into Moose Jaw with Grandad and Grandma, and went on relief. It was better than the ranch where there was nothing to do but watch tumbleweeds roll through the yard. We would have had to travel into town every week to collect the salted fish and government pork, anyway. Grandad was very happy to have us, because when my Dad went down to the railway yard to get our ration, he collected Grandad's too. My Dad never complained about waiting in line for the handout, but Grandad would've starved to death first. "The God-damned government drives us all to the edge," he would say. "Then they want us to queue up for the God-damned swill they're poisoning us with."

That was when we spent so much time listening to Grandad's radio. It came in a monstrous slab of black walnut cabinet he had swindled, so he thought, from a second-hand dealer on River Street. An incandescent green bulb glowed in the cente to show when the tubes were warming up. There was a row of knobs with elaborate-looking initials and a dial with the names of cities like Tokyo, Madrid, and Chicago. Try as we might on long winter evenings to tune the needle in to those stations and hear a play in Japanese or Russian, all we ever got was CHMJ Moose Jaw, The Buckle of the Wheat Belt. Even so, I spent hours lying on the floor, tracing the floral patterns on the cloth-covered speaker while I listened to another world of mystery and fascination.

When the time came that Grandad could find no more bricks to lay, he set a kitchen chair in front of the radio and stayed there, not moving except to go to the King William, where Uncle Fred now spent most of his time. My Dad had managed to get a job with the city, gravelling streets for fifty cents a day. But things grew worse. The Moose Jaw Light and Power Company came around one day in the fall of 1937 and cut off our electricity for non-payment. It was very hard on Grandad not to have his radio. Not only did he have nothing to do, but he had to spend all his time thinking about it. He stared out the parlour window, which looked over the alley running behind the hardware store. There was a grand view of the back of the Rainbow Laundry.

That was what he was doing the day of his discovery, just before Christmas. Uncle Fred and my Dad were arguing about who caused the Depression—R.B. Bennett or the C.P.R. Suddenly Grandad turned from the window. There was a new and strange look on his face.

"Where does that wire go?" he said.

"Wire?" said Uncle Fred, looking absent-mindedly around the room. He patted his pockets looking for a wire.

"What wire?" my Dad said.

Grandad nodded toward the window. "This wire running right past the window."

He pointed to a double strand of power line that ran from a pole in the back alley to the side of our building. It was a lead-in for the hardware store.

"Holy Moses Cousin Harry. Isn't that a sight now!" Grandad said, grinning like a crazy man.

"You're crazy," Uncle Fred told him. "You can't never get a tap off that line there. They'd find you out in nothing flat."

Grandma, who always heard everything that was said, called from the kitchen: "Father, don't you go and do some foolishness will have us all electrinated."

"By God," he muttered. He never paid any attention to a word she said. "Cut off *my* power, will they?"

That night, after they made me go to bed, I listened to him and Uncle Fred banging and scraping as they bored a hole through the parlour wall. My Dad wouldn't have anything to do with it and took my mother to the free movie at the co-op. He said Grandad was descending to the level of the Moose Jaw Light and Power Company.

Actually, Grandad knew quite a bit about electricity. He had known for a long time how to jump a wire from one side of the meter around to the other, to cheat the power company. I had often watched him under the meter, stretched out from his tip-toes at the top of a broken step-ladder, yelling at Grandma to lift the God-damned Holy Candle a little higher so he could see what the Christ he was doing.

The next day, Grandad and Uncle Fred were acting like a couple of kids, snorting and giggling and jabbing each other in the ribs. They were waiting for the King William beer parlour to open so they could go down and tell their friends about Grandad's revenge on the power company. They spent the day like heroes down there, telling over and over how Grandad had spied the lead-in, and how they bored the hole in the wall, and how justice had finally descended on the capitalist leeches. The two of them showed up at home for supper, but as soon as they ate they headed back to the King William where everybody was buying them free beer.

Grandma didn't seem to think much of their efforts, although now that she had electricity again, she could spend the evenings doing her housework if she wanted to. The cord came through the hole in the wall, across the parlour to the hall and the kitchen. Along the way, other cords were attached which led to the two bedrooms. Grandma muttered when she had to sweep around the black tangle of wires and sockets. With six of us living in the tiny suite, somebody was forever tripping on one of the cords and knocking things over.

But we lived with all that because Grandad was happy again. We might *all* have lived happily if Grandad and Uncle Fred could have kept quiet about their revenge on the power company. One night about a week later we were in the parlour listening to Fibber McGee and Molly when somebody knocked at the door. It was Mrs. Pizak, who lived next door in a tiny room.

"Goot evening," she said, looking all around. "I see your power has turnt beck on."

"Ha," Grandad said. "We turned it on *for* 'em. Damned rogues."

"Come in and sit down and listen to the show with us," Grandma said. Mrs. Pizak kept looking at the black wires running back and forth across the parlour, and at Grandad's radio. You could tell she wasn't listening to the show.

"Dey shut off my power, too," she said. "I alvays like listen de Shut-In. Now my radio isn't vork."

"Hmmm," Grandad said, trying to hear Fibber and the Old-Timer. Grandma and my Dad watched him, not listening to the radio any more either. Finally he couldn't stand it.

"All right, Fred," he said. "Go and get the brace and bit."

They bored a hole through one of the bedroom walls into Mrs. Pizak's cubicle. From then on, she was on Grandad's power grid, too. It didn't take long for everybody else in the block to find out about the free power, and they all wanted to hook up. There were two floors of suites above the hardware store, and soon the walls and ceiling of Grandad's suite were as full of holes as a colander, with wires running in all directions. For the price of a bottle of whiskey, people could run their lights twenty-four hours a day if they wanted. By Christmas Day, even those who *paid* their bills had given notice to the power company. It was a beautiful Christmas in a bad year—and Grandad and Uncle Fred liked to take a lot of credit for it. Nobody blamed them, either. There was a lot of celebration up and down the halls, where they always seemed to show up as guests of honour. There was a funny feeling running through the block, like being in a state of siege, or a revolution, with Uncle Fred and my Grandad leading it.

One late afternoon just before New Year's, I was lying on the floor of the front parlour, reading a second-hand Book of Knowledge I had got for Christmas. Grandma and my mother were knitting socks, and all three of us were listening vaguely to the Ted Mack Amateur Hour. Suddenly, out of the corner of my eye, I thought I saw Grandad's radio move. I blinked and stared at it, but the big console just sat there talking about Geritol. I turned a page. Again, it seemed to move in a jerk. What was going on?

"Grandma," I said. "The radio—"

She looked up from her knitting, already not believing a word I might have to say. I gave it up, and glared spitefully at the offending machine. While I watched, it slid at least six inches across the parlour floor.

"Grandma!" I screamed. "The radio's moving! It was sitting there—and it moved over here. All by itself!"

She looked calmly at the radio, then the table of wires spread across the floor, and out the front parlour window.

"Larry-boy, you'd best run and fetch your grandfather. He's over at McBride's. Number eight."

McBrides' suite was down the gloomy hall and across. I dashed down the corridor and pounded frantically at the door. Someone opened it the width of a crack.

"Is my Grandad in there?" I squeaked. Grandad stepped out into the hall with a glass in his hand, closing the door behind him.

"What is it, Larry?"

"Grandma says for you to come quick. The radio! There's something—"

"My radio!" Grandad was not a large man, but he had the energy of a buzz-saw. He started walking back up the hall, breaking into a trot, then a steady gallop, holding his glass of whiskey out in front at arm's length so it wouldn't spill. He burst through the door and screeched to a stop in front of the radio, which sat there, perfectly normal except that it stood maybe a foot to the left of the chair.

"By the Holy toe-nails of Moses—what is it?"

Grandma looked up ominously and jerked her chin toward the window. Her quiet firmness usually managed to calm him, but now, in two fantastic bounds, Grandad stood in front of the window, looking out.

"Larry," he said, glaring outside, "fetch your Uncle Fred."

I tore off down the hall again to number eight and brought Uncle Fred back to the suite. The two women were still knitting on the other side of the room. Grandma was doing her stitches calmly enough, but my mother's needles clattered like telegraph keys, and she was throwing terrified glances around the room.

"Have a gawk at this, will you, Fred?"

Uncle Fred and I crowded around him to see out. There, on a pole only twenty feet from our parlour window, practically facing us eye-to-eye, was a lineman from the power company. He was replacing broken glass insulators; God knows why he was doing it in the dead of winter. Obviously, he hadn't noticed our home-made lead-in, or he would have been knocking at the door. We could only pray he wouldn't look at the wire too closely. Once, he lifted his eyes toward the lighted window where we all stood gaping out at him in the growing darkness. He grinned at us, and raised his hand in a salute. He must have thought we were admiring his work.

"Wave back!" Grandad ordered. The three of us waved frantically at the lineman, to make him think we appreciated his efforts, although Grandad was muttering some very ugly things about the man's ancestry.

Finally, to our relief, the lineman finished his work and got ready to come down the pole. He reached out his hand for support—and my heart stopped beating as his weight hung on the contraband wire. Behind me, I could hear the radio slide another foot across the parlour floor. The lineman stared at the wire he held. He tugged experimentally, his eyes following it up to the hole through our wall. He looked at Grandad and

Uncle Fred and me standing there in the lit-up window, with our crazy horror-struck grins and our arms frozen above our heads in grotesque waves. Understanding seemed to spread slowly across his face.

He scrambled around to the opposite side of the pole and braced himself to give a mighty pull on our line. Simultaneously, Grandad leaped into action, grabbing the wire on our side of the wall. He wrapped it around his hands, and braced his feet against the baseboard. The lineman gave his first vicious yank, and it almost jerked Grandad smack against the wall. I remember thinking what a powerful man the lineman must be to do that to my Grandad.

"Fred, you feather-brained idiot!" he shouted. "Get over here and haul on this line before the black-hearted son of a bitch pulls me through the wall."

Uncle Fred ran to the wire just in time, as the man on the pole gave another, mightier heave. At the window, I could see the lineman stiffen with rage and determination. The slender wire sawed back and forth through the hole in the wall for at least ten minutes, first one side, and then the other, getting advantage. The curses on our side got very loud and bitter. I couldn't hear the lineman, of course, but I could see him—with his mouth twisted in an awful snarl, throwing absolutely terrible looks at me in the window, and heaving on the line. I know he wasn't praying to St. Jude.

Grandad's cursing would subside periodically when Grandma warned: "Now, now, father, not in front of the boy." Then she would go back to her knitting and pretend the whole thing wasn't happening, as Grandad's violent language would soar to a new high.

That lineman must have been in extra-good condition, because our side very quickly began to play out. Grandad screamed at Grandma and my mother, and even at me, to throw ourselves on the line and help. But the women refused to leave their knitting, and they wouldn't let me be corrupted. I couldn't leave my viewpoint at the window, anyway.

Grandad and Uncle Fred kept losing acreage. Gradually the huge radio had scraped all the way across the floor and stood at their backs, hampering their efforts.

"Larry!" Grandad shouted. "Is he weakenin' any?"

He wanted desperately for me to say yes, but it was useless. "It doesn't look like it," I said. Grandad burst out in a froth of curses I'd never heard before. A fresh attack on the line pulled his knuckles to the wall and

barked them badly. He looked tired and beaten. All the slack in the line
was taken up and he was against the wall, his head twisted looking at me.
A light flared up in his eyes.

"All right, Fred," he said. "If he wants the God-damned thing so
bad—let him have it!" They both jumped back—and nothing happened.

I could see the lineman, completely unaware of his impending disaster, almost literally winding himself up for an all-out assault on our wire.
I wanted out of human kindness to shout a warning at him. But it was too
late. With an incredible backward lunge, he disappeared from sight
behind the power pole.

A shattering explosion of wild noises blasted my senses, like a bomb
had fallen in Grandad's suite. Every appliance and electric light that
Grandma owned flew into the parlour, bounding off the walls and smashing against each other. A table lamp from the bedroom caromed off Uncle
Fred's knee. The radio collided against the wall and was ripped off its wire
by the impact. Sparking and flashing like lightning, all of Grandma's
things hurled themselves against the parlour wall. They were stripped like
chokecherries from an electric vine as it went zipping through the hole.
A silence fell—like a breath of air to a drowning man. The late afternoon
darkness settled through the room.

"Sweet Jesus Christ!" Grandad said. He had barely got it out, when
there came a second uproar: a blood-curdling barrage of bangs and
shouts, as our neighbours in the block saw all their lamps, radios, irons
and toasters leap from their tables and collect in ruined piles of junk
around the "free power" holes in their walls. Uncle Fred turned white as
a sheet.

I looked out the window. The lineman sat on the ground at the foot
of his pole, dazed. He looked up at me with one more hate-filled glare,
then deliberately snipped our wire with a pair of cutters. He taped up the
end and marched away into the night.

Grandad stood in the midst of the ruined parlour, trying in the
darkness to examine his beloved radio for damage. Grandma sat in her
rocking chair, knitting socks and refusing to acknowledge the disaster.

It was Grandad who finally spoke first. "They're lucky," he said. "It was
just God-damned lucky for them they didn't scratch my radio."

Two Kinds of Sinner

W.O. Mitchell

Ever since Ma quit cutting my hair for me, I go in to Repeat Golightly's.
He lets me sit right on the chair; he doesn't put that board across any
more. Most of the time Jake, our hired man, takes me to town in the
democrat, and he was in the barbershop the afternoon Doc Toovey got
to talking how his paint horse, Spider, could run the gizzard out of
Auction Fever.

The afternoon argument with Doc Toovey started, Jake had got his
shave and was sitting next to Old Man Gatenby whilst Repeat cut my hair.
I had my head tilted, with my chin on my chest, and was looking up from
under, the way you do, when Repeat swung me around. Then I could see
myself over the tonic bottles and the clock with its numbers all backward
and Doc Toovey just in the doorway.

Doc runs the Crocus Hay and Feed and Livery. He is a horse and cattle
vet, and he has very white hair and a very red face that is all the time
smiling. His eyes will put you in mind of oat seeds, sort of.

"Anybody ahead of me?" he asked. His voice is kind of smily too.

"There's four shaves waitin'," Repeat said; "there's four fellas waiting'
to git their shave."

"That's fine," Doc said, and he sat down in the chair between Old Man
Gatenby and Jake. Jake slid over a little; he isn't so fussy about Doc Toovey;
Doc would steal the well out of a person's yard when they weren't looking,
Jake says. Jake has old-timer eyes that are squinty from looking into the
sun an awful lot. He is pretty near always right.

Repeat went back to work on my hair. "She was smart," he said. "She
was a smart little mare." He was talking about Dish Face, the black hackney
he used to have in the early days.

"I knew a real smart horse once," Jake said. "Wasn't no hot blood neither—just an ordinary work horse. He run for Parliament on the Lib'ral ticket."

Doc stopped with a plug of tobacco halfway to his mouth. "That's plum foolish." He bit a corner off.

"The heck it is," said Jake. "He was a real bright horse, an' when he seen all the combines an' tractors comin' West he—what else was there fer him to do but go into politics?"

"Well—" Doc leaned sideways in his chair and spit into the spittoon. "I ain't interested in smart horses. But you take running horses, like my paint. He can run."

"'Bout as fast as a one-arm fella on a handcar," said Jake.

Doc Toovey smiled at Jake. "Ain't nothing around here can beat him."

"That right?" said Jake.

"The kid here has got a nice-looking horse," said Repeat. "I say this here kid's horse is a nice look—"

"I've seen him," said Doc. "He ain't no match for Spider." He smiled at me.

"He can nail Spider's hide to a fence post," I said. "Recess time out at Rabbit Hill he—"

"You wasn't int'rested in findin' out, was you?" Jake asked Doc real polite.

"Might be." Doc spit again. "Might even put a little bet on it."

"How much?" Jake asked him.

"Whatever you want."

"Fifty dollars," said Jake, "and Repeat holds the money."

"I'll hold her," said Repeat, letting me down out of the chair. "You fellas can give her to me and I'll hold her fer you."

"Fine," said Doc. Both him and Jake reached into their pockets.

They worked it out we were going to hold the race next Saturday along the CPR tracks behind Hig Wheeler's lumberyards. When they were done Doc climbed into the barber chair.

"You ain't next," said Repeat. "I say you ain't the next—"

"That's all right," said Doc. "Those others ain't in a hurry."

"I'm in a hell of a hurry," said Old Man Gatenby.

"I don't really need a four-bit haircut, Repeat." Doc smiled up at him. "Just give her a sort of neck trim. Fifteen cents."

Going out home I sat with Jake in the democrat, watching Baldy's hindquarters tipping first one side then the other, real regular but sort of jerky, like Miss Henchbaw when she leads the singing at Rabbit Hill with her stick. Jake didn't say anything for a long way. By the road a meadow lark spilled some notes off of a strawstack. A jack-rabbit next to the bar pit undid himself for a few hops then sat startled, with his black-tipped ears straight up.

Jake spit curvy into the breeze. "I wouldn't say nothin' to yer maw."

"About Fever racin' Doc's paint, Spider?"

"Yep."

The rabbit went bouncing to beat anything over the bald-headed prairie. Over to the right of the road a goshawk came sliding down real quiet, slipping his black shadow over the stubble.

"Way yer maw looks at it, bettin' ain't right. I guess next to eatin' tobacco, yer maw hates gamblin'. I wouldn't say nothin' to her—ain't like you was doing the bettin'. All you're doin' is racing." Jake turned to me. "Like she's always sayin', 'Gents don't bet, an' gents don't chaw.'" He spit, and slapped the reins. "Git yer nose out of it, Baldy."

Jake turned to me again. "Fever's gonna run that there long-geared Spider right into the ground!"

All that week I raced Fever—at recess—after four; and like he always does, he beat everything at Rabbit Hill. At home Jake worked on him till he started dandy nine times out of ten. When he finished the distance he wasn't blowing hardly at all, and stepped away all dancy, like he was walking on eggs.

"He'll do," Jake said.

Then Ma found out. She came out to the shed whilst I was washing up for supper.

"I was talking with Mrs. Fotheringham today, son." She waited like she wanted me to say something. I pretended I was getting soap out of my ears. "On the phone," Ma said.

I poured out the basin into the slop pail.

"Mrs. Fotheringham was talking to Doctor Fotheringham. He was talking with Mr. Golightly. She told me there was to be a race Saturday."

"Did she?" I said.

"Yes." Ma's dark eyes were looking right at me. "Between Fever and Dr. Toovey's horse."

I could feel my face getting burny.

"There is some money involved. Fifty dollars. Is that right?"

I jerked my head.

"Why did you do it, son?"

I didn't get any answer out.

"You knew I wouldn't approve. You know what I think of that sort of thing. You know it's wrong, don't you?"

I said, yes, I guessed I did.

"I blame you just as much as I do Jake. I'm beginning to think Auction Fever's not good for you."

"Oh yes he is, Ma!"

"Not if he's going to get you mixed up in—in—*gambling*."

I looked down at my boots.

"I honestly think I'd just as soon see you chewing tobacco, son!" Ma turned away. At the kitchen door she swung around again. "There's not to be a race Saturday or any day. Not with Doc Toovey's horse or any horse!"

She gave it to Jake too. She told him to call the race off because it was immoral. That means bad. Jake kicked, but it didn't do him any good.

We found Doc Toovey leaning against his livery stable. His tobacco cud had bulged out the side of his face, so his smile was sort of lopsided. "All set to get beat in that race?" he called.

"Ain't gonna be no race," Jake said.

"Huh!"

"Kid's maw won't let him."

"Well—" Doc smiled down to me— "that's just too bad."

"It is," Jake said.

"'Course, you'd have lost your fifty dollars anyway."

"Huh!"

"This way you don't prolong the agony."

"What do you mean?"

"You called off the race," said Doc. "I didn't. Don't expect to get your money back, do you?"

"I shore as hell do!"

Doc spit, and a little puff of dust came up. "Well, you ain't getting it."

Jake looked at Doc all smily; he looked at the manure fork leaning against the stable wall; he looked back at Doc Toovey again. Real quiet, he said, "You'd look awful funny with that there stickin' outa yer wishbone, Doc."

"Would I?" Doc kept right on smiling.

Later when Jake told Repeat Golightly, Repeat said:

"Ain't much you can do, Jake. I say if he don't want to leave you have the money there ain't much you can—"

Jake slammed out of the barbershop, me right behind.

Ma didn't give an inch. She's sure set against betting—and chewing tobacco.

The next time we were in to Crocus we met Doc Toovey in front of the Royal Bank.

"Got a new critter today, Jake," he said. "Bent Golly sold him to me. Figgered you might like to race the kid's buckskin against him."

Jake pushed on past.

"I'd have to get odds," Doc called after us. "He's a mule!"

The next time was in Snelgrove's bakery, when Doc saw me and Jake through the window, eating ice cream. He came in and he said he had a jack-rabbit he wanted to put up against Fever. A week later he asked Jake if he thought Fever might give a prairie chicken a good run. Jake mumbled something under his breath.

"'Course you might be scared, same as you were the time before, and want to back out of it," Doc said. "If you haven't got the guts—"

"Guts!" Jake yelled. "We got 'em all right! We'll show you! That there race is on again! Same place, same distance, and double the bet, you scroungin', stubble-jumpin', smily-faced son of a hardtail!"

Afterward I said to Jake:

"What'll Ma—"

"We're racin'," Jake said.

"But, Ma won't—"

"Yer maw figgers 'tain't right, but what that there—what that—what he's doin' to us is plum immoral too, an' if I got to take my pick between two kinds of a sinner, I know which kind I'm takin'!"

And that was how come we ended up behind Hig Wheeler's the next Saturday, all set to race Fever and the paint. Jake and me brought Fever in behind the democrat. At the last moment Ma decided to come with us. Jake told her we were getting Fever's hind shoes fixed.

We left Ma at Mrs. Fotheringham's, then we headed for the race.

Half the folks from Crocus were there, and nearly everyone from Rabbit Hill district. Jake and Doc Toovey weren't the only ones betting.

Mr. MacTaggart, that is mayor of Crocus, he was the starter and he sent Johnny Totcoal down to the Western Grain Elevator, where we had to make the turn. That turn had bothered Jake a lot when we were working out Fever. Spider was a cow horse and could turn on a dime. "He's got you there," Jake had said to me, "but I got a little trick to even that up." Then he'd showed me how to grab the horn with both hands and up into the saddle without touching a foot to the stirrup. Doc hadn't kicked when Jake told him the race ought to be from a standing start from beside the horses. I guess he figured a small kid couldn't get up as fast as he could with his longer legs.

"Now, fellas," Mr. McTaggart was saying, "you start from here, each one beside his horse. When I say 'go', into the saddle and down to the stake by the Western Grain Elevator, then around an' back."

Doc nodded and smiled; he had a chew of tobacco the size of a turkey hen's egg. Looking at the paint horse I felt sort of grasshoppery to my stomach; my knees weren't so good either. Doc's Spider was long in the leg, and he looked like he could line out if he wanted to.

"Real pretty." Doc had his hand on Fever's neck, stroking his gold hide and running his fingers through his silver mane. "But that don't make 'em run any faster."

If being ugly made a horse fast, I was thinking that jug-head of Doc's must be a whirlwind!

"How old is he?" Doc was up at Fever's head now.

"Two and a half."

Doc lifted Fever's lip and looked inside.

"Let that horse alone!" Jake had left Mr. MacTaggart and come up.

"Just looking at his teeth," said Doc.

"Only ones he's got," said Jake. "Keep your han's off that horse!"

"Ready, fellas?" Mr. MacTaggart called.

Doc jumped back beside Spider. I put both hands on top of the saddle horn.

"Go!"

I jumped into that saddle like a toad off a hot stove, and I dug my heels into Fever and gave him the leather both sides. He jumped straight into a gallop. Looking back I saw Doc's leg just coming down over the saddle.

Fever had his head up and was fighting like anything.

"Come on, Fever!" I yelled at him. His head came down again and he threw his shoulders into it. Then Spider and Doc were beside us, and

Fever had his head up again. Doc passed us, and Fever wasn't running at all! He was trying, but I'd seen old Baldy do better.

"Please, Fever—*please*!" I leaned down over his neck.

"Come on, boy!" He threw back his head, and I felt something wet on my cheek—foam blowing back.

Spider reached the stake five lengths ahead of us. He made the turn like you snap your fingers. We were halfway down the second lap when the paint went across the finish line. Doc was over by Repeat Golightly when I climbed down from Fever.

Poor Fever's sides were heaving, and he was still tossing his head, and me, I wished I wasn't a human being at all.

"He didn't run, Jake! He didn't run a bit."

"Some horses are like that," said Doc. He watched Jake feeling Fever's front legs. "When they get up against something good they quit."

"This horse ain't no quitter!" Jake had straightened up. "There's something fishy about this—"

"Jake!" That was Ma, with her face all red and her eyes brighter than anything. Jake saw Ma and he swallowed and kind of ducked. She grabbed me by the arm, hard. "You've deliberately disobeyed me, son! You've—Jake!"

Jake had hold of Fever's nose and was sticking his finger in it. "I'm lookin' fer somethin'," Jake said. "Somebody went an'—"

"I forbade you to race that horse and you went ahead, against my wishes! I—it—" Ma had got so tangled in her britching she couldn't talk.

"Mebbe a sponge," Jake said. "Cuts off their wind."

"Ma, Auction Fever he didn't run at—"

"That's enough!" Ma yanked on my arm. "I know now that I can't—" She stared at me, and it was like her face froze over all of a sudden.

"What have you got in your mouth?"

I didn't have anything in my mouth.

She jerked around to Jake. "The most despicable thing I've ever seen!"

"They claim water in their ear—"

"Teaching my son to chew tobacco!"

"Chew tobacco!" Jake's mouth dropped open and his eyes bugged.

Ma stepped forward and she stuck out her finger. It came away from the corner of my mouth, all brown. "There!"

"Now jist a minnit," said Jake. "Take it easy."

"Betting is bad enough—but—chewing—"

"Don't give him that money!" Jake's face was all lit up like he'd eaten a sunset. Repeat looked over at him, with the money he'd been going to give Doc still in his hand.

Jake walked across to Fever. He pulled out Fever's underlip. He looked, then he lifted the lip, grunted, and stuck his crooked finger in. It came out with the biggest jag of chewing tobacco I ever saw.

"Well, now," Jake said as he walked toward Doc, "ain't that interestin'? Horse that's fussy about chewin' tobacco. Wouldn't be Black Stag like you had in your mouth before the race—before you took a look at Fever's teeth?"

"I don't know what you're talking about." Doc was smiling, but it was a pretty sick-looking smile.

"The hell you don't!"

"Doctor Toovey!" That was Ma, and the way she was looking at Doc you could easy tell she used to be a schoolteacher. "Did you or did you not put a—a—cud of chewing tobacco in my—in that horse's mouth?"

I know how Doc felt—like when the whole room gets quiet and Mis Henchbaw is looking right at you and you know you're in for it.

"Makes 'em slobber," said Jake. "Then they swallow it down an' it cuts their wind."

"Will the horse be all right, Jake?" Ma asked.

"Shore," said Jake. "Won't hurt him none. 'Fact he's all right now."

Ma's face sort of tightened. She whirled back to Doc. "You are going to race! You will climb up on that horse and run an honest race against my son! Don't interrupt, Doctor Toovey."

"I ain't—that kid don't weigh more'n a grasshopper—"

"He hasn't put on any weight since you first arranged the race," Ma snapped.

Doc looked at Jake and the other folks around him; folks from our section aren't so fussy about seeing a kid and his horse get diddled.

You should of felt Fever under me that second race! He ran smooth, with his silver mane flying and his neck laid out. He ran like the wind over the edge of the prairie coming to tell everybody they can't live forever—slick as the wind through a field of wheat—slicker than peeled saskatoons. He's the only horse living, Jake says, with three gears in high. He's the only horse can make my throat plug up that way and my chest nearly bust.

Doc Toovey ought to have known better. My Fever is a Gent. and Gents don't chaw!

The Cure
E.G. Perrault

It all began with the stamp album though the Lord alone knows when it really began. Years and years, maybe, with him carrying on like that whenever her back was turned.

"I threw your stamp album in the furnace, Richard." She told him out of a clear blue sky after supper one night.

"You shouldn't have done that, Hilda," he said. That was all he said; didn't even raise his voice according to Mrs. Grindley.

"You can't say I haven't warned you time and time again," she told him. "Snippets of paper all over the living room table, people tracking through all the mud holes in town and then across my carpets just to look at your stamps. Didn't I warn you now?"

"Many times, dear," he said and walked out of the room and up the stairs as though the whole thing was over and done with.

She says he hadn't been right since he retired from the post office. Always mooning around, looking for something to do. His friends weren't exactly the kind you'd want in the house; mailmen mostly, all of them pipe smokers or tobacco chewers according to her. It didn't seem fair somehow for him to be visiting away at all hours without her so he stayed around the place most of the time doing nothing. The Devil finds work for that kind.

But the fact is she lay half an hour in bed that very same night, waiting for him to come in and turn the light off. Twice she called out, "Richard, come to bed this minute." Her voice is strong for a woman. No answer. So she climbed out of bed and went down the hallway to see what he was up to.

He was in the bathroom. She saw him through a crack in the door standing in front of the mirror looking at himself, preening like a peacock, making clown faces at himself, carrying on like a monkey in a cage.

"Richard," she said, "what do you think you're doing?"

"Shaving," he said, and started to take his shaving tools out of the cupboard.

"You never shaved at night in your life," she told him, "and you don't need to start now. Yesterday was your shaving day." He didn't argue with her; just followed along to bed not saying a word.

That's the first she remembers. Other things fit into the picture now. He became interested in the brass and silver in the house. I saw him with my own eyes many a time sitting at the kitchen table polishing the teaspoons with a chamois cloth.

Mrs. Grindley swears she didn't have a notion until the day she found a looking-glass in his trousers pocket. That's nothing, you say? Maybe so, but when another one turns up in his vest, and another in his dressing gown and still another one in the hip pocket of his gardening denims you'd be as surprised as she was. Little oblong mirrors they were, the kind you and I would carry in a purse. She waited until supper time to tell him about it.

"I see you have a new hobby, Richard," she said, throwing the mirrors on the table in front of him.

"I often wonder what I got for a husband. Carrying on like a drugstore dandy! What have you got to be proud of," she said. "Twenty years ago you were no beauty and time hasn't done you any favours." My, it must have been something to hear her give him his comeuppance. She's got a wonderful tongue, that woman!

He just sat there with his head bent over his teacup and let the words tumble down like brimstone on Sodom and Gomorrah. She thought he was taking it to heart until she noticed that he was smiling into his cup. It was plain enough what he was up to and she didn't waste any time pouring his tea back into the pot.

"You ought to be ashamed," she said, and broke the mirrors like soda crackers in front of his eyes. "Primping like a movie star actor! You try that sort of thing again and I'll do more than just talk."

She's a woman of her word; you know that as well as I do. Have you seen the place since she done it over? Richard was the reason for that.

She threw out everything that could make a reflection: that lovely walnut bookcase they used to have; the brass around the fireplace, vases, silverware. It must have broken her heart to do it, but then she had the house redecorated; new drapes and bric-a-brac, wallpaper in every room. When it was all over she gave him the bills and a good talking-to for the trouble he had caused. There was some satisfaction in that.

It seemed she had him beaten. For a week or more she watched his every move. There's no cure like a complete cure, they say. He seemed to come back to normal again and took to sitting in the kitchen in the evenings, staring out into the dark garden, saying never a word. She let him sulk; and then one night coming into the kitchen in a hurry she caught him with his face right up to the window glass, smiling at what he saw there.

I hate to tell it, but she threw the salt cellar across the room and knocked out a pane above his head. He was lucky to get away with a few splinter cuts. You can't blame her altogether. I ask myself what I would have done at a time like that.

She couldn't leave him alone for a minute. It might have looked harmless enough to watch them walking along on a Sunday afternoon, but you should have seen how she steered away from store-fronts and weighing scales, and that sort of thing. Poor woman!

She came to my house one day as close to tears as I've ever seen her.

"He was out in the backyard after the shower today," she said. "I caught him behind the tool house kneeling over a puddle of rain water. What can I do with the man?"

"Get his mind off himself," I told her. "Maybe his friends can help."

"You know how I feel about his friends," she said.

"Hasn't he got any interests—besides stamp collection," I said. "My John spends hours in the basement with his jigsaw."

"Noisy machinery gives me a headache," she said; and I know it's true for a fact; she has a bad time with migraine.

"Take him visiting," I told her. "Let him see how husbands should behave. Bring him over here and we'll have a nice evening together." She agreed to that and they came over one Saturday. I made up sandwiches and things. John and I didn't let on we knew about the trouble.

Richard just sat there saying nothing and Mrs. Grindley had to talk for both of them. I have to hand it to her she carried it off well, until Richard pulled his little surprise.

"Pardon me a moment," he says half-way through the evening; and he was gone before she could open her mouth.

Now what could we say under the circumstances. You can't go following a guest through the house. Mrs. Grindley began to fidget and look over her shoulder in the middle of sentences. John and I suffered along with her; but he was back soon enough smiling and contented.

"I believe I'll have another of your macaroons," he said to me as natural as you please, and from that time on he talked right along with us. You never saw such a change. John thinks he stopped a few minutes in front of the hall mirror. Whatever he did it picked him up like a nip of toddy on a winter's night. Mrs. Grindley didn't take him visiting again. Couldn't run the risk.

Imagine the poor soul with such a responsibility. She couldn't leave the house for more than a few minutes at a time. I phoned her two, three times a day and visited when I could to see how she was making out.

"You can't go on like this," I told her finally. "Someone should be called in, one of those doctor fellows that knows about these things."

"I do believe he's not quite right," she said.

"It's as plain as can be," I said. "What normal healthy man would carry on like that? You talk to a mind doctor about him."

"I believe I will," she said.

That doctor shouldn't be allowed to practise. He started to blame the whole thing on her.

"You don't give him a chance," he told her. "You don't take any interest in what he does or what he wants to do. I really believe you're not in love with the man."

"Nonsense!" she shot right back at him. "I married him, didn't I? He's had the best years of my life."

"Why didn't you have a family?" he asks her, although the question had nothing to do with Richard.

"On a mailman's wages I could have a dozen children, I suppose," she said.

Oh, he told her a good deal more; and the harder she tried to make him see reason the more confused he got. He had it figured that Richard had no friends, or interests, or recognition. All he had left was himself— which is little enough at that. When Mrs. Grindley explained that Richard was probably trying a new way to aggravate her he wouldn't hear of it. "You give that man a little love," he said, "and he'll be well in no time."

He was wrong as wrong can be, she knew it, but she had to clutch at straws. It was terrible the way she tried. I was over there many a time and saw her, fetching his slippers, pouring him a second cup of tea, and smiling at him when there was no need at all to be nice.

The strain showed on her face but she knew her duty and she did it. As for him, I'm sure he didn't understand what was going on. He let her know he was suspicious.

"What do you want from me?" he'd say.

"Nothing, darling, just for you to be happy," she'd say.

"You're working too hard at it," he told her. "I'd rather have you the other way." Oh he said mean, cruel things; flew into rages which was something he'd never done before. But Mrs. Grindley stuck to her guns. The worse he got the nicer she became.

"I'm knitting Richard a pair of socks," she'd say, and smile across at him slumped in the window seat. "Hold your foot up 'til I see how this is going to be."

"You know my size," he'd say.

"Green's his favourite colour," she'd say, letting on she hadn't heard him.

"Green's your favourite colour," he'd snap. "Talk about something else."

I wonder now that she didn't leave him; but then neither of them have any place to go. The house is all they've got and they're not spring chickens. Mrs. Grindley isn't the kind to run away at any rate. She tried everything she knew to win him over; took to wearing bright flouncy dresses instead of the good practical greys and purples that she's partial to; had her hair curled up a new way and wore a touch of colour in her cheeks. She'd walk up to him right in front of me and peck him on his forehead.

"It's Yorkshire pudding for lunch, Richard," she'd say. If she got a growl out of him she was lucky. He just couldn't see what she was up to.

And then overnight everything changed. You've seen them yourself. Remember last week at the bazaar—embracing like newlyweds in front of the fish pond with half the town milling around them? That happened overnight.

"It's a miracle," she said to me over the phone that morning. "He's like a schoolboy with his first lover. Last evening I tried to kiss him goodnight—he started to push me away and then such a change came over him I couldn't believe it. He pulled me back and squeezed me 'til I fairly begged for breath."

Oh I'll tell you she was excited. It's been the same ever since with him playing lovey-dovey every hour of the day. I don't see how she puts up with it really—him stepping out of closets when she least expects it to plant kisses on her that would put Rudolph Valentino to shame. He gives no thought to who might be watching.

"Let me look at you," he says, and he gazes at her with such a tender expression that it sends the shivers up my spine. It's not fitting in a man his age.

"It's too good to be true!" she tells me. "I'll put up with any amount of his nonsense so long as he forgets about his looking-glasses."

Too good to be true indeed! I see through his game plain enough, and I haven't the heart to tell her. I wouldn't breathe a word of it to you either except I know you can be trusted to keep it to yourself.

Watch how he gazes at her. Watch how he looks deep into those big, shiny eyes of hers. What will happen in a year or two when old age dulls them? What will he do then? Love! He loves what he sees in her eyes, and he sees himself there, twice over. It's a sin and a shame the way that man has treated her.

The Babysitter

Brenda Riches

FRIDAY

"Eat your egg," Megan says.

Seth says no. Why should he eat his egg when he can see his mom through the window, driving the truck out the yard? One red light winks at him. The dust behind is swallowing it up like Old Joe in the whale.

"I want my mom," he whines. His mouth is a skeeter. He hopes Mad Megan won't squish it dead. Skeeters bleed a lot if they're squished after their supper.

"Well, tough shit. She's not here."

Seth looks at the yellow yolk and kills it with his fork. Now the egg is bleeding yellow blood all over the plate and Seth is The King. He feels better. Kings feel good all the time. They don't have to do anything they don't want to do. And now that his mom's not here, Seth is The King who stabs eggs to death.

Rude Megan snatches up the plate, slaps Seth across the head, and scrapes his supper into the garbage.

"You're going to bed," she yells. Her yell feels like the barbed wire fence that ripped his shirt and made his mom so mad.

"No."

Mean Megan is an octopus and all her arms are slimy around him. Up the dim skinny staircase she carries him. King Seth is put to bed.

Seth is left alone with the spiders the sun has dumped into the room the way Seth dumps his toys in his closet when his mom yells at him to clean up his filthy mess. Slowly the spiders creep across the chair, the table, the bed, creep and crawl till they're on Seth's face. He can't go to sleep now. If he does, the shadows will kill him dead. When the sun has gone and left one huge shadow in the room, Seth decides to go and see what Megan's doing.

The yard is a coffin with a hole in the lid for the moon to get in. Seth walks into it down the stone steps that always trip him because they're breaking to bits, past the bad cat that goes pee on the bedcover. Megan is somewhere, singing a song about the moon. Seth follows Megan's song past the spooky granaries that shine like cans with the labels pulled off, and thinks of the smacks his mom gives him when she can't tell what's in the cans any more. The chicken coop comes and goes in the dark of the moon that hides then peeks go seek behind the clouds. The chickens in the dark coop make noises like Seth's mom did after Seth's dad became a dead person who couldn't hug Seth any more.

Megan comes out of the coop, holding a chicken in her arms. The moon shining on the chicken makes it look like a ghost. The moon shining on the long knife in Megan's hand makes it look like lightning. Megan's face is sad like the moon's face. She holds the chicken against her cheek, and it squawks and wiggles.

"I hope it pecks your eyes out," he says. She drops it. "You get back to bed," she yells, as the chicken flaps away in the dark. White feather ghost. Seth does as he's told, but only because he wants to.

The spider is waiting for him. If he lies ever so still on the bed, it won't get him. Maybe Megan will come and get in the bed with him, and when she opens the door with a big bang the spider will run away because Megan's bigger than the spider. But waiting for Megan gives him a crick in the neck. He has to be brave. He has to get up and cross the wide brown carpet road.

Seth has made it to the bedroom door and is walking across the hall to his mom's room because the door is open and he can see Megan lying on his mom's bed.

Should he wake her?

Seth is hungry, but he's afraid to make a sandwich because he might chop his fingers off with the long knife and there's no apples left and he can't get himself cookies because he has to show Megan how many he's taking and milk is BORING and if he wakes Megan up she'll do something to him he won't like, because she's bigger than he is. Seth doesn't know what's worse—a hungry hole inside him or Crazy Big Megan outside him.

He sits cross-legged on the floor and hold his hands palms up. The yellow ball is his hunger. Witch Megan is the red ball. For hours and hours he juggles them, hoping he'll drop one and it'll break and he'll be left with the other one to tell him what to do. But all the balls do is get bigger and in the end he drops them both and they're two splatted messes on his mom's clean floor.

Megan's green eyes are watching him. "Go to bed," she cackles. Witches make him tired. He thinks he'll go to bed.

SATURDAY

Seth buries his face in the bowl of his melon and sucks. Then bites. If he breathes it'll go up his nose and choke him. He feels melon on his eyelids. He eats and eats until he can't reach any more. He sees the kitchen through juicy eyelashes. He hears the word *pig*, and tells Megan he isn't, but secretly that's what he wants to be now that his mom's not here to tell him. He doesn't give a care what *Megan* says. Seth is King Pig and can do anything he wants to do.

Nasty Megan's washcloth makes his face sore. It's too hot and it burns his skin. Sometimes Pigkings cry.

Megan doesn't care. She won't feel sorry for poor Seth. She just turns the radio up louder and goes and sits in his mom's rocker like an old witch granny, and listens to that dumb music. She's picking at her chin. If she keeps doing that, her face will get sick and then her face will die like Snow White. Seth decides he won't eat an apple, you never know what's in them.

The dumb cat likes Megan's lap, especially when she's on the rocker rocking. She keeps on rocking to that dumb old music. She must be dizzy now. Dizzy Old Witch Granny Megan. She makes him feel tired. He'd better go take a nap.

But first Seth sneaks to the fridge and opens the door. The milk carton is a soldier on guard. There's half a can of pear-halves-in-syrup. He could have *one* half. She'd never miss *one* half. Quick as a thief, Seth slurps up two halves, takes the little glass jug of cream and goes to the door. Megan doesn't see; she's got her eyes closed. Perhaps she's dead. The cat leaves Megan's lap and follows Seth. Fat bitch Lucy is a pile of yellow turds on the front steps. Who will clean her up? Not Seth.

This is Seth's other bed high up on top of the straw bales near the high window where the sun pours in like barfwater only golden and dusty and

not wet. Here is where the wind can't get him and the rain only in little
bits and the sun is hot but can't burn his skin off, and the cat loves him
even though its claws scratch him.

There's straw up his nose and claws in his neck and fur in his mouth
and purring in his ears. The cat's tongue feels good, licking the cream
off his mouth. Seth doesn't want the licking to stop, but the cream's all
cleaned away and the cat's running off down the bales and out the door.
Seth hopes the cat isn't going to tell Megan he took the cream from the
fridge.

It's lonely in the sunshine. He'd better take his nap.

Seth wakes up from a dream about fried spider sandwiches eating him
and remembers he's Seth and his sandwiches are always made from
peanut butter and ketchup, and *he* eats *them*. The hole in his stomach has
grown so big there'll be no Seth left in a minute and then Mean Megan
will be sorry. He slides down the staircase of bales. Bump, bump goes his
bum, too fast. CRACK at the bottom of the bales.

When he hobbles out of the barn, Lucy waddles up to him like a fat
yellow slop, dragging the calf's head she's been chewing on for years, the
calf Seth fed from a bottle once upon a time, drops it on his toes, OWCH
and bangs his leg with her tail. She's grinning with all her teeth. *She* can
grin okay. She's had *her* lunch.

Lucy keeps poking his legs with her nose all the way across the yard,
which is hot and dusty and quiet, all the way up the steps, poke poke
through the door into the kitchen where Megan should be standing at
the counter making Seth a sandwich, but she isn't. The only thing in the
kitchen is a big buzzing fly trying to get out through the glass. And she
isn't in the barfroom where Seth pees and splashes the rim, who gives a
care, his mom's not there to yell at him to wipe it off. She's not in his
mom's room where the curtains are all closed and it's dark like the inside
of the pocket where Seth keeps his dead moths, squashed snails and alive
toads. Seth sits down on the bed. Does he dare go down and take some
cookies from the tin? Criminy! He's left the cream jug in the straw!

Megan is lying in the grass without her clothes on, getting red like
raspberries in the sun. That skeeter must like Megan's raspberry skin a
lot. Should he squish it dead? Megan would get mad if he woke her up,
he'd better leave her be. She looks funny with that skeeter and two flies

crawling over her. Now they're on her bum. If Seth was a bug, he'd crawl up to the top of Megan's bum and slide all the way down. If Seth was a bug on Megan's bum, he'd be Bug King of the Castle, and the skeeter would be the Dirty Rascal.

Seth the Bug King squats in the long grass that blows like Megan's hair around him, and plans the death of skeeters, soap, washcloths and barfs. Bug Kings can do anything they want, so Seth goes to the puddle at the back of the house, the one that never dries up, where Seth must never play or he'll get a whack he won't forget in a hurry. When he's cooled himself off in the puddle, he makes a tower cake. For the five candles he will chop off the fingers of Megan's hand, the one that holds the washcloth, the hand that's OW pulling him up by his hair.

"You filthy little bugger. Get on up to the bathroom." Megan's voice hangs over him like the hawks that never go away till the summer and the rabbits do.

"Get in that tub." Megan's voice sounds like his mom's door banging shut. "And if I catch you in the mud again, I'll make you really sorry. What's your mom going to say when I tell her, eh?"

Under the water that's pouring from the mug Megan's holding, Seth sits, head bowed, nose pinched between his filthy finger and his filthy thumb, snatching for air when he has to. He longs for the mug to be put back on the edge of the barf where it belongs. It doesn't belong in Megan's nasty hand. In Megan's hand it pours water to drown him.

Seth looks at the water growing grubby, feels Megan's claws on his shoulder keeping him still so she can do her nasty work. At last she pulls the plug out and Seth's dirt is sucked down into the black hole.

"Now get yourself dried off, put on clean clothes, and go play somewhere clean, do you hear?"

Seth is hanging by his knees from the chicken roost and looking at the dumb old chickens who sing worse than Megan does, and peck around in their own shit all day. "Shit. Shit. Shit." Seth spits the words out like cherry pits and watches them fly through the air.

The floor is the shitty ceiling and the chickens are stuck to it, hanging there, thinking they're the right way up, dumb clucks. Any minute now those dumb birds will crash on their stupid heads kersplat and their blood will paint the white floor red.

Through the stink of chicken shit and the pain at the back of his knees, Seth is the only one in the world who is the right way up. Any minute now the sky will fall and one of those dumb chickens will come and tell King Seth all about it.

Seth doesn't feel like talking with those dummies. He's going out to see what Megan's doing.

Seth the Worm King wriggles between cornstalks so quietly Megan will never find out he's here. The wind tugs at the leaves. They're like those flags people wave when the King rides by in his new clothes. But worms don't ride. Worms slide. Megan looks as sore as a bear with no honey pot. She's tearing the face of a sunflower to bits. Seth knows how she feels. Sometimes he'd like to smash the sun and watch it bleed all over the sky, then tell his mom to wipe up the mess, it's *gusting*. Megan says a word Seth gets slapped for. Seth doesn't know what's wrong with that word. His mom said it when she saw the clean shirt he'd worn when he ripped his arm on the barbed wire fence. But Seth's a worm now, and worms don't bleed. Neither do kings.

Megan's lying under a tree now. The skeeter must have bitten her between her legs, because that's where she's scratching herself. It must hurt—tears are making her face all shiny. She's closed her eyes. Good. Now Seth can go into the house and take a few raisins out of the jar, and a spoonful of brown sugar. Seth's going to have a feast.

Seth at the bedroom window chews on raisins and brown sugar and watches the big black clouds growing far away but getting closer. The longer he stands looking, the more the world turns into a Nowhere Land where the black dragon will come any minute, breathing a long flame. Who will put it out? Soon Seth's face is hot with tears. If he cries long enough, that will put the dragon out, won't it?

Megan's still outside, and Seth is King of the Lonely Castle with only Lucy asleep to guard him and the whole wide yard to cross if he wants to hide in the chicken coop. Who will rescue the cat if the dragon attacks? When will Megan come in? Isn't it supper time?

The sky is getting blacker. Soon it will rain frogs and warty toads. If Seth find a warty toad today, he'll keep it forever because his mom's not here to tell him to get rid of the gusting thing or she'll get rid of it for him, and he won't like *that*.

That's rain smacking the window, but the window doesn't turn red like Seth when *he* gets smacked. The rain drops into the yard, more and more rain till the weeds lie down. The rain is making so much noise, Seth opens the window and tells it to piss off. Then he lies down and hopes he can sleep till supper time.

Eggs again, slimy old eggs. But he's hungry, so he mashes it into a sandwich and kills it with ketchup and eats it like the good boy he doesn't want to be, while Megan sits in that dumb old rocker drinking his mom's beer and listening to that dumb old radio. Rock, rock, up and down, it makes him want to throw up.

The door's bangshut and the Witch has turned the light off. She's left Seth with the Spider again. If he hides under the blanket, he won't be able to breathe. If he just shuts his eyes, that won't keep the spider from coming up close. He lies in the dark, closing and opening his eyes and waiting for the first skinny leg to touch his mouth.

Seth can't do as he's told. Who gives a care. He's getting out of bed, but he's only going to look out the window.

Megan will catch her death. She's out there bare naked, dancing in the pouring rain. If she doesn't catch her death of cold, lightning will strike her the way it struck his dad and shrivelled him up, and then who will make Seth his breakfast? He wants to yell at her from the window, but if she finds out he's not in bed, she'll throw a nasty spell and turn him into a toad, and his mom will get rid of him when she gets back, and he won't like *that*.

Maybe if Seth's a very good boy and says his prayers now I lay me down to sleep and goes back to bed and falls asleep and does everything that Megan tells him to and tells her about everything he stole and promises to put it all back . . . Criminy! He'd have to throw *up* to do that . . . Maybe he won't be a toad when his mom comes back with the present for Seth, if he's been good.

Oh cripes! Here comes his mom's truck with yellow-moon lights in the rain. Naughty Megan's going to get caught. But the truck comes all the way into the yard and Megan's not there any more. She must have thrown a spell on herself and disappeared. He'd better get back into bed quick before his mom gets in.

Seth lies in the dark and wonders what to tell his Mom when she asks him where Megan is.

Troller

Kevin Roberts

The sea burst against the bow where Bill lay on the starboard bunk, and the boat timbers shivered and trembled the full thirty-six-foot length of the *Pacific Maid*. Mel, the skipper, had been sick for three days now and so had his son, Bert, and the fishboat was barely under control. Bill lay there in his floater jacket, the rubber tailpiece drawn up between his thighs and hooked to the front. Bert had made a number of cracks about that, but as soon as the wind hit the boat, when they passed the moaning fog horn of Tofino harbour, Bill'd put the jacket on and left it on. This was his first trip as a deck-hand on the outside and the sheer size of the Pacific disturbed him deeply. Two bad seasons on the inside coast, no sockeye run, no pinks worth a damn, and his small fishboat had been claimed by the Royal Bank. He'd had no choice but to find a job, start again at the bottom, as a deck-hand on a large Pacific troller. And he was lucky to get on with Mel, he knew. But he didn't want to be here.

He had been stunned on that first day out when Mel had confessed that he was always seasick for the first couple of days, and sometimes for longer in bad weather. It seemed crazy, even dangerous, to put yourself into a job where you suffered so much, where control over your body was in such jeopardy. But, Mel had added, seasickness was a lot more common than most fishermen admitted. Greed and pride kept them at it; that, and the strange attraction the sea had for some men. That was the hardest to believe.

Above him, outside in the dark, the wind thrummed on the wires of the poles like a mad guitarist. Beside him on the other bunk, Bert moaned, and above and behind him, Mel lay suffering in the wheelhouse bunk. The gale rose and fell in wild bursts and he was glad he could not see the swells, topped with flying white lace, that rolled ominously and endlessly from the heart of the dark Pacific.

Four days ago, they'd smashed and rolled their way fifty miles out from Tofino, the weather channel voice predicting falling winds and sea. They'd fished that first morning, their thighs braced hard against the sides of the fish-well in the stern, slapping the gurdies in on only half the lines because the yawing, pitching boat could not be held straight, even on the Wagner autopilot. It was a monstrously unstable world, where the sky swung like a mad chandelier, and at the bottom of a swell, the boat seemed totally enveloped in the seething grey sea. He had not realized how totally enveloped in the pitching bowl of the Pacific they were, until they encountered another fish boat, the *Ocean Rambler*, about the same size, and its toy-like struggle to lift up from the weight of the sea, smashing endlessly on its bow, caused him to fear that this other frail cockle of wood, a quarter of a mile away, could not, would not rise this time, or the next, out of the green mass that rolled again and again and again, pushing the whole boat down and down, until, when both boats were on the bottom of the swell, the *Ocean Rambler* would disappear completely from sight. It was then, too, that he realized that the *Pacific Maid*, his own boat, must also look a frail shell waiting for one great wave to take it under.

They had caught fish that first day, coho and a few medium springs, but the big fish broke the lines or ran amok with ease about the barely controllable boat. He had brought one big spring alongside, thirty pounds, maybe more, and swung the gaff down and into its head, but, instantly, the boat yawed and the gaff and fish pulled beyond his strength and he let go before he too was tipped into the maelstrom. The skipper's curses were torn from his lips by the wind as he came aft in a running crouch. He shouldered Bill aside, and with huge hands, criss-crossed with the white scars from nylon fish-line, manhandled the flapping spring with the gaff still in its head into the checkers, and expertly killed it with a single blow behind the head.

Though he could not hear Bert's jibes from the other side of the boat, he was embarrassed, but not for long. The skipper, with a sudden lurch, pushed by him again, green-faced, and vomited into the spume. Bert soon followed his father and both of them leaned over the side and vomited time and time again.

It was then that he'd taken charge, scuttled to the wheelhouse to adjust the Wagner, crouched and run back to run the lines, pulled the salmon,

ran out the lines again, cleaned the fish and stocked them in the checkers.
But the wind and sea grew and the main line and the deep line of the
starboard side crossed and tangled and for half an hour he struggled to
bring both of them in and clear the gear. The skipper watched, red-eyed,
and finally told him to pull all the lines in and lash them down.

Incredibly, though the skipper stopped regularly to retch overboard,
Mel worked with him until all the gear was on board and the lines and
lead cannonballs lashed down with cutty hunk. Together they pulled the
prostrate Bert into the wheelhouse and down into the bunk. Bill went out
again to the stern, staggered back with armful after armful of salmon,
crawled deep down into the hold of the boat, stuffed handfuls of ice into
the cleaned bellies of the fish and stacked them into the waiting ice.

"Sea-anchor, Bill," mumbled Mel, pointing to the bow. "I'll run the
boat up, you drop it." Bill looked through the window. The weighted
parachute with the red Scotsman buoy was lashed to the foredeck. It had
to be eased overboard so it sank and opened deep beneath the sea. A long
rope, coiled now on the bow, then ran from the capstan on the bow down
to the chute flowering under the sea. With this down, the boat rode easily,
moving with the tide a mile or so in and out, on the ballooned tension of
the underwater anchor. But it was dangerous to put out in a high wind.
If the chute snapped open in the gale the rope would whip out like a snake
striking. If the boat was not held tight against the smashing swell, the rope
jerked about and the feet and body of the man, already threatened by the
great wash of water pounding against it, could be washed overboard
instantly. The very idea of walking out there, out to where the grey sea
bounded onto the bow, was almost too much for him, except for the
haggard look of the skipper, white-faced and red-eyed. He knew then that
he had to do it, not just for them on the boat, but for himself, because
the sea was building relentlessly and it was doubtful if they could turn and
run safely before it back to Tofino. The danger of broaching, or of the
stern going under in the massive rolling seas was such that he looked an
instant at Mel, and saw in his watering eyes that there was only one choice.

And he had shuffled grimly out along the deck, gripping the handrail
tightly with both hands, past the wheelhouse and out onto the bow. There,
the first burst of swell knocked him soaking and breathless to his knees.
Worse, the suck of the sea off the deck rushed about him and loosened
his footing. In the second or two before the next wave burst upon him,
he worked with one hand on the lashed parachute. He timed his work so

that in the brief dip of the bow, before the next swell deluged him, the parachute and its chain and rope were freed. He hooked one foot about a stanchion, braced the other, and in the same two-second dip, let the parachute and rope slip through his left hand over the side. Despite his effort the rope kicked and jumped and burnt his wrist and hand.

It was not classic seamanship. There were many men of the West Coast fishing fleet for whom this act was daily bread, but for him, the final "tung" of the rope tight against the capstan, the red Scotsman floating before the boat now easing back, was a gong of triumph. He sat, hanging onto the rail, his knees braced against the stanchion, totally exhausted, wet through, and not at all jubilant. His hands were scored and torn by the rope. He thought of the poached salmon steaks he'd seen once for an exorbitant price, served in silver chafers in a restaurant on Sloane Square in London, and the enormity of the callous economics of it made him burst out with laughter. Eventually, he crawled back on his knees, gripping the rail, and got into the wheelhouse.

He told himself through clenched teeth that this was it, that never again would he risk the plunge and certain death in that cold and bitter sea. It was over. He'd get a shore job, pumping gas, unloading fish, anything to avoid this pulse and roll and madness of the sea.

The skipper sat with his head down on the wheel, and Bill crawled past him and down into the bunk next to Bert. The boat now rode more easily, tossing like a massive child whose fever has broken and, even though the sea still smashed and burst against the hull, he fell quickly asleep. He dreamed he was in a strange moving bed with a beautiful green woman who undulated under and away from him every time he tried to possess her.

A rumbling sound growing nearer brought him to wakefulness. He got up unsteadily, his limbs rigid with cold, and stepped up into the wheelhouse. Mel lay asleep on the wheelhouse couch, his white face garish every second or two from the flash of the strobe light on the mast top. The sea was unabated. Green frills ran constantly up and down the wheelhouse window, obscuring the bow light. On the port bow half a mile and closing, at the tops of the massive swells, he could see a row of lights in the whirling darkness. He fervently hoped the radar operator on the freighter out there was awake and that the many blips of the fishing fleet tossing at anchor were clear in the stormy night. The freighter passed quickly, unperturbed it seemed by the muscular walls of water in which it moved.

He wished then, as many fishermen have, for a boat so big the sea could not threaten it. He thought, too, of the wreaths rotting on the Anglican Church wharf at Bamfield, and the inscription, "O lord your sea is so strong, and our boat is so frail."

He looked about him at the unutterable darkness, the wild wind and crashing sea, and felt a great loneliness, until, in the distance, the quick flash of a tiny strobe appeared, another fishboat, anchored too in this hissing vortex, and another flash, and another, and suddenly all about, at the top of the swells, the flick, flick, sometimes miles away, sometimes closer, magical in the storm. Bill felt strangely and utterly comforted by the pattern their lights made, flickering, miles away from home and warmth and safety. Again he looked at his hands, throbbing now with the red lines of the chafe marks. He knew it was a mark, along with the lights, of a community; the boats of the West Coast fishing fleet, held by the flowers of their sea anchors, a pattern of faith one with the other in this arduous endeavour upon the encircling sea.

I. Paintings
II. Water-colours
III. Hand-Painted Flowers, All You Can Carry, 25¢

Leon Rooke

I told the woman I wanted that bunch down near the pine grove by the rippling stream.

Where the cow is? she asked.

I told her yep, that was the spot.

She said I'd have to wait until the milking was done.

The cow mooed a time or two as we waited. It was all very peaceful.

How much if you throw in the maiden? I asked.

Without the cow? she asked, or *with*?

Both would be nice, I said.

But it turned out a Not For Sale sign had already gone up on the girl. Too bad. It was sweet enough with her out of the picture, but not quite the same.

I took my cut bunch of flowers and plodded on behind the cow over to the next field. I wanted a horse too, if I could get one cheap.

Any horses? I asked.

Not today, they said.

Strawberries?

Not the season, I was told.

At home, I threw out the old bunch and put the new crop in a vase by the picture window so the wife might marvel at them when she came in from her hard day's grind.

I staked the cow out front where the grass was still doing pretty well.

It was touch-and-go, whether we'd be able to do the milking ourselves. It would be rough without a shed or stall.

Oh, hand-painted! the wife said when she came in.

I propped her up in the easy chair and put up her feet. She looked a trifle wind-blown.

Hard day? I asked.

So-so, she said.

I mixed up a gin and tonic, nice as I knew how, and lugged that in.

A touch flat, she said—but the lemon wedge has a nice effect.

I pointed out the cow, which was tranquilly grazing.

Sweet, she said. Very sweet. What a lovely idea.

I put on the stereo for her.

That needle needs re-doing, she observed. The tip needs re-touching, I mean.

It will have to wait until tomorrow, I told her.

She gave me a sorrowful look, though one without any dire reproach in it. She pecked me a benign one on the cheek. A little wet. I wiped it off before it could do any damage.

The flowers were a good thought, she said. I appreciate the flowers.

Well, you know how it is, I said. What I meant was that one did the best one could—though I didn't really have to tell her that. It was what she was always telling me.

She was snoozing away in the chair as I tip-toed off to bed. I was beginning to flake a little myself. Needed a good touch-up job from an expert.

We all do, I guess. The dampness, the mildew, the *rot*—it gets into the system somehow.

Not much to be done about it, however.

I thought about the cow. Wondered if I hadn't made a mistake on that. Without the maiden to milk her, there didn't seem to be much *point* in having a cow. Go back tomorrow, I thought. Offer a good price for the maiden, the stream, and the whole damned field.

Of course, I could go the other way: find a nice seascape somewhere. Hang that up.

Well, sleep on it, I thought.

The wife slipped into bed about two in the morning. That's approximate. The paint job on the hour hand wasn't holding up very well. The undercoating was beginning to show through on the entire clock face, and a big crack was developing down in the six o'clock area.

Shoddy goods, I thought. Shoddy artisanship.

Still, we'd been around a bit. Undated, unsigned, but somewhere in the nineteenth century was my guess. It was hard to remember. I just wished the painter had been more careful. I wished he'd given me more chin, and made the bed less rumpled.

Sorry, baby, she said. Sorry I waked you.

She whispered something else, which I couldn't hear, and settled down far away on her side of the bed. I waited for her to roll into me and embrace me. I waited for her warmth, but she remained where she was and I thought all this very strange.

What's wrong? I said.

She stayed very quiet and did not move. I could feel her holding herself in place, could hear her swallow, irregular breathing, and I caught the sweep of one arm as she brought it up to cover her face. She started shivering.

I am so sorry, she said. I am so sorry. She said that over and over.

Tell me what's wrong, I said.

No, she said, please don't touch me, please don't, please don't even think about touching me. She went on like this for some seconds, her voice rising, growing in alarm, and I thought to myself well I have done something to upset her, I must have said or done something unforgivable, and I lay there with my eyes open wide, trying to think what it might be.

I am so sorry, she said. So very very sorry.

I reached for her hand, out of that hurting need we have for warmth and reassurance, and it was then that I found her hand had gone all wet and muddy and smeary.

Don't! she said, oh please don't, I don't want you to hurt yourself!

Her voice was wan and low and she had a catch in her voice and a note of forlorn panic. I lifted my hand away quickly from her wetness, though not quickly enough for I knew the damage already had been done. The tips of my fingers were moist and cold, and the pain, bad enough but not yet severe, was slowly seeping up my arm.

My drink spilled, she said. She snapped that out so I would know.

Christ, I thought. Oh Jesus Christ. God help us.

I shifted quickly away to the far side of the bed, my side, away from her, far as I could get, for I was frightened now and all I could think was that I must get away from her, I must not let her wetness touch me any more than it had.

Yes, she said shivering, do that, stay there, you must try and save yourself, oh darling I am so sorry.

We lay in the darkness, on our backs, separated by all that distance, yet I could still feel her warmth and her tremors and I knew there was nothing I could do to save her.

Her wonderful scent was already going and her weight on the bed was already decreasing.

I slithered up high on the sheets, keeping my body away from her, and ran my good hand through her hair and down around her warm neck and brought my face up against hers.

I know it hurts, I said, you're being so brave.

Do you hurt much? she said. I am so terribly, terribly sorry. I was dozing in the chair and opened my eyes and saw the dark shape of the cow out on the lawn and for an instant I didn't know what it was and it scared me. I hope I haven't hurt you. I've always loved you and the life we had in here. My own wounds aren't so bad now. I don't feel much of anything any more. I know the water has gone all through me and how frightful I must look to you. Oh please forgive me, it hurts and I'm afraid I can't think straight.

I couldn't look at her. I looked down at my own hand and saw that the stain had spread. It had spread up to my elbow and in a small puddle where my arm lay, but it seemed to have stopped there. I couldn't look at her. I knew her agony must be very great and I marvelled a little that she was being so brave for I knew that in such circumstances I would be weak and angry and able to think only of myself.

Water damage, I thought, that's the hardest part to come to terms with. The fear that's over you like a curse. Every day you think you've reconciled yourself to it and come to terms with how susceptible you are, and unprotected you are, and then something else happens. But you never think you will do it to yourself.

Oil stands up best, I thought. Oh holy Christ why couldn't we have been done in oil.

You get confident, you get to thinking what a good life you have, so you go out and buy yourself flowers and a goddamn cow.

I wish I could kiss you, she moaned. I wish I could.

My good hand was already behind her neck and I wanted to bring my head down on her breasts and put my hand there too. I wanted to close my eyes and stroke her all over and lose myself in the last sweetness I'd ever know.

I will too, I thought. I'll do it.

Although I tried, I couldn't, not all over, so I stroked my hand through her hair and rolled my head over till my lips gently touched hers.

She sobbed and broke away.

It's too much, she said. I'm going to cry. I am, I know I am.

Don't, I said. Don't. If you do that will be the end of you.

The tears burst and I spun above her, wrenching inside, gripping the sheet and wiping it furiously about her eyes.

I can't stop it! she said. It's no use. It burns so much but I can't stop it, it's so sad but I've got to cry!

She kept on crying.

Soon there was just a smear of muddled colour on the pillow where her face had been, and then the pillow was washing away.

The moisture spread, reaching out and touching me, filling the bed until at last it and I collapsed on the floor.

Yet the stain continued widening.

I had the curious feeling that people were already coming in, that someone already was disassembling our frame, pressing us flat, saying, Well here's one we can throw out. You can see how the house, the cow, etc. have all bled together. You can't recognize the woman any more, or see that this once was a bed and . . . well it's all a big puddle except those flowers. Flowers are a dime a dozen but these are pretty good, we could snip out the flowers, I guess, give them their own small frame. Might fetch a dollar or two, what do you say?

The scissors took off my arm and leg, they got my wife straight down the middle. Then where the flowers were there was only a big rectangular hole.

"Too bad," they said, "though it happens sometimes. Water-colours, you know . . ."

The Painted Door

Sinclair Ross

Straight across the hills it was five miles from John's farm to his father's. But in winter, with the roads impassable, a team had to make a wide detour and skirt the hills, so that from five the distance was more than trebled to seventeen.

"I think I'll walk," John said at breakfast to his wife. "The drifts in the hills wouldn't hold a horse, but they'll carry me all right. If I leave early I can spend a few hours helping him with his chores, and still be back by suppertime."

Moodily she went to the window, and thawing a clear place in the frost with her breath, stood looking across the snowswept farmyard to the huddle of stables and sheds. "There was a double wheel around the moon last night," she countered presently. "You said yourself we could expect a storm. It isn't right to leave me here alone. Surely I'm as important as your father."

He glanced up uneasily, then drinking off his coffee tried to reassure her. "But there's nothing to be afraid of—even if it does start to storm. You won't need to go near the stable. Everything's fed and watered now to last till night. I'll be back at the latest by seven or eight."

She went on blowing against the frosted pane, carefully elongating the clear place until it was oval-shaped and symmetrical. He watched her a moment or two longer, then more insistently repeated, "I say you won't need to go near the stable. Everything's fed and watered, and I'll see that there's plenty of wood in. That will be all right, won't it?"

"Yes—of course—I heard you—" It was a curiously cold voice now, as if the words were chilled by their contact with the frosted pane.

"Plenty to eat—plenty of wood to keep me warm—what more could a woman ask for?"

"But he's an old man—living there all alone. What is it, Ann? You're not like yourself this morning."

She shook her head without turning. "Pay no attention to me. Seven years a farmer's wife—it's time I was used to staying alone."

Slowly the clear place on the glass enlarged: oval, then round, then oval again. The sun was risen above the frost mists now, so keen and hard a glitter on the snow that instead of warmth its rays seemed shedding cold. One of the two-year-old colts that had cantered away when John turned the horses out for water stood covered with rime at the stable door again, head down and body hunched, each breath a little plume of steam against the frosty air. She shivered, but did not turn. In the clear, bitter light the long white miles of prairie landscape seemed a region strangely alien to life. Even the distant farmsteads she could see served only to intensify a sense of isolation. Scattered across the face of so vast and bleak a wilderness it was difficult to conceive them as a testimony of human hardihood and endurace. Rather they seemed futile, lost. Rather they seemed to cower before the implacability of snow-swept earth and clear pale sun-chilled sky.

And when at last she turned from the window there was a brooding stillness in her face as if she had recognized this mastery of snow and cold. It troubled John. "If you're really afraid," he yielded, "I won't go today. Lately it's been so cold, that's all. I just wanted to make sure he's all right in case we do have a storm."

"I know—I'm not really afraid." She was putting in a fire now, and he could no longer see her face. "Pay no attention to me. It's ten miles there and back, so you'd better get started."

"You ought to know by now I wouldn't stay away," he tried to brighten her. "No matter how it stormed. Twice a week before we were married I never missed—and there were bad blizzards that winter too."

He was a slow, unambitious man, content with his farm and cattle, naïvely proud of Ann. He had been bewildered by it once, her caring for a dull-witted fellow like him: then assured at last of her affection he had relaxed against it gratefully, unsuspecting it might ever be less constant than his own. Even now, listening to the restless brooding in her voice, he felt only a quick, unformulated kind of pride that after seven years his absence for a day should still concern her. While she, his trust and earnestness controlling her again:

"I know. It's just that sometimes when you're away I get lonely . . . There's a long cold tramp in front of you. You'll let me fix a scarf around your face."

He nodded. "And on my way I'll drop in at Steven's place. Maybe he'll come over tonight for a game of cards. You haven't seen anybody but me for the last two weeks."

She glanced up sharply, then busied herself clearing the table. "It will mean another two miles if you do. You're going to be cold and tired enough as it is. When you're gone I think I'll paint the kitchen woodwork. White this time—you remember we got the paint last fall. It's going to make the room a lot lighter. I'll be too busy to find the day long."

"I will though," he insisted, "and if a storm gets up you'll feel safer, knowing that he's coming. That's what you need, Ann—someone to talk to besides me."

She stood at the stove motionless a moment, then turned to him uneasily. "Will you shave then, John—now—before you go?"

He glanced at her questioningly, and avoiding his eyes she tried to explain, "I mean—he may be here before you're back—and you won't have a chance by then."

"But it's only Steven—he's seen me like this—"

"He'll be shaved, though—that's what I mean—and I'd like you too to spend a little time on yourself."

He stood up, stroking the heavy stubble on his chin. "Maybe I should all right, but it makes the skin too tender. Especially when I've got to face the wind."

She nodded and began to help him dress, bringing heavy socks and a big woollen sweater from the bedroom, wrapping a scarf around his face and forehead. "I'll tell Steven to come early," he said, as he went out. "In time for supper. Likely there'll be chores for me to do, so if I'm not back by six don't wait."

From the bedroom window she watched him nearly a mile along the road. The fire had gone down when at last she turned away, and already through the house there was an encroaching chill. A blaze sprang up again when the drafts were opened, but as she went on clearing the table her movements were furtive and constrained. It was the silence weighing upon her—the frozen silence of the bitter fields, and sun-chilled sky—

lurking outside as if alive, relentlessly in wait, mile-deep between her now and John. She listened to it, suddenly tense, motionless. The fire crackled and the clock ticked. Always it was there. "I'm a fool," she whispered hoarsely, rattling the dishes in defiance, going back to the stove to put in another fire. "Warm and safe—I'm a fool. It's a good chance when he's away to paint. The day will go quickly. I won't have time to brood."

Since November now the paint had been waiting warmer weather. The frost in the walls on a day like this would crack and peel it as it dried, but she needed something to keep her hands occupied, something to stave off the gathering cold and loneliness. "First of all," she said aloud, opening the paint and mixing it with a little turpentine, "I must get the house warmer. Fill up the stove and open the oven door so that all the heat comes out. Wad something along the window sills to keep out the drafts. Then I'll feel brighter. It's the cold that depresses."

She moved briskly, performing each little task with careful and exaggerated absorption, binding her thoughts to it, making it a screen between herself and the surrounding snow and silence. But when the stove was filled and the windows sealed it was more difficult again. Above the quiet, steady swishing of her brush against the bedroom door the clock began to tick. Suddenly her movements became precise, deliberate, her posture self-conscious, as if someone had entered the room and were watching her. It was the silence again, aggressive, hovering. "All farmers' wives have to stay alone. I mustn't give in this way. I mustn't brood. A few hours now and they'll be here."

The sound of her voice reassured her. She went on: "I'll get them a good supper—and for coffee tonight after cards bake some of the little cakes with raisins that he likes . . . Just three of us, so I'll watch, and let John play. It's better with four, but at least we can talk. That's all I need—someone to talk to. John never talks. He's stronger—he doesn't understand. But he likes Steven—no matter what the neighbours say. Maybe he'll have him come again, and some other young people too. It's what we need, both of us, to help keep young ourselves . . . And then before we know it we'll be into March. It's cold still in March sometimes, but you never mind the same. At least you're beginning to think about spring."

She began to think about it now. Thoughts that outstripped her words, that left her alone again with herself and the ever-lurking silence. Eager and hopeful first; then clenched, rebellious, lonely. Windows open, sun

and thawing earth again, the urge of growing, living things. Then the days
that began in the morning at half-past four and lasted till ten at night; the
meals at which John gulped his food and scarcely spoke a word; the
brute-tired stupid eyes he turned on her if ever she mentioned town or
visiting.

For spring was drudgery again. John never hired a man to help him.
He wanted a mortgage-free farm; then a new house and pretty clothes for
her. Sometimes, because with the best of crops it was going to take so long
to pay off anyway, she wondered whether they mightn't better let the
mortgage wait a little. Before they were worn out, before their best years
were gone. It was something of life she wanted, not just a house and
furniture; something of John, not pretty clothes when she would be too
old to wear them. But John of course couldn't understand. To him it
seemed only right that she should have the clothes—only right that he,
fit for nothing else, should slave away fifteen hours a day to give them to
her. There was in his devotion a baffling, insurmountable humility that
made him feel the need of sacrifice. And when his muscles ached, when
his feet dragged stolidly with weariness, then it seemed that in some
measure at least he was making amends for his big hulking body and
simple mind. That by his sacrifice he succeeded only in the extinction of
his personality never occurred to him. Year after year their lives went on
in the same little groove. He drove his horses in the field; she milked the
cows and hoed potatoes. By dint of his drudgery he saved a few months'
wages, added a few dollars more each fall to his payments on the mortgage; but the only real difference that it all made was to deprive her of
his companionship, to make him a little duller, older, uglier than he
might otherwise have been. He never saw their lives objectively. To him
it was not what he actually accomplished by means of the sacrifice that
mattered, but the sacrifice itself, the gesture—something done for her
sake.

And she, understanding, kept her silence. In such a gesture, however
futile, there was a graciousness not to be shattered lightly. "John," she
would begin sometimes, "you're doing too much. Get a man to help
you—just for a month—" but smiling down at her he would answer simply,
"I don't mind. Look at the hands on me. They're made for work." While
in his voice there would be a stalwart ring to tell her that by her thought-
fulness she had made him only the more resolved to serve her, to prove
his devotion and fidelity.

They were useless, such thoughts. She knew. It was his very devotion that made them useless, that forbade her to rebel. Yet over and over, sometimes hunched still before their bleakness, sometimes her brush making swift sharp strokes to pace the chafe and rancour that they brought, she persisted in them.

This now, the winter, was their slack season. She could sleep sometimes till eight, and John till seven. They could linger over their meals a little, read, play cards, go visiting the neighbours. It was the time to relax, to indulge and enjoy themselves; but instead, fretful and impatient, they kept on waiting for the spring. They were compelled now, not by labour, but by the spirit of labour. A spirit that pervaded their lives and brought with idleness a sense of guilt. Sometimes they did sleep late, sometimes they did play cards, but always uneasily, always reproached by the thought of more important things that might be done. When John got up at five to attend to the fire he wanted to stay up and go out to the stable. When he sat down to a meal he hurried his food and pushed his chair away again, from habit, from sheer work-instinct, even though it was only to put more wood in the stove, or go down cellar to cut up beets and turnips for the cows.

And anyway, sometimes she asked herself, why sit trying to talk with a man who never talked? Why talk when there was nothing to talk about but crops and cattle, the weather and the neighbours? The neighbours, too—why go visiting them when still it was the same—crops and cattle, the weather and the other neighbours? Why go to the dances in the schoolhouse to sit among the older women, one of them now, married seven years, or to waltz with the work-bent, tired old farmers to a squeaky fiddle-tune? Once she had danced with Steven six or seven times in the evening, and they had talked about it for as many months. It was easier to stay at home. John never danced or enjoyed himself. He was always uncomfortable in his good suit and shoes. He didn't like shaving in the cold weather oftener than once or twice a week. It was easier to stay at home, to stand at the window staring out across the bitter fields, to count the days and look forward to another spring.

But now, alone with herself in the winter silence, she saw the spring for what it really was. This spring—next spring—all the springs and summers still to come. While they grew old, while their bodies warped, while their minds kept shrivelling dry and empty like their lives. "I mustn't," she said aloud again. "I married him—and he's a good man. I mustn't keep on this way. It will be noon before long, and then time to think about supper . . . Maybe he'll come early—and as soon as John is finished at the stable we can all play cards."

It was getting cold again, and she left her painting to put in more wood. But this time the warmth spread slowly. She pushed a mat up to the outside door, and went back to the window to pat down the woollen shirt that was wadded along the sill. Then she paced a few times round the room, then poked the fire and rattled the stove lids, then paced again. The fire crackled, the clock ticked. The silence now seemed more intense than ever, seemed to have reached a pitch where it faintly moaned. She began to pace on tiptoe, listening, her shoulders drawn together, not realizing for a while that it was the wind she heard, thin-strained and whimpering through the eaves.

Then she wheeled to the window, and with quick short breaths thawed the frost to see again. The glitter was gone. Across the drifts sped swift and snakelike little tongues of snow. She could not follow them, where they sprang from, or where they disappeared. It was as if all across the yard the snow were shivering awake—roused by the warnings of the wind to hold itself in readiness for the impending storm. The sky had become a sombre, whitish grey. It too, as if in readiness, had shifted and lay close to earth. Before her as she watched a mane of powdery snow reared up breast-high against the darker background of the stable, tossed for a moment angrily, and then subsided again as if whipped down to obedience and restraint. But another followed, more reckless and impatient than the first. Another reeled and dashed itself against the window where she watched. Then ominously for a while there were only the angry little snakes of snow. The wind rose, creaking the troughs that were wired beneath the eaves. In the distance, sky and prairie now were merged into one another linelessly.

All round her it was gathering; already in its press and whimpering there strummed a boding of eventual fury. Again she saw a mane of snow spring up, so dense and high this time that all the sheds and stables were obscured. Then others followed, whirling fiercely out of hand; and, when at last they cleared, the stables seemed in dimmer outline than before. It was the snow beginning, long lancet shafts of it, straight from the north, borne almost level by the straining wind. "He'll be there soon," she whispered, "and coming home it will be in his back. He'll leave again right away. He saw the double wheel—he knows the kind of storm there'll be."

She went back to her painting. For a while it was easier, all her thoughts half-anxious ones of John in the blizzard, struggling his way across the hills; but petulantly again she soon began, "I knew we were going to have a storm—I told him so—but it doesn't matter what I say. Big stubborn fool—he goes his own way anyway. It doesn't matter what becomes of me. In a storm like this he'll never get home. He won't even try. And while he sits keeping his father company I can look after his stable for him, go ploughing through snowdrifts up to my knees—nearly frozen—"

Not that she meant or believed her words. It was just an effort to convince herself that she did have a grievance, to justify her rebellious thoughts, to prove John responsible for her unhappiness. She was young still, eager for excitement and distractions; and John's steadfastness rebuked her vanity, made her complaints seem weak and trivial. Fretfully she went on, "If he'd listen to me sometimes and not be so stubborn we wouldn't be living still in a house like this. Seven years in two rooms— seven years and never a new stick of furniture . . . There—as if another coat of paint could make it different anyway."

She cleaned her brush, filled up the stove again, and went back to the window. There was a void white moment that she thought must be frost formed on the window pane; then, like a fitful shadow through the whirling snow, she recognized the stable roof. It was incredible. The sudden, maniac raging of the storm struck from her face all its pettishness. Her eyes glazed with fear a little; her lips blanched. "If he starts for home now,"she whispered silently— "But he won't—he knows I'm safe— he knows Steven's coming. Across the hills he would never dare."

She turned to the stove, holding out her hands to the warmth. Around her now there seemed a constant sway and tremor, as if the air were vibrating with the violent shudderings of the walls. She stood quite still, listening. Sometimes the wind struck with sharp, savage blows. Sometimes it bore down in a sustained, minute-long blast, silent with effort and intensity; then with a foiled shriek of threat wheeled away to gather and assault again. Always the eavestroughs creaked and sawed. She started towards the window again, then detecting the morbid trend of her thoughts, prepared fresh coffee and forced herself to drink a few mouthfuls. "He would never dare," she whispered again. "He wouldn't leave the old man anyway in such a storm. Safe in here—there's nothing for me to keep worrying about. It's after one already. I'll do my baking now, and then it will be time to get supper ready for Steven."

Soon, however, she began to doubt whether Steven would come. In such a storm even a mile was enough to make a man hesitate. Especially Steven, who, for all his attractive qualities, was hardly the one to face a blizzard for the sake of someone else's chores. He had a stable of his own to look after anyway. It would be only natural for him to think that when the storm rose John had turned again for home. Another man would have—would have put his wife first.

But she felt little dread or uneasiness at the prospect of spending the night alone. It was the first time she had been left like this on her own resources, and her reaction, now that she could face and appraise her situation calmly, was gradually to feel it a kind of adventure and responsibility. It stimulated her. Before nightfall she must go to the stable and feed everything. Wrap up in some of John's clothes—take a ball of string in her hand, one end tied to the door, so that no matter how blinding the storm she could at least find her way back to the house. She had heard of people having to do that. It appealed to her now because suddenly it made life dramatic. She had not felt the storm yet, only watched it for a minute through the window.

It took nearly an hour to find enough string, to choose the right socks and sweaters. Long before it was time to start out she tried on John's clothes, changing and rechanging, striding around the room to make sure there would be play enough for pitching hay and struggling over snowdrifts; then she took them off again, and for a while busied herself baking the little cakes with raisins that he liked.

Night came early. Just for a moment on the doorstep she shrank back, uncertain. The slow dimming of the light clutched her with an illogical sense of abandonment. It was like the covert withdrawal of an ally, leaving the alien miles unleashed and unrestrained. Watching the hurricane of writhing snow rage past the little house she forced herself, "They'll never stand the night unless I get them fed. It's nearly dark already, and I've work to last an hour."

Timidly, unwinding a little of the string, she crept out from the shelter of the doorway. A gust of wind spun her forward a few yards, then plunged her headlong against a drift that in the dense white whirl lay invisible across her path. For nearly a minute she huddled still, breathless and dazed. The snow was in her mouth and nostrils, inside her scarf and up her sleeves. As she tried to straighten a smothering scud flung itself against her face, cutting off her breath a second time. The wind struck from all sides, blustering and furious. It was as if the storm had discovered her, as if all its forces were concentrated upon her extinction. Seized with panic suddenly she threshed out a moment with her arms, then stumbled back and sprawled her length across the drift.

But this time she regained her feet quickly, roused by the ship and batter of the storm to retaliative anger. For a moment her impulse was to face the wind and strike back blow for blow; then, as suddenly as it had come, her frantic strength gave way to limpness and exhaustion. Suddenly, a comprehension so clear and terrifying that it struck all thoughts of the stable from her mind, she realized in such a storm her puny insignificance. And the realization gave her new strength, stilled this time to a desperate persistence. Just for a moment the wind held her, numb and swaying in its vise; then slowly, buckled far forward, she groped her way towards the house.

Inside, leaning against the door, she stood tense and still a while. It was almost dark now. The top of the stove glowed a deep, dull red. Heedless of the storm, self-absorbed and self-satisfied, the clock ticked on like a glib little idiot. "He shouldn't have gone," she whispered silently. "He saw the double wheel—he knew. He shouldn't have left me here alone."

For so fierce now, so insane and dominant did the blizzard seem, that she could not credit the safety of the house. The warmth and lull around her was not real yet, not to be relied upon. She was still at the mercy of the storm. Only her body pressing hard like this against the door was staving it off. She didn't dare move. She didn't dare ease the ache and strain. "He shouldn't have gone," she repeated, thinking of the stable again, reproached by her helplessness. "They'll freeze in their stalls—and I can't reach them. He'll say it's all my fault. He won't believe I tried."

Then Steven came. Quickly, startled to quietness and control, she let him in and lit the lamp. He stared at her a moment, then flinging off his cap crossed to where she stood by the table and seized her arms. "You're so white—what's wrong? Look at me—" It was like him in such little situations to be masterful. "You should have known better than to go out on a day like this. For a while I thought I wasn't going to make it here myself—"

"I was afraid you wouldn't come—John left early, and there was the stable—"

But the storm had unnerved her, and suddenly at the assurance of his touch and voice the fear that had been gripping her gave way to an hysteria of relief. Scarcely aware of herself she seized his arm and sobbed against it. He remained still a moment, unyielding, then slipped his other arm around her shoulder. It was comforting and she relaxed against it, hushed by a sudden sense of lull and safety. Her shoulders trembled with the easing of the strain, then fell limp and still. "You're shivering,"— he drew her gently towards the stove. "There's nothing to be afraid of now, though. I'm going to do the chores for you."

It was a quiet, sympathetic voice, yet with an undertone of insolence, a kind of mockery even, that made her draw away quickly and busy herself putting in a fire. With his lips drawn in a little smile he watched her till she looked at him again. The smile too was insolent, but at the same time companionable; Steven's smile, and therefore difficult to reprove. It lit up his lean, still-boyish face with a peculiar kind of arrogance: features and smile that were different from John's, from other men's—wilful and derisive, yet naïvely so—as if it were less the difference itself he was conscious of, than the long-accustomed privilege that thereby fell his due. He was erect, tall, square-shouldered. His hair was dark and trim, his young lips curved soft and full. While John, she made the comparison swiftly, was thickset, heavy-jowled, and stooped. He always stood before her helpless, a kind of humility and wonderment in his attitude. And Steven now smiled on her appraisingly with the worldly-wise assurance of one for whom a woman holds neither mystery nor illusion.

"It was good of you to come, Steven," she responded, the words running into a sudden, empty laugh. "Such a storm to face—I suppose I should feel flattered."

For his presumption, his misunderstanding of what had been only a momentary weakness, instead of angering quickened her, roused from latency and long disuse all the instincts and resources of her femininity. She felt eager, challenged. Something was at hand that hitherto had always eluded her, even in the early days with John, something vital, beckoning, meaningful. She didn't understand, but she knew. The texture of the moment was satisfyingly dreamlike: an incredibility perceived as such, yet acquiesced in. She was John's wife—she knew—but also she knew that Steven standing here was different from John. There was no thought or motive, no understanding of herself as the knowledge persisted. Wary and poised round a sudden little core of blind excitement she evaded him, "But it's nearly dark—hadn't you better hurry if you're going to do the chores? Don't trouble—I can get them off myself—"

An hour later when he returned from the stable she was in another dress, hair rearranged, a little flush of colour in her face. Pouring warm water for him from the kettle into the basin she said evenly, "By the time you're washed supper will be ready. John said we weren't to wait for him."

He looked at her a moment, "But in a storm like this you're not expecting John?"

"Of course." As she spoke she could feel the colour deepening in her face. "We're going to play cards. He was the one that suggested it."

He went on washing, and then as they took their places at the table, resumed, "So John's coming. When are you expecting him?"

"He said it might be seven o'clock—or a little later." Conversation with Steven at other times had always been brisk and natural, but now suddenly she found it strained. "He may have work to do for his father. That's what he said when he left. Why do you ask, Steven?"

"I was just wondering—it's a rough night."

"He always comes. There couldn't be a storm bad enough. It's easier to do the chores in daylight, and I knew he'd be tired—that's why I started out for the stable."

She glanced up again and he was smiling at her. The same insolence, the same little twist of mockery and appraisal. It made her flinch suddenly, and ask herself why she was pretending to expect John—why there should be this instinct of defence to force her. This time, instead of poise and excitement, it brought a reminder that she had changed her dress and rearranged her hair. It crushed in a sudden silence, through which she heard the whistling wind again, and the creaking saw of the eaves. Neither spoke now. There was something strange, almost terrifying, about this Steven and his quiet, unrelenting smile; but strangest of all was the familiarity: the Steven she had never seen or encountered, and yet had always known, always expected, always waited for. It was less Steven himself that she felt than his inevitability. Just as she had felt the snow, the silence and the storm. She kept her eyes lowered, on the window past his shoulder, on the stove, but his smile now seemed to exist apart from him, to merge and hover with the silence. She clinked a cup—listened to the whistle of the storm—always it was there. He began to speak, but her mind missed the meaning of his words. Swiftly she was making comparisons again; his face so different to John's, so handsome and young and clean-shaven. Swiftly, helplessly, feeling the imperceptible and relentless ascendancy that thereby he was gaining over her, sensing sudden menace in this new more vital life, even as she felt drawn towards it.

The lamp between them flickered as an onslaught of the storm sent shudderings through the room. She rose to build up the fire again and he followed her. For a long time they stood close to the stove, their arms almost touching. Once as the blizzard creaked the house she spun almost sharply, fancying it was John at the door; but quietly he intercepted her. "Not tonight—you might as well make up your mind to it. Across the hills in a storm like this—it would be suicide to try."

Her lips trembled suddenly in an effort to answer, to parry the certainty in his voice, then set thin and bloodless. She was afraid now. Afraid of his face so different from John's—of his smile, of her own helplessness to rebuke it. Afraid of the storm, isolating her here alone with him in its impenetrable fastness. They tried to play cards, but she kept starting up at every creak and shiver of the walls. "It's too rough a night," he repeated. "Even for John. Just relax a few minutes—stop worrying and pay a little attention to me."

But in his tone there was a contradiction to his words. For it implied that she was not worrying—that her only concern was lest it really might be John at the door.

And the implication persisted. He filled up the stove for her, shuffled the cards—won—shuffled—still it was there. She tried to respond to his conversation, to think of the game, but helplessly into her cards instead she began to ask, Was he right? Was that why he smiled? Why he seemed to wait, expectant and assured?

The clock ticked, the fire crackled. Always it was there. Furtively for a moment she watched him as he deliberated over his hand. John, even in the days before they were married, had never looked like that. Only this morning she had asked him to shave. Because Steven was coming—because she had been afraid to see them side by side—because deep within herself she had known even then. The same knowledge, furtive and forbidden, that was flaunted now in Steven's smile. "You look cold," he said at last, dropping his cards and rising from the table. "We're not playing, anyway. Come over to the stove for a few minutes and get warm."

"But first I think we'll hang blankets over the door. When there's a blizzard like this we always do." It seemed that in sane, commonplace activity there might be release, a moment or two in which to recover herself. "John has nails to put them on. They keep out a little of the draft."

He stood on a chair for her, and hung the blankets that she carried from the bedroom. Then for a moment they stood silent, watching the blankets sway and tremble before the blade of wind that spurted around the jamb. "I forgot," she said at last, "that I painted the bedroom door. At the top there, see—I've smeared the blankets coming through."

He glanced at her curiously, and went back to the stove. She followed him, trying to imagine the hills in such a storm, wondering whether John would come. "A man couldn't live in it," suddenly he answered her thoughts, lowering the oven door and drawing up the chairs one on each side of it. "He knows you're safe. It isn't likely that he'd leave his father, anyway."

"The wind will be in his back," she persisted. "The winter before we were married—all the blizzards that we had that year—and he never missed—"

"Blizzards like this one? Up in the hills he wouldn't be able to keep his direction for a hundred yards. Listen to it a minute and ask yourself."

His voice seemed softer, kindlier now. She met his smile a moment, its assured little twist of appraisal, then for a long time sat silent, tense, careful again to avoid his eyes.

Everything now seemed to depend on this. It was the same as a few hours ago when she braced the door against the storm. He was watching her, smiling. She dared not move, unclench her hands, or raise her eyes. The flames crackled, the clock ticked. The storm wrenched the walls as if to make them buckle in. So rigid and desperate were all her muscles set, withstanding, that the room around her seemed to swim and reel. So rigid and strained that for relief at last, despite herself, she raised her head and met his eyes again.

Intending that it should be for only an instant, just to breathe again, to ease the tension that had grown unbearable—but in his smile now, instead of the insolent appraisal that she feared, there seemed a kind of warmth and sympathy. An understanding that quickened and encouraged her—that made her wonder why but a moment ago she had been afraid. It was as if the storm had lulled, as if she had suddenly found calm and shelter.

Or perhaps, the thought seized her, perhaps instead of his smile it was she that had changed. She who, in the long, wind-creaked silence, had emerged from the increment of codes and loyalties to her real, unfettered self. She who now felt suddenly an air of appraisal as nothing more than an understanding of the unfulfilled woman that until this moment had lain within her brooding and unadmitted, reproved out of consciousness by the insistence of an outgrown, routine fidelity.

For there had always been Steven. She understood now. Seven years—almost as long as John—ever since the night they first danced together.

The lamp was burning dry, and through the dimming light, isolated in the fastness of silence and storm, they watched each other. Her face was white and struggling still. His was handsome, clean-shaven, young. Her eyes were fanatic, believing desperately, fixed upon him as if to exclude all else, as if to find justification. His were cool, bland, drooped a little with expectancy. The light kept dimming, gathering the shadows round them, hushed, conspiratorial. He was smiling still. Her hands again were clenched up white and hard.

"But he always came," she persisted. "The wildest, coldest nights—even such a night as this. There was never a storm—"

"Never a storm like this one." There was a quietness in his smile now, a kind of simplicity almost, as if to reassure her. "You were out in it yourself for a few minutes. He would have five miles, across the hills . . . I'd think twice myself, on such a night, before risking even one."

Long after he was asleep she lay listening to the storm. As a check on the draft up the chimney they had left one of the stovelids partly off, and through the open bedroom door she could see the flickerings of flame and shadow on the kitchen wall. They leaped and sank fantastically. The longer she watched the more alive they seemed to be. There was one great shadow that struggled towards her threateningly, massive and black and engulfing all the room. Again and again it advanced, about to spring, but each time a little whip of light subdued it to its place among the others on the wall. Yet though it never reached her still she cowered, feeling that gathered there was all the frozen wilderness, its heart of terror and invincibility.

Then she dozed a while, and the shadow was John. Interminably he advanced. The whips of light still flicked and coiled, but now suddenly they were the swift little snakes that this afternoon she had watched twist and shiver across the snow. And they too were advancing. They writhed and vanished and came again. She lay still, paralyzed. He was over her now, so close that she could have touched him. Already it seemed that a deadly tightening hand was on her throat. She tried to scream but her lips were locked. Steven beside her slept on heedlesly.

Until suddenly as she lay staring up at him a gleam of light revealed his face. And in it was not a trace of threat or anger—only calm, and stonelike hopelessness.

That was like John. He began to withdraw, and frantically she tried to call him back. "It isn't true—not really true—listen, John—" but the words clung frozen to her lips. Already there was only the shriek of wind again, the sawing eaves, the leap and twist of shadow on the wall.

She sat up, startled now and awake. And so real had he seemed there, standing close to her, so vivid the sudden age and sorrow in his face, that at first she could not make herself understand she had been only dreaming. Against the conviction of his presence in the room it was necessary to insist over and over that he must still be with his father on the other side of the hills. Watching the shadows she had fallen asleep. It was only her mind, her imagination, distorted to a nightmare by the illogical and unadmitted dread of his return. But he wouldn't come. Steven was right. In such a storm he would never try. They were safe, alone. No one would ever know. It was only fear, morbid and irrational; only the sense of guilt that even her new-found and challenged womanhood could not entirely quell.

She knew now. She had not let herself understand or acknowledge it as guilt before, but gradually through the wind-torn silence of the night his face compelled her. The face that had watched her from the darkness with its stonelike sorrow—the face that was really John—John more than his features of mere flesh and bone could ever be.

She wept silently. The fitful gleam of light began to sink. On the ceiling and wall at last there was only a faint dull flickering glow. The little house shuddered and quailed, and a chill crept in again. Without wakening Steven she slipped out to build up the fire. It was burned to a few spent embers now, and the wood she put on seemed a long time catching light. The wind swirled through the blankets they had hung around the door, and struck her flesh like laps of molten ice. Then hollow and moaning it roared up the chimney again, as if against its will drawn back to serve still longer with the onrush of the storm.

For a long time she crouched over the stove, listening. Earlier in the evening, with the lamp lit and the fire crackling, the house had seemed

a stand against the wilderness, against its frozen, blizzard-breathed implacability, a refuge of feeble walls wherein persisted the elements of human
meaning and survival. Now, in the cold, creaking darkness, it was strangely
extinct, looted by the storm and abandoned again. She lifted the stove lid
and fanned the embers till at last a swift little tongue of flame began to
lick around the wood. Then she replaced the lid, extended her hands,
and as if frozen in that attitude stood waiting.

It was not long now. After a few minutes she closed the drafts, and as
the flames whirled back upon each other, beating against the top of the
stove and sending out flickers of light again, a warmth surged up to relax
her stiffened limbs. But shivering and numb it had been easier. The bodily
well-being that the warmth induced gave play again to an ever more
insistent mental suffering. She remembered the shadow that was John.
She saw him bent towards her, then retreating, his features pale and
overcast with unaccusing grief. She re-lived their seven years together
and, in retrospect, found them to be years of worth and dignity. Until
crushed by it all at last, seized by a sudden need to suffer and atone, she
crossed to where the draft was bitter, and for a long time stood unflinch-
ing on the icy floor.

The storm was close here. Even through the blankets she could feel a
sift of snow against her face. The eaves sawed, the walls creaked. Above it
all, like a wolf in howling flight, the wind shrilled lone and desolate.

And yet, suddenly she asked herself, hadn't there been other storms,
other blizzards? And through the worst of them hadn't he always reached
her?

Clutched by the thought she stood rooted a minute. It was hard now
to understand how she could have so deceived herself—how a moment
of passion could have quieted within her not only conscience, but reason
and discretion too. John always came. There could never be a storm to
stop him. He was strong, inured to the cold. He had crossed the hills since
his boyhood, knew every creek-bed and gully. It was madness to go on like
this—to wait. While there was still time she must waken Steven, and hurry
him away.

But in the bedroom again, standing at Steven's side, she hesitated. In
his detachment from it all, in his quiet, even breathing, there was such
sanity, such realism. For him nothing had happened; nothing would. If
she wakened him he would only laugh and tell her to listen to the storm.
Already it was long past midnight; either John had lost his way or not set

out at all. And she knew that in his devotion there was nothing foolhardy. He would never risk a storm beyond his endurance, never permit himself a sacrifice likely to endanger her lot or future. They were both safe. No one would ever know. She must control herself—be sane like Steven.

For comfort she let her hand rest a while on Steven's shoulder. It would be easier were he awake now, with her, sharing her guilt; but gradually as she watched his handsome face in the glimmering light she came to understand that for him no guilt existed. Just as there had been no passion, no conflict. Nothing but the sane appraisal of their situation, nothing but the expectant little smile, and the arrogance of features that were different from John's. She winced deeply, remembering how she had fixed her eyes on those featues, how she had tried to believe that so handsome and young, so different from John's, they must in themselves be her justification.

In the flickering light they were still young, still handsome. No longer her justification—she knew now—John was the man—but wistfully still, wondering sharply at their power and tyranny, she touched them a moment with her fingertips again.

She could not blame him. There had been no passion, no guilt; therefore there could be no responsibility. Suddenly looking down at him as he slept, half-smiling still, his lips relaxed in the conscienceless complacency of his achievement, she understood that thus he was revealed in his entirety—all there ever was or ever could be. John was the man. With him lay all the future. For tonight, slowly and contritely through the day and years to come, she would try to make amends.

Then she stole back to the kitchen, and without thought, impelled by overwhelming need again, returned to the door where the draft was bitter still. Gradually towards morning the storm began to spend itself. Its terror blast became a feeble, worn-out moan. The leap of light and shadow sank, and a chill crept in again. Always the eaves creaked, tortured with wordless prophecy. Heedless of it all the clock ticked on in idiot content.

They found him the next day, less than a mile from home. Drifting with the storm he had run against his own pasture fence and overcome had frozen there, erect still, both hands clasping fast the wire.

"He was south of here," they said wonderingly when she told them how he had come across the hills. "Straight south—you'd wonder how he could have missed the buildings. It was the wind last night, coming every which way at once. He shouldn't have tried. There was a double wheel around the moon."

She looked past them a moment, then as if to herself said simply, "If you knew him, though—John would try."

It was later, when they had left her a while to be alone with him, that she knelt and touched his hand. Her eyes dimmed, still it was such a strong and patient hand; then, transfixed, they suddenly grew wide and clear. On the palm, white even against its frozen whiteness, was a little smear of paint.

Hunting Season

Helen J. Rosta

She saw the footprints early one morning, directly below her cabin in the soft muck around the beaver dam, first one, and then a few yards farther on, another. She followed them until they disappeared on the hard ground that led into the trees. Then she turned back, and straddling one of the prints, stood for a long time looking at it. It was sunk deeply into the mud, a large oval heel and five toes, the big toes nearly the size of her hand, as if, during the night, a giant had walked across her field. She wondered what they had used to make it.

She heard the putt-putt of his truck and looked up just as it was rising over the brow of the hill. For a moment she thought of moving into the shadow of trees and waiting . . .

She could imagine him with his ear close to the cabin door listening to the sound of his knocking reverberate through the two rooms, and when he was satisfied that she wasn't there, turning away, his hand shading his eyes, slowly scanning the countryside for a sight of her . . . then sauntering, heavy-footed, to the corral where Star would whinny to him, stopping to pet her, whistling softly through his gap teeth . . . continuing on to the barn, peering into the stalls, climbing the stairs to the hayloft . . . down again . . . and over to the garage, which was locked, and windowless . . .

He got out of the truck. She could hear the tinny sound as the door slammed shut. When his back was toward her, she started away from the trees at a dead run, circling the hill so that when he saw her he wouldn't know where she had come from. He was still pounding on the door when she walked up behind him.

"There's nobody in there," she said.

He turned and a smile spread over his long, sun-reddened face. "Some people are up and about early."

The cabin was warm inside. She stirred the fire and set the coffee pot on the stove. He pulled up a chair to the table, took off his red hunter's cap, placed it on his knee and clasped his hands around it. His hands were large and square, the fingernails flat and rimmed with grease.

"When hunting season starts you shouldn't wander around without something red on," he told her.

"My land's posted," she said.

"They don't always pay attention to that ... There's lots of game hiding out in this bush."

"But it is my land ..."

"Doesn't matter whose land it is ... during hunting season you wear something red." He smiled, showing big, gap teeth and then covered his mouth with his hand, speaking from behind it. "They say this year maybe they'll bag the old maid over on the Coulter place."

"It's not the Coulter place any more," she said and then added, "Nobody's going to bag anything on my land."

"Now don't go getting mad. You know how people talk." He took his hand away from his mouth.

"I just don't want them tramping all over the place ... " She thought of the tracks down by the beaver pond and for a moment considered taking him down and showing them to him but then the image of the hand covering his smile came to her ... probably he knew about the footprints already, had helped to plot them, and was waiting for her to say something so that he could go back and tell his buddies. Maybe he had been one of them, skulking about her place in the dead of night.

"I came to help you trim the mare's feet," he said.

"But you've been here nearly every day doing something for me." Every day, every day ... and he's the only one. "I can do them."

"I came to help," he said. He stood up, smoothed his hair and set the red cap on his head.

She led the way out to the corral. "You're doing too much for me," she continued. "I appreciate it, but you have your own work ..." He whistled and Star whirled about, ran toward them and then stood stock-still, ears pricked, watching their approach.

"Trimmers still in the barn?" He started toward it. He knows where everything is, she thought. She climbed over the railing into the corral and put an arm around the mare's neck. She could feel a quiver moving like a ripple under the skin. He emerged from the barn, watched for a moment, then unfastened the gate and came into the corral, the hoof trimmers in one hand.

"You hang onto the halter," he said. "I'll take care of the feet." He ran his hand over the horse's neck and shoulder, bent down, slid his hand along the leg, straddled it, and grabbing the fetlock pulled the leg back toward him. The horse reared up, jerking the halter from her hand and knocking him to the ground. He swore, picked himself up, and lunged for the halter.

"Don't!" She grabbed his sleeve. "Leave it for now. She's trembling . . . something's frightened her." They did, prowling around . . .

"Shouldn't let her get away like that. She'll try it next time." He seemed undecided, standing, slightly stooped, the hoof trimmers still in his hand.

"She's too nervous."

"Shouldn't let her get away."

"Something's frightened her," she repeated. "Do you have any idea what it might have been?"

"Horses spook easy . . . maybe one of those wild animals you've been harbouring scared her."

She saw the beginnings of the smile, turned her back and walked ahead of him. "It *is* my land. I don't have to let them hunt it."

"They've always hunted this land." He paused and gazed toward the dark line of trees behind the beaver dam. "You know how they are."

"No," she said. "I don't know how they are. I never see any of them."

"They're kind of shy," he said, "that is the bachelors are shy, and the married ones . . ." The hand went over his mouth. "Course being a widower, none of that applies to me . . ." He looked away, letting the words hang in the air. "And the women . . . people don't like what they don't understand."

"What don't they understand?"

"They wonder what's a woman doing out here all alone."

"I've got as much right to be here as anyone."

"Oh, it isn't a question of right. They wonder, that's all."

"How do they feel about your coming here?"

"Oh, I get teased but I can take a joke."

"I imagine," she said, "that everyone around here really loves . . . a good joke."

He waved his hand toward the craggy, sombre hills covered with dense clumps of trees. "To survive in this country, you've got to have a sense of humour."

After he left, she rushed down to the beaver dam and inspected the tracks, again following them to where they disappeared, pausing on the margin of the trees, peering into the shadows, listening, turning back . . . They must have gone to a lot of trouble to make the footprints, she thought, and how could they be sure she'd even find them . . unless they were watching her . . . knew her habits, the walk by the beaver dam in the early mornings, the rides along the fence lines.

Two days later she found her mailbox, still attached to its post, lying in the ditch beside the road. The side with her name on it was shoved in, the lid ajar. She dragged the box up to the roadbed, reached inside and felt for the letter which she had placed there the previous evening. She found the envelope. It was covered with black smudges and one end had been slit. The letter was gone. She held the envelope gingerly by one corner and studied it. They've left fingerprints, she thought. She was standing beside the road, the envelope still in her hand when he drove up. He stopped the truck beside her, jumped out, and started to throw tools from the back.

"Aren't you lucky," he said, "that I've been carting around all this fencing stuff?"

She didn't move. "How did you know it was torn down?"

"Didn't. Just happened to be going by and saw you standing here. Like I said, you're lucky." He got a hammer from his tool kit and started to tap out the side of the box. "Guess you'll have to do without mail today."

"If I had any, the mailman could have brought it to me."

"Maybe when he saw the box gone, he figured that you didn't want any." He gave the box a final tap with the hammer, stood up and rubbed his hands on his trousers. "Good as new. Now all we have to do is dig another hole and set it up again." He picked up the post-hole auger, leaned his weight on it, and began to move rhythmically in a circular motion.

"This time they've gone too far." She shoved the envelope under his nose. "They've stolen my letter and that's a criminal offence."

"I wouldn't go making a fuss about it . . . it's nothing serious."

"Serious! They could go to jail for this." She waved the envelope at him. "Fingerprints all over. Look at it."

He snatched the envelope from her, wadded it up and stuffed it in his pocket. "When I get the box up, you can send another letter easy enough." He lifted the auger out of the hole and emptied the dirt from it. "Ground's moist. It won't take any time at all to get that thing standing." He set the auger back in the ground.

"They stole my letter!"

He gave a violent twist to the auger, stopped and looked straight at her. "Was there anything in that letter you wouldn't want people to see?"

She kicked the ground angrily. "It's nobody's business what's in my letters."

He reached into his pocket, extracted the envelope and smoothed it out on the auger handle. When he had finished examining it, he put it back in his pocket and smiled at her. "That looks like a business letter to me. I've been to Edmonton. Think I've even been in that store."

"I was ordering a gun."

He started working again. "Any money in that letter?"

"No . . . but it's stealing anyway . . . it's a Federal offence to tamper with the mail."

"A gun won't do you any good," he said.

"What do you mean?"

"Can't hunt on your own land if it's posted."

"I wasn't going to hunt."

"Then what do you want a gun for?"

"Target practice."

"You don't need practice to hit a target," he said, "as long as it isn't moving."

He set up the mailbox in silence. She helped him tamp dirt and gravel around its base and carry the tools back to the truck.

"They could go to jail."

He started to load the tools into the truck as if he hadn't heard her. When he had finished, he said, "You know, maybe you should get yourself a gun after all." He paused and gazed in the direction of her cabin. "Seems like they've noticed some kind of funny tracks leading into your land."

"What kind of tracks?"

"You noticed anything?"

"What kind of tracks?" she asked again.

He shrugged. "I don't know . . . funny tracks . . . maybe you should take a look for them."

"Why are they doing this to me?"

"Nobody's doing anything to you." He gestured toward the mailbox. "That's nothing."

"They've done other things."

"A few jokes . . ."

"My letter was no joke."

He climbed into the truck, started the engine, then rolled down the window and leaned out. "You didn't thank me," he said.

"I'm thanking you, but as far as I'm concerned, the rest of them should go to jail."

He started to roll up the window and his words drifted back to her over the roar of the engine. "Hunting season starts tomorrow."

That afternoon, she saddled Star and rode around the fence lines. South of the beaver dam, she found a dead tree lying across the wire.

She dismounted, tied the horse to a sapling and, thinking that they had pushed the tree onto the fence, examined the ground for footprints. She found none. She grasped the trunk and tried to swing the tree off the wire. It moved slowly in an arc, its limbs catching in the branches of the trees surrounding it. She struggled with it, her breath coming in short, quick gasps. Star snorted and pawed impatiently. Suddenly, the tree broke loose and crashed to the ground. The mare reared back, nostrils flaring.

She approached the horse, speaking softly. "Whoa Star . . . easy girl . . . take it easy." She ran her hand along the quivering side. All at once, the mare became rigid, head up, ears forward. She turned slowly, following the mare's gaze.

It didn't move, just stood, looking at her, its hairy body towering among the trees, its hands resting at its sides, its eyes a pale translucent amber, large, luminous, and full of fear.

The horse, as if she'd finally caught an alien scent, snorted and plunged. The creature stepped back, turned, and with huge strides, vanished into the shadows like an apparition.

Early next morning, the shots started. The first one was faint, far to the northeast. The next was louder, and the next. By dawn, they were sounding in a steady, staccato rhythm, closer, closer, one after the other. By nightfall, she imagined that they had advanced to the borders of her property.

That evening when she heard his truck, she waited silently behind the closed curtains, listening to the sound of his fist on the door. After a time, she heard him move away from the door, around the cabin, in front of the window, pause, then on . . . She thought she heard Star whinny softly and the thin sound of whistling. Finally, she heard the truck door slam and the roar of his engine as he drove away.

She listened to the roar fading in the distance, then opened the door and peered out. The moon was high, a large silver disc in the black sky. Below the cabin, the beaver pond gleamed like a pale circle of light. Behind it, the trees lay in impenetrable darkness. She thought of the creature crouching among the trees, its long arms resting on its knees, hands motionless, eyes large and luminous as the moon, staring into darkness.

Shortly after midnight, she heard the trucks. The sound cut through the cold air like the thud of wings. She ran to the window and looked out. The trucks came slowly up the road, gleaming shapes, lights extinguished, moving like a caravan. One by one they stopped outside the cabin and the dark figures alighted. At first she thought he wasn't with them, but then she saw his truck, saw him step down.

He joined the others, and they all walked together, their long, black shadows moving ahead of them.

The Tree

Andreas Schroeder

He was an old man, though just how old was quite impossible to tell; he belonged to one of those aboriginal tribes whose members grow old at an early age and then seem to stop having anything to do with time at all. He was introduced to me simply as a "displacer of stones," a man who spent most of his time down at the beach lifting and replacing the jagged chunks of coral in search of whatever he could find. It was mentioned that his father had lowered the first fishing nets into the Macumba River.

He was an unperturbed old man, almost always smiling and nodding his head, trying to interest me in this or that triviality, often raising his calloused, almost black finger and delivering himself of little wisdoms which were translated to me as "People have more fun than anybody" and "In the days after the Great Heat, the heron sticks his legs into his pockets and flies elsewhere" or even the more unfathomable "In a land of little water, men weep less but take more women." Day after day I saw him wading along the beach at low tide, patiently turning over rocks, his fingers making quick darts into the water as whatever lurked beneath the stones blinked in the unaccustomed light and was caught. He dropped everything he apprehended into a smelly brown flour sack which he dragged into his hut at the end of the day, then lowered the curtain. I was never able to discover what he did with all he caught.

It was several weeks after I had met him that I was informed: "the old man has been told." At first I couldn't understand the information and no one seemed to understand my incomprehension, but eventually I discovered that the old man's death had been "officially forecast" by the tribal fortune-teller that day. After that there were no more smiles. When I saw the old man later that afternoon, his eyes gloomed and his face hung dully from his skull like his empty sack. He announced to me sadly that he would soon be turning into a tree; that the fortune-teller had divined his fate by looking at the seasons to come through the eyes of a dying rooster.

I asked if he knew exactly when this would occur, but he merely shook his head and muttered that "one would have to be careful where one stood from now on; one would have to be careful where one stood."

From that time on the old man became increasingly clumsy at displacing his stones; his attention was constantly divided between the water and the land, and he appeared always on the verge of making a dash for the line of trees just above the beach. Whenever he stopped to talk on the trail, villagers admonished him that "that is not a good place for a tree to stand", and he would hurriedly step aside among the bushes, continuing the conversation through the branches. His main concern was that when death became imminent, he would be able to reach an advantageous place where he could continue his life in tree form with relative comfort. For this reason he rarely dared to stray farther than a quick sprint away from such a spot.

Then the days began to grow longer and the tides receded farther from the land each day. Food grew more plentiful in the village and the fishermen risked deeper and deeper forays into the ocean's belly for sponge. Now, in the afternoons, the reef lay exposed for miles in every direction, baring an ever-increasing expanse of formerly concealed and mysterious sea-life. Every day saw the capture of new, colourful and obscure monstrosities which the villagers dried and added to their constantly growing string of temple gods. Only Katunga, the old displacer of stones, crouched near his tree-line and refused to hunt. The villagers made sympathetic, sorrowful clucking noises and brought the new spirits for him to see. Each time Katunga fingered the grotesque eyes and ornate scales of each new god, his eyes glowed darkly with the longing to join the search, as a displacer of stones should do. But he held grimly on beneath the trees, turning away.

It was one or two days after the kaantung, the Hottest Day, that I woke from my afternoon sleep to a frenzied shouting and clanging of pots through the village; children screamed, footfalls thudded rapidly past my curtain toward the beach, and everywhere I heard the name "Katunga." I pushed my curtain aside, the villagers pointed excitedly toward the reef and motioned me to hurry. Far across the treacherous maze of coral I saw a scattering of people straggling toward what appeared to be an unusually tall gaunt man flailing wildly about himself with his arms and legs.

"Katunga, Katunga," the villagers shouted, and as the tall gaunt man erupted into strange, jerking convulsions on the distant reef, I began to run.

As I jumped and stumbled across coral-encrusted boulders I remember thinking angrily, why couldn't he have resisted that temptation; should've stayed near the other trees where he was safe, the damn fool, to go that far out has to be madness, and I almost rammed my foot down on a cluster of poison-filled spine coral and realized I was running much too fast for my own safety; when I looked up again he was already twice his original size.

I stopped. Katunga staggered as if jolted by enormous bursts of electricity, like a giant epileptic; what I had at first assumed to be reflections of his arms in the trembling heat were in fact many arms, some longer than others, some already very thick; his torso grew wider, heavier, rippling with straining, rebelling muscles; he was trying to run, to return, but his legs had already become too stiff to give him leverage and he tottered about until his feet entwined in the coral and anchored him fast. Above, his head disappeared in a burst of leafy green.

Now the transformation slowed, the struggled appeared resolved, the tree had asserted itself and the only movement I could still discern was the steady rising and unfolding of its crown, like the opening of a huge flower in the first rays of morning sun. A tentative breeze from the ocean riffled through the branches, swaying it slightly, and I thought for a moment I could still see Katunga trying to find more solid footing on the slippery reef, but that might have been only my imagination. By the time the first villagers arrived, they found nothing more than an implacable tree.

A dark tribesman standing next to me shook his head with a mixture of impatience and sadness. "This is not a good thing," he muttered, looking with some anxiety at the sky. "He has chosen a foolish place. Tonight the winds will be angry from the west, and the tides will leap high. He will drown."

I hooded my eyes and looked back at the strange tree of Katunga, standing improbably where in a few hours the ocean would return and find him there, a giant plant in a sea-meadow, clutching grimly to the rainbow molluscs and rubbery brain-coral underneath.

"He will be swept away," the tribesman muttered again. "It was a foolish place, he does not know the sea; he will be swept away."

Emily

Lois Simmie

Every year we rented the same cottage at the west end of the lake. All through the dry, cold winter, when snow lay thick on the town, I dreamed about the lake; and in the summer, too, when parched prairie grass crackled under my feet and the caragana hedges were covered with dust. And still I was surprised, every year, by the shimmering immensity of it; you could barely make out the hills on the far side, and cottages were mere specks on the horizon.

On the first of July we were always up by six-thirty to get an early start. That year my sister, who was fourteen, complained about getting up, but I didn't mind. In a corner of the back seat, made fort-like by a stack of pillows and blankets, I hugged my bathing suit and imagined how it would be. The imagining was always the same, made familiar by months of practice: I would run along the warm wooden pier, dive into the cold water and swim—just like that I would know how, my body as easy and casual in the water as a fish's. Sometimes I saved someone from drowning, most often my mother, though how she was in danger of drowning when she never went near the water I had never worked out satisfactorily. She was always wearing a jersey print dress and a straw hat, so I supposed she had fallen in.

But when we arrived and I raced into the water, I sank like a stone. It didn't matter, it never mattered, the lake itself was enough, the luxurious wetness of the water, as clear as a crystal glass—no matter how deep you walked in, you could always see the hard ribs of sand on the bottom. I splashed in it, wallowed in it, soaked it up through my pores, longing to pull off my tanksuit but afraid my father or Val would catch me. I dogpaddled furiously, arms and legs churning foam, breath held hurting in my chest, but when I stood up and looked back, the stirred-up water extended only a few feet behind me.

I was building a sand castle when Emily floated into my life. A movement made me look up. She was floating in the water about fifteen feet from shore, enormous mounds of breasts and belly above the water, the back of her head completely submerged, long hair drifting out around her face like strings of brown weed. Just floating there, without a sound, in that clear, still water. She passed silently by, parallel to the beach, and I shaded my eyes to see her better.

She must be dead, drowned bodies rose to the top, I knew that, and was just going to run for my father when I saw her white foot move, just a flicker but still a movement, and farther on another, stronger flicker, like a fish's tail, and she began to move faster. I watched her for a long time, and then she rolled over and began to swim. Until I saw her white arms gleaming rhythmically in the sun I still half believed she was dead. I watched for her all that day but she still hadn't appeared by bedtime.

Ours was a plain two-bedroom cottage with a screened verandah, its board siding weathered to a pale silver-grey, soft and fuzzy to the touch, like suede. It was set back in the trees, close enough to the lake to hear the waves on a windy night, and fat spiders hung outside the screens. The trees gave us the illusion of privacy, though in fact we were close enough to our neighbours to hear them talking at night, their screen door and toilet door slapping open and shut, bursts of laughter. And sometimes other sounds in the night. My father always reserved the cottage on the day we left for the first of July the following year. It gave us a proprietary feeling and made it easier to leave.

Mr. Jacobson, the man who owned the cabins, called renters "summer people", which made us sound faintly glamorous. In fact we were quite ordinary, and this didn't bother me but it bothered my sister considerably. She had met some kids from the city last year, and was afraid that we were going to shame her in some way, do something horribly gauche or gross that she could never live down. I swore I would never be a dumb snot like her, but of course I was, a few years later.

It was almost dark when my father came in from fishing that first night and told us he'd had the scare of his life. He was fishing in the rowboat, a long way from shore, when a fat girl came floating by. He'd almost snagged her with his fish hook. It was downright spooky, he said, seeing someone that far out in the lake, just floating along as if she was ten feet from shore. He asked her if she wanted a ride but she didn't answer, didn't even lift her ears out of the water when she saw him speaking to her. She smiled and swam off, he said, and he followed her in to shallow water to make sure she didn't drown. She floated in and out of my dreams that night, a strange little smile on her lips.

"That's Dummy Morrow's daughter," Mr. Jacobson said the next morning in answer to my father's question. "Your wife would know the family." Mother had grown up only a few miles from the lake. "Floats like a cork," he said, aiming a stream of tobacco juice into the long grass beside our cottage. A sturdy dandelion swayed, straightened, and dripped brown. "Emily, her name is, you'll get used to her. Swims like a fish and floats like a cork—swim clean across the lake if she takes the notion. And that ain't all." He didn't explain what he meant.

My mother had finished the dishes and was rolling cigarettes on the oilcloth-covered table when I went in. She was expecting company later and her hair was twisted onto hard metal curlers with rubber knobs. Because she had grown up near there she had a lot of company.

"Dummy Morrow," she said thoughtfully, lighting a clumsy, hand-rolled cigarette, "I haven't thought of him for years." She blew smoke toward the ceiling while charred bits of paper and tobacco drifted onto her wine chenille robe. "In fact I thought they'd moved away." She absently scooped the loose tobacco into a pile on the table. Not many women smoked in those days, and Val had asked Mother not to smoke in front of her new friends, but she just laughed and went on lighting up whenever she felt like it.

"Did you know Emily?" I asked.

"No, I wouldn't know her. But I remember her father. He used to come around to the farm, sharpening knives and scissors and mower blades. He knew everything you said by watching your lips. And when he wanted to tell you something, he wrote a note."

"Was he deaf and dumb?"

"Of course," said my mother, "that's why he was called *Dummy* Morrow."

I accepted this without question or surprise, that was the way people talked then—Chinny Sawyer had a huge chin, Gimp Brown had one leg shorter than the other, Fat Faber weighed three hundred pounds. No one seemed to think anything of it, not even the Chinnys and Gimps and Fats, who waved and grinned when they were hailed by name.

"Do you think Emily is deaf and dumb?" Mother was putting things away in the bright blue cupboards on which someone had painted fat yellow fish with bubbles rising from their open mouths.

"She probably is," she said. "It's hereditary."

Emily was sitting on what I thought of as my stretch of beach when I got there. Even sitting, there was something of the same stillness about her, but she looked up and smiled as I went past her into the water. She was wearing a faded blue bathing suit and her wavy brown hair hung past her shoulders. Because of her size, I found it difficult to guess her age, she could have been thirteen or twenty. I attacked the water headlong, willing it to hold me up, but I could not keep my feet from touching bottom for more than a few seconds. Each time I glanced ashore, Emily was watching me intently.

And then she was in the water, gesturing for me to lie down, supporting me with her hand on the small of my back. I was stiff and awkward and she set me on my feet, shook her head and arms and legs and let them go limp, then she flopped back in the water and lay there. She put her hand on her chest so I would notice that she was breathing naturally. She was able to tell me with gestures what she wanted me to do, and I did it. There was authority in her manner, firmness in her hands, and before that first lesson was over, I trusted her completely. She smiled broadly when I managed to stay up for a while without support, and then she signalled the end of the lesson.

While we were building an elaborate sand castle, my father walked down the dock with his green tackle box and fishing pole. I waved. "My Dad," I said, making sure Emily could see my lips. She smiled and nodded.

"Do you want to go fishing, Bethie?" he called, his voice sounding different across the water, distant, remote.

"No," I called back, "we're going swimming again." I pointed to Emily and myself and made swimming motions with my arms.

He nodded and lifted his arm. "Be careful," he said, and stepped down into the rowboat, almost losing his balance before he sat down. As he rowed away, I promised myself I would go with him the next time he asked.

I don't know why, but we were not a family who did many things together. I've heard it said that the Depression made families close, but it was not that way with us. For one thing, there were four years between my sister and me. There had been a baby who died two years before I was born, a girl, too. She was beautiful, I'd heard my mother say, with thick black hair and a perfect little face. Her name was Elizabeth and they named me for her; you'd think my mother would be afraid to do that, afraid it would bring bad luck.

No, we didn't do that many things together. For that matter, my parents didn't do many things together that I remember. Certainly not at the lake, where my father fished and my mother visited friends or read on the screened verandah, drinking iced tea and fanning herself with a cardboard fan with DRINK COCA-COLA printed on it in red and white. She liked the stories in Liberty magazine and saved them all up to bring to the lake. She enjoyed the company she had there, too. She was a woman who liked to talk and my father was a quiet man; maybe it was years of poring over figures in the small office in the back of the Co-op Store, maybe he just got out of practice.

I discovered that first day that Emily was a fine person to build sand castles with. When we needed a flag for the turret, she raked the sand with her fingers and unearthed a small piece of silver paper, which she folded into a triangle. A quick raking on her other side produced a small twig which she split part way down with her strong fingernail, and sliding the paper into place, she poked it into the wet sand. She laughed when the wind caught it and turned it around. The sun was hot on my neck and arms, between my shoulder blades, and the warm wind fluttered and dried the wet sand on my legs.

Val came down to swim, walking in carefully, riffling the water with her fingers. In her white two-piece bathing suit, her blonde hair in a green net snood with small green bows on it, even I could see that she was pretty. "My sister," I told Emily, and she smiled and rolled her eyes in a complimentary way.

"Can I come in with you?" I called. It was always better to ask, with Val.

"Sure. But don't splash me," she said, as I ran in. And I kept my distance, fearful she'd change her mind. I capered around her, telling her about the swimming lesson, telling her who Emily was, scarcely able to contain the huge bubble of joy in my stomach; I had to expand my chest to the limit to hold it. The sun, the lake, the absence of school, the swimming lesson, Emily, my sister . . . sometimes things were so good you could hardly stand it. I fell in the water face down and slowly sank to the bottom, my arms flung wide to take in the whole lake, the whole world.

Emily and I went in a half dozen more times that day, and while she sat on the beach, I went on practising. By the end of the day I could float on my back easily, though I had to move my arms and legs more than Emily did.

Once, while I was in the water, two boys came down to the beach and seemed to be asking Emily to go somewhere. She jumped up and ran off with them, her long hair flying, joy in the pumping of her fat legs. They disappeared into a clump of dense bush down the beach. They were gone about twenty minutes and then Emily was running back, looking over her shoulder and waving at the boys who didn't wave back, but who were giggling hysterically as they staggered off up the beach the other way, shoving each other into the water every so often, and they weren't even in bathing suits, they were wearing pants and shirts and shoes.

I wonder if anyone else ever learned to swim as quickly and easily as I did, for there could be no other teachers like Emily. We were together every day, and almost as easily as she had taught me to float, she taught me how to breathe, how to move my arms and legs. I never wondered who had taught Emily, it seemed as if she must have been born knowing how, as if her mother had birthed her in the lake and she had swum easily from one fluid to another. Sometimes, with motions for me to stay close to shore, she would strike straight out toward the centre of the lake until I couldn't see her for the reflection of the sun on the water. She always came back. And every day we floated, side by side, wrapped in water, the sun warm on our faces, open-beaked gulls hanging in the blue air above us.

Val got a boyfriend, a boy from the city. I didn't like him, though I couldn't have said why. He was polite and good-looking but there was something about him I didn't trust. They wound up the old Victrola gramophone on the cottage verandah and danced to Bing Crosby singing "Moonlight Bay" and "Sioux City Sue". My mother grumbled about being relegated to the back yard with her books and her visitors, but you could tell she was pleased.

More boys came for Emily, they beckoned to her from down the beach almost every day, and I soon accepted these interruptions as part of our routine. I put in the time while she was gone perfecting moats, straightening flags—we had one on every turret, all different colours—and squinting at the bushes now and then to see if she was coming. If there were more boys, Emily was gone longer. She always came back smiling, and sometimes there were leaves in her hair.

Once her father came to the beach just as Emily and two boys emerged from the trees. He was a thin, bald man with thick glasses, and his hands moved so fast they were almost a blur at times. I knew he was shouting at her in his way. Emily's hands, which were slim and graceful compared to the rest of her, moved more slowly and there was no anger in her face. When he started pulling on her arm, she just shook him off, walked into the water and swam away.

Emily was not there when we went back the next year. She had been sent away to a special school for the deaf, we were told.

I could make a collage of that summer with Emily if I had to, and I know exactly how I would do it. There would be the immense shimmering blue of the lake, and on the far shore, my father in the rowboat, fishing. My mother and another woman are in deck chairs, words falling out of their mouths into their laps; they are wearing dark glasses. Off to the left, my sister in her white two-piece bathing suit is dancing with her boyfriend and there are notes rising from the gramophone. From a clump of bushes on the edge of the shore, boys' faces are grinning.

And right in the centre of that blue water, Emily and I are floating, floating in the silence like a strange pair of sea creatures. Emily's eyes, the colour of the lake, are open, and her long hair is drifting out around her face.

Delusions of Agriculture

Fred Stenson

John Percy found his heaven on the lee side of a foothill in an elbow crook of mountains. He left a lucrative practice to get there, a good fifteen years before most dentists even think of retiring. John looked at it this way: what purpose to pry more money out of people's teeth when it would only mean more time spent away from agricultural bliss?

He made the move in the summer of 1979, with his wife in tow. Anne saw it all as some form of menopausal male mania, and put up with it only because she thought the alternative might be John's pursuing young girls with exceptional teeth or his demanding that she wear a tutu to bed.

When they arrived at their farm, the reception given them by their neighbours was nil. John had expected this and was in one way pleased about it. It was dramatic proof that this was the real country! Much too far from the nearest city to be a cozy haven for commuters who longed to own a cow. To the third- and fourth-generation tillers of this deep, black soil, John and Anne must have looked like conquistadores, the beginning of a trend, perhaps the beginning of the end. John did not want the natives to come too readily bearing gifts; he wanted to earn their respect with painstaking toil. He wanted his well-fed, shining brood cows to plead his case from the lush hills upon which they grazed, tranquilly announcing to the neighbours who drove by: "Behold the unmistakable signature of a farmer. Does this look like the handiwork of a dentist with delusions of agriculture?"

The first token of acceptance came one month to the day after the Percy arrival: a jar of beet jelly delivered to their door by Mrs. Cal Dornly. The woman did not announce herself. She did not stay to talk. She merely set the jar on the front step and walked back across the field toward home, her babushkaed head moving above the heads of ripening grain like a preamble to Millet.

Anne was somewhat suspicious of the offering. "Jelly made out of beets?" she cried when John finally came back to the house after digging in a gate post.

"What's the matter with that, dear? I think it's wonderful."

"But John. The beet is a vegetable."

"Marvellous resourcefulness." And to prove that he thought so, John smashed through the wax seal with his jack-knife and slathered a piece of bread with a thick layer of the purple stuff. It was the first indication beyond his own confidence that this foray into foreign territory was destined to be a success.

Cal Dornly himself came to call two days later. He pulled into the yard in his half-ton truck, the cab rearing and plunging on the chassis like a wild stallion. The truck crunched to a steaming halt beside John, who was kneeling in the shade of his swather, squirting grease into nipples as prescribed in the operator's manual.

Dornly and one grubby-chinned child dismounted. Dornly plunked himself down on the frame of the swather, picked at a decaying tooth with a brittle stalk of alfalfa, and swung his gaze from building to freshly painted building.

"Place looks nice, Mr. Percy."

"Thank you, Mr. Dornly. I'm determined to make this a success."

"Sure you will." Dornly worked his mouth as if there was something distasteful under the upper lip. "Those other fellas went broke here were lazy as hell."

This was the first John had heard of a chain of financial failures on his farm. He was daunted, but not so much that he forgot his common touch.

"Would you care for a cup of tea, Mr. Dornly? Or coffee?"

Dornly shook his head.

John remembered the Mormon contingent in these parts. "Kool-Aid?"

"Gosh, no. Actually I'm here to apologize is all."

"Apologize! Good Lord, Mr. Dornly, for what?"

"That damn jelly! I told my wife you weren't likely to want any of her stupid jelly when you're perfectly capable of buying store-bought, but she brought the damn stuff anyway. I don't know how she could have been so damn dumb."

"On the contrary, Mr. Dornly. We were delighted. It was wonderful hospitality and wonderful jelly!"

"I'm awful sorry," Dornly said for the fourth or fifth time. "It'll probably flush down the toilet, if you want the jar. If not, put the whole works in the outdoor john."

It went on a bit longer: Dornly denigrating the jelly, John pleading to be listened to as he praised it, along with Cal's wife, local hospitality, and home-made confections. He was still pelting Dornly's greasy backside with thanks even as it was hoisted back behind the wheel of the decrepit half-ton.

It was after the truck had bucked out of the yard that John turned to his swather and discovered the grubby-chinned child still there. Boy or girl, he couldn't quite decipher. It was about nine years old and had been forgotten by both Dornly and himself.

The child corrected him on the last point. "Supposed to help," it said.

For the rest of the afternoon, John tinkered uncertainly with his swather, bothered more than a little by the silent child. The only communication consisted of the child's walking to the tool box and coming back with a needed tool each time John turned his attention to another part of the machine.

At five o'clock, John declared with relief that it was time to quit. He begged the child to come in for Kool-Aid and cookies, but was coldly refused. In desperation he produced his wallet and plucked out a ten. The child examined it briefly as if it might be counterfeit, deposited it somewhere in the tattered coveralls, then turned and started for home. That small, spiritless back parting the grain sent a wave of unmistakable failure rushing through John, the first he had felt on his farm.

Pigs had never occurred to John in the planning of his farm. He had always seen himself on horseback, riding astern contented Herefords. Riding astern a herd of contented pigs lacked charisma somehow.

But cattle hadn't been living up to John's expectations. For one thing, they didn't sweetly low. They roared, and did so with ear-shattering intensity, often right outside the bedroom window at dawn. He had also somewhat overrated their quiet dignity. In truth, anything at all could put them in a state of frenzy—milk-tight udders, lightning, rabbits—and once frantic, they would take off directly over or through whatever or whomever stood in their way.

Sometimes when John went to count them or check their health, one would scramble right up to him, as if deputized by the herd to complain, and, giving out with a wild-eyed cough, would whip great, mucousy tangles of saliva onto his cowboy shirt and coveralls.

He began to consider pigs seriously. For one thing, they were smaller, less likely to break the bones in your feet if they stampeded over you. Then there was that favourite old wives' tale about their impeccable cleanliness relative to other beasts. John lulled himself into believing this, a happy alternative to his cows, who seemed to delight in dragging their bags through filth just prior to milking. Yes, pigs. There was much to be said for them. If the bastards got mutinous, you could lock them up. Also, they require no milking.

"Pigs?" Anne said. "This place smells bad enough as it is!"

John reminded her that the pig is one of the cleanest animals in Christendom.

"Have you taken a deep breath going past the Dornlys'?"

John had indeed experienced the sweet, rotting reek that was manu-factured for export at his neighbour's farm. He began to tack left in his argument. Perhaps smell was not a sure indicator of cleanliness. He reminded Anne of the many halitosis sufferers he had dealt with in his former profession. Most of them swore up and down that they were frequent brushers, garglers, sprayers and flossers.

Anne glared at him. "Smell," she said, "is still an excellent gauge of smell."

Defeated in argument, John remained strong in conviction. He put the stock racks on the truck and drove from farm to farm in search of pigs. On this tour, he avoided the Dornlys' farm. Not because he doubted the excellence of Cal's herd; rather he feared he would appear ignorant. After the jelly-and-child incident, John had come to crave Dornly's re-spect.

Methodically he perused hundreds and hundreds of local pigs, but he couldn't find what he wanted. The pigs he looked at seemed to be a pretty undistinguished lot, rooting, ranting, vulgar beasts that ate, slept, slopped, and screwed with equal indifference. He did see the odd York-shire that impressed him slightly, but he didn't care for the way their ears pointed forward and shielded their eyes. The last thing he needed were pigs who went around running into things and injuring themselves.

John was about to give up when he ventured onto the farm of Orin

Werner and his two brothers. Theirs was an enormous pig farm with literally thousands to choose from; but there were as usual none about whom John would have written home to mother.

"I want the best," he implored them, after an extensive search. "Registered purebred beasts that would turn a person's head if he were to pass one on the street."

The Werners looked at one another, some silent message passing. They signalled John to follow. He was led to a large A-pen, freshly painted and set apart from the others—clearly the throne room. John felt a tingle of excitement as the low door was unlatched and Herman Werner pounded the cherry-red walls to fetch the inhabitants out.

Two black heads poked out. Finally, the full body of one pig emerged. Its tall back scraped the lintel of the door. Regally, it paced to the centre of the yard and stood like a Roman senator, surveying the Werners and John. The second sow followed, young, enormous, and proud.

The Werners listed their virtues for John. Both the young sows had yet to produce their first litter. They had genealogical virtues galore—sired by Somebody III, grandsired by Somebody Else VI. John was barely listening. His eyes were too busy soaking up the sleek blackness of the beasts, the snow-white ring around their middles. He interrupted Orin Werner's recitation to announce that he'd take them.

Gently, John urged the pigs up the chute to his truck. Neither one seemed eager to race into this change of ownership. The larger of the two lay down, and its flesh spread so broadly as to fill the chute from side to side. Still, John would not hear of letting the Werners jolt his beauties with an electric prod. For his new-bought sows he waited, and eventually they saw fit to move up the gangplank and into the deep, clean straw of the truckbox.

All the way home John muttered statements biblical in nature, about the rocks upon which he would build his herd and the various wonders they would beget. He also named the pigs: Rosebud and Tulip.

At home, John would not rest until Anne came to look at his wondrous purchase. He took her by the hand and tugged her across the yard to the A-pen. Anne stared at the sows in silence. Finally, frostily, she turned to John.

"Call them whatever you like. They're still pigs, and they still smell."

In twelve years of marriage, this was the low point, but John spent little time brooding about it. He had work to do. According to the cycle of the moon and the complex charts kept by the Werners, he had but two weeks before his sows became fertile. Between now and then, it was up to John to find a sire suitable for the spawning of peerless piglets.

In his search for the sows, John had already seen most of the boars of the region, and not one had struck him as being noble enough for the job. He talked to the district agriculturist and the local vet. Their only suggestion was that he resort to artificial insemination. They showed him the credentials and a picture of one Ebony VI, whose living semen was banked in some quantity. But, though the brute was handsome and the same breed as Tulip and Rosebud, John had qualms. The idea of his two beauties having for their first affair of the flesh a test-tube romance withered him. John decided to press his search outward another thirty-mile radius.

Meanwhile, to the east, Cal Dornly was having his own problems. It had been a rough summer. Though he was more than willing to hire his brood of six children out, no one was willing to hire them in—some horsecrap about their being too young. Cal himself had worked and brought money home to his own layabout father from the age of six, and had usually been able to steal a fair bit to boot. But people had since gone all soft, mainly in the head.

There was also Dornly's wife. Ordinarily she brought in a good dollar doing laundry for town people. But this summer she was well on her way to producing a seventh child for the litter. She complained often of fatigue and yelled blue murder at any mention of laundry.

This all shifted the onus squarely onto Dornly, a place he was not fond of having onuses put. His business was pigs and chickens, and the chicken end of that business had been wiped out by a thieving skunk. What's more, Cal's oldest boy had been rendered unfit for human company when Cal sent him under the coop with a shotgun to give the skunk what-for.

As for pigs, because of his wife's being pregnant and his kids too young or smelly for work, Dornly had completely run out of feed for them. And he hadn't a cent to buy more. For most of the summer he'd been out by the light of the moon, chasing his pigs over the hills to dine on road allowances and other people's grass.

Lately, though, with the Hutterites' wheat beginning to fill right across the fence from his barn, he couldn't get his pigs to forage any farther than that nearby feast. The moment he opened the barn door after dark, he was bowled over by the anxious lot of them. They made straight for the Hutterites' wheat and couldn't be budged until they'd eaten their gluttonous fill. That was all fine and good—the pigs were flourishing and fattening on the fine feed—but the Hutterites' wheat crop had come to look downright mangy. What's more, the Hutterites had noticed.

"You von't be renting us from much long more else you keep doze shtinkink pigs in der wheat field out!" was the sum total of what the Hutterite colony's wheat boss had had to say.

Cal couldn't afford to lose the farmstead, what with the naïvely low rent the Hutterites charged. And, as his own yard was bare of grass, and the fence between the Hutterites and himself was no match for a starving pig, he had no choice but to lock his pigs in the barn day and night.

At John Percy's the critical moment had arrived. Rosebud and Tulip had announced themselves ripe for breeding just a day apart, and were restlessly searching the horizon for beaux. John loaded their trough with grain, hoping to distract them as he scoured the countryside in a final, vain search for the ideal boar. He had seen so many pigs in the last two weeks that his head swam with snouted visions, but his determination not to compromise had become perverse. Better to sacrifice the month's fertility altogether than to expose his darlings to a pig with inferior genes.

In Cal Dornly's barn, things had also reached crisis proportions. Every edible straw was eaten. Dornly had not even swung open the upper half of the barn door in three days, his financial condition having shown no improvement.

The pigs were literally starving to death. Some took to the corners to conserve their energy. Others stood in stupefied disbelief. Still others hovered by the door, having in their extreme condition hallucinated Dornly walking across the yard with the beaten-in slop buckets.

But one of the pigs, a small boar the children had named Rhino for a minor deformity on the upside of his snout, continued day and night to pace the inner perimeter of the barn. Rhino was the type of pig who would burn the last calorie his body had to offer before giving up the ghost. He was practically down to that, too, when he discovered a tiny dot of daylight where a knot had fallen out of the parched wood. Baring vestigial tusks, Rhino attacked. He widened the hole, split the wood, and chewed his way to freedom.

When the others realized what was happening, they crowded up to follow. Soon all forty-two of them were happily gorging in the Hutterites' wheat. All, that is, save Rhino. He took but one life-sustaining mouthful and started chugging across the field. As he poked his head out into sunlight, there had been a faint but unmistakable something in the air, the one thing in the world that meant more to him than food. With the same doggedness that had carried him to freedom, he pursued that something west.

Rhino had begun life as the runt of the litter, the type of pig that rarely lives because its siblings won't let it suckle. But Rhino's approach to life had been truly pig-headed from the first, and no amount of chewing or throttling could subdue him. He made it through piglethood with his ears chewed down to stubs, and remained part of the Dornly herd only because he was too scrawny and ugly to sell.

The logical thing would have been to rob the runt of his ability to reproduce long before he had the opportunity or the wherewithal to pass on his shortcomings. But Rhino's wiliness in combination with his master's laziness saved him time and again. Whenever Dornly emerged from the house with sharpened knife to do the deed, Rhino would head for the burdock, the only plant that flourished on the Dornly farm. The chase would always end with Dornly and Rhino looking into each other's beady eyes from opposite sides of the burr-bearing wall of weed.

Now, stomach curving up against his spine, Rhino hurtled westward, casting his head from side to side, stripping heads of grain into his maw. The spoor grew ever stronger, and soon he was within view of John Percy's gleaming, recently painted farmstead. To this eater of walls, the fence that corralled Percy's champion sows was hardly an obstacle. He found an enlarged square in the page wire, drove into it snout first, and thrashed until he was through.

The sows became suddenly coy. They crammed together in the farthest corner of the pen and faced out at the intruder. Both emitted low groans of fear.

Rhino stood heaving, catching his wind, swinging his gaze from the fertile sows to the grain-heaped trough. Finally, his goals in order, he dashed to the trough and scooped up a jawful of chop. He choked it down with no time lost for chewing and, new life and lust roaring through his veins, approached the far corner of the pen.

Rhino seemed not the least bit abashed by the fact that Rosebud and

Tulip were both at least twice his height and weight. He mastered one and then the other with not a moment between, then returned to the trough to prepare for another bout.

John Percy returned to his farm, exhausted from another morning's fruitless search for a suitable boar. Anne tried to call him in for lunch, but John would not rest until he had checked on his sows. He headed for the pen, head down and mind full of problems, when a snort of a sort he had never heard before brought him to attention. There before him, *flagrante delicto*, was Tulip, prize of prizes, bemounted by the thinnest, most ravaged nightmare of a boar John had ever seen.

It is a credit to Percy that he did not faint, a credit to his general health that he did not take apoplexy. What did happen was that a volcanic rage unlike anything he had ever felt roared upward through him and exploded in obscene oaths. He ran to the fence and grabbed the coal shovel he used to clean the pen, ran back, and brought the shovel down as hard as he could on the boar's awful, pitch-roof back.

Rhino slid from Tulip, his ardour momentarily dampened, and ran around the pen with Percy in hot pursuit. Another pig might have fled for the hole through which it had entered, but Rhino was no stranger to this type of thing. Beatings were a commonplace in his life, and things were going to have to get a damn sight worse before he abandoned two majestic, fertile sows and a trough of grade A barley chop. Half of Percy's blows he dodged, the other half he absorbed, scooping another mouthful of chop each time he passed the trough.

Rhino's dogged masochism drove John to even greater frenzy. The mild-mannered dentist had found a well of molten violence deep within. He rained blow after blow on the raping cretin, leaving bloodied bruises by the dozen. When at last he was too weary to raise the shovel one more time, he stood and stared at his red-eyed adversary. The little boar, a welted mess, still had that undaunted look in his eyes. John got the disquieting feeling that if he didn't leave promptly, he himself might become the prey.

When he first saw his wife at the fence waving her sweater in the air to get his attention, Cal Dornly figured she'd found the most inopportune time to produce their seventh child. It was inopportune because, at that moment, Dornly was knee-deep in ravished Hutterite wheat, field-marshalling his six kids in a last-ditch effort to get his pigs back in the barn. The whole business had been given a desperate dimension by the vision, not less than a half-hour ago, of three self-propelled swathers cresting Hatfield Ridge. On the other side of the ridge was the Hutterite colony, and the Hutterites were the only operators around who owned three swathers. There could be no doubt that they were on their way to swathe the grain that forty-one of Dornly's pigs were gulping down with bright delight.

"What the hell do you want?" he cried, approaching his wife on the dead run. "This is no time to drop a kid. Go bite on a piece of wood or something."

His wife explained that that was not the nature of the problem. The problem was John Percy, who was on the phone and mad as hell—something about pigs. At that moment the Hutterite swathers roared over the hill, no more than three hundred yards away. Dornly sounded a general retreat and he, his pregnant wife, and six kids headed hell-a-whooping for the house.

After barricading the doors and pulling the blinds, he noticed that the phone was still off the hook. Cal took it up and found Percy still on the line. It was necessary to hold the receiver at arm's length for the next several minutes. Even at that, Percy's voice could be heard, furiously going on about the rape of Tulip and Rosebud. The really nasty bit was that Percy intended to charge Cal two hundred dollars per ravished sow, the estimated difference between the worth of piglets by Rhino and those they could have had by a more distinguished sire. Dornly apologized humbly and said he'd be down some time after dark to talk.

He went on foot, dodging the lights of the swathers as they wheeled around looking for something worth cutting. He found John sitting on top of an inverted chop bucket in the centre of the pigpen. The yellow light from the lantern at his feet illuminated several things: Rosebud and Tulip lying contentedly together in the mud; the sleeping smile of Rhino, who lay tucked up against the vast, warm flank of Tulip; the exhaustion and defeat on Percy's sunken face.

When John lifted his eyes to Dornly, a large tear glistened in one of them. "I want that money right now, and I want that boar out of here tonight."

Dornly gave John a long look pregnant with sympathy. He pushed his hand up under his cap and scratched for some time. "Gosh, Mr. Percy," he said at last. "This is a hell of a note. I can't tell you how sorry I am. But I had that damn boar penned in the barn and he ate his way right out through the wall."

He shifted his gaze from Percy to Rhino, a blood-encrusted mass, snoring gently. With the air of a local magistrate, Dornly said, "There's no doubt you've got something coming here. You've suffered a loss, I agree. Problem is, Mr. Percy, I don't have a red cent to give you. And, at the moment, I don't have a single way of getting you one either."

He paused again, screwed up his face in thought. He scratched a great deal here and there, looking all the while at the devastated Rhino. Then he smiled a sudden, lightbulb smile and turned quickly to John.

"I'll tell you what," he said. "You can have the boar."

A week after John put his farm up for sale, it was purchased by a French noblewoman representing some shadowy consortium of Paris business-men. He hoped not to have to see Dornly again, but as he was starting off with the loaded U-Haul trailer in tow, Dornly's bucking half-ton—also full of furniture—met him at the gate. Dornly jerked to a halt, causing one child to fall from a tattered chesterfield at the top of the load. Dornly jumped from the cab and flagged John to a stop.

John sat rigid behind the wheel of his car.

"Just wanted to wish you well, Mr. Percy. And missus of course. Been a pleasure knowing you, although I can't say I actually ever did meet you, missus . . ."

"Why is that furniture on your truck?" growled Percy.

"Well, I had a kind of disagreement with the Hutterites about the other place. Had to move. And then I heard those Frenchmen were looking for someone to live in this place and kind of keep an eye on—"

Dornly didn't have a chance to finish. John popped the clutch and roared off over the hill with the trailer swinging on the hitch and bouncing over the ruts. Cal, shaking his head, walked back to the truck and sat beside the missus, who was suckling their new-born son.

"Those city people," he said as the engine shivered and caught. "They sure make poor neighbours. Just when you're startin' to get to know them, they always seem to leave."

The Summer Visitor
Gertrude Story

When Uncle Emil Beckmann moved Gerda and Auntie Elizabeth and the new little boys to town, it hurt me. I never said it, but it hurt me. Hurt me lots and lots.

He moved them to town because Grampa Schroeder said to do it. He bought them the house, secret, private, only he told Papa. Told Papa his little Elizabeth had by The Holies suffered enough. And Papa was a careful man, he never told things, only if you were sitting quiet in his big chair with the high back in the parlour, people sometimes didn't know it when they came in and talked, or else they thought you had no ears, no ears to understand them.

Papa was a careful man and never told things. Mama got too excited. I learned it early. But Gerda was a teller, sometimes; only sometimes. My Cousin Gerda was mostly a listener. When people came she listened too, washing dishes hard, hard, her eyes only on the dishes—she told me once how to do it—or folding towels and sheets, later, in her Mama's new bedroom off the kitchen in town, Gerda listened and sometimes told things.

She had to be sore when she did. She had to be so sore, most likely at Uncle Emil, and then she told things. Otherwise Gerda hardly ever talked.

But before Uncle Emil moved them all to town and it hurt me, Gerda would walk over to our place sometimes, Sunday afternoons. And she most likely would have that lightning in her eyes, that lightning that made her eyes like pale slough ice—Uncle Emil eyes. But she always hung her head quick if it was Mama opened the door to her; I guess it was a danger if somebody like Mama saw the lightning in her eyes. So she always hung her head quick if it was Mama opened the door to her and said, real quiet to Mama, "Mother said I could come play with Alvena a while, so long as it's all right with you."

"She's always hanging her head like that, like a whipped dog," Mama said to Papa this day. "Hanging her head like a whipped dog, like she was the cause of it all. Why doesn't your sister leave that man if she can't get along with him; a lot of women would like the chance to get along with him, but my, she thinks she's so modern, won't go to church, just like your father, she's too good for God, I guess, just like your father, no wonder Emil Beckmann gets ornery now and then, so why doesn't she just leave him, she's modern enough to do it, and your father will give *her* money for a house in town even though *we,* my goodness, can't get the loan of a few dollars for three new milk cows, my goodness, why doesn't she just leave him and go live in town with your father, he always favoured her, you know, you're just too blind to see it, and she can stop looking so long-necked skinny and put-upon all the time and that young Gerda wouldn't have to come around here looking like a whipped dog all the time, it isn't healthy, it affects others, you know, not to mention any names," Mama said, "it hurts others."

When Mama got going, she talked; she never quit. If you tried to say anything, even like, "But Mama, I never broke the pitcher, honest," she just put her voice up another squeaky holler louder and went right on, and if Papa came in, she right away cried a little.

Papa was a quieter one, and he hardly ever interrupted.

But now he said, "Well now Tina, it seems to me there's likely lots of things affects girls Alvena's age. Twelve years or not, it seems to me there's better things for her to do than sit in the house on a nice summer day with her nose in a book. No sunshine likely affects people too, seems to me; she should be out there."

"It's Sunday, leave her alone," Mama said, "she has her good church clothes on; there's more to life than running around outside like a tomboy, riding horses bareback and pretending at cowboys like all the Schroeders. Besides, she's at that stage, you know; she's already had the back pains some, and it could be any time now."

"Oh," Papa said, and got a little bit red behind the beard, and stuffed his hands in the pockets where he stood and chewed on the end of one side of his moustache where it drooped and always got wet in his coffee if Mama didn't warn him first to lift it.

"Well," he said, "I wonder what's the use to talk all the time about things. Things are what they are and we got them cows anyway, remember? A man who has got to go beg from his father is no man. I always said I'd squeeze the money for the cows if you wanted them, so what was the use, really, of mentioning it to him, it might have been better not to do it."

"Oh sure," Mama said, "blame me! I was only trying to help, you know. It's not that I take pleasure squeezing tits on three more cows."

"I know, I know, I know," Papa said quick. And he took one hand out of a pocket and held it, sort of, out to her, but a little like he knew she wouldn't take it. "So come on," he said, "how about it? How about at least *you* come out and ride a little horseback like the crazy Schroeders and we'll go check the crop for wild oats; it's quite a while since we did that together."

"Hmph," said Mama, standing a little straighter, like a queen, but letting her mouth be glad just a little to be asked. "You're a goof sometimes," she said, "and it would be more like checking the crop for crop. If it doesn't rain pretty soon there'll be no green oats even to feed the cows we had, and here's us with three new ones giving milk like rain and eating oat chop by the gallon."

"You worry too much," Papa said. "Come on now, put on some overalls, why not, and come show me how the Uhriches used to play a little cowboy too."

Mama smiled a little when he said that, even smiled wide enough to show the teeth nice, even though she pressed her mouth together quick to shut out the smile. "It's Sunday," she said.

"God don't stop the wild oats because it's Sunday," Papa said. "We could handpick a few down there by the north slough where the wild mint grows. Surprising," Papa said, "how handpicking helps to small up that patch of wild oats."

"Well, I don't know," Mama said, looking at me.

"She's twelve," Papa said. "Nearly a woman. Or are you afraid somebody's gonna come steal her if you go away one little hour?"

And he went out to the porch himself and brought in Mama's little outside chore overalls and held them out to her. And Mama put them on over her dress saying, "Now Alvena, if Gerda comes, you stay in the house and play the organ, only hymns, mind you; or play the little blue *Gospel Songs* book, there's nice ones in there, they're safe." And she gave a little yank to the overalls' braces and Papa stepped over quick to help. "And if I have to say it myself," she said, looking up at him and letting the smile come wide, "I could always rope a calf better than Elizabeth Schroeder or even Abe Schroeder." And she bent and rolled up the pants cuffs three sharp turns apiece. "And if you get back pains again," she said to the pants cuffs, "make a hot water bottle and send Gerda home, she's a little too young yet; and go to bed and stay there and read *Marjorie May's Twelfth Birthday* again, it will help. Papa and I won't be long, only maybe a little hour is all."

"She's OK," Papa said. "She has good sense, just like all the Schroeders." And Mama opened her mouth to be a little sore about that, but Papa gave her a swat on her little overalled hinder and said, "How about them wild oats, then?" And the swat got her going out the door and then she started talking and I couldn't hear what but I heard "roped Papa's bull once" and then there was laughing, Papa's was no surprise but Mama's was, even if it wouldn't of been Sunday.

And I guess I didn't really think it was fair, in a way, not getting asked to go pick wild oats—for a long time *I* was the one had got to go with Papa. Anyway, just all at once the *Ulysses* seemed dull, dull, dull; they'd got old Helen of Troy in there again and it all seemed so stupid, all that killing and for only one woman, who maybe even had a prissy little mouth like Mama—it sure looked like it in the picture.

And so I got up out of Papa's big chair, and the crocheted chair back slipped off and I didn't even care if Mama came home and saw it, I just left it. And I picked up the little blue book of *Gospel Songs* and all at once I kind of hated even Jesu. And I went out and had a slice of saskatoon berry kuchen; Mama made it good no matter what she put inside it, except she'd got stingy with the sugar again and it didn't taste right, so I left it.

And my back and legs felt draggy, felt like somebody else's, and I went back to Papa's big chair and sat in it, it was still warm from me, and I pulled my feet up under. And there was something caught in the chair back, I thought it was the crocheted chair back and I thought, Darn Mama's darn old doilies! But it was *Marjorie May's Twelfth Birthday* stuck there instead, and I hauled it out and turned the pages again, it was dull, dull, dull; after the first page of it you could tell it wasn't about anybody's birthday, it was a trick to teach you something. I got tired of learning, school was plenty, and so I threw it, but it was so puny little it only fluttered a little ways and then flopped down in the middle of Mama's all-colour parlour rug, its plain blue with a simpy Marjorie May on the cover lying there saying, And what's Mama gonna say when she sees it when she comes?

And then, sure enough, Gerda came. And she had on her Sunday dress, too; not fancy, never anything fancy—Auntie Elizabeth didn't believe in it, and it was only Sundays or to concerts Gerda ever wore a dress, any kind at all. Gerda didn't like dresses, but I did.

To dress up in a clean new dress—or even one still hot from the iron because Mama had washed it out special for the school picnic when you'd got berry pie on it—to dress nice was to feel like a princess, or a queen, only not Helen of Troy. To be a real queen you had to do good things for the ordinary people and give God all the credit besides, not go have somebody make a war because he thought you were too beautiful to be a queen to anybody else but him.

And Gerda even wore a pinafore over her dress, not very nice but a good idea all the same. Gerda had real sweaty hands and she was always wiping them. You try wiping sweaty hands in summer down the sides of your Sunday dress all day and see what your mother tells you come washday.

And Gerda came in and threw her hat on the kitchen table. She swirled it onto the kitchen table like Uncle Abe did his cowboy hat when he came in to wash and eat when he and Papa were cutting pigs or something. Gerda's hat used to be Grampa Schroeder's Sunday one, and she liked it a whole lot. And she said, real quiet, but with those slough-ice eyes flashing lightning sparks, "It's so goddam bastardly hot, it's gonna burn all the crops again, and then there'll be some fun."

And I knew Uncle Emil Beckmann was off again to ride his big white stallion over at Elmyra Bitner's. When Gerda came and swore right away, swore a lot all day, before the day was done you'd hear Uncle Emil was off again to ride his big white stallion over at Elmyra Bitner's.

"Mama and Papa went to pick wild oats," I said.

"I saw," said Gerda.

My legs were so darn draggy.

"Wanna play organ?" I said. I wanted to sit.

"Nah," Gerda said. She went ahead of me into the parlour and flopped on the all-colour rug there and so did I.

"What's this?" Gerda said. She'd flopped on simpy old *Marjorie May*. She hauled it out. "Sonofabitch," she said, "I bent it all to hell. I didn't mean to. It's a book." Gerda had this real respect for books.

"It's no book," I said. "It's one of those tricks to teach you stuff, like Uncle Emil's *Brotherhood of Man* books he keeps in his bottom dresser drawer."

"Hmm," said Gerda. And she thumbed through and pressed it back together, flat, flat, flat. "It's just about rags," she said.

"What kind of rags?" I said. I didn't remember anything about rags in there, I guess I hadn't read in it far enough. I didn't really care, though. I asked but I didn't really care. I lay flat on my back on the parlour rug. My legs were somebody else's.

"*No* kind," said Gerda. "It's just a something that happens. Blood and stuff. So girls can have babies. Mother said."

I sat up. "*I* don't want to have babies," I said. "*I* don't want to have blood. What does the blood do? When do the babies come? Babies come out of the hinder, like calves and kittens. I don't want any dull old babies coming out of *my* hinder," I said, and I felt myself getting sorer and sorer about it. And there were Papa and Mama gone off on horseback to pick wild oats in the sun.

"I don't know and I don't care," said Gerda. "*I'm* never gonna have it. Wanna go out?"

"Mama said not," I said. And then I thought of Mama off on horseback with Papa and how she'd said about roping her papa's bull. So Mama roped calves when she was a Uhrich still, and now I wasn't supposed to, I was supposed to rope only a fence post or sometimes, sneak, sneak, one of the dull old milk cows in the pasture. So I said to Gerda, "Can you rope a calf?"

"Can God spit?" said Gerda, jumping up.

"Don't be stupid," I said. "And don't take God's name in vain, either; you're gonna get caught out one of these times and once the pastor hears I bet you ten cents you go to hell."

"*He* can go to hell," Gerda said. "Pastor and Papa and God can all go to hell, for all of me; see if I give so much as a sonofabitch about it."

When Gerda was that way, what was the use of talking? "Can you rope a calf?" I said again.

"Got a rope?" Gerda said.

So I got up too, and we went out into the sun. It was hot, hot as hell, after the dark coolness of Mama's parlour. So I went back for my sun hat, it was pretty, I liked it, but Gerda seemed to look pretty nice with just Grampa Schroeder's old Sunday hat on her head. And then we walked to the barn and I put my arm around Gerda. She never put her arm around, not on anybody, and she carried herself stiff all the time *you* did it. But all the same, when you were telling her hard something from the *Ulysses* and so forgot somehow to put an arm around her while walking out to the pasture or the north mint slough or something, she would pick up your arm and put it around herself and walk stiff close beside you, listening.

But this day we went out to the calf corral, not the pasture. And from the lean-to by the chop bin, we got some rope; it was new, almost, full of oily binder-twine smell and smooth and sweat-shiny yet.

And the calves came prancing up to watch us. They came stiff-legged and hopgoblin prancy to watch us. And one stuck his cold wet pink slobby nose up against my bare leg and behind me. And I yelled, "Hey," surprised as anything, and spun around and grabbed him, grabbed him around the neck, so hard he made a aw-w-gh from deep down in the throat where I was hard-squeezing him. And we sort of wrestled, he and I, and Gerda laughed and laughed, and hollered, "Hang on to the little bugger, and I'll rope you both!"

And the calf and I went down then, down together on the hot dirt and straw and you-know-what-maybe-else of the calf corral. And the calf aw-w-ghed again and thrashed and I was under him but I somehow hung on to his neck, wanting him to say aw-w-gh even harder. And Gerda hollered, full of giggles, "You're buggin' his eyes, Alvena; that'sa way! Here comes the rope!"

And it whanged and was there. And the calf was yanked off me; it was like something had got stolen from me somehow, and I felt a warm warmness worm-crawling slow slow down between my legs. And I got up and lifted my dress, my Sunday dress. And there was the blood.

And the pain was a hurt that went all through me; there wasn't a part of me, not even the part that always used to stand there outside me and never felt things but only watched them, even that part of me felt pain, and knew it, and *was* it, somehow.

And the calf was gurgling aw-w-gh! deep and low and terrible; terrible loud and hard inside his throat. Gerda had the rope around his neck and snubbed around a fence post. The calf was up and had set his clean little growing feet fierce as fierce into the hot dirt of the calf corral and was putting his everything into pulling his own head off.

"Let him go," I said to Gerda. I never knew before that pain had a colour. Now I knew it was all-colour, just like Mama's parlour rug.

"Won't," said Gerda.

"Let him go," I said, "or I'll kill you where you stand."

And Gerda looked at me, and it seemed her eyes lost their lightning for a minute, a whole acre and a year of a minute, while we stood and looked at each other through the all-colour pain of the calf's aw-w-gh.

And then she let him go. And he ran, ran, ran, head-wobbling away from us to the far end of the calf corral where he stood and looked at us, still shaking his head.

It was a hot day but now I was shivery. I lifted my dress again and showed Gerda the blood.

"It's the rags," she said. "You have to go in the house and wash up good, Mother said, and tear up an old sheet, make sure it's an old one, and stuff yourself there, she didn't really say how, and lie down." And Gerda put her arm around me and we went to the house and she helped me do all that.

She didn't know about the hot water bottle, but I remembered it all of a sudden, out of the pain that stood outside of me and was good at remembering. And so Gerda lit the stove and got the water so boiling hot in a big flat pan for the hot water bottle, she had to wrap it in a piece of old sheet to lay it on my belly; and there was hardly enough hot water bottle for all the pain.

And Mama said afterwards, "My goodness, didn't the girl know enough to light the coal oil stove instead to get hot water in this heat? She's made it like an oven in this kitchen. To light a wood stove in this heat, it makes you wonder," Mama said afterwards, "where the famous Schroeder brains have got to in that Gerda."

But before Mama and Papa came Gerda kept saying, "Did it quit yet? Do you hurt yet? Why don't you look at yourself and see if it's nearly done!" And I told her I hurt too much. I could still see the calf trying to pull his head off. I could see him there, about three feet in front of my eyes, while I lay there on the kitchen couch and was glad it was so warm in there.

"Oh Gerda," I said, "it hurts too much to look at it."

Then Gerda's eyes got the lightning in them again and she said, "Well, it's never gonna happen to *me!*" And just then we heard Mama and Papa ride jangling and laughing into the yard. "It's never bloody sonofabitchen hell ever gonna happen to *me!*" said Gerda. And she grabbed her Grampa Schroeder's old Sunday hat and clapped it on her head and slammed the door and was gone.

"She had her head hanging down like a whipped dog again," Mama said as soon as she stepped in the door. "Just like a whipped dog again. Now whatever in the world happened between you and your Cousin Gerda here today?"

"Nothing," I said. "Just nothing," I said. And I turned my face to the wall so that she couldn't see me crying: crying for Gerda, and me, and the blood, and the calves; crying for the way things used to be when Gerda came over and Mama was outside for a while and we sneaked the key to the organ and played "There Was an Old Man and He Had an Old Sow" even though it was Sunday, and laughed so hard we nearly killed ourselves, and switched to "Komm Jesu Schōn" the minute Mama came in, and laughed again, later, when she was gone, because she told us we were good little girls to sing so nice on Sundays.

Once upon a time, my Cousin Gerda and I, we had sure had a lot, a lot, of laughs, I told the crying part of me; and I held myself steady so that Mama, if she was watching, wouldn't see and know how I was crying all through me now that Gerda was gone.

Coughs, Memory Lapses, Uncle's Hands
Wayne Tefs

Staring into the bottom of a whisky glass, as he sat in his favourite chair waiting for the midnight news, Arnold decided it was thinking about his uncle's hands that caused him to break into a clammy sweat.

Arnold remembered the visits of his uncle clearly, because living in isolated Red Rock, the family made any relative's appearance in their drab mining town an occasion to celebrate. Uncle Ed was his mother's brother and had been born late enough to miss the War against Hitler from which Arnold's father returned with a wounded leg and a sad face. A decade or more younger than his sister, Uncle Ed cashed in on the postwar boom; he leapt from cabs to bulldozers in the first months of "agonizing reappraisal." When he first came to Red Rock he had the flushed open face of the youth eager to make his way in the world. That was in the early fifties.

It was a happy time. After the penury of the war, consumption burned at fever pitch. Arnold's father bought a 1952 Meteor with the "flat-head" eight-cylinder engine. Arnold's mother got a new refrigerator. The newspapers were filled with talk of expansion and progress, and when Red Rock built a new high school the mayor placed a plaque over its main door reading *Educatio Est Successui Ianua*. Everyone was infected with the allure of profits and the giddiness of unrestrained spending: hula hoops, whiffle balls, fizzies.

Talk of money, too, was in the air. Dollars, dollars. Arnold got a paper route and delivered the *Winnipeg Free Press* to the frame houses springing up in the newly developed area of Red Rock called Birch Heights. (His parents competed with the neighbours, artlessly mimicking the affectations of the *nouveaux arrivés*: teak tables, naugahyde chairs.) They bought a television and watched "Leave It to Beaver" and "Father Knows Best."

Arnold saved his collections for a CCM bicycle. There were hockey sticks to buy, too, the kind with straight blades, good for backhand shots, and Arnold's first baseball glove which he rubbed with oils to make the new leather soft. But most of all it was the bicycle.

That's where Uncle Ed came in. One summer afternoon he arrived from the city in his gleaming car (everything in Red Rock was coated in red iron dust). It was the week Arnold bought his CCM Roadster. There was nothing backward about Uncle Ed. He slammed the car door and shouted hello to Arnold from across the street. He had black hair and a scar on his chin that made him look tough. In one hand he carried chocolates and in the other a bottle of whisky which he waved at Arnold's mother when he looked in the kitchen window. He was back from a stint on the DEW Line where, according to Arnold's mother, he'd amassed a king's ransom. His flashy red Oldsmobile bore witness. From his back pocket he produced a silver bicycle bell which he brandished at Arnold even as he hugged his sister, chocolates clutched in one big hand, the whisky bottle already installed on the kitchen table. He shook hands with Arnold's father and mumbled something about being dry as a tumble-weed.

Arnold fetched the tool box while Uncle Ed and his father toasted each other with whisky. Bent over the handlebars, screwdriver tuned to the bright metal slots, Arnold inhaled the burnt wood mist from their breath as they appraised his work. After he'd taken a turn around the block, ringing his bell at Sandy Russell coming out of the grocery, he stood between the two men while his mother snapped a photograph. Then Uncle Ed took the Roadster for a spin and on his return drifted up to the curb in a shower of pebbles, a leer on his face like a motorcycle tough. Arnold's mother pursed her lips.

Later, when the supper dishes were put away and the men were talking politics in the living room, she shook her head. They'd opened a second bottle of whisky. "You see," she said to Arnold, playing on the floor with plastic soldiers from cereal boxes. "It's the same as my father." Her eyes seemed greyer then. "First it's only a few harmless glasses of beer, but before you know it . . ." She stood in the archway between the rooms. A lock of blonde hair kept falling loose and she tucked it behind one ear with automatic precision. She caught her husband's attention with one of her black looks. She returned and began to make sandwiches. "I expect you to understand this," she said to Arnold, one finger waggling. "Because it's something that passes from generation to generation. Because I won't have it happening to you." She muttered some words about her father and then she helped Arnold gather up his soldiers and tucked him in bed.

He would never forget the warmth of her breath as she bent over to kiss him, steam of freshly ironed shirts pressed against his cheek.

The next day they bought accessories for the Roadster at Sokol's Hardware. A red reflector for its rear fender. Uncle Ed punched a hole through the fender with an electric drill and Arnold filed off the metal burrs before bolting down the reflector. They attached a mileage counter to the front wheel and took turns going around the block. Each circuit added two tenths of a mile. Uncle Ed showed him how to drift into curves with one leg out like motorbikers, scattering gravel. They took turns wearing a black leather cap; they were reckless champions of Red Rock's roads.

Finally the news came on but Arnold listened with only one ear. He was thinking of Sokol's Hardware, of loose gravel on curves, of sweet oak mist from an uncle's breath. His glass was filled again. In Japan a famous poet had jumped to his death from a high-rise. Somebody was contesting the election in El Salvador. The dollar had plummeted by a record amount—was it really eleven cents?—and traders were predicting a world-wide crash. Nothing from the art world. Typical, thought Arnold. A team of doctors had separated Siamese twins. A man in Cleveland had accidentally shot himself with a pistol he'd put on a bedside table near the phone—had he been awakened by ringing and picked up the pistol instead of the phone? A cold front was moving in.

Arnold finished his whisky. The back of his throat felt raw. He stared into the bottom of the glass. He was tired. He could feel a headache building behind his ears but he decided not to think about that. He fiddled with the radio dial but all he could find was rock and roll. His hands trembled. To still them he poured another whisky and rolled it over his tongue before drifting off into a sleep punctuated by the word "Roadster."

Uncle Ed died at forty-eight. It should have been in a motorcycle pileup where the rider, giddy with speed, loses control navigating a hairpin curve and sails past the guard rails in a cloud of smoke and gravel. It might at least have been an air disaster. Shrieks, groans, sudden revelations. Instead he died attached to a ticking machine in a hushed hospital. His sister was by his side. And Arnold. At the end his eyes had gone away as if he had given up. His big hands were swollen and wrinkled with fat. No more trembling. The machine had been unable to sustain his liver and kidneys any longer. But something else had gone before that.

After the weeping his mother had said, "You see? From one generation to the next. So don't pity him. Learn from his stupidity, his weakness." She was holding onto Arnold's arm to steady herself and she squeezed it as she repeated, "Yes, weakness." They had stood in a north wind by the graveside. Her nose was red. She blew it and said, "If you must, love him. But for heaven's sake don't pity him."

This was her way of making a bleak prediction about the two bottles of beer Arnold drank every night while listening to the late news. He was finishing his degree in art history, then. Planning a career in writing. Already two of his articles had been published in glossy magazines. He laughed her off. He barely had time for his meagre meals and the odd movie with a friend. But for complexities like love? Or pity? Anyway, he was different from his uncle. He was a young man in control. He was popular, successful, dynamic.

There was a time when he had pitied Uncle Ed. At forty, the age Arnold was approaching, his uncle had seemed older than Arnold's father. Stooping shoulders, wattles at his throat. His hands trembled, and when he lit a cigarette he had to place it in his mouth and then bring the flame up to it, one hand steadying the other. (He smoked Exports, without filter.) At family gatherings the cousins imitated his cough and laughed at him. Later they poured glasses full of water and then shook them until the table was dotted with little pools. More loud hooting. Arnold's mother scolded them but they only laughed at her too.

His uncle was a sad man and also powerless, and no one paid much attention to his sadness. Between him and Arnold there had grown the silence of men guilty of having failed the same woman.

At first when Arnold discovered the trembling, he took measures. For several months he paid close attention to his diet. Practised exercises to strengthen the muscles in the wrist—exercises he learned about in a pamphlet circulated by the Canadian Air Force. (He was living on his own then, in an apartment on Stradbrook.) He mastered certain relaxation techniques recommended by Reveen, the hypnotist. When he visited his parents he kept both hands folded in his lap, feigned disinterest in photographs, passed newspapers quickly through his hands. He avoided the eyes of his mother. Declined refills from his father. In an effort to gain control over his body he read about autosuggestion and trained himself to repeat a phrase that was supposed to induce a healing trance. But he never stopped drinking whisky.

Then one day his mother said, "Stop pretending." And she left Arnold and his father in the living room and fled to the kitchen where she cried quietly while she fixed sandwiches. When she came back she said to her husband, "Say something to him." She glared at the bottle installed on the table between them. She picked it up and revolved it in her hands, looking as if she meant to throw it. "I hate to think what'll happen. I just hate to think," she said.

"Then don't," Arnold's father said, "if it bothers you so much. Don't think." They were into one of their wrangles before Arnold had his coat on and was out the door.

That was when he used to see his parents every week. They gossiped about the cousins. About Uncle Ed, who was often drunk and constantly losing jobs on account of his drinking. He would turn up on his sister's doorstep every six months or so, barely able to stand after ringing the bell. These visits developed a predictable pattern. First he would berate Arnold's father for being a dull success; after some incoherent shouting he'd leave; later he'd weep apologies to his sister over the phone. The whole charade embarrassed her. It disgusted Arnold's father. But they gleefully treated Arnold to every detail of each episode. His mother fixed coffee which they had with cinnamon buns and then the talk flowed. Sometimes Arnold's father poured whisky and they got on to politics. (The Conservatives had swept to power with the largest majority in history but were busy self-destructing from corruption and mismanagement.) There was a lot of laughter among them. Their favourite pastime was looking through old photograph albums.

Now Arnold rarely went there. For years his mother had had that certain look in her eyes. She had stopped dropping hints about his drinking but he knew she was thinking black thoughts about her father. About his Uncle Ed. Blaming herself, probably, in the way of mothers.

He stayed in his room and wrote pieces on the latest painters for avant-garde magazines. In the mornings he drank coffee and talked to editors on the phone. His pieces were in demand from London to Paris to New York. Evenings he went to the galleries and afterwards he sipped

whisky at the cafés. When he could afford it he travelled to Paris or
Florence, and he always sent his mother a package before he left these
places: silk kerchiefs, linens. For his father he brought back Glenlivet, and
once a bottle of Rémy Martin, which his father didn't like. He'd never
seen his Uncle Ed drink it either; like himself, he preferred rawer brands,
and had been reduced in his final days to Saskatchewan Number One
Hard Liquor. Arnold had tried it once. Corn whisky. As coarse and
unsubtle as the prairie itself. Bold as death. Mornings when he woke with
a headache Arnold thanked god he'd never taken to smoking. But
sometimes when he coughed a certain way or found himself listening
absently to an editor whom he couldn't remember having called, he grew
suddenly cold and he started to sweat. Well, he said to himself, it's
probably nothing, a little lapse, the first tremor of mortality. He said that
but his eyes blinked and his mouth went dry and he decided to stop
thinking about things, like coughs, memory lapses, uncle's hands. They
were as deadly as they were compelling, yes, deadly is what those thoughts
were. So he decided to stop thinking them.

Goalie

Rudy Thauberger

Nothing pleases him. Win or lose, he comes home angry, dragging his equipment bag up the driveway, sullen eyes staring down, seeing nothing, refusing to see. He throws the bag against the door. You hear him, fumbling with his keys, his hands sore, swollen and cold. He drops the keys. He kicks the door. You open it and he enters, glaring, not at you, not at the keys, but at everything, the bag, the walls, the house, the air, the sky.

His clothes are heavy with sweat. There are spots of blood on his jersey and on his pads. He moves past you, wordless, pulling his equipment inside, into the laundry room and then into the garage. You listen to him, tearing the equipment from the bag, throwing it. You hear the thump of heavy leather, the clatter of plastic, the heavy whisper of damp cloth. He leaves and you enter. The equipment is everywhere, scattered, draped over chairs, hung on hooks, thrown on the floor.

You imagine him on the ice: compact, alert, impossibly agile and quick. Then you stare at the equipment: helmet and throat protector, hockey pants, jersey, chest and arm protectors, athletic supporter, knee pads and leg pads, blocker, catching glove and skates. In the centre of the floor are three sticks, scattered, their broad blades chipped and worn. The clutter is deliberate, perhaps even necessary. His room is the same, pure chaos, clothes and magazines everywhere, spilling out of dresser drawers, into the closet. He says he knows where everything is. You imagine him on the ice, focused, intense, single-minded. You understand the need for clutter.

When he isn't playing, he hates the equipment. It's heavy and awkward and bulky. It smells. He avoids it, scorns it. It disgusts him. Before a game, he gathers it together on the floor and stares at it. He lays each piece out carefully, obsessively, growling and snarling at anyone who comes too close. His mother calls him a gladiator, a bullfighter. But you know the truth, that gathering the equipment is a ritual of hatred, that every piece represents, to him, a particular variety of pain.

There are black marks scattered on the white plastic of his skates. He treats them like scars, reminders of pain. His glove hand is always swollen. His chest, his knees and his biceps are always bruised. After a hard game, he can barely move. "Do you enjoy it?" you ask, "Do you enjoy the game at least? Do you like playing?" He shrugs. "I love it," he says.

Without the game, he's miserable. He spends his summers restless and morose, skating every morning, lifting weights at night. He juggles absent-mindedly; tennis balls, coins, apples, tossing them behind his back and under his leg, see-sawing two in one hand as he talks on the phone, bouncing them off walls and knees and feet. He plays golf and tennis with great fervour, but you suspect, underneath, he is indifferent to these games.

As fall approaches, you begin to find him in the basement, cleaning his skates, oiling his glove, taping his sticks. His hands move with precision and care. You sit with him and talk. He tells you stories. This save. That goal. Funny stories. He laughs. The funniest stories are about failure: the goal scored from centre ice, the goal scored on him by his own defence-man, the goal scored through a shattered stick. There is always a moral, the same moral every time. "You try your best and you lose."

He starts wearing the leg pads in September. Every evening, he wanders the house in them, wearing them with shorts and a T-shirt. He hops in them, does leg lifts and jumping jacks. He takes them off and sits on them, folding them into a squat pile to limber them up. He starts to shoot a tennis ball against the fence with his stick.

As practices begin, he comes home overwhelmed by despair. His skill is an illusion, a lie, a magic trick. Nothing you say reassures him. You're his father. Your praise is empty, invalid.

The injuries begin. Bruises. Sprains. His body betrays him. Too slow. Too clumsy. His ankles are weak, buckling under him. His muscles cramp. His nose bleeds. A nerve in his chest begins to knot and fray. No one understands. They believe he's invulnerable, the fans, his teammates. They stare at him blankly while he lies on the ice, white-blind, paralyzed, as his knee or his toe or his hand or his chest or his throat burns.

To be a goalie, you realize, is to be an adult too soon, to have too soon an intimate understanding of the inevitability of pain and failure. In the backyard, next to the garage, is an old garbage can filled with broken hockey sticks. The blades have shattered. The shafts are cracked. He keeps them all, adding a new one every two weeks. You imagine him, at the end of the season, burning them, purging his failure with a bonfire. But that doesn't happen. At the end of the season, he forgets them and you throw them away.

You watch him play. You sit in the stands with his mother, freezing, in an arena filled with echoes. He comes out without his helmet and stick, skating slowly around the rink. Others move around him deftly. He stares past them, disconnected, barely awake. They talk to him, call his name, hit his pads lightly with their sticks. He nods, smiles. You know he's had at least four cups of coffee. You've seen him, drinking, prowling the house frantically.

As the warm-up drills begin, he gets into the goal casually. Pucks fly over the ice, crashing into the boards, cluttering the net. He skates into the goal, pulling on his glove and blocker. He raps the posts with his stick. No one seems to notice, even when he starts deflecting shots. They come around to him slowly, firing easy shots at his pads. He scoops the pucks out of the net with his stick. He seems bored.

You shiver as you sit, watching him. You hardly speak. He ignores you. You think of the cost of his equipment. Sticks, forty dollars. Glove, one hundred and twenty. Leg pads, thirteen hundred dollars. The pads have patches. The glove is soft, the leather eaten away by his sweat.

The game begins, casually, without ceremony. The scoreboard lights up. The ice is cleared of pucks. Whistles blow. After the stillness of the face-off, you hardly notice the change, until you see him in goal, crouched over, staring.

You remember him in the back yard, six years old, standing in a ragged net, wearing a parka and a baseball glove, holding an ordinary hockey stick, sawed off at the top. The puck is a tennis ball. The ice is cement. He falls down every time you shoot, ignoring the ball, trying to look like the goalies on TV. You score, even when you don't want to. He's too busy play-acting. He smiles, laughs, shouts.

You buy him a mask. He paints it. Yellow and black. Blue and white. Red and blue. It changes every month, as his heroes change. You make him a blocker out of cardboard and leg pads out of foam rubber. His mother makes him a chest protector. You play in the backyard, every evening, taking shot after shot, all winter.

It's hard to recall when you realize he's good. You come to a point where he starts to surprise you, snatching the ball out of the air with his glove, kicking it away with his shoe. You watch him one Saturday, playing with his friends. He humiliates them, stopping everything. They shout and curse. He comes in, frozen, tired and spellbound. "Did you see?" he says.

He learns to skate, moving off the street and onto the ice. The pain begins. A shot to the shoulder paralyzes his arm for ten minutes. You buy him pads, protectors, thinking it will stop the pain. He begins to lose. Game after game. Fast reflexes are no longer enough. He is suddenly alone, separate from you, miserable. Nothing you say helps. Keep trying. Stop. Concentrate. Hold your stick blade flat on the ice.

He begins to practice. He begins to realize that he is alone. You can't help him. His mother can't help him. That part of his life detaches from you, becoming independent, free. You fool yourself, going to his games, cheering, believing you're being supportive, refusing to understand that here, in the rink, you're irrelevant. When you're happy for him, he's angry. When you're sad for him, he's indifferent. He begins to collect trophies.

You watch the game, fascinated. You try to see it through his eyes. You watch him. His head moves rhythmically. His stick sweeps the ice and chops at it. When the shots come, he stands frozen in a crouch. Position is everything, he tells you. He moves, the movement so swift it seems to strike you physically. How does he do it? How? You don't see the puck, only his movement. Save or goal, it's all the same.

You try to see the game through his eyes, aware of everything, constantly alert. It's not enough to follow the puck. The position of the puck is old news. The game. You try to understand the game. You fail.

He seems unearthly, moving to cut down the angle, chopping the puck with his stick. Nothing is wasted. You can almost feel his mind at work, watching, calculating. Where does it come from, you wonder, this strange mind? You try to move with him, watching his eyes through his cage, and his hands. You remember the way he watches games on television, cross-legged, hands fluttering, eyes seeing everything.

Suddenly you succeed, or you think you do. Suddenly, you see the game, not as a series of events, but as a state, with every moment in time potentially a goal. Potentiality. Probability. These are words you think of afterwards. As you watch, there is only the game, pressing against you, soft now, then sharp, then rough, biting, shocking, burning, dull, cold. No players. Only forces, feelings, the white ice, the cold, the echo, all joined. A shot crashes into his helmet. He falls to his knees. You cry out.

He stands slowly, shaking his head, hacking at the ice furiously with his stick. They scored. You never noticed. Seeing the game is not enough. Feeling it is not enough. He wants more, to understand completely, to control. You look out at the ice. The game is chaos again.

He comes home, angry, limping up the driveway, victorious. You watch him, dragging his bag, sticks in his hand, leg pads over his shoulder. You wonder when it happened, when he became this sullen, driven young man. You hear whispers about scouts, rumours. Everyone adores him, adores his skill. But when you see his stiff, swollen hands, when he walks slowly into the kitchen in the mornings, every movement agony, you want to ask him why. Why does he do it? Why does he go on?

But you don't ask. Because you think you know the answer. You imagine him, looking at you and saying quietly, "What choice do I have? What else have I ever wanted to do?"

A Latin for Thieves

Aritha van Herk

But he does not have the hands of a thief. Instead, his are the hands of a lover, with the long cool warm fingers that every woman conjectures brushing slowly tenderly ever-so-lightly over the secret and most unexpected of places: the small bump on the forehead, the bossy and pliable skin over the elbow, the slight indentation below the navel, the callus on the edge of the outer toe. His fingers are not stealthy but lingering, the kind that hesitate over even inanimate objects, that cannot tell time without caressing a watch face, that cannot dial a telephone without rubbing the dial and the receiver, as if touch contains a message beyond its object. He runs his palms over the surfaces of desks and counters. At the supermarket, he secretly compares the skins of oranges and eggplant. His fingers centre no rings and he never smooths on a pair of gloves—he wants no interference between his hands and their profession. And his constant piano touch is his way of reminding his hands of control. He cuts his fingernails short and neat: you would never imagine he chews them, although it will eventually be discovered that (in private) he does chew his fingernails, fastidiously but nevertheless. And he is always rubbing his thumb and forefinger together, with delicate attention, as though testing the grain of his own fingerprints. Which have been variously dusted from the innumerable places where he has abandoned them, and which occur on various police sheets, but no one has ever thought to connect him, *this* thief, with his own particular and beautifully whorled fingerprints. He is careless with them, so palpably unconnected to his act that he can afford to flaunt them, to leave them enigmatically behind. The most obvious evidence is the most difficult to believe.

He is, however, an orderly thief, and perhaps it is this orderliness that makes him truly sinister.

He keeps everything he steals, never fences or re-sells one piece of stolen property. He keeps his thefts indelibly—filed according to subject and content, perhaps even cross-referenced, he is that methodical, that purposeful. Those objects too large to fit inside a folder in one of his many double-wide filing cabinets, he keeps in his basement, a cement-block room lined with shelves of graduated size, and with movable partitions so that each object and thought has its own small box or nest, its own cubbyhole, a spot where it juxtaposes with other objects in an ineffable order. This cool damp room, these shelves, these compartments and their contents, are breath-taking in their strange variety, that variety adding immensely to the power that the thief has over those he steals from. For they are only one of many, only a small cipher in the thief's gallery of passion, and they have no right to think themselves special.

Nor does he have the body of a thief. You predicate them as having supple, infinitely bendable bodies, spider-like bodies capable of slipping through the smallest of windows, the slightest crack of a door ajar. You think of them wearing black turtlenecks and tights, with the soft-soled shoes of a dancer and a nylon stocking revealing only their eyes and the possible bones of the face. You think of them lounging against a mantle-piece with wonderful nonchalance, of tickling a safe dial into submission. You imbue them with infinite dexterity, the adroitness that you are not capable of.

But this thief, I confess, is clumsy, a bumbler, one who drops *hors d'oeuvres* on the floor, who never has a handkerchief, and whose brown shoes are always in need of a spit or a shine. He gangles and gawks, his bones jut out at awkward angles, and were it not for his beautiful hands, you would consider him quite adolescent. You know better than to stand close to him when he is holding a cup of coffee. He tends, in his abstracted way, to bump into walls and to tumble down steps. He has a shy smile and a chipped front tooth that adds to his innocence, the wonderful innocence of the truly devious.

He is, when he appears on the doorstep of a house having a social gathering, seldom invited but welcomed with pleasure, though not the unreserved delight meant for true party sparklers. He is curiously useful: frantic hostesses find him trying to fit all the dirty dishes into the over-loaded dishwasher, and will stop to peck his cheek, to cry, "Angel, you're wonderful, you can come and live here anytime." And he grins and brushes back the lock of black hair that has fallen into one eye, and at exactly that moment, he tucks into his suit jacket pocket her wooden pepper mill.

But do not make the mistake of believing that he steals things that are useful, or things that he needs, or things that are valuable. The pepper mill is because the hostess is a peppery woman, short and spicy with greying hair, a woman who loves pepper, hot pepper and lemon pepper and mixed pepper and white pepper and the scent of freshly-ground black peppercorns, so much so that her husband often thinks he smells them in the bed. The thief takes what matters, he steals what is important, what counts, some indicator, some intimate affiliate of its owner.

He is a thief of private reconditenesses.

This might lead you to believe that he spends a fair amount of time gauging the contents of dresser drawers and closets, that his fingers snag themselves on the lace and satin of underclothing. Oh he has those too, women's lingerie, but not what you would expect, the frothy stuff, the black strapped stuff. He knows instinctively a woman's favourite bra, the one she has worn almost thin, its seams fraying. He knows the pair of panties that she likes to wear every month when she is menstruating, without caring if the tampax leaks, the bloodstains carefully soaked into faint blossoms. He knows the t-shirt she likes to wear when she reads in bed, propped against the pillows with the book resting on her knees. He finds these secret items effortlessly, almost as if his fingers are sensors, can anticipate what the woman will miss most, will search for, will be puzzled at losing and yet resigned: it has been used so well, so carefully, so long.

How does he do this, how does he manage to find those things that are not replaceable, your biggest revelations? He knows the owners of his thefts more or less well, sometimes only slightly. Certainly, he does not rely on personal knowledge of your habits or your possessions. He has an instinct, a sweet sharp stab of instinct that tells him to take, yes, that fat coffee mug, so good to hold between the hands, that flat tack from a pin-up board, that button which you intend to sew on your red coat before the snow appears, that scarf—you had it tied around your waist, but have pulled it off and dropped it in a corner so that you can dance more freely—that bar of apple soap from the bathtub soap dish, that small cork coaster from the table beside the soft chair, a nail, a twist-tie, a half-full jar of chutney from the fridge, the brown leaf of an inconsolable house-plant, a dust-ball from under a shelf. He has even gone on his knees and taken between his impressionable fingers the residual bubbles left behind on the surface of the tub.

He has, he knows, sometimes gone too far, been unable to resist a cherished brass doorknob or an embroidered footstool, a pinch of ash from a cremation urn. He himself barely dares to remember how he managed to get away with these items, or the obvious gaps they left behind, especially the doorknob, the round confession of the hole in the door. And yet, things that are readily missed are sometimes overlooked for days. That doorknob, for instance, was never missed so much as the door's ability to open and close, and the family's discussion over the strange thief who required entrance completely missed the doorknob as the object of that thief's desire. They thought he was after their stereo and television, which the thief, of course, disdains. He refuses to steal appliances, mechanical objects, or screens; he despises the winking eyes of microwaves and VCRs, sees them as instruments of depersonalization, when he is after that rare essence, the *crème de la crème* of the personal.

He has, for instance, quite a number of pairs of shoes. And mittens—he prefers mittens (the objects of the rejected lover) to gloves, something fuzzy and sweet about fingers clenched in a ball. Needles and thread too: he enters the sewing room of women with an ache in his crotch. Mostly he loves the needles that he can unscrew from sewing machines—he imagines their rapid piercing with a kind of ecstasy. He seldom takes jewellery. Gold and silver are too impersonal, but there is a faint sexiness about those round button-like earrings made of plastic. He has acquired several pairs.

His favourite room for theft is the bathroom, and not because it is a safe place to put things in your pocket. Bathrooms reveal so much—the innocence of a frayed toothbrush, the setting on the scale, the shells that crowd a ledge, the small fat candle used for midnight baths. He loves the moment when he stands in front of a sink, just before he opens the medicine cabinet. He cannot resist just one tablet from a prescription bottle, a sleeping pill, an analgesic, an antibiotic. He has, and oh he felt wicked for days afterwards, knowing the consternation he must have caused, taken one contact lens, the left, from a neatly scooped double case. He had to buy a small container and some solution in order to keep it pliable and corrective.

He takes rubber frogs and fishes. He finds the erotic magazine stuffed in the towel closet. But more than anything else, he loves makeup, the tube of carmine lipstick showing the very creases of the woman's lips, the last of mascara brushes, perfume bottles with only a few drops left, face creams and false eyelashes. The kinds of things it is easy for a woman to misplace or to imagine that she has thrown away, not realizing how intimate, how unbearably revealing these things are.

He tags the items with their owners, knows the ears, the feet, the breaths of the bodies who have used them; no, not with their names but with their essence, the capsicum of their possession, and that is what he remembers and counts, tells over in his myriad orderings of his stolen goods, his secret fingering of the items of revelation. It is the intimacy of his theft that makes him so perfect an artist. Knowing what to steal is as important as the act. Doing it is easy, but knowing, ah, knowing enough about the secret life of his victims is the trick.

And yes, how does he do it? How does he appear at all the neighbourhood parties? It is shameful to omit him, he cannot be left out because he is so much a part of your social lives, although he comes always unattended, attending no one himself, unescorted, with only that shy grin and perhaps a bunch of flowers in one hand. Certainly, he always brings the canonical bottle of wine; he can be relied upon. Not one of your loud-mouthed guzzlers who decimates the Courvoisier before he stumbles out the door. He is awkward and polite, infallibly courteous, and if he is there, standing in the bedroom, looking at the picture over the bed with his head cocked to one side, you are never suspicious, never nervous. He is simply looking at your art, and if it is true that he bends to sniff the pillowcase before you appear (fetching a sweater for one of your guests— the night air is getting chilly), does it worry you? Not at all.

Although he seems so lonely sometimes, in his solitary manner, that you want to match him up, find him a friend or a woman, possibly a wife. Which leads to dinner parties and further revelations on your part, and which leads him into another woman's life. And curiously, although he always goes home alone, although none of the matchmaking works, all those women that he is introduced to, who subsequently marry someone else, always invite him to their parties and give him more scope for his perverse profession. Of course he cannot marry. It would intefere with his perpetual theft, capture, collection. His craft requires such intimacy that he has nothing left over for a lover or a wife. He is engaged to thievery, the intricate collection of what belongs to others, an artist absolute.

For he is a thief of more than objects. He steals smell, taste (his tongue on the bristles of a hairbrush), he steals the images of a photograph of your daughter when she was twelve, he hears the small gurgle of your tap when it is shut off, he feels the rough edge of an unsanded door. He has even, to capture more fully the essence of one woman's shape, hung all her heaped and flung clothes on hangers in her closet. He takes away the texture of your carpet on his bare feet, he harbours the creak of an old chair. He steals all of these things, knowledge that you think you alone have, no one else can comprehend, let alone take away. Which you only discover after it is missing, perhaps weeks later, when you realize it is gone.

And you never suspect him, despite the fact that he is often found, alone, standing in the middle of a room with his hands in his pockets, you are never suspicious. He is innocent, so sweet, a loner, he smiles at you and reaches to your left shoulder to pick off a piece of lint. And you are grateful; his attention is so pure. That too is a theft.

If you were to try and steal intimacy in his way, what would you take? The small scoop in the laundry soap? Several blank sheets from the notepad by the telephone? A silver spoon? A lunchbag? It has nothing to do with worth, but with value. A tea bag from the counter canister, an ad torn from the weekend newspaper? He does no damage, only minimal, that moment of irritation when you discover something that you expected to be in one place missing, or that moment of surprise when you suddenly realize that something you have come to think unremovable has vanished.

For he steals the sorrow that has grieved in the corner for years, he steals the pleasure you take in the way your husband pulls up his socks, he steals the pride that keeps the furniture polished. He steals lies and unwritten love letters and forgotten messages and unfinished homework and unmade dinners, he steals the very unused space between your walls. You only discover that it was there after it is gone. Sometimes you are relieved.

You never imagine him, hunched over a single grey sock, smoothing it with his lover's hands, shaping it into his thief's use for it, to be a thing that once had one owner and now has another—to whom it yields its own purposeful emanation.

And he does no harm, does he?

Even when he steals work in progress, that half-written letter to your mother, that half-baked cake, that half-hung wash and half-drunk cup of coffee, a half-read book, a halved apple, there is always a half left for you.

And by now, you've guessed his fatal flaw, the one that will bring him to light, expose him for the thief he is. He steals only from women, from safely, happy or unhappy, married women, whom he judges to be, accurately enough, the keepers of the intimate world. He is a domestic thief. He is a thief of intimacy and he has marked his quarry well. For those same women who hold within their circled lives all of the smells and tastes and sounds he wants are never believed when they complain about their losses. Their husbands send them to doctors; their children suggest aerobics classes. And they only discuss their private losses with each other, over their half-incomplete chores and house husbandry, puzzled that they should be considered the owners of something worth stealing.

And they never suspect him.

Of course, once you think about it, his guilt is self-evident. He manages to be so sweet, so guileless, his appearance steady enough but somehow always in disguise. His eyes change colour, with the sky, from grey to blue, and even to that rosy green you sometimes see at the end of portentous days. He grows taller or shorter than the last time you saw him, and the only consistent trait he reveals is that endearing awkwardness. He has arranged a life to suit theft: alone, but trusted, well-liked. He is his own fence. He harbours the artistry of theft.

And indeed, it has been a family profession for centuries. He can trace his ancestry back, back, through bank robbers and publicans and gold miners, their special expertise, through pickpockets and graverobbers, ancestors who lost one or both hands. He can trace his blood all the way back to Dysmus, one of the two thieves crucified with Jesus—those two, one on his right and one on his left, one mocking and one repentant. He is a product of his history, and it is possible that he will come to the same end—recognition, trial, punishment.

Yet, his ultimate theft is still unknown, untried, a horizon he pushes toward. For he is, after all, the ultimate lover, the one who finds out what counts, and who cherishes that as much as you do, with your pragmatic approach to what is important and what will last of yourself, and what you own. And he might be the ultimate arbiter of your memories, those memories you manage to keep instead of squander, and those memories others keep of you when you are gone, lost or forgotten or dead.

He will steal your self-respect, but never the imprint of an open palm upon your guilty conscience.

What I Learned from Caesar

Guy Vanderhaeghe

The oldest story is the story of flight, the search for greener pastures. But the pastures we flee, no matter how brown and blighted—these travel with us. They can't be escaped.

My father was an immigrant. You would think this no penalty in a nation of immigrants, but even his carefully nurtured, precisely colloquial English didn't spare him much pain. Nor did his marriage to a woman of British stock (as we called it then, before the vicious-sounding acronym, WASP, came into use). That marriage should have paid him a dividend of respectability, but it only served to make her suspect in marrying him.

My father was a lonely man, a stranger who made matters worse by pretending he wasn't. It's true that he was familiar enough with his adopted terrain, more familiar than most because he was a salesman. Yet he was never really *of* it, no matter how much he might wish otherwise. I only began to understand what had happened to him when I, in my turn, left for greener pastures, heading east. I didn't go so far, not nearly so far as he had. But I also learned that there is a price to be paid. Mine was a trivial one, a feeling of mild unease. At odd moments I betrayed myself and my beginnings; I knew that I lacked the genuine ring of a local. And I had never even left my own country.

Occasionally I return to the small Saskatchewan town near the Manitoba border where I grew up. To the unpracticed eye of an easterner the countryside around that town might appear undifferentiated and monotonous, part and parcel of that great swath of prairie that vacationers drive through, pitying its inhabitants and deploring its restrooms, intent only on leaving it all behind as quickly as possible. But it is just here that the prairie verges on parkland, breaks into rolling swells of land, and here, too, that it becomes a little greener and easier on the eye. There is still more sky than any country is entitled to, and it teases the traveller into believing he can never escape it or find shelter under it. But if your attention wanders from that hypnotic expanse of blue and the high clouds drifting in it, the land becomes more comfortable as prospects shorten, and the mind rests easier on attenuated distances. There is cropland; fields of rye, oats, barley and wheat; flat, grassy sloughs shining like mirrors in the sun; a solitary clump of trembling poplar; a bluff that gently climbs to nudge the sky.

When I was a boy it was a good deal bleaker. The topsoil had blown off the fields and into the ditches to form black dunes; the crops were withered and burnt; there were no sloughs because they had all dried up. The whole place had a thirsty look. That was during the thirties when we were dealt a doubly cruel hand of drought and economic depression. It was not a time or place that was kindly to my father. He had come out of the urban sprawl of industrial Belgium some twenty-odd years before, and it was only then, I think, that he was coming to terms with a land that must have seemed forbidding after his own tiny country, so well tamed and marked by man. And then this land played him the trick of becoming something more than forbidding; it became fierce, and fierce in every way.

It was in the summer of 1931, the summer that I thought was merely marking time before I would pass into high school, that he lost his territory. For as long as I could remember I had been a salesman's son, and then it ended. The company he worked for began to feel the pinch of the Depression and moved to merge its territories. He was let go. So one day he unexpectedly pulled up at the front door and began to haul his sample cases (which he had driven off with) out of the Ford.

"It's finished," he said to my mother as he flung the cases out of the car and onto the lawn. "I got the boot. I offered to stay on—strictly commission. He wouldn't hear of it. Said he couldn't see fit to starve two men where there was only a living for one. I'd have starved that other son of a bitch out. He'd have had to hump his back and suck the hind tit when I was through with him." He paused, took off his fedora and nervously ran his index finger around the sweat-band. Clearing his throat, he said, "His parting words were, 'Good luck, Dutchie.' I could have spit in his eye. Jesus H. Christ himself wouldn't dare call me Dutchie. The bastard."

Offence compounded with offence. He thought he was indistinguishable, that the accent wasn't there. Maybe his first successes as a salesman owed something to this naïvety. Maybe in good times, when there was more than enough to go around, people applauded his performance by buying from him. He was a counterfeit North American who paid them the most obvious of compliments, imitation. Yet hard times make people less generous. Jobs were scarce, business was poor. In a climate like that perceptions change, and perhaps he ceased to be merely amusing and became, instead, a dangerous parody. Maybe that district manager, faced with a choice, could only think of George Vander Elst as Dutchie. Then again, it might have been that my father just wasn't a good enough salesman. Who can judge at this distance?

But for the first time my father felt as if he had been exposed. He had never allowed himself to remember that he was a foreigner, or if he did, he persuaded himself he had been wanted. After all, he was a northern European, a Belgian. They had been on the preferred list.

He had left all that behind him. I don't even know the name of the town or the city where he was born or grew up. He always avoided my questions about his early life as if they dealt with a distasteful and criminal past that was best forgotten. Never, not even once, did I hear him speak Flemish. There were never any of the lapses you might expect. No pet names in his native language for my mother or myself; no words of endearment which would have had the comfort of childhood use. Not even when driven to one of his frequent rages did he curse in the mother tongue. If he ever prayed, I'm sure it was in English. If a man forgets the cradle language in the transports of prayer, love and rage—well, it's forgotten.

The language he did speak was, in a sense, letter perfect, fluent, glib. It was the language of wheeler-dealers, and of the heady twenties, of salesmen, high-rollers and persuaders. He spoke of people as live-wires, go-getters, self-made men. Hyphenated words to describe the hyphenated life of the seller, a life of fits and starts, comings and goings. My father often proudly spoke of himself as a self-made man, but this description was not the most accurate. He was a remade man. The only two pictures of him which I have in my possession are proof of this.

The first is a sepia-toned photograph taken, as nearly as I can guess, just prior to his departure from Belgium. In this picture he is wearing an ill-fitting suit, round-toed, clumsy boots and a cloth cap. The second was taken by a street photographer in Winnipeg. My father is walking down the street, a snap brim fedora slanting rakishly over one eye. His suit is what must have been considered stylish then—a three-piece pin-stripe— and he is carrying an overcoat casually over one arm. He is exactly what he admired most, a "snappy dresser." The clothes, though they mark a great change, aren't really that important. Something else tells the story.

In the first photograph my father stands rigidly with his arms folded across his chest, unsmiling. Yet I can see that he is a young man who is hesitant and afraid; not of the camera, but what this picture-taking means. There is a reason why he is having his photograph taken. He must leave something of himself behind with his family so he will not be forgotten, and carry something away with him so that he can remember. That is what makes this picture touching; it is a portrait of a solitary, an exile.

In the second picture his face is blunter, fleshier; nothing surprising in that, he is older. But suddenly you realize he is posing for the camera; not in the formal European manner of the first photograph but in a manner far more unnatural. You see, he is pretending to be entirely natural and unguarded; yet he betrays himself. The slight smile, the squared shoulder, the overcoat draped over the arm, all are calculated bits of a composition. He has seen the camera from a block away. My father wanted to be caught in exactly this negligent, unassuming pose, sure that it would capture for all time his prosperity, his success, his adaptability. Like most men he wanted to leave a record. And this was it. And if he had coached himself in such small matters, what would he ever leave to chance?

That was why he was so ashamed when he came home that summer. There was the particular shame of having lost his job, a harder thing for a man then than it might be today. There was the shame of knowing that sooner or later we would have to go on relief, because being a lavish spender he had no savings. But there was also the shame of a man who suddenly discovers that all his lies were transparent, and everything he thought so safely hidden had always been in plain view. He had been living one of those dreams. The kind of dream in which you are walking down the street, meeting friends and neighbours, smiling and nodding, and when you arrive at home and pass a mirror you see for the first time you are stark naked. He was sure that behind his back he had always been Dutchie. For a man with so much pride a crueller epithet would have been kinder; to be hated gives a man some kind of status. It was the condescension implicit in that diminutive, its mock playfulness, that made him appear so undignified in his own eyes.

And for the first time in my life I was ashamed of him. He didn't have the grace to bear an injustice, imagined or otherwise, quietly. At first he merely brooded, and then like some man with a repulsive sore, he sought pity by showing it. I'm sure he knew that he could only offend, but he was under a compulsion to justify himself. He began with my mother by explaining, where there was no need for explanation, that he had had his job taken from him for no good reason. However, there proved to be little satisfaction preaching to the converted, so he carried his tale to everyone he knew. At first his references to his plight were tentative and oblique. The responses were polite but equally tentative and equally oblique. This wasn't what he had hoped for. He believed that the sympathy didn't measure up to the occasion. So his story was told and re-told, and each time it was enlarged and embellished until the injustice was magnified beyond comprehension. He made a damn fool of himself. This was the first sign, although my mother and I chose not to recognize it.

In time everyone learned my father had lost his job for no good reason. And it wasn't long before the kids of the fathers he had told his story to were following me down the street chanting, "No good reason. No good reason." That's how I learned my family was a topical joke that the town was enjoying with zest. I suppose my father found out too, because it was about that time he stopped going out of the house. He couldn't fight back and neither could I. You never can.

After a while I didn't leave the house unless I had to. I spent my days sitting in our screened verandah reading old copies of *Saturday Evening Post* and *Maclean's*. I was content to do anything that helped me forget the heat and monotony, the shame and the fear, of that longest of summers. I was thirteen then and in a hurry to grow up, to press time into yielding the bounty I was sure it had in keeping for me. So I was killing time minute by minute with those magazines. I was to enter high school that fall and that seemed a prelude to adulthood and independence. My father's misfortunes couldn't fool me into believing that maturity didn't mean the strength to plunder at will. So when I found an old Latin grammar of my mother's I began to read that too. After all, Latin was the arcane language of the professions, of lawyers and doctors, those divinities owed immediate and unquestioning respect. I decided I would become either one, because from them, respect could never be stolen as it had been from my father.

That August was the hottest I can remember. The dry heat made my nose bleed at night, and I often woke to find my pillow stiff with blood. The leaves of the elm tree in the front yard hung straight down on their stems; flies buzzed heavily, their bodies tip-tapping lazily against the screens, and people passing the house moved so languidly they seemed to be walking in water. My father, who had always been careful about his appearance, began to come down for breakfast barefoot, wearing only a vest undershirt and an old pair of pants. He rarely spoke, but carefully picked his way through his meal as if it were a dangerous obstacle course, only pausing to rub his nose thoughtfully. I noticed that he had begun to smell.

One morning he looked up at me, laid his fork carefully down beside his plate and said, "I'll summons him."

"Who?"

"Who do you think?" he said scornfully. "The bastard who fired me. He had no business calling me Dutchie. That's slander."

"You can't summons him."

"I can," he said emphatically. "I'm a citizen. I've got rights. I'll go to law. He spoiled my good name."

"That's not slander."

"It is."

"No it isn't."

"I'll sue the bastard," he said vaguely, looking around to appeal to my mother who had left the room. He got up from the table and went to the doorway. "Edith," he called, "tell your son I've got the right to summons that bastard."

Her voice came back faint and timid. "I don't know, George."

He looked back at me. "You're in the same boat, sonny. And taking sides with them don't save you. When we drown we all drown together."

"I'm not taking sides," I said indignantly. "Nobody's taking sides. It's facts. Can't you see . . ." but I didn't get a chance to finish. He left, walked out on me. I could hear his steps on the stairway, tired, heavy steps. There was so much I wanted to say. I wanted to make it plain that being on his side meant saving him from making a fool of himself again. I wanted him to know he could never win that way. I wanted him to win, not lose. He was my father. But he went up those steps, one at a time, and I heard his foot fall distinctly, every time. Beaten before he started, he crawled back into bed. My mother went up to him several times that day, to see if he was sick, to attempt to gouge him out of that room, but she couldn't. It was only later that afternoon, when I was reading in the verandah, that he suddenly appeared again, wearing only a pair of undershorts. His body shone dully with sweat, his skin looked grey and soiled.

"They're watching us," he said, staring past me at an empty car parked in the bright street.

Frightened, I closed my book and asked who was watching us.

"The relief people," he said tiredly. "They think I've got money hidden somewhere. They're watching me, trying to catch me with it. The joke's on them. I got no money." He made a quick, furtive gesture that drew attention to his almost naked body, as it it were proof of his poverty.

"Nobody is watching us. That car's empty."

"Don't take sides with them," he said, staring through the screen. I thought someone from one of the houses across the street might see him like that, practically naked.

"The neighbours'll see," I said, turning my head to avoid looking at him.

"See what?" he asked, surprised.

"You standing like that. Naked almost."

"There's nothing they can do. A man's home is his castle. That's what the English say, isn't it?"

And he went away laughing.

Going down the hallway, drawing close to his door that always stood ajar, what did I hope? To see him dressed, his trousers rolled up to midcalf to avoid smudging his cuffs, whistling under his breath, shining his shoes? Everything as it was before? Yes. I hoped that. If I had been younger then and still believed that frogs were turned into princes with a kiss, I might even have believed it could happen. But I didn't believe. I only hoped. Every time I approached his door (and that was many times a day, too many) I felt the queasy excitement of hope. I hope. I hope.

It was always the same. I would look in and see him lying on the tufted, pink bedspread, naked or nearly so, gasping for breath in the heat. And I always thought of a whale stranded on a beach because he was such a big man. He claimed he slept all day because of the heat, but he only pretended to. He could feel me watching him and his eyes would open. He would tell me to go away, or bring him a glass of water; or, because his paranoia was growing more marked, ask me to see if they were still in the street. I would go to the window and tell him, yes, they were. Nothing else satisfied him. If I said they weren't, his jaw would shift from side to side unsteadily and his eyes would prick with tears. Then he imagined more subtle and intricate conspiracies.

I would ask him how he felt.

"Hot," he'd say. "I'm always hot. Can't hardly breathe. Damn country," and turn on his side away from me.

My mother was worried about money. There was none left. She asked me what to do. She believed women shouldn't make decisions.

"You'll have to go to the town office and apply for relief," I told her.

"No, no," she'd say, shaking her head. "I couldn't go behind his back. I couldn't do that. He'll go himself when he feels better. He'll snap out of it. It takes a little time."

In the evening my father would finally dress and come downstairs and eat something. When it got dark he'd go out into the yard and sit on the swing he'd hung from a limb of our Manitoba maple years before, when I was a little boy. My mother and I would sit and watch him from the verandah. I felt obligated to sit with her. Every night as he settled himself on to the swing she would say the same thing. "He's too big. It'll never hold him. He'll break his back." But the swing held him up and the darkness hid him from the eyes of his enemies, and I like to think that made him happy, for a time.

He'd light a cigarette before he began to swing, and then we'd watch its glowing tip move back and forth in the darkness like a beacon. He'd flick it away when it was smoked, burning a red arc in the night, showering sparks briefly, like a comet. And then he'd light another and another, and we'd watch them glow and swing in the night.

My mother would lean over and say to me confidentially, "He's thinking it all out. It'll come to him, what to do."

I never knew whether she was trying to reassure me or herself. At last my mother would get to her feet and call to him, telling him she was going up to bed. He never answered. I waited a little longer, believing that watching him, I kept him safe in the night. But I always gave up before he did and went to bed too.

The second week of September I returned to school. Small differences are keenly felt. For the first time there was no new sweater, or unsharpened pencils, or new fountain pen whose nib hadn't spread under my heavy writing hand. The school was the same school I had gone to for eight years, but that day I climbed the stairs to the second floor that housed the high school. Up there the wind moaned more persistently than I remembered it had below, and it intermittently threw handfuls of dirt and dust from the schoolyard against the windows with a gritty rattle.

Our teacher, Mrs. MacDonald, introduced herself to us, though she needed no introduction since everyone knew who she was—she had taught there for over ten years. We were given our texts and it cheered me a little to see I would have no trouble with Latin after my summer's work. Then we were given a form on which we wrote a lot of useless information. When I came to the space which asked for Racial Origin I paused and then, out of loyalty to my father, numbly wrote in Canadian.

After that we were told we could leave. I put my texts away in a locker for the first time—we had had none in public school—but somehow it felt strange going home from school empty-handed. So I stopped at the library door and went in. There was no school librarian and only a few shelves of books, seldom touched. The room smelled of dry paper and heat. I wandered around aimlessly, taking books down, opening them, and putting them back. That is, until I happened on Caesar's *The Gallic War*. It was a small, thick book that nestled comfortably in the hand. I opened it and saw that the left-hand pages were printed in Latin and the right-hand pages were a corresponding English translation. I carried it away with me, dreaming of more than proficiency in Latin.

When I got home my mother was standing on the front step, peering anxiously up and down the street.

"Have you seen your father?" she asked.

"No," I said. "Why?"

She began to cry. "I told him all the money was gone. I asked him if I could apply for relief. He said he'd go himself and have it out with them. Stand on his rights. He took everything with him. His citizenship papers, baptismal certificate, old passport, bank book, everything. I said, 'Everyone knows you. There's no need.' But he said he needed proof. Of what? He'll cause a scandal. He's been gone for an hour."

We went into the house and sat in the living-room. "I'm a foolish woman," she said. She got up and hugged me awkwardly. "He'll be all right."

We sat a long time listening for his footsteps. At last we heard someone coming up the walk. My mother got up and said, "There he is." But there was no knock at the door.

I heard them talking at the door. The man said, "Edith, you better come with me. George is in some trouble."

My mother asked what trouble.

"You just better come. He gave the town clerk a poke. The constable and doctor have him now. The doctor wants to talk to you about signing some papers."

"I'm not signing any papers," my mother said.

"You'd better come, Edith."

She came into the living-room and said to me, "I'm going to get your father."

I didn't believe her for a minute. She put her coat on and went out.

She didn't bring him home. They took him to an asylum. It was a shameful word then, asylum. But I see it in a different light now. It seems the proper word now, suggesting as it does a refuge, a place to hide.

I'm not sure why all this happened to him. Perhaps there is no reason anyone can put their finger on, although I have my ideas.

But I needed a reason then. I needed a reason that would lend him a little dignity, or rather, lend me a little dignity; for I was ashamed of him out of my own weakness. I needed him to be strong, or at least tragic. I didn't know that most people are neither.

When you clutch at straws anything will do. I read my answer out of Caesar's *The Gallic War*, the fat little book I had carried home. In the beginning of Book I he writes, "Of all people the Belgae are the most courageous . . ." I read on, sharing Caesar's admiration for a people who would not submit, but chose to fight and see glory in their wounds. I misread it all, and bent it until I was satisfied. I reasoned the way I had to, for my sake, for my father's. What was he but a man dishonoured by faceless foes? His instincts could not help but prevail and, like his ancestors, in the end, on that one day, what could he do but make the shadows real, and fight to be free of them?

In One Ear and Out the Other
Edwin Varney

A little girl sits beside the stove petting a black cat which purrs and stretches and falls asleep. As she is sitting there, a huge bird flies in the window, snatches the sleeping cat from her lap and flies back out the window with it clutched in its talons. The girls runs into the bathroom screaming where her mother is making grotesque faces in front of the mirror. "What's the matter, dear?" she soothes. "A bird took my cat," the little girl sobs. "Never mind, dear, we'll get you another one," her mom says. "I don't want another one," screams the girl. "Go to your room until you stop crying," scolds her mother. The little girl runs thru the house crying and slams the door to her room behind her. Her room is large and filled with shelves of canned goods, pop bottles, bags of potato chips and cookies, a freezer full of frozen vegetables, orange juice, blocks of margarine, ice cream and frozen pizzas. At the opposite end of the room, a man in a white uniform stands next to a cash register watching as an old grey-haired lady counts out pennies for a can of dog food. As she reaches into her purse for more pennies, her false teeth slip out of her mouth and drop wide open over the can of dog food. When she tries to retrieve them, she finds that they are stuck tight. She picks up the can and the teeth, drops them both into her bag and runs out the door. The man at the cash register seems to suddenly wake up. "What the?" he says, then "Stop thief!" and runs out the door after her. A policeman halfway down the street comes running and sets off in pursuit of the old lady. As she runs, she reaches into her bag and pulls out a chrome-plated 45 calibre automatic and fires three shots at the policeman. The first two shots ricochet harmlessly off the pavement in front of the policeman but the third bullet hits him right in the centre of his forehead. Instead of a bloody hole, an

312 In One Ear and Out the Other

eye appears, blinks, and rolls up white in ecstatic trance. The policeman stops short and immediately sits down crosslegged on the sidewalk and begins to meditate. As he is sitting there, a large bird with a cat in its claws flying overhead drops the cat which lands in his lap, stretches, and falls asleep.

The Angel of the Tar Sands

Rudy Wiebe

Spring had most certainly, finally, come. The morning drive to the plant from Fort McMurray was so dazzling with fresh green against the heavy spruce, the air so unearthly bright that it swallowed the smoke from the candy-striped chimneys as if it did not exist. Which is just lovely, the superintendent thought, cut out all the visible crud, shut up the environmentalists, and he went into his neat office (with the river view with islands) humming, "Alberta blue, Alberta blue, the taste keeps—" but did not get his tan golfing jacket off before he was interrupted. Not by the radio-telephone, but Tak the day operator on Number Two Bucket in person, walking past the secretary without stopping.

"What the hell?" the superintendent said, quickly annoyed.

"I ain't reporting this on no radio," Tak's imperturbable Japanese-Canadian face was tense, "if them reporters hear about this one they—"

"You scrape out *another* buffalo skeleton, for god's sake?"

"No, it's maybe a dinosaur this time, one of them—"

But the superintendent, swearing, was already out the door yelling for Bertha who was always on stand-by now with her spade. If one of the three nine-storey-high bucketwheels stopped turning for an hour the plant dropped capacity, but another archaeological leak could stop every bit of production for a month while bifocalled professors stuck their noses . . . the jeep leaped along the track beside the conveyor belt running a third empty already and in three minutes he had Bertha with her long-handled spade busy on the face of the fifty-foot cliff that Number Two had been gnawing out. A shape emerged, quickly.

"What the . . ." staring, the superintendent could not find his ritual words, ". . . is that?"

"When the bucket hit the corner of it," Tak said, "I figured hey, that's the bones of a—"

"That's not just bone, it's . . . skin and . . ." The superintendent could not say the word.

"Wings," Bertha said it for him, digging her spade in with steady care. "That's wings, like you'd expect on a angel."

For that's what it was, plain as the day now, tucked tight into the oozing black cliff, an angel. Tak had seen only a corner of bones sheared clean but now that Bertha had it more uncovered they saw the manlike head through one folded-over pair of wings and the manlike legs, feet through another pair, very gaunt, the film of feather and perhaps skin so thin and engrained with tarry sand that at first it was impossible to notice anything except the white bones inside them. The third pair of wings was pressed flat by the sand at a very awkward, it must have been painful—

"The middle two," Bertha said, trying to brush the sticky sand aside with her hand, carefully, "is what it flies with."

"Wouldn't it . . . he . . . fly with all six . . ." The superintendent stopped, overwhelmed by the unscientific shape uncovered there so blatantly.

"You can look it up," Bertha said with a sideways glance at his ignorance, "Isaiah chapter six."

But then she gagged too for the angel had moved. Not one of them was touching it, that was certain, but it had moved irrefutably. As they watched, stunned, the wings unfolded bottom and top, a head emerged, turned, and they saw the fierce hoary lineaments of an ancient man. His mouth all encrusted with tar pulled open and out came a sound. A long, throat-clearing streak of sound. They staggered back, fell; the superintendent found himself on his knees staring up at the the shape which wasn't really very tall, it just seemed immensely broad and overwhelming, the three sets of wings now sweeping back and forth as if loosening up in some seraphic 5BX plan. The voice rumbled like thunder, steadily on.

"Well," muttered Tak, "whatever it is, it sure ain't talking Japanese."

The superintendent suddenly saw himself as an altar boy, the angel suspended above him there and bits of words rose to his lips: "*Pax vobis . . . cem . . . cum,*" he ventured, but the connections were lost in the years, "*Magnifi . . . cat . . . ave Mar . . .*"

The obsidian eyes of the angel glared directly at him and it roared something, dreadfully. Bertha laughed aloud.

"Forget the popish stuff," she said, "it's talking Hutterite, Hutterite German."

"Wha . . ." The superintendent had lost all words; he was down to syllables only.

"I left the colony . . ." But then she was too busy listening. The angel kept on speaking, non-stop as if words has been plugged up inside for eons, and its hands (it had only two of them, in the usual place at the ends of two arms) brushed double over its bucket-damaged shoulder and that appeared restored, whole just like the other, while it brushed the soil and tarry sand from its wings, flexing the middle ones again and again because they obviously had suffered much from their position.

"Ber, . . . Ber . . ." the superintendent said. Finally he looked at Tak, pleading for a voice.

"What's it saying," Tak asked her, "Bertha, please Bertha?"

She was listening with overwhelming intensity; there was nothing in this world but to hear. Tak touched her shoulder, shook her, but she did not notice. Suddenly the angel stopped speaking; it was studying her.

"I . . . I can't . . ." Bertha confessed to it at last, "I can understand every word you . . . every word, but I can't say, I've forgotten . . ."

In its silence the angel looked at her; slowly its expression changed. It might have been showing pity, though of course that is really difficult to tell with angels. Then it folded its lower wings over its feet, its upper wings over its face, and with an ineffable movement of its giant middle wings it rose, straight upward into the blue sky. They bent back staring after it, and in a moment it had vanished in light.

"O dear god," Bertha murmured after a time. "Our elder always said they spoke Hutterite in heaven."

The three contemplated each other and they saw in each other's eyes the dread, the abrupt tearing sensation of doubt. Had they seen . . . and as one they looked at the sand cliff still oozing tar, the spade leaning against it. Beside the hole where Bertha had dug: the shape of the angel, indelible. Bertha was the first to get up.

"I quit," she said. "Right this minute."

"Of course, I understand." The superintendent was on his feet. "Tak, run your bucket through there, get it going quick."

"Okay," Tak said heavily. "You're the boss."

"It doesn't matter how fast you do it," Bertha said to the superintendent but she was watching Tak trudge into the shadow of the giant wheel. "It was there, we saw it."

And at her words the superintendent had a vision. He saw like an opened book the immense curves of the Athabasca River swinging through wilderness down from the glacial pinnacles of the Rocky Mountains and across Alberta and joined by the Berland and the McLeod and the Pembina and the Pelican and the Christina and the Clearwater and the Firebag rivers, and all the surface of the earth was gone, the Tertiary and the Lower Cretaceous layers of strata had been ripped away and the thousands of square miles of black bituminous sand were exposed, laid open, slanting down into the molten centre of the earth, O *miserere, miserere*, the words sang in his head and he felt their meaning though he could not have explained them, much less remembered Psalm 51, and after a time he could open his eyes and lift his head. The huge plant, he knew every bolt and pipe, still sprawled between him and the river; the brilliant air still swallowed the smoke from all the red-striped chimneys as if it did not exist, and he knew that through a thousand secret openings the oil ran there, gurgling in each precisely numbered pipe and jointure, sweet and clear like golden brown honey.

Tak was beside the steel ladder, about to start the long climb into the machine. Bertha touched his shoulder and they both looked up.

"Next time you'll recognize it," she said happily. "And then it'll talk Japanese."

Fog

Ethel Wilson

For seven days fog settled down upon Vancouver. It crept in from the ocean, advancing in its mysterious way in billowing banks which swallowed up the land. In the Bay and the Inlet and False Creek, agitated voices spoke one to another. Small tugs that were waylaid in the blankets of fog cried shrilly and sharply "Keep away! Keep away! I am here!" Fishing-boats lay inshore. Large freighters mooed continuously like monstrous cows. The foghorns at Point Atkinson and the Lions' Gate Bridge kept up their bellowings. Sometimes the fog quenched the sounds, sometimes the sounds were loud and near. If there had not been this continuous dense fog, all the piping and boo-hooing would have held a kind of beauty; but it signified danger and warning. People knew that when the fog lifted they would see great freighters looking disproportionately large riding at anchor in the Bay because passage through the Narrows into the harbour was not safe. Within the harbour, laden ships could not depart but remained lying fog-bound at great expense in the stream ... booo ... booo ... they warned, "I am here! Keep away!" All the ships listened. The C.P.R. boat from Victoria crashed into the dock. Gulls collided in the pathless air. Water traffic ceased and there was no movement anywhere offshore.

In the streets, cars crawled slowly. Drivers peered. Pedestrians emerged and vanished like smoke. Up the draw of False Creek, fog packed thick on the bridges. Planes were grounded. People cancelled parties. Everyone arrived late for everything.

Mrs. Bylow was an old woman who lived in a small old house which was more cabin than cottage in an unpleasant part of Mount Pleasant. For the fifth day she sat beside her window looking into the fog and cracking her knuckles because she had nothing else to do. If she had owned a telephone she would have talked all day for pastime, repeating herself and driving the party line mad.

Mrs. Bylow frequently sat alone and lonely. Her diurnal occupations had narrowed down to sleeping, waking to still another day, getting up, making and swallowing small meals, belching a little, cleaning up (a little), hoping, going to the bathroom, going to the Chinaman's corner store, reading the paper (and thank God for that, especially the advertisements), becoming suddenly aware again of the noise of the radio (and thank God for that, too), and forgetting again.

This, and not much more, was her life as she waited for the great dustman and the ultimate box. So Mrs. Bylow's days and months slid and slid away while age—taking advantage of her solitariness, her long unemployment of vestigial brain, her unawareness of a world beyond herself, her absence of preparation for the grey years—closed down upon her like a vice, no, more like a fog. There had been a time about ten years ago when Mrs. Bylow, sitting on her small porch, beckoned to the little neighbour children who played on the sidewalk. "Come," said Mrs. Bylow, smiling and nodding.

The children came, and they all went into the kitchen. There was Mrs. Bylow's batch of fresh cookies and the children ate, looking around them, rapacious. They ate and ran away and once or twice a child hovered and said, "Thank you." Perhaps that was not the child who said "Thank you," but parents speaking through the child ("Say Thank you to Mrs. Bylow!") so the child said "Thank you" and Mrs. Bylow was pleased. Sometimes the children lingered around the little porch, not hungry, but happy, noisy and greedy. Then Mrs. Bylow rejoiced at the tokens of love and took the children into the kitchen. But perhaps she had only apples and the children did not care for apples. "Haven't you got any cookies?" asked a bold one, "we got lotsa apples at home."

"You come Tuesday," said Mrs. Bylow, nodding and smiling, but the children forgot.

So within Mrs. Bylow these small rainbows of life (children, cookies, laughing, and beckoning) faded, although two neighbours did sometimes stop on their way home and talk for a few minutes and thus light up her day. Miss Casey who worked at the People's Friendly Market and was a smart dresser with fine red hair, and Mrs. Merkle who was the managing type and had eyes like marbles and was President of the Ladies' Bowling

Club dropped in from time to time and told Mrs. Bylow all about the illnesses of the neighbours which Mrs. Bylow enjoyed very much and could think about later. Mrs. Merkle told her about Mr. Galloway's broken hip and Miss Casey told her about her mother's diabetes and how she managed her injections, also about the woman who worked in her department when she didn't need to work and now her kid had gone wrong and was in the Juvenile Court. Mrs. Bylow was regaled by everything depressing that her two friends could assemble because she enjoyed bad news which was displayed to her chiefly against the backdrop of her own experience and old age. All these ailments, recalling memories of her own (" . . . well I remember my Uncle Ernest's . . .") provided a drama, as did the neglect and irreponsibility of the young generations. Like an old sad avid stupid judge she sat, passing judgment without ill will. It is not hard to understand why Mrs. Merkle and Miss Casey, hastening past Mrs. Bylow's gate which swung on old hinges, often looked straight ahead, walking faster and thinking I *must* go in and see her tomorrow.

During long periods of bad weather, as now in this unconquerable fog, time was a deep pit for Mrs. Bylow. Her hip was not very good. She should have belonged to a church (to such base uses can the humble and glorious act of worship come) or a club, to which she would at least look forward. Gone were the simple impossible joys of going to town, wandering through the shops, fingering and comparing cloth, cotton and silk. Gone was the joy of the running children. Life, which had been pinkish and blueish, was grey. And now this fog.

So it was that on the fifth day of fog, Mrs. Bylow sat beside her window in a sort of closed-up dry well of boredom, cracking her knuckles and looking into the relentless blank that pressed against her window panes and kept her from seeing any movement on the sidewalk. Mrs. Merkle and Miss Casey were as though they had never been. I'm not surprised they wouldn't drop in, thought Mrs. Bylow modestly and without rancour, it couldn't be expected, it'll be all they can do to get home; and she pictured Miss Casey, with her flaming hair, wearing her leopard coat, pushing through the fog home to her mother. Diabetes, thought Mrs. Bylow, and she was sorry for old Mrs. Casey. Her indulgence of sorrow spread to include Miss Casey hurrying home looking so smart. Not much in life for her, now, is there, really, she thought, rocking. Mrs. Bylow peered again. She was insulted by this everywhere fog, this preventing fog.

She needed a cup of cocoa and she had no cocoa. She repeated aloud a useful phrase, "The fog is lifting"; but the fog was not lifting.

Mrs. Bylow creaked to her feet. She wrapped herself up well, took her walking stick and went unsteadily down her three steps. Then, not at all afraid, she turned to the left and, in a silence of velvet, she moved slowly along beside the picket fence which would guide her to Wong Kee's store. At her own corner a suggestion of sickly glow in the air told her that the street lamps were lighted. She moved on, screwing up her eyes against the greyish yellow fog that invaded eyes, nose, mouth. At last another pale high glimmer informed her that she was near Wong Kee's store and, gasping, leaning now and then against the outside wall of the store itself, she reached the door with the comfortable knowledge that, once inside, she would find light and warmth. She would ask Wong Kee for his chair or a box and would sit down and take her ease while the Chinaman went with shuffling steps to the shelf where he kept the tins of cocoa. Wong Kee was a charming old man with good cheek-bones and a sudden tired Oriental smile. After Mrs. Merkle and Miss Casey he was Mrs. Bylow's third friend. She pushed the door open and waddled in to where there was this desired light and warmth, puffing a little.

Something was happening inside the store, a small whirlwind and fury. Mrs. Bylow was roughly pushed by large rushing objects. She lost her balance and was thrown, no, hurled violently to the ground. The person or persons rushed on, out and into the fog. The door slammed.

The store was empty. Everything was still. The old woman lay in a heap, bewildered and in pain. Gradually she began to know that someone or some people had rushed out into the fog, knocking her down and hurting her because she happened to be in the way. She whimpered and she thought badly of Wong Kee because he did not come to help her. Her body gave her massive pain, and as she looked slowly about her in a stupefied way she saw that a number of heavy cans of food had rained down upon her and lay around her. As she tried clumsily to heave herself up (but that was not possible), a customer came in.

"Well well well!" said the customer, bending over her, "whatever ..." then he straightened himself and listened.

A faint sound as of a bubbling sigh came from behind the counter on which was the till. The till was open and empty. The customer went behind the counter and again bent down. Then he drew himself up quickly. Wong Kee lay like a bundle of old clothes from which blood seeped and spread.

The sound that the customer had heard was the soft sound of the death of Wong Kee who was an honest man and innocent. He had worked all his life and had robbed no one. He had an old wife who loved him. In a way hard to explain they were seriously and simply happy together. This was now over.

The customer paid no further attention to Mrs. Bylow on the floor but, stepping round Wong Kee's body, reached the telephone.

A small woman parted the dingy curtains which separated the store from the home of Wong Kee and his wife. She held in her arms a bundle of stove wood and stood motionless like a wrinkled doll. Then the stove wood clattered to the ground and she dropped to her knees uttering high babbling noises. She rocked and prostrated herself beside the impossible sight of her husband's dead body and his blood. The customer regarded her as he talked into the telephone. Then he too knelt down and put his arm round her. He could find nothing to say but the immemorial "There there . . ."

Mrs. Bylow, lying neglected on the floor, endeavoured to look behind her but she had to realize as people do in bombardment, flood and earthquake that she was at the mercy of whatever should happen to her and could not do anything about it, let alone look behind her.

"They're slow coming," said the customer. "It's the fog."

The old Chinese woman wrenched herself from him. "I tarryphome," she cried out, "I tarryphome my son . . ."

The door opened and there seemed to be some policemen. The outside fog poured in with this entrance and some other kind of fog pressed down upon Mrs. Bylow's understanding and blurred it. "I'm a very old woman," she mumbled to a constable who had a little book, "and they knocked me down . . . they mighta killed me . . . they shouldn't a done that . . . they've broke my hip . . . aah . . . !"

"Yes, lady, we'll look after you," said the constable, "who was it?"

"It was . . ." (well, who was it?) "I guess it was some man . . . no . . ." she breathed with difficulty, she should not have to suffer so, "I guess it was a boy . . . they knocked me down . . ."

A constable at the door said to a crowd which had gathered from somewhere in the fog and now pushed against the front of the store, "Now then, you can't come in here, there's been a robbery, see? You best go on home," but someone battered on the pane with both hands enough to break it, and Miss Casey burst in at the door, her red hair wet with fog.

"She's here! Yes there she is!" said Miss Casey, talking to everyone in her loud voice and bringing into the muted shop a blazing of bright eyes and hair and leopard coat and humanity, "—that's what I thought! I thought right after I left the store I'd better go in and see was she O.K. because she shouldn't be out and the fog was just *awful* and I prett' near went past her gate but I kinda felt something was wrong and my goodness see what happened . . . Mrs. Bylow honey, what happened to you," and Miss Casey dropped on her knees and took Mrs. Bylow's hand in hers. "Say, what's been going on around here anyway?" she said, looking up at the constable, ready to accuse.

"She's not so good," said the constable in a low tone in Mrs. Bylow's dream and a high noise came into the night ("That's the syreen," said Miss Casey) and some men lifted her and took her somewhere on a bed. It did not occur to Mrs. Bylow that perhaps she had been killed inadvertently by two youths who had just killed her old friend, but if a policeman had said to her "Now you are dead," she would have accepted the information, so unfamiliar was the experience of boring horizontally through a fog at top speed very slowly in a high and unexplained swelling noise. She opened her eyes and saw a piece of Miss Casey's leopard coat and so she was not dead.

"Is it reel?" she whispered, because she had always wanted to know.

"Is what reel?" said Miss Casey, bending her flaming head. "Sure it's reel. The collar's reel anyway." Mrs. Bylow closed her eyes again for several years and said "But I never got my cocoa." Then she began to cry quietly because she felt old and helpless and the pain was something cruel, but it was good to feel Miss Casey beside her in her leopard coat. She did not know that Wong Kee was dead—slugged on the head, pistol-whipped, stabbed again and again in the stomach with a long knife—all because he had summoned his small strength and fought like a cat and defended himself for his right to his thirty dollars and some loose change and a handful of cigarettes and his life. "Well, here we are," said Miss Casey, standing up, very cheerful.

In a week or two, while she was better and before she got worse, Mrs. Bylow began to remember the two boys whom she had never seen and, as she constructed their leather jackets and their faces, she said she would know them anywhere. Of course she would not, and the murderers of Wong Kee were never found but carried the knowledge of their murder into the fog with them on their way from the betrayal of their youth to whatever else they would soon violently undertake to do. When they arrived back, each at his own home, their parents said in pursuance of their habit of long years past "Where you bin?" and the hoodlums said in pursuance of their habit of long years past "Out." This satisfied the idiot parents. They said "My that fog's just terrible," and the hoodlums said "Sure is." They were excited and nervous because this was the first time they had killed, but they had the money. One of the young hoodlums did not go into the room where his parents were but went upstairs because he was pretty sure there was still some blood on his hands and so there was. Wong Kee's blood was on his parents' hands too but they, being irresponsible, did not know this. And on their hands was the blood of Mrs. Bylow who was soon to die, and of Mrs. Wong Kee who could no longer be said to live, and of their own hoodlum children.

Before Mrs. Bylow died, wiped out by forces quite outside herself like a moth in a storm (not much more and no less), she began to be a little proud of almost being present at a murder.

"It's not everyone who's been at a murder, Miss Casey, love, is it?"

"No honey," said Miss Casey, seeing again that sordid scene, "it isn't everyone."

"I always liked that coat of yours," said Mrs. Bylow.

"And then," said Miss Casey to Mrs. Merkle, "d'you know what she said? She said if ever I come to die—just like she wasn't ever going to—would you please wear your leopard coat. She's crazy about that coat. And then she said she often thought of those two boys that killed the storekeeper and knocked her down and she guessed it was more their parents' fault and not their fault. It made the tears come to your eyes," said Miss Casey who was kind as well as noisy and cherished a sense of personal drama.

"Sure," said Mrs. Merkle who had eyes like marbles that did not weep.

Mrs. Bylow's death was obscure and pitiful. Miss Casey got the afternoon off and so there were two people at her funeral. Miss Casey wore her leopard coat as promised.

NOTES

EDNA ALFORD was born in 1947 in Turtleford, Saskatchewan, and now resides in Livelong, Saskatchewan. "Head" appears in the collection *The Garden of Eloise Loon* (1986). Alford is also author of the short story collection *A Sleep Full of Dreams* (1981), for which she was declared co-recipient of the 1981 Gerald Lampert Award. Both books are published by Oolichan.

DAVID ARNASON was born in 1940 in Gimli, Manitoba, and now resides in Winnipeg. "The Event" appears in *50 Stories and a Piece of Advice* (1982). Arnason's other books include *Marsh Burning* (1980), *The Circus Performers Bar* (1984), and *The Happiest Man in the World* (1989).

SANDRA BIRDSELL was born in 1942 in Morris, Manitoba, and now lives in Winnipeg. "Flowers for Weddings and Funerals" appears in *Night Travellers* (1982), which won the Gerald Lampert Award. *Night Travellers* and Birdsell's other collection of stories, *Ladies of the House* (1984), were republished as *Agassiz Stories* (1987). All are from Turnstone Press.

LOIS BRAUN was born in 1949 in Winkler, Manitoba, and now lives on a farm near Altona, Manitoba. "Golden Eggs" appears in the collection *A Stone Watermelon* (1986) which was nominated for the Governor-General's Award.

BRIAN BRETT was born in 1950 in Vancouver, B.C., and now resides outside Vancouver in White Rock. "The Thing That Grows in the Gasoline Tank" previously appeared in *The New Quarterly*. Brett has published the novel *The Fungus Garden* (1988) and five books of poetry.

SHIRLEY BRUISED HEAD was born on the Peigan Reserve in Alberta in 1951, and now lives in Coaldale, Alberta. "An Afternoon in Bright Sunlight" first appeared in the Native Authors issue of *Canadian Fiction Magazine* (No. 60, 1987). Bruised Head, who is a member of the Blackfoot Nation, has had her poetry published in *Fireweed* and *Whetstone*.

BONNIE BURNARD was born in 1945 and now lives in Regina. "The Knife Sharpener" appears in *Women of Influence*, a collection of short stories published by Coteau in 1988.

MEL DAGG was born in Vancouver in 1941 and now resides in Calgary, Alberta. "The Museum of Man" first appeared in *Fiddlehead* and then in his collection *Same Truck, Different Driver* (1982). The story is on the Distinctive American Short Story List.

JAMES MICHAEL DANCE was born in Kamloops, B.C., in 1953 and now lives in Nanaimo, B.C. "A Plague of Armadillos" appeared in the *Canadian Short Fiction Anthology* (1977).

SANDY FRANCES DUNCAN was born in Vancouver and now lives on Gabriola Island, B.C. "Flowers for the Dead" first appeared in *Room of One's Own*. Duncan is the author of many books, among them *Dragonhunt* (1981), *Finding Home* (1982), and *Kap-Sung Ferris* (1982).

CECELIA FREY was born in 1936 in Padstow, Alberta, and now resides in Calgary. "How I Spent My Summer Holidays" first appeared in *Dinosaur Review* in 1986. It is included in the short story collection *The Nefertiti Look* (1987), which won the Writers Guild of Alberta Award for Short Fiction. Frey is the author of the novel *Breakaway* (1974) as well as a collection of poetry, *The Least You Can Do Is Sing* (1982).

KRISTJANA GUNNARS was born in 1948 in Reykjavik, Iceland, and now lives in Winnipeg. "Ticks" appears in the short story collection *The Axe's Edge* (1983). Gunnars has published the novel *The Prowler* (1989) as well as several collections of poetry.

ERNEST HEKKANEN was born in 1947 in Seattle, Washington, and now lives in Vancouver, B.C. "The Fatal Error" first appeared in *The Malahat Review* in 1980 and then in his first collection of short stories, *Medieval Hour in the Author's Mind* (1987). Hekkanen has also produced the collection *The Violent Lavender Beast* (1988). Both books are published by Thistledown Press.

RICK HILLIS was born in 1956 in Nipawin, Saskatchewan, and immediately moved to Moose Jaw; he now lives in Saskatoon. "Rumours of Foot" first appeared in *Canadian Fiction Magazine* and then in Oberon's annual collection of stories by new writers, *Coming Attractions*, for 1988. Hillis is the Wallace Stegner Fellow at the Creative Writing Centre of Stanford University for 1988-90.

JACK HODGINS was born in 1938 on Vancouver Island and resides in Victoria, B.C. "By the River" appears in his first short story collection, *Spit Delaney's Island* (1976). His fiction works include *The Invention of the World* (1977), *The Resurrection of Joseph Bourne* (1979), *The Barclay Family Theatre* (1981), and *The Honorary Patron* (1987). He received the Eaton's B.C. Book Award for *Spit Delaney's Island* in 1977, the Gibson First Novel Award in 1978, the Governor-General's Award for Fiction in 1980, and the Canada-Australia Literary Award in 1986.

LIONEL KEARNS was born in 1937 in Nelson, B.C., and now lives in Vancouver. "Blue Moon" appeared in *New: West Coast Fiction* (West Coast Review/Pulp Press, 1984). Kearns has published numerous collections of poetry.

THOMAS KING was born in 1943 in Sacramento, California, and now lives in Lethbridge. "Magpies" appears here for the first time; it is part of the collection *One Good Story, That One*. Dr. King received the Whetstone Short Fiction Prize for 1989 and was nominated for the 1989 Journey Prize. He was guest editor for the *Canadian Fiction Magazine* Native Authors issue and co-editor with Helen Hoy and Cheryl Calver of *The Native in Literature*, a volume of critical essays, in 1987. His novel *Medicine River* will appear in January, 1990.

W.P. KINSELLA was born in Edmonton in 1935 and now resides in White Rock, B.C. "The Thrill of the Grass" appears in the collection of the same name. Kinsella is the author of many novels and short story collections, including *Dance Me Outside* (1977), *Scars* (1978), *Shoeless Joe Jackson Comes to Iowa* (1980), *Born Indian* (1981), *The Moccasin Telegraph* (1983), *The Thrill of the Grass* (1984), *The Iowa Baseball Confederacy* (1986), and *The Fencepost Chronicles* (1986). He was awarded the Houghton Mifflin Literary Fellowship, the Books in Canada First Novel Award and the Writers Guild of Alberta Novel Award, all in 1982.

HENRY KREISEL was born in Vienna in 1922 and now lives in Edmonton. "The Broken Globe" first appeared in *The Literary Review* and then in his collection *The Almost Meeting* (1981). His publications also include the novels *The Rich Man* (1948) and *The Betrayal* (1964). He is the recipient of the 1983 J.I. Segal Foundation Award for Literature and the 1986 Sir Frederick Haultain Prize from the Government of Alberta for Significant Achievement in the Fine Arts.

MARGARET LAURENCE was born in 1926 in Neepawa, Manitoba. She resided for many years in Lakefield, Ontario, and died there in 1985. "The Loons" appears in *A Bird in the House* (1970), which was published by McClelland and Stewart, as was the collection *The Tomorrow Tamer* (1963). Laurence's novels are *The Stone Angel* (1964), *A Jest of God* (1966), *The Fire Dwellers* (1969), and *The Diviners* (1974), similarly published by McClelland and Stewart. Laurence was the recipient of many honours and awards, most notably the Molson Award and the Governor-General's Award for *The Diviners*. She was named a Companion of the Order of Canada.

LESLIE LUM was born in Vancouver in 1952 and makes Richmond, B.C., her home base. "Old Age Gold" appeared in the *Canadian Short Fiction Anthology II* (1977). Although Lum has no other fiction credits, her poetry has been published in a number of small magazines.

DAVE MARGOSHES was born in 1941 in New Brunswick, New Jersey, and now lives in Regina, Saskatchewan. "The Caller" appeared in *Descant* and was later published as part of the collection *Small Regrets* (1986). Margoshes is also the author of a collection of poetry, *Walking at Brighton* (1988). Both books are published by Thistledown Press.

EDWARD McCOURT was born in Ireland in 1907 and died in Saskatoon in 1972. "Cranes Fly South" first appeared in *Weekend Magazine* in 1955. McCourt's novels are *Music at the Close* (1947), *Home is the Stranger* (1950), *The Wooden Sword* (1956), *Walk Through the Valley* (1958), and *Fasting Friar* (1963). He also produced the critical work, *The Canadian West in Fiction* (1949).

KEN MITCHELL was born in 1940 in Moose Jaw, Saskatchewan, and now resides in Regina. "The Great Electrical Revolution" appeared in *Prism international* in 1970. Mitchell is the author of poems, plays, novels, stories and screenplays. He has published the novels *Wandering Rafferty* (1972) and *The Con Man* (1979); the short story collection *Everybody Gets Something Here* (1977); and the omnibus collection *Ken Mitchell Country* (1984).

W.O. MITCHELL was born in Weyburn, Saskatchewan, in 1914 and now lives in Calgary, Alberta. "Two Kinds of Sinner" was first heard on CBC Radio's "Jake and the Kid" series, and later appeared in the short story collection of the same name. Mitchell's novels are *Who Has Seen the Wind* (1947), *The Kite* (1962), *The Vanishing Point* (1973), *How I Spent My Summer*

Holidays (1981), *Since Daisy Creek* (1984), and *Ladybug, Ladybug* (1988). He has received numerous honorary degrees, the Order of Canada, and the Leacock Medal for Humour for *Jake and the Kid* (1961).

E.G. PERRAULT was born in Penticton, B.C., in 1922 and now lives in North Vancouver, B.C. "The Cure" appeared in *Raven*, the U.B.C. literary magazine. Perrault's novels are *The Kingdom Carver*, *The Twelfth Mile*, and *Spoil!*.

BRENDA RICHES was born in India and educated in England; she now lives in Regina. "The Babysitter" appears in *New: West Coast Fiction* in 1984. Riches has published the short fiction collections *Dry Media* (1981) and *Rites* (1989).

KEVIN ROBERTS was born in Australia and immigrated to Canada in 1966; he resides in Lantzville, B.C. "Troller" appears in *Picking the Morning Colour* (1984). Roberts has published another short story collection titled *Flash Harry* (1980).

LEON ROOKE was born in North Carolina in 1934, immigrated to Canada in 1969, and now resides in Victoria, B.C. "I. Paintings II. Watercolours III. Hand-Painted Flowers, All You Can Carry, 25¢" appears in *New: West Coast Fiction* (1984). Rooke has published the short story collections *The Last One Home Sleeps in the Yellow Bed* (1968), *The Love Parlour* (1977), and *Sing Me No Love Songs I'll Say You No Prayers: Selected Stories* (1984); his novels are *Fat Woman* (1981) and *Shakespeare's Dog* (1983), which earned him the Governor-General's Award for Fiction.

SINCLAIR ROSS was born in Shellbrook, Saskatchewan, in 1908 and now lives in Vancouver, B.C. "The Painted Door" first appeared in *Queen's Quarterly* in 1939 and is included in the collection *The Lamp at Noon and Other Stories* (1968). Ross's novels are *As For Me and My House* (1941), *The Well* (1958), *Whir of Gold* (1970), and *Sawbones Memorial* (1974). He has also published the short story collection *The Race and Other Stories* (1982).

HELEN J. ROSTA lives in Edmonton, Alberta. "Hunting Season" appears in the anthology *Getting Here* and later was reprinted in her own short story collection, *In the Blood* (1982).

ANDREAS SCHROEDER was born in Germany in 1946, came to Canada in 1951, and now lives in Mission, B.C. "The Tree" appears in his collection *The Late Man* (1971). Schroeder's publications also include the novel *Dustship Glory* (1986).

LOIS SIMMIE was born in Edam, Saskatchewan, in 1932 and now resides in Saskatoon. "Emily" appeared in the anthology *Sundogs* and in her short story collection *Pictures* (1984). Simmie has also written the novel *They Shouldn't Make You Promise That* (1981) and the short story collection *Ghost House* (1976), as well as several children's books.

FRED STENSON was born in 1951 in Pincher Creek, Alberta, and now lives in Calgary. "Delusions of Agriculture" appeared in *Saturday Night* in 1981. Stenson has also published the novels *Lonesome Hero* (1974) and *Last One Home* (1988).

GERTRUDE STORY was born in 1929 in Saskatoon, Saskatchewan, and lives there now. "The Summer Visitor" appeared in *Saskatchewan Gold* and was then published in the collection *It Never Pays to Laugh Too Much* (1984). Story has produced several collections of stories, *The Way to Always Dance* (1983), *The Need of Wanting Always* (1985), and *Black Swan* (1986), as well as the volume of personal reminiscences *The Last House on Main Street* (1988), all from Thistledown Press.

WAYNE TEFS was born in 1947 in Winnipeg, Manitoba, where he currently resides. "Coughs, Memory Lapses, Uncle's Hands" first appeared in *Dandelion*. Tefs is the author of two novels, *Figures on a Wharf* (1983) and *The Cartier Street Contract* (1985).

RUDY THAUBERGER was born in Saskatoon in 1961 and now resides in Burnaby, B.C. "Goalie" appeared in *The Rocket, the Hammer, the Flower and Me* (1988), an anthology of hockey stories edited by Doug Beardsley. The story earned Thauberger the first prize for fiction in the B.C. Federation of Writers Literary Rites Competition.

GUY VANDERHAEGHE was born in 1951 in Esterhazy, Saskatchewan, and now resides in Saskatoon. "What I Learned from Caesar" appeared in *The Malahat Review* in 1979 and subsequently in his collection *Man Descending* (1982), which won the Governor-General's Award for Fiction. Vanderhaeghe's other short story collection is *The Trouble with Heroes* (1984); his novels are *My Present Age* (1984) and *Homesick* (1989).

ARITHA VAN HERK was born in 1954 near Edberg, Alberta, and now lives in Calgary. "A Latin for Thieves" was first published in *Dandelion* in 1987. Van Herk's novels are *Judith* (1978), *The Tent Peg* (1981), and *No Fixed Address* (1986). *Judith* earned van Herk the 1978 Seal First Novel Award.

EDWIN VARNEY was born in the East towards the end of World War II. He now lives in Vancouver. "In One Ear and Out the Other" first appeared in *Canadian Short Fiction Anthology* (1977). Varney was founder and director of Intermedia Press until it closed in 1981. He is the author of three collections of poetry, *Openings* (1969), *Summer Sings* (1971), and *Human Nature* (1974), and editor of *Contemporary Surrealist Prose* (1978) and *The Poem Country* I and II (1972 and 1977). Currently he is editor of *Bite*, a poetry magazine, and is himself working in visual art.

RUDY WIEBE was born near Fairholme, Saskatchewan, in 1934 and now lives in Edmonton. "The Angel of the Tar Sands" appears in the collection *The Angel of the Tar Sands and Other Stories* (1982). Wiebe has also published the collection *Where Is the Voice Coming From?* (1974). His novels are *Peace Shall Destroy Many* (1962), *First and Vital Candle* (1966), *The Blue Mountains of China* (1966), *The Temptations of Big Bear* (1973), *The Scorched Wood People* (1977), and *My Lovely Enemy* (1983). Recently he published the essay collection *Playing Dead* (1989). He received the 1973 Governor-General's Award for *The Temptations of Big Bear*.

ETHEL WILSON was born in South Africa in 1888 and immigrated to Canada in 1898. She lived in Vancouver until her death in 1980. "Fog" appears in the collection *Mrs. Golightly and Other Stories* (1961). Wilson also published a number of novels: *Hetty Dorval* (1947), *The Innocent Traveller* (1949), *The Equations of Love* (1952), *The Swamp Angel* (1954), and *Love and Salt Water* (1956). She was awarded the Canada Council Medal in 1961 and the Order of Canada Medal of Service in 1970.

ACKNOWLEDGEMENTS

EDNA ALFORD. "Head" © Edna Alford. Reprinted from *The Garden of Eloise Loon* by Edna Alford, with permission of the publisher, Oolichan Books.

DAVID ARNASON. "The Event" reprinted with permission from *50 Stories and a Piece of Advice* (Turnstone Press, 1982). © David Arnason.

SANDRA BIRDSELL. "Flowers for Weddings and Funerals" reprinted with permission from *Night Travellers* (Turnstone Press, 1982). © Sandra Birdsell.

LOIS BRAUN. "Golden Eggs" reprinted with permission from *A Stone Watermelon* (Turnstone Press, 1986). © Lois Braun.

BRIAN BRETT. "The Thing That Grows in the Gasoline Tank" © Brian Brett. Previously published in *The New Quarterly.*

SHIRLEY BRUISED HEAD. "An Afternoon in Bright Sunlight" © Shirley Bruised Head.

BONNIE BURNARD. "The Knife Sharpener" © Bonnie Burnard. Originally published in *Women of Influence* by Bonnie Burnard (Coteau, 1988).

MEL DAGG. "The Museum of Man" © Mel Dagg. From *Same Truck, Different Driver* (Westlands Book Express Ltd., 1982).

JAMES MICHAEL DANCE. "A Plague of Armadillos" © James Michael Dance. First published in *Canadian Short Fiction Anthology* (Intermedia Press, 1977, ed. Cathy Ford).

SANDY FRANCES DUNCAN. "Flowers for the Dead" © Sandy Frances Duncan. First published by the author as Frances Duncan in *Room of One's Own* 1:2, reprinted in *Canadian Short Fiction Anthology*, Vol. 2 (Intermedia Press, 1982).

CECELIA FREY. "How I Spent My Summer Holidays" by Cecelia Frey reprinted from *The Nefertiti Look* (Thistledown Press, 1987) with permission.

KRISTJANA GUNNARS. "Ticks" by Kristjana Gunnars reprinted from *The Axe's Edge* (Press Porcepic, 1983) with permission.

ERNEST HEKKANEN. "The Fatal Error" by Ernest Hekkanen reprinted from *Medieval Hour in the Author's Mind* (Thistledown Press, 1987) with permission.

RICK HILLIS. "Rumours of Foot" © Rick Hillis.

JACK HODGINS. "By the River" by Jack Hodgins from *Spit Delaney's Island.* Reprinted by permission of Macmillan of Canada, a Division of Canada Publishing Corporation.

LIONEL KEARNS. "Blue Moon" © Lionel Kearns.

THOMAS KING. "Magpies" © Thomas King.

W.P. KINSELLA. "The Thrill of the Grass" from *The Thrill of the Grass* by W.P. Kinsella. © W.P. Kinsella, 1984. Reprinted by permission of Penguin Books Canada Limited.

HENRY KREISEL. "The Broken Globe" by Henry Kreisel © 1981. From *The Almost Meeting and Other Stories*, published by NeWest Publishers Ltd., Edmonton.

MARGARET LAURENCE. "The Loons" from *A Bird in the House* by Margaret Laurence. Used by permission of the Canadian Publishers, McClelland and Stewart, Toronto.

LESLIE LUM. "Old Age Gold" © Leslie Lum.

THE EDITORS

ALLAN FORRIE teaches English at Evan Hardy Collegiate in Saskatoon. For more than a decade he has been an editor and book designer for Thistledown Press. He co-edited the poetry anthology *Dancing Visions*.

PATRICK O'ROURKE teaches English at Evan Hardy Collegiate in Saskatoon. He is the Editor-in-Chief of Thistledown Press. He co-edited the poetry anthology *Dancing Visions*.

GLEN SORESTAD is a Saskatoon writer and editor. He has published several books of poetry, most recently his selected poems, *Hold the Rain in Your Hands*. As an anthologist he has co-edited three short story anthologies. Glen Sorestad is one of the founders of Thistledown Press.